STALKED

BLOOD OF THE CHOSEN TRILOGY

D.L. BLADE

To my amazing mother. Please skip over the naughty content.

SOCIAL MEDIA

Goodreads:
@D_L_Blade
TikTok:
@authordlblade
Facebook:
@dlblade
Instagram:
@booksbydlblade
Pinterest:
@DLBlade
YouTube:
@DLBlade
Newsletter:
www.linktr.ee/dlblade

AUTHOR NOTE

Though the prologue was written from Dorian's POV in 1692, the remaining chapters are only from Mercy's POV, which is set in the present day.

Stalked is a retelling, adult edition of my novel, *The Dark Awakening*, published in 2018. The young adult edition is published under my second pen name, Diana B. Lynn. *Stalked* features mature themes and content.

Full content warnings can be found on my website, www.dlblade.com

PROLOGUE

DORIAN

Salem, Massachusetts 1692

The ringing of the church bells had announced the beginning of yet another trial, masking the loud wails and screams from the village's main square. I gritted my teeth and turned away from the sound, heading deeper into the forest. But no matter how hard I tried to drown out the cries of grief and pain, I knew they would always stay with me.

I wasn't sure why I behaved so differently from the other vampires that had been turned. Most of the undead looked at humans as dispensable food sources, nothing more. For me, they were prevalent reminders that I was once human. They represented the fact that I still had a choice whether I wanted to be a monster by shutting off my humanity, so I didn't feel that heavy guilt or embrace what compassion I had left by not losing myself entirely to frenzied blood lust.

Tonight would mark one year of regaining a semblance of a life I thought was forever out of my reach. One year with her ... the one who saved me.

And the one who stole my heart.

My Mercy.

The acrid smell of burning wood filled the air as I approached the stables where I knew Mercy's coven had planned to gather. Through the window of the stables, I watched three of the Chosen Ones gathered in a circle, and candles spread out along the dirt. It looked like preparations for the ritual were nearly complete. I kept myself flush against the wall, concealing myself in the growing shadows of the building. I was close enough to stay hidden but not close enough that the coven could spot me watching them. Aside from Mercy, they never trusted me. Not even a tiny bit. I was a monster in their eyes, and nothing could convince them otherwise.

As the moonlight filled the woods with a silver glow, illuminating the pine trees, I spotted Roland stepping out from the shadows. "Careful, Dorian. If they see you—" Roland warned.

"They won't see me, Roland," I said. "Just because I don't drink blood from a human vein does not mean I've lost my skills as a predator. I know how to stay hidden." Turning to the forest, I watched the ghostly haze of fog creep through the trees.

"There isn't much time," Roland whispered, reaching into his cloak and handing me a dagger. My eyes grew wide as I caught a glimpse of the handle.

"Is that—?"

Roland nodded, pressing the handle into my palm. "If she goes through the ritual, you must stick this dagger into her chest and end it. Do you understand?"

I paled at the sight of the dagger in my hand, unable to avert my eyes from the dangerous blade as I shook my head from side to side. "You're out of your damn mind if you believe I'd ever hurt her."

Roland rolled his eyes and curled my fingers around the handle. "Don't be ridiculous, Dorian. It's an act of mercy. If you could see into the heart of the clan's leader, you'd beg her to do it herself. I've heard the vile things that monster wants to do to her. Trust me when I say that we're saving her from a fate worse than death." We stood in silence before Roland took a step back and turned away. He scoffed quietly. "For a vampire, I'm surprised how easy it is for you to *feel*. That guilt will weigh you down, if not suppress your natural instincts. It will consume you, Dorian."

"Do you not feel anything?" I asked. "You kill for pleasure while your own son fights to protect the world from creatures like us."

Roland winced at the comment. "It's easier not to care about them. You have to shut it off."

"Not with her," I growled. "I can't *shut it off* with her!"

A loud boom that echoed through the sky interrupted our heated conversation. The wind howled as the thunder crashed again, the moon's light fading under heavy clouds, throwing the forest into complete darkness. A storm was upon us.

Roland peered inside the barn and smiled at the sight of the coven. The children he helped raise and taught were now young adults, ready to be sent off into the world. It shocked me to see that kind of sentimental look on Roland's face, but I kept my words behind my teeth.

"All these years of training, and this is how it must end." He looked at me and placed a hand on my shoulder. "When all this is over, you can join the clan, you know?"

I shook my head. "So, I feed on human blood for all of eternity while being in the presence of the man who plans to abduct the woman I love, forcing me to kill her before he does something worse?"

Roland huffed. "Oh, Dorian, so noble of you. If you think you're going to survive on just animal blood, you're blind to your desires. They're always there; you just have to release them." A smile flitted across his features. "Nothing is more satisfying than the feeling of your fangs piercing the delicate skin of your victim and draining them until their body goes limp in your arms. No other blood will make you feel alive."

It was true, but I couldn't admit that to him.

"I shall pass on your offer, Roland," I said, placing my hand on the windowsill, leaving the dagger for the coven to find. "How much time do we have before they come for her?"

"They're already on their way," Roland replied, his mouth set in a hard line, looking perturbed.

The scent of freshly spilled blood drifted in the air, coming in with the wind, and settled around us. I closed my eyes as I desperately fought down the urge to give in to the uncontrollable desire for human blood.

The clan was close, *very* close. We were prepared for that night since we first heard the prophecy—a centuries-old prophecy that predicted the downfall of the vampiric era. The ruling clan was all-powerful, and they would get what they wanted. They wouldn't stop until they trapped the coven behind the gates of their hidden lair. Maurice's top priority was to capture Mercy, for she was the key to their destruction. The bloodlust they all felt for her went beyond anything they had experienced in the past when they hunted witches. She meant a lot more than any other witch, especially to the clan's master.

"There has to be a way to stop him." My voice was only a whisper as I fought down my growing despair, hoping I wouldn't have to bear the weight of Mercy's unfortunate destiny.

Roland snickered at my remark. "Maurice is determined and dangerously ruthless. The only way to stop him is a stake through his heart," Roland mocked, "but I wish you luck trying. The master will always be better as an ally than an enemy." Roland glanced again at the dagger's sharp blade, his stony gaze conveying a message. "You ought to decide now, Dorian, before they get to her first. Then consider joining us once you set her free from him."

To join a vampire clan went against everything I stood for, but if I didn't, a stake through my own heart was the best punishment. I hated that I needed human blood to survive, and no matter how much animal blood I drank, it wasn't enough to satisfy me. I'd never survive on my own without human blood, and I didn't trust myself enough to control the beast I felt within, waiting to be set free. That beast lurked beneath the surface of my control every time I made love to Mercy. It made me not only crave to sink my fangs into her throat as she climaxed, but I fantasized about draining her blood as I reached my own peak.

Loving a woman as deeply and passionately as I did Mercy would be my ultimate death. I didn't deserve her.

Maurice, the very man who had been stalking Mercy for months now, waiting for her ascension, would become my master. The thought of serving that cruel bastard made me feel ill. But reasonably, belonging to a clan would help control the urge to kill.

Vampires were monsters, that was the truth, but they lived by a code—they were careful.

I looked over to the path leading to the town's main square, hearing angry voices in the distance.

"Try to stall them as long as you can," I said. "I won't make this decision for her, Roland, but I'll give her the warning she needs to decide for herself."

Roland let out a heavy sigh. "I have faith you'll do the right thing, boy. But don't think that just because of what I am, she doesn't mean something to me, too."

Roland disappeared into the forest before I could respond. There wasn't a moment to spare, so I ran to find Mercy.

After arriving at her home, I crept to her window—peering inside. I breathed a sigh of relief when I noticed she was still in her house, speaking with her mother. I listened intently—her mother was pleading with Mercy to run away, to stay mortal and flee. Maybe if enough people were warning her, she would listen.

I climbed through the windowpane, slipping into the room silently so as not to be detected. Time was running out, and every passing second meant the clan was getting closer. I stood in the corner of her room for a moment longer before I heard footsteps coming up the stairs. To not startle her, I swiftly rounded to the edge of the doorframe, staying flush with the wall.

I watched Mercy rush to the dresser and sift through her clothes and other items in her room. Quietly, I tapped on the door. "Mercy," I called softly.

She turned around, her eyes widening at seeing me in the doorway. I had never been to her home before. We always met in my lair when we were together, as she was afraid her parents and the coven would find out about me. "Dorian, what are you doing here?"

My heart skipped a beat when I saw her face. I searched her features, trying to remember every detail of her beauty and warmth. We both knew what this night meant and that whatever she chose to do would forever change the course of history. This moment would be the last time I would see her face. This clear night would be the last time I would hear her voice. A lone tear escaped down my cheek. Right then and there, I swore that I'd never love another woman as I had loved her.

How could I tell the love of my life to sacrifice herself, so she'd be free from being enslaved by the most powerful vampire clan? Was I wrong to do so?

I pushed away from the wall and walked over, stopping by her bed, and breathed in her scent. "Your mother is right, Mercy—you cannot allow Caleb to make you immortal. The vampires know you're doing the ritual tonight, so I came here to warn you. Maurice is on his way. Once the ritual is completed, his men plan to take all five of you and enslave you behind their walls. I'm not strong enough to stop them." I took her hand, pulling her closer to me. "You saved my life once, love. Let me save yours."

The look on her face pained me.

How can I ask her to do such a thing?

"I'm dead either way." She gripped my hand and placed it over my heart. "Do you feel that, Dorian? My heart is steady. I'm not afraid. At least if I were immortal, I'd be stronger, fight back, and not need you to protect me anymore."

I will always fight for her, whether she is immortal or not.

My breath hitched as I forced the words out, "I'd rather for you to be dead than tortured by them. At least if you're dead, you'll be free."

Mercy shrugged. "We'll be apart either way." She squeezed my hand and released it.

I wanted to reach out and hold her, knowing the moments we had for over a year would be taken from us.

She stepped closer to me, touching her forehead to mine. Then she drew a deep breath, as if taking in my scent for the last time, treasuring every moment she could before saying goodbye.

I closed my eyes but hesitated to pull her closer to me. Of course, I wanted to, but the pain I felt, even for a vampire, was too much to bear. Vampires didn't have that kind of emotion toward humans, especially witches, but I did. She was my everything.

She stepped back, picked up her bag, and walked to the door. "The coven is waiting for me, Dorian. I ... I must go." I watched as she rushed down the stairs.

No, I can't let her do this. They're going to catch her.

I moved swiftly, using my vampire speed, rushing down the stairs before she reached the door. My speed caused her hair to fly back over her shoulder as if caught in a breeze. "Mercy." My voice wavered as I whispered, "You don't have to do this. You can choose death. If the vampires catch you after you become immortal, you'll want to die, believe me."

Mercy dropped her leather bag at her feet, and silver tears shone in her eyes. She didn't speak as she closed her eyes tightly, her mouth hardening into a thin line. I wondered what she was thinking in that heavy silence. But when she opened her eyes, the tears had dried, and she gave me a nod. My heart leaped and broke simultaneously; I knew what she had decided.

"I love you, Dorian," she said. "I love you more than my own life. Nothing in this world has ever meant more to me than the moments we've shared this last year. Every kiss. Every touch. Every moment of pleasure." Her smile was small before she turned from me and slowly opened the door.

I saw the sky crash with lightning, outlining the tall pines and her silhouette. I heard screams and shouts coming from the line of trees to the front of her house and lit torches appearing from the wooded glen behind her home. The villagers, not the vampires, had come for Mercy.

She turned on her heel, rushing back to me and leaping into my arms. Her lips collided with mine with raw passion, and our emotions flowed down our cheeks.

Mercy released our embrace, stepping back to create distance. "Don't forget me, Dorian," she said before walking out the door and into the night.

Mercy fell to her knees and put her hands up in the air as crowds of angry villagers formed around her, carrying ropes to bind her wrists behind her back.

She had chosen death. Mercy had trusted my warning and chose freedom.

I backed away from the open door and watched the crowd grow around her. Though it was the only way she would not suffer, I wanted to stop it from happening. How could I watch the woman I love die in front of me?

I silently crept out and followed the crowd like another greedy peasant waiting for Death's show. They brought her onto a platform and pulled a noose around her neck that dangled from a large oak tree.

A man standing next to me shouted, "Witch! Witch!"

"Hang her now!" another bellowed.

Mercy stood calmly on the platform, scanning the faces of the rage-fueled villagers as if taking in their bloodlust and religious fervor. Her eyes were shining, but she did not weep, nor did she scream for her life. Instead, they fell upon my face, and her lips twitched just a little. A small smile for me and my grief.

I looked into her eyes one last time and whispered, "Come back to me, Mercy. Promise you'll come back to me."

CHAPTER I

MERCY

East Greenwich, Rhode Island – Present Day

The fragrance of cologne stung my senses as a man hustled by toward the kegs in the far-right room. I craned my neck to look up at the tall spiral staircase, watching my best friend Riley head to the second floor of the fraternity house. Snuggling up under his armpit was a dainty blonde girl with an hourglass figure and long, slender legs.

My anxious heartbeat thumped against my ribcage when I realized I was alone again. I massaged my thighs nervously, swallowing down my spit to moisten my achingly dry throat.

Then I realized I'd had too much to drink, and going to the party was an idiotic idea.

The Kappa Nu fraternity house was one of the few homes off campus near Brown University. They decorated the walls with old yellow wallpaper with sand-sized golden dots covering it from floor to ceiling. It made it appear as if tiny stars were glimmering around the room. All the antique furniture and paintings gave it character—but the old rustic piano that stood proudly in the corner of the room appeared out of place. It didn't belong in a room filled with boisterous men getting drunk and coked out on a Friday night.

This may have been the last night of my junior year at Brown, but I still had another year left before I graduated. Everyone here would see me again, and this would be their last memory over the summer until the fall semester—too drunk and having a silent panic attack.

I looked up from my jeans and cocked my head to the right as a well-built man came sauntering over to me. All black clothing covered his body, with tattoos reaching from his elbow to his chin. His bulky muscles strained against the way-too-small shirt he tucked tightly into his pants. The flutter in my stomach clenched again as he bent his knee to be at eye level with me.

"Mercy Brawling," he hummed, his cheekbones stretching high into a smile. "Are you still alive in there?"

It gave me a sense of pleasure that I couldn't remember his name after the fifth time he had reminded me that night. With the number of times I had told him to leave me the fuck alone, it surprised me he was still around, trying to make small talk.

"You ..." My voice trailed off, trying desperately to search my hazy memory for what he had called himself earlier that night.

"Nick," he said, as if reading my thoughts. His eyes heated as his cocky smile dropped. "Let me take you upstairs to sleep this off." Nick reached out to grab my arm, but I slapped it away.

That wasn't what he wanted to do with me up there.

"Whoa, buddy," I said. That shiver of fear had rippled up my spine again. My instincts screamed throughout my body to move, to get up, but the damn alcohol kept my limbs numb.

Run, my thoughts yelled. *Get out!*

The stone-cold look on his face at the rejection caused every hair on my body to stand straight. I had seen him several times around campus. I never knew his name, though. He was notorious for being a total dick to women, and apparently that night, I was his new conquest.

Not a chance, asshole.

I met his gaze and flashed him a mocking smile, all the while trying to adjust my shirt higher on my chest so he couldn't look at my cleavage. The expression on Nick's face was predatory at this point, and I could see his hand balled into a tight fist.

Sheer panic suddenly flooded me when I searched the room. It was empty. All the partygoers had moved to the kitchen for what sounded like beer pong, and my girlfriends, Shannon and Cami, were nowhere to be found.

Fucking hell, did they leave me?

Nick leaned forward until his lips touched my ear, his fingers wrapping around my thighs. "Let me get you some water, then." After removing one hand from my thigh, he placed the tip of his index finger under my chin to tilt it up, forcing me to look at his pretty face.

The only thoughts going through my head at this moment were that the room was starting to spin and that I really should have eaten something before I started drinking. My stomach churned.

"I think I'm going to be sick, so you might want to back up," I told him, squinting my eyes, but it only made the dizziness worse.

Riley, get your ass back down here!

Riley and I officially called it quits four months ago, but he wasn't out of my life forever; he was my best friend, too. I practically begged him to move on and find someone else, even for just a night. He deserved to be happy.

"Riley," I said aloud, forcing my eyes to stay open. "Who did he go upstairs with?"

The Nick guy flashed me another forced, bitter smile. "Oh, it seemed you were shifting from his touch all night," he said, almost sounding genuine. "I thought maybe you needed rescuing, so I sent my friend Nadia to take care of him. Don't worry." He moved back, giving us space. "She'll be really gentle. Just as he likes it."

I squinted again, my blurry vision clouding over my eyes. "How would you know?" I asked, hearing the slur in my speech getting worse. I gave him a friendly wink. Maybe if I played fun, he'd tone down his intensity, and I wouldn't feel so freaked out.

He sported a tiny smile, but it wasn't friendly. "It's not too difficult for men like him to get off on bimbos who pay attention to them."

Well, I'm becoming less afraid and way more annoyed by this douchebag.

I didn't like the way he was talking about Riley. We may not be together anymore, but he was still my best friend, and the fact some stranger sent a random girl to suck him off was really pissing me off.

Was I jealous? Probably. Did I care? Fuck no.

"I need you to—" I blinked once, feeling my hands tingle at the tips. It felt like electricity vibrating violently under my fingernails, aching to be released. Pressing my hands to my chest, I concentrated on willing the feeling away.

That wasn't the first time it had happened. My body no longer felt like mine anymore. It hadn't felt like mine in a long time. However, in the last few months, a lot of weird shit had been happening to me. Unexplained tingly fingers when I was upset were one of them. It wasn't a nerve issue or something medically explainable, but it felt as if there was a cloud of smoke beneath my fingers, trying to push through my skin.

It was just one more strange thing happening in my life.

For real, though, why does it keep doing that?

"What the hell is wrong with you?" he asked, his face growing hard, as if I had offended him somehow. His eyes, though, his eyes were on my fingers. I glanced down to see what I thought looked like green moss coating my fingertips. I blinked rapidly, and one moment it was there, and then it wasn't.

What the hell?

"Did you slip me something?" I asked him, trying to stand, but Nick moved back as if I suddenly repulsed him.

"I changed my mind about you, you freak," he said, turning on his heel and heading up the stairs to another room.

I clambered to my feet, focusing on the sound of a door opening and footsteps on the stairs. Relieved, I watched as Riley hurried down the steps while Nadia emerged from a bedroom, her arms folded tightly over her chest.

I scoffed, sizing him up. "Seriously, Riley?"

A shy smile adorned his face. "We just talked."

I rolled my eyes at the response that I had no right to be upset about. Right then, my body fell forward, the floor reeling under my feet. Riley's hands reached out to catch me, but the moment his hands found purchase on my arm, I pulled back, stumbling over my feet and landing on my backside. The ceiling fan spun, and so did my head. Everything, and I mean everything, climbed up to my throat.

It's just today. Tomorrow, everything will go back to normal.

Three years ago, I was a completely different person. I always looked forward to dressing up for parties like this. The old Mercy was popular, beautiful, with lots of friends and a great outlook on life, but I wasn't that girl anymore. The person who stared back at me in the mirror was a stranger. All I could see were the horrors hidden in the depths of her emerald eyes and the long, dark brown hair that didn't quite shine anymore. She was merely the shell of the person I used to be.

"Riley, I'm going to be sick," I said quickly, jumping to my feet to rush outside and then vomiting right over the front porch railing. There were a few obnoxious chuckles and jeers from some of the frat boys to the right of me. Cami and Shannon called my name while simultaneously telling the guys to eat shit.

I leaned back up, wiped my mouth, and held my stomach in a tight grip. Taking a deep breath, I stepped down from the porch and walked to the back of the house. Thankfully, I could get some peace and quiet as the backyard had already cleared out.

As I glanced around the yard, my eyes strained as I caught a figure between the tall grove of trees that lined the river. I felt my face pale as I bent forward to get a better look, hoping it was only a hallucination caused by the drinks.

But no, it was *him*, watching in the shadows again. It was the third time this week that I felt his eyes on me in the darkness. Their constant gaze felt like icy fingers trailing up my back, eliciting fear from the depths of my soul.

When the stalking first started, I convinced myself it was only my imagination. But after hearing the rustling of leaves and the soft crackling sound of twigs breaking the last two weeks, I knew someone was there—watching me.

Last Sunday, I felt this warm breath on my neck, causing the hairs on my skin to stand up straight. My body stiffened as I twisted around to see who it was, but they had vanished.

I'm not imagining this. I can't be.

It happened again two nights later when I stepped out of my car after class. My blood ran cold as ice as the sensation touched me again.

"Who's there?" My voice had cracked, fear choking me.

Clutching my phone, I fumbled for the flashlight, but the battery died before I could turn it on. I grabbed my purse and bag, then sprinted into my apartment, locking all the doors and windows. I didn't sleep that night.

I snapped out of the grim memory, my focus turning back to the backyard fence—spotting the dark figure again. They were still there. I wanted it to be a student taking out the trash or a neighbor walking a dog. But the silhouette stood there—motionless. The only movement was the wind blowing through the trees and the river's rippled waves gliding across the water.

The threat of something violent was in the night air, and I lifted my hands, watching that same green light from earlier shine lightly, barely over my fingertips. It was mesmerizing. Whatever Nick had slipped into my drink was starting to freak me out. There was a sound of footsteps in the grass behind me, and I felt the fear surging through my body again. I opened my mouth to scream.

"Mercy!"

Riley gripped my arms from behind, twirling me around to look into his panic-filled eyes, and for the first time that night, I felt safe again.

CHAPTER 2

"What are you staring at, Mercy?" Riley asked, with concern in his eyes. He took one tiny step back to create space between us.

I blinked once. "Did you see that?" I asked, looking over my shoulder through the trees and then back at my hands. Everything was normal again.

Cami, who stood behind Riley with Shannon, brushed her long blonde hair away from her pearl-toned face. She let out a breath to blow a strand away. "We should get you back to the apartment, Mercy. You're drunk as hell and freaking everyone out right now." She adjusted the strap of her yellow sundress while putting her weight on her right heel.

Shannon's smooth, golden brown skin glistened in the moonlight while stifling a yawn. "I'm tired, anyway. These guys are boring as fuck," she said, straightening her back while braiding her raven-black hair over her shoulder.

Riley turned around slowly, giving her a playful sneer.

"You don't count, babes," Shannon added, winking at Riley.

With Riley's light blue eyes glued on mine, he said, "Cami, start the car. Just give Mercy and me a minute, and I'll bring her back."

The girls nodded, turned around, and headed to where they parked, leaving us alone.

Once they had left, Riley threw his hands out in frustration. "What the hell is going on with you tonight?" He gestured to me as I wrapped my arms around my waist.

At least the nausea was beginning to pass.

The dimly lit deck lights glimmered in the reflection of Riley's eyes. I didn't want to put this on him or my girlfriends, but not talking about it would be a thousand times worse.

"Three years ago today, Riley," I told him, waiting for it to register. I didn't expect any of them to remember, of course; enough time had passed for them to let it slip into their subconscious memories.

His eyes widened before he drew in a shallow breath. "Ah, shit, Mercy, I had completely forgotten."

I stepped back until my rear hit a nearby deck swing and sat down, gesturing with my head for him to sit next to me.

He sat down but gave us enough space.

It had been exactly three years since my attack. Three years of trying to rebuild myself again and repair every relationship that I had pushed so far away because I was afraid.

I honestly thought heading out tonight with my friends would help me forget it, allowing me to have fun as a distraction. But it wasn't fun; it was a horrible mistake. All I wanted to do was go home and sleep the memory off.

There was also the fact that someone had been following me in the last month, and I couldn't even share that with the ones I loved and trusted—the three friends I had known since we were five years old. I convinced myself it was only paranoia—living my nightmare all over again by creating something that wasn't there.

If it wasn't the sensation of hands on my skin or the faintest sound of footsteps behind me, causing a harrowing chill to run down my spine, it was the dreams that kept me up at night.

Something terrible was going to happen, and I was about to be in the middle of it all. This was a sense of doom I couldn't shake or free myself from.

"Talk to me, Mercy," Riley spoke before I could tell him I was sorry for drinking so much and for causing a scene out on the porch by being sick.

I reached over and gently took his hand in mine. The action caused him to look at me, and I saw genuine concern in his eyes.

"I *do* want to talk to you. I want to tell you everything." My attempt to mask the fear would only work for so long. That agonizing guilt tore through me as I watched Riley's expression fall; it made me feel sick. This was *my* fault, and it wasn't fair to either of us that I kept causing pain.

He gave me a half smile. "I saw how you reacted in the house when I touched you," he said.

"Sorry about that," I said shamefully. "I'm on edge tonight."

The grimace on his face was too painful to look at, so I turned my attention toward the water behind the frat house and gently pulled my hand away, cradling it to my chest as I took it all in.

The breathtaking view was what I needed to help settle the emotions running through me. It was calm, almost entirely serene. The river reflected the moonlight, and the slight breeze caused small ripples to wash over the rocks at the shoreline. There was no sign of the shadow figure, and I felt my fear ease a little.

"I wish it was different, Riley." I ran my hand through my unruly hair. "God, we've been dating since we were kids. I honestly tried. I tried to make *us* last, but it hasn't been the same between us ever since that night, and I don't know why. The last three years feel like I've imagined it, you know?"

He nodded and slid closer until we almost touched.

"I know you think you did something wrong, but you didn't," I said. "Our situation—not being together anymore—has never been your fault."

Riley had to have felt it, too. The way we had grown apart. We graduated from high school three years ago. After I almost died, we both pulled away from each other, but I felt like I still needed him around in some way. What I really needed was to heal myself alone, and I was using him to mask that pain and fear. Sex between us wasn't even the same. My mind would go to a different place despite the pleasure and intimacy. Something was suddenly missing between us, and I couldn't figure out what it was.

Not until now.

I'm not in love with him anymore.

Riley smiled and held out his hand to me. I slipped my fingers through his, feeling the heat from the simple touch as he traced circles on my hand with his thumb. I both craved that feeling and hated it.

"I know. It's not either of our faults. It's hers," Riley said, nearly whispering the last two words.

He didn't need to say *her* name for my vision to blur.

Riley's firm grip on my hand seemed to anchor me. "What she did to you was fucked up, and I'll never be able to fully understand how you feel. I'll never know what that was like, but I can be here for you. Okay? Please accept *good* when it comes to you." He got up and kneeled in front of the bench, keeping my hand wrapped between his own. His light blue eyes were clear as he looked up at me. "I want to take care of you, even as your friend. I always have."

I couldn't force a sound to get past the lump in my throat. He kneeled there patiently, and I let my free hand cup his cheek for a moment. The wind tousled his blond hair over his eyes, and I gently tucked a few strands behind his ear before pulling my hands away.

I gripped the sleeves of my sweater and hugged my arms tight to my chest again. "Okay," I said. "Understand that today is different, that's all. I'll be fine in the morning."

His expression turned grim, but he nodded.

The two of us had been in so much pain that the happiness we both needed flickered like a small light in the far distance.

Riley stood up and leaned against the pole of the swing, a smile adorning his face. "I still love you."

"I know. I love you, too," I hummed, standing up from the bench. I unzipped my red sweater, letting the sleeves fall off my shoulders. Taking a deep breath, I let the moonlight hit my upper chest. Riley's breath hitched as he watched me trace the two-inch scar; the ugly pink scar rose above my skin. "When I see this scar in the mirror, it reminds me of that night. *Tonight*, three years ago. It will never go away. The scar might fade or lighten, but it will always be there, strengthening me. I feel more powerful today than I ever have in my entire life, even before the attack." A tiny smirk touched my lips. "Maybe not tonight, but this anniversary is an exception."

He reached out, hovering his fingers over the scar. "Does it still hurt?" he asked with genuine concern.

I shrugged. "Not really. It's just a scar now. It's not like she can hurt me anymore through this wound." I took a deep breath and closed my eyes. "I do dream about it, though, from time to time," I said. "I replay the scenes repeatedly in my head. I can still hear the music from the graduation party. All of it."

My mind drifted to that night, the memories pouring in.

Cami and Shannon hosted our school's after-graduation party at Cami's home, and it was everything I hoped it would be. We danced until we couldn't feel our legs; we sang until our voices cracked. I had given my finals everything, and I had nothing else to worry about.

I remember every moment I had with Riley that night in the back of his dad's pickup truck. We had snuck out of the party to have a moment alone. I remember how his hands roamed down my body and between my legs, inching their way to the spot that ached for his touch. The heat from his mouth caressed up and down my neck, sending a tingling sensation through my entire body until I surrendered to him. The pleasure was warm and full of love, awakening every fragment of my body.

I left Cami's house shortly after two in the morning, dead on my feet. Between dancing all night and pulling all-nighters for finals earlier that week, I wanted nothing more than to pass out on my bed.

I quietly made my way through the house, walking straight to my room—face-planting onto my pillow without getting undressed.

The sound of the ticking clock was starting to lull me asleep, and I let my mind wander. The wind could be heard through my open bedroom window, and I had nearly drifted off when I heard a floorboard creak.

Rubbing my eyes, I called out, "Mom? I just got back. Sorry if I worried you."

I turned to face her in the doorway, but she wasn't there. The moonlight lit up the door, and I blinked in confusion, feeling a growing sense of panic. I rolled over when I heard heavy breathing, only to see my mother kneeling over the bed. An object, shiny and silver, sparkled by her hip. My eyes widened when I realized what it was—a large kitchen knife.

"Close those little eyes of yours, Mercy," my mom whispered softly. "I'll make it quick, so you don't suffer too long."

The next few moments were a blur as searing pain took over my senses. I felt the blade go through my chest; the cold metal felt smooth as it pierced my skin. I had no time to react, fight back, or even scream.

The warmth of my blood trickled down the side of my body, soaking the bed sheets, and I blacked out.

After I awoke in the hospital, they told me I had managed to call 911, and an ambulance picked me up. Those memories of the aftermath had now been buried so deep within my subconscious. It was a typical response caused by trauma, the doctors had told me.

For months, my brain struggled to process the thought that my own mother had tried to kill me—a woman who had sworn to protect her only child—a woman who loved me with all her heart.

They had found her in our backyard, sitting in the middle of the overgrown lawn, covered in blood—*my* blood.

I wanted to know why she did it, but she refused to utter a single word until her trial. The only words I had heard her say since that night were spoken in court as she turned to face the judge.

Guilty, Your Honor.

To make matters worse, her fancy lawyer had pleaded insanity. He had collected enough documentation from doctors that declared my mom wasn't in her right mind, and they gave her a life sentence at Raven's Mental Institution in Salem, Massachusetts. It was one of the most secure hospitals where the most unstable criminals were sent. The judge promised never to set her free.

I felt uneasy the entire two hours the trial lasted. I could still see my mother's eyes when I closed mine and feel the ghost touch of the blade as it pierced my skin. Sorrow filled me as I realized I'd never get my answers as to why she tried to kill me.

My eyes opened to the wave of panic coursing through my veins. I tried to take a deep breath, but I couldn't. Then I saw Riley—poor Riley, who still wanted me, despite everything that had happened.

He didn't deserve this.

I wiped away my tears and watched as Riley took a step closer. He was careful not to touch my skin so close to the scar as he gently pulled the sweater over my shoulder and zipped it up.

"Promise me that if those feelings you once had for me never return ..." Tears threatened to fall down my face again as his voice trailed off. "... you'll find someone so much better than me."

I swallowed down a sob. I needed my best friend, but the thought of us only being friends was weird. We had been in a relationship since junior high, technically even before. He was my first and only boyfriend and had been a part of my life for so long.

I could see the hope in his eyes, hoping that one day we could be each other's forever. The forever that will never come.

He smiled and held his hand out for me to take. "Time to get you to bed, Mercy."

elle

As I crawled under my blanket that night, my mind reeled over everything that had happened. That night was supposed to be the best night of my life, as I celebrated new beginnings, but instead, it turned into a nightmare I couldn't escape.

I closed my eyes, slowly drifting off to sleep. The darkness faded away, and I saw myself sitting in a meadow. I gasped. _He_ was back. I had no idea who he was, but it comforted me to see him in my dream again. About a year ago, he started appearing in my dreams, a man with glossy, deep brown hair that fell just below his shoulders and light brown eyes that always put me at ease.

His fingers gently brushed my hair away from my eyes. I shivered as the tips of his nails caressed my skin. He gently tilted my chin up seconds before his lips captured mine. His kiss was soft and teasing at first, but it quickly deepened as lust and hunger consumed our bodies. Nothing else mattered as I could feel his pulse under my hands—his soft skin touching my own. The man's large hand trailed down my chest, gliding over my skin before it finally settled on my breast, teasing me. He let out a moan as if the expression of pleasure on my face was alone enough to satisfy him. I softly whimpered as he pulled away, wanting more.

"So greedy," he purred, his lips lingering on mine. I could practically feel his warm breath against my mouth.

"Do you blame me?"

My God, he made me feel alive, even if he was just a figment of my imagination.

His other hand trailed up between my thighs and under my dress, spreading my legs apart. They instantly obeyed, allowing him easier access to my throbbing center. The man's soft caresses trailed between my folds, prodding at my entrance before his finger entered me. My lips parted at the sensation, and he gave me a moment to adjust before moving his wrist. He thrust in and out while his thumb ran circles over the delicate bundle of nerves. Pleasure roamed through my body as my legs clenched around his knee, bringing him closer to me. I never wanted him to be so far away.

I wanted more than just his hand inside me. God, I wanted more.

In my dreams, I could be myself and not hide from the world because I knew he would keep me safe. My body hummed whenever he was near. My head cleared, and I blushed.

He gradually built up the pace of his motion, bringing me closer to that blissful state I ached for. His eyes were glued to mine; he observed my reaction to how he touched me—my head tipped back slightly, my lips parted, and my eyebrows furrowed together. My body shuddered as he tipped me over that glorious edge, and I finally found my release. Momentarily, the pleasure that he provided flooded me. I struggled to catch my breath, and then my head dropped back to relax on the grass.

The beautiful man slowly dragged his finger out of me, creating space between us. This mysterious, gorgeous man made me feel things I had never felt with anyone.

He murmured, "Well, now that we have gotten that out of the way." His smile reached his eyes. "What are you thinking about right now?"

Shouldn't he know? He was a part of my own mind.

Sighing, I replied, "You." I tore away my gaze from his beautiful eyes to glance up at the dark clouds forming above us.

His breath tickled my ear as he whispered, "I'll see you again tomorrow."

"I know."

He reached out and caressed my cheek, and I gladly soaked up the warmth of his touch. He moved his hand and tilted my chin again. I closed my eyes and leaned into the chaste kiss. Unfortunately, the moment was cut short as my eyes popped open to the sound of my alarm.

CHAPTER 3

The towering trees swayed from the wind within the vast forest surrounding my childhood home. The pleasant aroma of lavender buds spilled into the gentle breeze from the front porch. Despite my college only being twenty-five minutes away, it had been almost three years since I stepped inside.

After they locked my mom away, the courts had turned the house over to my aunt Lily. I spent my summers and between semesters with my uncles in New York. Lily often joined us, making the trip much more enjoyable when we were all together as a family.

I continued to stare at the front door of the house I had grown up in all my life. Lily had repainted the charming white picket fence, and the wooden shutters were changed from blue to black. The window panels were now slightly teal, and the front door was a metallic black with an elaborate, golden-bronze door handle.

One unique feature was all the decorative patio furniture that wrapped around the entire front of the house. Brightly colored tapestries draped to the sides with vibrant green vines that climbed up the walls, intertwining with fairy lights, creating a peaceful oasis on a cloudy, stormy night.

Looking back, I recalled all the moments Lily wanted to visit so she could make something of our dull-looking home. My mom and I were never good at creating an earthy ambiance, but Lily had a knack for decor. New-age pagan aesthetics surrounded Lily's entire life. She believed in using the surrounding earth to bring peace into her world. It wasn't that I thought it was strange; I just didn't understand the significance.

Lily took guardianship of me after my mom was locked away, but it was only a few weeks before my eighteenth birthday, so it was just legal paperwork at that point. When it was time to start college, I packed up the room where my blood had spilled on that hellish night, and I hadn't been back since.

Lily shouted my name through the open window screen, jolting me to awareness. I thought she had seen me and was calling me inside, but I didn't see her standing at the window. It sounded like Lily was shouting my name at someone in anger. I was too far away to understand what she had said afterward, so I walked up toward the house. Stepping onto the porch, I peered inside, watching her pace around the kitchen table. I quietly opened the back door and eased inside the house, my heart pounding with growing anxiety. I swallowed hard and looked around.

The scent of incense through the hallway stung my senses as it permeated into the first-floor bedrooms. Everything was dark around me, aside from a few candles lit on the sconces in the foyer and the light above the kitchen stove. I spotted Lily just inside the kitchen, near the doorway, pressing the phone to her ear. She seemed really agitated.

After Lily disappeared around the corner, I moved closer, staying flush against the wall until I was within earshot.

I glanced through the kitchen doorway. Lily tucked her brown hair behind her ear and listened intently to someone on the other side of the landline, her foot tapping impatiently. "There's no way I'd let that happen! Joel and I will tell her!" she said harshly, her voice climbing an octave.

Lily still hadn't seen or heard me come in, or at least, I didn't think she had. I wanted to listen to more of the phone call, so I stayed silent, not wanting to alert her to my presence yet.

In my haste to remain hidden, the wooden floor creaked under my foot. I backed up farther behind the wall, hoping she hadn't heard.

"Oh, give me a fucking break," Lily continued. "All of this is your fault." Her voice was icy now, and I could feel the anger radiating from her. Her fingers were white as she gripped the phone and hissed, "Two weeks, Daniella! I have two weeks!"

My body froze, and my chest tightened—my mother. The only image I could conjure was her face as she held the knife over my body and the sound of her heavy breathing as she drove it into my chest. I felt panic wash over me, and my stomach twisted into a painful knot.

She's not here.

"Never call here again. I'm done taking these calls, and I'm done with you!" She slammed the phone down before taking a few deep breaths. Lily, always soft-spoken and forbearing, had just lost her temper with my mom. My mother had contacted her, and they had spoken! I hadn't realized those admitted to the asylum could even make outside calls. Lily had never mentioned it.

This couldn't have been the first time, though. Lily and Joel had an obligation to protect me, so something as triggering as this would have been kept a secret.

I swallowed the lump that reached my throat as my foot stepped forward, but Lily was there in the doorway, staring right at me.

"I thought you were coming home tomorrow morning," she said calmly, glancing at the clock as if she had lost track of time.

My thoughts could only focus on my sweaty palms and the rapid heartbeat in my ear as I moved past her. "Well," I said, taking a seat at the table, "you kind of have to tell me now. I heard you and my mom talking."

Her expression fell, and her brown eyes glistened. "It's not that I don't want to tell you about that call, Mercy. It's more complicated than that. Your mom isn't well."

"Yeah," I said. "The scar on my chest reminds me of that every single day." I gestured with my head for her to sit by me. I could feel my hands shaking in my lap as Lily moved to sit down. I wasn't mad, just taken aback by it all, that she had kept the fact that my mom had been calling her for who knows how long. The question had to be asked. "How many times, Lily?"

She blinked. "Oh, um, at least once a month." A row of lines creased her forehead like she was lost in thought. "The doctors said it was good for her. That it might help her in some way. But every time she calls, it feels less and less like the woman we knew."

We sat in silence for a beat. The weight of the conversation hung thickly in the air. I eagerly wanted to know everything my mom had said and what had transpired in that conversation to make Lily so angry.

Keeping my face blank, I watched her reach for the glass of wine sitting on the table and sip slowly before she said, "Daniella wants me to put you on the list at the hospital." She licked her lips. "Because she wants you to visit her." She took a deep breath and gazed back into her wine glass, shaking her head. "But it doesn't matter, Mercy. I'm not authorizing the hospital to let you go inside. It would completely erase everything you have done to heal these last three years."

Lily's eyes locked with mine. I could see the fear behind them. She quickly looked away, unaware I was on the verge of another panic attack.

I lowered my brow and exhaled slowly. "Lily, I'm not a child anymore," I said, not believing the words that were about to leave my lips. "What if she wants to tell me she's sorry? I should let her, right?" I could hear the doubt in my own voice, and the last time I had gone to see her, she was anything but apologetic. That day didn't just affect me; it affected Lily, too.

Right after they incarcerated my mom, I sat down with her to get answers as to why she tried to kill me. Minutes of silence passed before I gathered enough courage to ask the question I desperately wanted an answer to. While my hands shook nervously in my lap, I asked my mother why she wanted me dead. Her eyes looked dull, and she twitched when I said the word 'dead.' Large bags hung under her eyes, and she stared at her cuffed hands in complete silence. I searched her face for any sign that it wasn't my fault but found none on her emotionless face.

My mom showed me no compassion or empathy. Her silence proved that she didn't care about me at all. That thought hurt me more than the feeling of a blade slicing my chest open.

I couldn't tell if they had drugged her or if she had simply lost her mind. As she looked up, it felt like she was looking through me; I remember wondering if anything was happening inside her head. It was in that moment of thought that she came after me like a tiger attacking its prey, leaping over the table she was still chained to and knocking over her chair. Somehow the chains of the cuffs snapped, and she freed herself. She lashed out at me, and all I could do was shield myself with my arms so she didn't cut my face with her sharp, unkempt nails. Her shrieks of rage and hatred filled the small room before the guards ran and grabbed her. Yanking her off me, they dragged her out of the room, where the asylum doctor quickly sedated her. I could still hear her shrieks fade as they carried her back to her cell.

Lily's voice pulled me out of my memory. "Mercy, I'm begging you not to go."

I leaned forward and reached out, placing my hands over hers for comfort.

"Please, Lily."

There was a brief expression of doubt on her face before her words caught me off guard. "I'll sleep on it," she said.

That's good enough for now.

I gave her an agreeable nod to settle her worries and let go of her hands. If I had to go through the courts, I would. Lily was hiding something else from that conversation, and I was determined to find out.

She took a deep breath and slowly released the air from her lungs. Lily looked exhausted and worn down as she lowered her head to her hands.

"As upset as I am at what your mother did, I miss how close we all used to be," she said, glancing up at me. "I miss the woman she used to be."

Guilt tore through me then. I was so blind. Lily was hurting just as much as I was—she had lost her only sister.

We all needed to focus on the good times we used to have as a family. Talking or even thinking about what my mom did only brought pain to both of us.

My favorite day with my mom was when the city dedicated a bench to my grandfather. My uncle Joel and his husband, Derek, had flown in from New York, and we were all together, laughing and crying while sharing memories of what a great man he had been.

I hummed, "Hey, do you still have that photo we took that last day together? The one in front of the bench?"

She sat there for a moment, and then her face lit up. "Scallop-town Park!"

I was fifteen years old. Two years after my grandfather passed away, the city installed a bench in his honor for all his service to our community. We had gone together for the unveiling and dedication.

"Yeah, it's on my Facebook page, I think," she said while grabbing her phone and scrolling through her photo albums. "Ah. Here it is." She brought her phone in front of us. We looked at the picture for a few seconds as if replaying the memory. "I'll text it to you," she said.

"Thank you." I needed a reminder on my phone that we were all happy once. My phone made a small chime as a new message popped on the screen.

I opened the attached image, saving it in my picture gallery. My mom and I were sitting on that same bench with Lily, Joel, and Derek standing behind us. We had asked a jogger, who was passing by, to snap a quick photo.

My grandfather, William Winchester, was an important figure in our community. He was a city councilman and business owner who devoted his time and money to various projects around town. Before he got sick, he was about to expand his hotel chain nationwide. He was only married to my nana, Helen, ten years before she passed. Together, they had three children, all a year apart from one another. The oldest was my uncle Joel, who lived in New York. Their second child was my mother, Daniella, and their youngest, my aunt Lily. After my grandfather died, they split the inheritance equally between the three of them. My mom took her share and set up a trust fund so that when I turned twenty-one, I would be able to access the money.

Lily opened her café a little over four years ago with her part of the inheritance. She had contemplated using the funds for traveling or opening a boutique. Ultimately, she decided a small café was what our town needed.

Joel, an artist, opened a gallery of the work he'd been creating since he was a kid. He painted abstract art, while Derek, a photographer, focused on real-life portraits, from *The Barber on Main Street* to *The Prostitute on 22nd Avenue*. Together, they incorporated their projects into works of art that drew national acclaim. They agreed that their spare room would be available for me to rent after I graduated from college until I found a more permanent place to live.

Even after everything that had happened, I wasn't going to let this stop me from living my dreams. I would graduate with my friends from Brown University with a degree in marketing and, someday, open my own firm in New York.

Lily finished the last sip of her wine and placed the glass next to the sink.

"I need to open the café early tomorrow morning. Are you going to be alright hanging out alone, or do you plan to head into town?" she asked.

I shrugged. "Oh, right. Uh, breakfast with the girls at nine."

"They're doing good?" she asked.

I nodded. "Well, Cami plans to avoid her mom as much as possible this summer, so we'll just have to keep her busy." A smile reached my lips.

"I checked on Laurie a few times this last spring," Lily said. "She seems to be doing okay. Drinking less. Working hard."

My smile grew. "Cami knows her mother loves her; she's just terrible at showing it."

Lily smiled and nodded. "At least she's trying." She placed her phone in her robe's pocket. "Stop by the café on your way back, and don't forget to lock up when you leave in the morning, okay?" She perked up. "Also, I'd like to take you out for an early birthday dinner. How about La Masseria tomorrow night?"

I nodded.

"Be back by six, okay?" she added.

I flashed her a warm smile. "Sounds good. Night, Lily."

After Lily retired to her room, I attached the family photo at the park in a text message for Joel.

Me: *Sorry for texting so late. You and Derek need to get your asses out here. I miss you guys.*

Joel: *I may be able to fly out for your birthday next week. I have a few projects I'm working on, but if I can wrap them up, I'll come out. Thanks for the picture. Man, I've aged.*

Me: *Dork, you and Derek still look amazing. Anyway, no problem. That would be great if you could come out for my birthday. I can go out drinking with you guys this time. Well, legally, anyway. Tell Derek I said hi.*

Joel: *Will do. Take care, kiddo.*

Nothing had changed in my room except for the freshly cleaned sheets and the scent of citrus surface cleaner from the bathroom. All the old belongings that I didn't want to take to college that I had left behind were still stacked in boxes in my walk-in closet. My guitar still sat in the corner of the room.

I plopped on my bed, placed my phone on the charger, and then lay back, staring up at the ceiling.

She isn't here. You're safe.

Turning back to the nightstand, I reached for my purse, pulled out a container of melatonin, and popped a few to help me sleep. Many would wonder why I'd sleep in this room after what happened. Lily had asked me a million times before I came here today if I was sure. But I told her I'd be okay because I would be. I have to be.

My eyes felt heavy before I slipped into my dreams.

His hands gently caressed my neck. Those soft lips reached my collarbone and tickled my skin, creating a mountain of goosebumps up my back. A small sound escaped my lips, my back instinctively arching. My body ached to be touched everywhere by his powerful hands. However, something felt different tonight, like he was fading slowly from my dream. Yet his touch still lingered over every curve of my naked body.

"God, I've missed you," he breathed, stroking my cheek with the back of his fingers. I moaned at his touch and placed my hand over his, stretching out his fingers and leaning into his palm.

"You know I would have come sooner if I could," I said, gripping his hand more firmly. My fingers locked with his. "Be patient with me right now. It won't always be like this."

He grinned and kissed me gently. "It's worth the wait," he whispered. "I'll always be here when you come."

Suddenly, a black cloud of smoke crept between us, and when the wind blew from my right, it took the image of him with it. A sudden panic hit me at my core. Why was everything suddenly changing after a year of him coming into my dreams?

The gentle breeze felt warm as it tickled my skin, but something was missing. I looked around and saw a beautiful field full of bright-colored flowers. I heard the birds chirping and saw the lush green trees swaying in the wind. But it felt empty—like I was looking at a painting. I walked over to the trees to take a closer look. The thick trunks of the trees were hard to the touch; they didn't feel like trees.

As the branches shook, I pulled my hand away and watched the leaves quickly change colors. The bright green faded into blood-red and radiant amber. It was like seeing the seasons in a time-lapse. I reached out to touch the tip of the leaves when they suddenly darkened and curled, eventually vanishing, leaving the tree bare.

One tree stood out among the others. Dark red leaves fell slowly from their branches onto the ground, leaving me transfixed by their hypnotic beauty.

A gray, smoky mist crept through the trees and wrapped around my body. I walked closer to the tree as each leaf dripped what looked like thick red liquid.

Is this blood?

The puddled liquid at the base of the tree turned from red to black, swirling clockwise and becoming thicker and thicker like molten lava, making it harder for me to walk as it closed tightly around my legs.

I looked ahead, and there stood a mausoleum in the center of a cemetery. I freed my legs from the thick, black lava and moved forward. My legs inexplicably gave way as I approached the entryway, causing me to stumble through the door. I stood up and brushed the remaining thick liquid off my pants. I saw a black onyx coffin at the center of the room and approached cautiously. The lid was opened slightly, and I peered inside, expecting to see a rotting corpse.

Instead, I saw a secret passageway that led down into a dark and mysterious tunnel. Wrought iron stairs were hooked to the top of the opening, but I couldn't see how far down they went. I pushed the lid further open and lifted myself up to look deeper inside. Before I could peer all the way in, I felt a force grab me by the neck and push my body forward and into the coffin. I was nearing the bottom of the tunnel when my eyes shot open to the light coming in from my bedroom window.

"Holy shit!"

What the hell was that?

CHAPTER 4

While slowly sipping my coffee, my eyes honed in on the necklace dangling between my fingers and the note Lily had left me on my nightstand.

Mercy,

Happy early birthday! This gem is a family heirloom passed down to each firstborn female in our bloodline. The stone belonged to your mother. She had planned to give it to you right before your eighteenth birthday. I found it recently going through her storage. Please don't be upset. It's from me, not her.

The stone itself is called a jet stone, and the pentagram engraved on it is our family crest.

We are descendants of Salem witches, after all.

The pentagram is more than just a symbol of witch-craft. I know you don't believe in all this, but I do, so giving it to you will mean the world to me. It also meant something to our family back then. They believed it had the power to protect them from evil, as each point of the pentagram represented a different universal element: earth, air, water, fire, and spirit. Some history books spoke of the witches of Salem being able to harness powers drawn from those elements. Without those elements, magic would cease to exist.

Okay. I know what you're thinking. Magic isn't real. I get it. But the necklace is still a part of who we are. Who you are.

We all should believe in something, shouldn't we? Wear it if not for you, then for me.

I love you,

Lily

I latched the necklace around my neck, then placed the gem against my chest, feeling the engraving between my fingers.

Maybe Lily just ran out of ideas on what to get me for my birthday.

Honestly, a case of beer would have been perfect.

Fresh out of the shower, I put on light makeup, pulled my thick hair into a wet ponytail, and headed downstairs to go into town.

The wind had picked up, causing the wooden deck to shake as I stepped outside.

A storm is coming.

As I walked under the oak tree next to our front yard fence, a leaf fell in front of my eyes, and for a moment, it drew me back to last night's dream, wondering what it all meant.

Once I got into my car and secured my seatbelt, I turned on the radio, settling for the local rock station. I let the music drown out my thoughts about the tree from my dream as I pulled out of the driveway and onto the street.

I focused on the road straight ahead, narrowing my eyes to the white lines in the center of the two lanes. My mind zoned out, counting each line as I drove past them as if I were on autopilot. It didn't feel as if I had an entire night's sleep.

Moments before turning on Howland Drive, an animal dashed in front of my car so fast that I couldn't quite make out what it was, but the distraction was enough that I swerved into the left lane and slammed on my brakes.

Fuck!

The wheels turned sharply to the right, but this only caused my car to spin around in circles.

I was going to crash!

My body was thrown hard into the steering wheel and then up against the window, smashing my head violently against the glass. Then, blackness.

—⁓⁓—

When I awoke, my car was at the bottom of a ditch on the side of the road. I looked around, and the only way I could see to get out of the car was through the shattered window. I felt the warmth of blood pumping from my forehead and dripping over my left eye, and my sight began to blur.

No. No. No, this isn't happening.

I looked through the window, assessing the surrounding environment, trying to figure out where I was or if there were any passersby I could call out to. My car was on its left side, leaning against a small tree that had nearly been knocked down when I crashed. I tried to move, even just an inch, but I couldn't. My left leg was lodged between the dashboard and my seat. My ankle was stuck, and I thought about moving it slightly back and forth to wiggle out of my shoe. When I went to move my foot to get free, a sudden surge of excruciating pain shot up my leg. I let out a scream of pain and twisted my body to see what had happened to my leg. A closer examination revealed a cracked piece of plastic from the dashboard had pierced into my calf. Blood was pouring from the puncture wound, and the plastic shard was lodged fairly deep in my skin.

Shit!

"Help!" I screamed as loudly as I could. "Someone, help me!"

My head spun, and there was a tight pinch in my chest. It was as if I had to think about every breath I took, and the rapid breathing caused my lips to tingle.

Great, I'm having another panic attack.

My lungs suddenly felt clogged, and I desperately gasped for air.

Slow breaths, Mercy. You can do this.

As I tried again to move my leg out of its stuck position, I heard a snap in my ankle. A new, fiery burst of pain rocketed up my leg, stealing the breath out of my lungs.

"Fuck!" Tears stung my eyes. "Oh my God, this isn't happening." My body ached from head to toe, and I felt that at any moment, I would pass out from the amount of blood I felt pouring out of my leg.

I managed to drag my foot out from under the dashboard, crying out in pain as the pressure increased on my bloody calf and broken ankle. The adrenaline coursing through my body was starting to wear off, and I could feel myself getting colder and colder. I gripped my arms until I could see marks on my skin from my nails—anything to draw away from the pain.

At this point, I could barely move. There was no way I was getting out of the ditch. I tried looking for my cell phone, but it had fallen from my purse and was nowhere to be seen. Defeated, I tilted my head back, staring at the leaves hanging above me, trying to ignore the sticky feeling of the blood running down my leg.

The small hope that someone would see my car and help me had vanished.

Someone, please find me.

Suddenly, I heard movement from behind my car, causing me to look back through the window. But no one was there. The slight movement had sent another wave of pain. I bit down hard on my bottom lip, attempting to breathe through it.

I heard a small, barely audible breath from right outside my door. My eyes blurred at the pain when the door flew off the hinges, causing the car to shake. I glanced at the metal door lying on the forest floor.

The hell?

A sudden movement caught my eye, and I tried to follow it, but I could only move so much. I watched as an arm came into the car and reached toward me. I waited for them to speak or touch me, but instead, they grabbed the piece of plastic and yanked. It was gentle and fast, completely removing the plastic from my leg. The movement sent another wave of nausea and pain through me as I watched more blood pouring out of the gushing wound. My eyes began to close as the pain was too much to bear.

I forced myself to look over at the person who appeared to be a man. At least, I think they were—everything seemed so blurred. In an instant, I felt strong, muscular arms wrap around me, bringing me tight against a hard and flat chest. The touch was gentle as he cradled me to his body, lifting me out of my seat.

Yes, they are most definitely a man.

The musky scent made my head spin into a euphoric daze. The heat from his skin warmed my own, and a sudden comfort surrounded me like a relaxing, soothing bath.

My eyes blinked open, focusing on the arm before me, and I noticed a flame-shaped tattoo above his right wrist. The stranger laid me gently on the ground, releasing his hold.

I still hadn't looked up. "Thank you." My voice didn't sound like my own. "I'm pretty sure my ankle broke—"

"Why aren't you healing?" The man's voice was steady, his nails gingerly gliding down my arm into a tender caress.

Goosebumps spread along my wrist to my shoulder as he ran his calloused hand along my soft skin. He reached my neck, weaving his fingers under my hair and against my scalp, taking hold of the back of my neck to keep me from falling back.

The stranger's heavy breath fanned my skin as he said, "Mercy!" My name on his tongue was spoken with such urgency.

He knows me.

That knowledge caused my spine to stiffen involuntarily.

"Heal yourself, dammit," the man said in a low, tender voice as if he wanted no one else to hear but me.

I looked up, confused, but in an instant, he was gone—vanishing before I could blink. That awareness that he was no longer holding me felt bare, lonely, and scary.

My head pounded so hard that I forced my eyes closed and lay all the way down on the ground, feeling the dried leaves and twigs scratch against my tender skin and the mud soaking into my clothes.

I felt my eyes roll back against my eyelids, and my mind drifted into the darkness of another haunting and ominous dream.

A sensation of relief hit me as my body felt pain-free again, except everything around me felt suffocating. I tried to take a few breaths, but my lungs were restricted.

I looked around and saw that I was in a dark forest. The sky was cloudy, and flashes of lightning flickered over the tops of the trees. I walked a few feet until I entered a clearing where a woman with a rope wrapped around her neck stood on a wooden platform below a large tree. The rope was secured to a thick branch above her. There was no escape for the woman, only certain death. When I looked more closely at her, I noticed her face was like mine.

The only difference between us was the color of her hair, which was light auburn, and the clothes she wore were not from this era. An angry crowd surrounded the woman, hoisting up flaming torches.

I jumped back at the sudden chaos, watching the surrounding scene.

"Witch!" they chanted in unison.

"Hang her now!" a man bellowed.

The woman closed her eyes as the platform opened from under her. Her feet dropped, and her body went limp. The shock of her death made me scream, closing my eyes tightly, unable to tolerate the sight of watching someone die. When I opened my eyes again, all I saw was a white-painted ceiling above me.

CHAPTER 5

"Oh, thank God," Lily whispered. "Shannon, please go find a nurse, and tell them Mercy's awake."

I lay in a hospital bed, wearing nothing but a flimsy white gown and a plastic band around my wrist with my name on it. Riley and Shannon stood by the back wall while Lily stayed by my side. Shannon quickly walked out of the room to grab a nearby nurse.

Lily grabbed my hand. "Minor injuries, Mercy. You're okay."

I didn't feel okay. I felt achy, but it wasn't nearly as painful as it had been in the car.

They must have me on some pretty powerful painkillers.

I looked down at my leg and noticed my ankle wasn't in a cast, either. I placed my fingertips on my forehead, gliding them gently across the skin, but felt nothing.

What the fuck?

I looked up at Lily. "Jesus, what happened to me?"

"You were in an accident not too far from our house. Someone saw your car from their home across the street and called 911," she said. "Before the ambulance reached you, they saw you stumbling into the woods, collapsing about twenty feet from your car. The doctor thinks you may have passed out."

"What do you mean that I was walking?" I shook my head. "No, that isn't what happened. My ankle broke when I crashed. I remember now. There's no way I would have been walking after that." I tried to recall what had happened, but my mind wasn't making sense of it.

Lily and Riley looked at each other and then back at me. I glanced down at my foot again, moving my ankle from side to side. "Or I thought I did."

"You scared the hell out of us," Riley said, coming to my side. "From what the nurses have said, nothing's broken, though." He inched closer until we almost touched. "Kind of surprised, though, you destroyed your car."

"Shit," I said, closing my eyes to calm the room from spinning.

"The door had been completely ripped off in the crash," he added.

"What?" My jaw dropped. The stranger who saved me was real. Everything I remember happening was real.

I glanced around the room. "Is Cami here, too?" I asked Lily.

"She's here, somewhere," Lily replied. "The last I saw her was in the waiting room, speaking with her mom on the phone."

Before Lily opened her mouth again, Shannon followed in with the nurse, who checked my monitors.

"Your doctor will be right in," the nurse assured me.

I shot Shannon a weak smile, then shifted my body back to Riley again. "Hey, you," I said to him. His fingers lightly touched my arm, running along my forearm.

"God, the moment Lily called me—" he said, placing his hand higher on my arm but dropping it to move away, but only slightly.

"I know, Riley," I said, seeing the fear in his eyes. "But I'm okay."

After a few seconds, I turned from Riley to face Lily on my other side. "I hate to ask," I said. "But I may need to borrow your truck. If that thing is still alive." I snickered at my joke, despite the situation I was in.

She smiled and rolled her eyes. "Oh please, it's not *that* bad. Plus, I need someone to drive it every now and then anyway, so that helps me out." She folded her arms across her chest. "But only when you're healed, alright?" Lily leaned back against her chair and crossed her legs, running her hands down her light brown hair. "What can you remember from the accident?"

My thoughts raced through the images swirling in my mind. *What did I see?*

I bit my bottom lip. "An animal ran across the street, but I didn't have time to avoid it. The car spun out after I swerved, landing in a ditch on the side of the road. I—" I hesitated again because what had happened after that seemed impossible.

I'll leave out the part about some guy having superhuman strength as he ripped off my door and tossed it into the forest like it was made of air.

"This guy found me and pulled me from the car," I said. "He ... then he just left me there like a fucking asshole." My face paled at the realization. He left me there. As tender as he was with me, and the fact he saved me from lying dead in a trapped car, he *left* me. Abandoning me in the hopes that I would survive on my own from my injuries. Who the hell does that? I could have died ... alone.

"What? No, Mercy." Confusion crossed over Lily's face. "The person who called 911 said they didn't see anyone else at the scene."

As I tried to make sense of everything—tried to figure out what was real and what wasn't—a doctor entered the room.

"Mercy, glad to see you're awake," the doctor said as he walked in. "Sorry for the long wait; the hospital is pretty busy tonight." He reached out to shake my hand. "I'm Doctor Reid. How's your head feeling now?"

It wasn't my head I was worried about.

I looked down at my ankle again. "Well, my head feels fine, but I would have sworn I had broken my ankle. I—" I stopped, confusion clouding my thoughts. "Did you guys take an x-ray to make sure I didn't break anything?"

"I examined you myself. There's a minor wound on your calf and your forehead. Aside from that, you're fine," the doctor explained.

That's impossible.

"Please check my ankle." I looked at him nervously. "I broke it. I know I did."

Was I losing my goddamn mind?

Doctor Reid sucked in a breath as if he were humoring me at that point and pulled a chair to the end of the bed. He lifted the blanket, gently placing his hands on my ankle, and moved it slightly right.

"Alright. How's that? Any pain?" I shook my head. He turned it to the left. "And that?" I shook my head again. There was no pain, not even a tiny bit. "Is it possible you dreamed you broke it when you passed out?" he asked.

My eyes dropped to the foot of the bed, moving my ankle from side to side on my own. "I guess it's possible." A ghost of a smile touched my lips, thinking about how ridiculous I must have sounded to everyone in the room. Dreaming of the injuries was more realistic than a broken ankle healing itself within an hour.

The doctor crossed his arms and leaned back into his swivel chair. "My only real concern is that you passed out at the scene, so I'd like to keep you here for twenty-four hours to monitor you. After you head home tomorrow, just take it easy. If you pass out again or get headaches, call my office, and I'll refer you to a neurologist," he instructed.

"Maybe you fell asleep at the wheel?" Shannon, sitting quietly in the back of the room, suggested. "You lost a lot of sleep this week between finals and the party."

Her theory made sense, too. I remembered zoning out and feeling incredibly tired. Maybe there hadn't been an animal. Perhaps I fell asleep, crashed my car, and dreamed about everything after that.

"Mercy, I'll stay here for as long as you need. I can keep the café closed for the rest of the day," Lily told me.

I shook my head. "No way, please don't do that. As the doctor said, I'm fine. It's just routine monitoring." I looked up at Shannon and Riley. "God, I love you guys. I appreciate you being here. Really."

Doctor Reid excused himself, informing Lily that the nurse would be in shortly to check on me.

Shannon opened her mouth to say something, but Cami barged through the door. "Oh my God, Mercy!" she yelled.

I giggled at her dramatic response. "It's not that serious, Cami, really. I'm fine. They want to keep me here overnight, though."

"Well, that doesn't sound like you're fine," she huffed, folding her arms across her chest.

"How's your mom?" I asked, changing the focus away from me.

She frowned and shook her head. "I should probably get back to her. She's having another shitty morning again."

I turned to Riley, giving him a small smile. "I'll text you later, okay?"

I could see the disappointment in his eyes, but I wanted to be alone. He solemnly nodded and signaled for the girls to head out.

—ee—

A few hours after everyone had left the hospital, I was getting restless. Once I climbed out of bed, the sudden urge to pee took over. After relieving myself, I washed my hands and turned my gaze up at the mirror. I brought my hands to my forehead and pulled the bandage off to reveal ... nothing.

What?

My face paled as the bandage hung limply in my hand. I quickly tossed the bloodied Band-Aid into the trash and rubbed my forehead. After the pink smudge washed away, there was no trace of the large cut. There was nothing but unblemished skin. I pinched myself, wincing at the pain.

This isn't a dream.

I scrambled to pull at the bandage on my leg, ripping it off. I felt the tearing pain from the tape but fear quickly overshadowed it. There was no gash, not even a faint scar, from where the plastic embedded itself in my leg.

Had I just imagined it?

Sweat pooled in my hands as my heart raced faster and faster. I looked around the bathroom, quickly spotting a bag of the clothes I had been wearing when I had my accident. My hands shook as I pulled out my pants, fingering the large tear in the fabric. There was a two-inch hole right where the plastic had been. I could see that the nurses could have missed the blood staining my pants where the tear was, as mud completely covered my dark jeans.

No, I thought. *I didn't dream of those injuries.*

I hustled out of the bathroom, crawled back into bed, and bent my knees, hugging my legs to my chest. My hands trembled slightly from the realization that something was happening to me—something unnatural that I couldn't explain.

I had a sickening feeling I was about to find out sooner rather than later.

That man held me so close to him as if he *knew* me, knew my name. Not just knowing me but caring enough to soothe my pain away, putting me into the dream of the dark forest. That stranger was still out there, and every gut feeling I had said he would be back, and there would be no way for me to escape him a second time.

I checked my phone notifications before rolling over and shutting my eyes. But, of course, it was impossible to shut my thoughts off. I was too wound up to go to sleep.

I turned back around and sat up. When I pressed the bed controls to sit upright, there was a noise coming from the door. The handle turned to the left and then stopped. I sat there waiting for the on-call nurse to come in, but she didn't. I got up from my bed and waited again.

"Yes?" My lips trembled around my words. "Can I help you?"

You're just paranoid, Mercy. You're safe in a hospital. A nurse just changed their mind about coming in.

Even though that was the rational explanation, my heartbeat picked up, my breath catching sharply in my throat.

To put my nerves at ease, I steadily walked to the door and opened it. Looking down the hall, the only hospital employee was a female nurse sitting at the desk from a short distance, her eyes focusing intently on a computer monitor. I stepped out of the room and walked a few feet toward the nurses' station.

I glanced at the nurse at the front desk, gently clearing my throat. "Excuse me?" I muttered.

She looked up and smiled. "Hey, Mercy. How can I help you?"

"Yes ... um ... did you just try to come inside my room?"

She looked slightly concerned. "No. I've been sitting here for at least thirty minutes. Why?"

"Oh, it's not a big deal. I'm fine. Goodnight." I turned to walk back to my room but only took one step before I stopped, turning back to face her. There were more questions than answers, and I wouldn't be able to sleep until I felt satisfied with what those answers were. I swallowed. "Are there any other nurses working right now on this floor and ..." The words faded on my lips when she shook her head.

"Just me." She stood up, giving me a reassuring smile. "I'll walk you back to your room. You need to be resting right now."

They'll think I'm hallucinating, I thought. *Then they'll keep me here longer if I don't stop acting so paranoid.*

My body screamed at me, telling me I needed to get out of the hospital as soon as possible. I climbed into the bed, and the nurse eased my legs up, even though I didn't need help.

"Mercy, if you need anything, ring the monitor on your bed. Try to sleep. Okay?"

"Alright, thank you." I rolled back over while listening to the door click shut.

Once I heard her footsteps continue down the hall, my pulse picked up again. No one else was in the room, but a sense of foreboding washed over me.

CHAPTER 6

The sky was hazy, with only a tiny light trickling down onto the cove. The hospital felt so suffocating that coming to the park to meet Riley was all I needed to help me breathe.

Pulling into the marina at Goddard Park, I spotted Riley sitting on our bench. He looked out, facing the rippling waves from the water in the cove.

The park was one of my favorite places near East Greenwich, stretching across four hundred acres along Greenwich Cove. There were beautiful trails, canoeing, and spots to picnic. In high school, my friends and I would come to look out over the water, drink, party, and have sex.

The patrol had to crack down on us as word had gotten out about how much shit we got away with out here, and they weren't having it anymore.

All of that didn't matter, though, not anymore. There were moments like this—today—where we could escape a bit from the chaos in our lives and be us. Just Riley and me. Like we used to.

"It's been a while since we've come here together like this," I said as I approached him.

"Don't you miss it?" Riley asked solemnly, turning around and handing me the bag of food. "Two plain bean burritos for you. Extra packets of mild sauce."

My eyes captured his. "This was exactly what I needed."

Riley matched my smile, slapping his hand on the bench next to him. "Sit."

Leaning back on the bench, I stretched out my legs while we ate silently, watching the water become as still as a sheet of ice.

When I slowly turned to face Riley, I noticed the change on his face—a thoughtful frown as his brows pulled together.

"Riley," I started, "what's wrong?"

He glanced at me and then back to the water. His eyes were filled with sadness and pain.

"Everything," he said. "I mean, not everything, but ... fuck. Life has been really hard for me lately, Mercy. How do we go every day without breaking down?"

I shrugged. "To be honest, I haven't a clue." My dark brows drew together in thought. "I'm working on that myself. You know?"

He nodded and ran his hand through his blond hair. "Hey, remember how my dad and I used to come out here when my mom was still alive and fish on our little paddle boat?"

I nodded. "Yeah, I remember. Your dad was so excited when you caught your first fish that he cooked it up that night. He didn't realize my mom and I didn't eat fish, but he tried to serve us what you guys caught that day, anyway." We both snickered at the memory.

His laughter dwindled as he looked back out at the cove. "Yeah. Everything changed after my mom died. We no longer have those kinds of moments that a father should have with his son. God, he really is a shit of a father. Now, if I go home and visit, he stays in his room and doesn't come out until dinner. Constantly talks about my mom and reminds me every fucking day how unhappy she was and what we could have done to help her but didn't these last twelve years."

I watched as his shoulders sagged, no longer tense. How long had he been waiting to share that with someone? He looked like a child who had lost everything and never had the chance to grieve properly. I saw the small child who stared at his father's back, waiting for that parent to turn around and give him a hug.

Riley shuddered. "I was on my way to Goddard Park yesterday morning before I got the call about your accident." He sighed and leaned forward, resting his elbows on his thighs. "I was going to take my boat out myself and hopefully catch something."

He pointed to a group of trees on our left, farther into the cove than the rest. I saw a few wooden paddle boats tied to a tree that reached over the water.

"There isn't an official dock on this side, so people just keep their boats tied to the trees. I'm pretty sure strangers have taken ours out before." He chuckled, but I couldn't join his laughter. I knew he was hurting—and that hurt me.

Riley had been alone for so many years. The sadness in his eyes was somewhat always present, and I didn't see it until now. I had been his girlfriend and never noticed the pain he felt from the absence of his father's love. He must have felt me pulling away these last years, way before what happened with my mom. I saw that now. He hadn't had a father to give him affection. He'd had me, and now I had taken that from him.

We relaxed on the bench for over an hour, staring at the waves and talking about the times when life wasn't so complicated. Time moved so quickly that I hadn't realized the sun was already setting. I glanced at my phone to note the time.

"Riley, I need to get back," I said. "Lily and I were supposed to head to dinner tonight on Main, but most likely, she'll force me to stay in until she feels I'm fully healed."

Right then, I reached out, opening my palm for him to take.

He gave me a curt nod and wrapped his fingers in mine.

Riley held my hand for a few minutes longer, allowing me to relax before I let go, releasing our touch. "Thank you for sharing that with me," I said while standing up. "We need to do this more often than we have been."

We locked eyes, and I saw the strength behind them and gave him a reassuring nod before we said our goodbyes for the night.

When we were both in our cars, I waved at him and turned the key, but Lily's truck stood still.

"Oh, you stupid truck, don't do this," I whined. "Not today, please. Not today."

I tried again, and nothing happened. I opened the door to flag Riley down, but he had already rounded the corner, disappearing down the road.

Dammit. Dammit. Dammit.

I ran to the car to grab my phone, hoping I could get him to come back for me, but I didn't see it anywhere—not in my purse or under the seat.

"Dammit," I swore out loud that time.

Back at the cove where we had been sitting, I kneeled on the floor, my jeans digging into the dirt and rocks. I peered underneath the bench and let out a frustrated grunt when I didn't see it there, either. Right as I clambered to my feet and wiped the dirt off my pants, I noticed a shadow on the ground in front of me. Instinctively, I stepped back and looked up into the eyes of a man standing right in front of me.

My heart leaped at the startling appearance of a stranger appearing out of nowhere. Yet despite that, my eyes were drawn to take in the face and form of the man before me.

He was gorgeous. Beautiful even.

A smile of amusement reached his lips. "Sorry to startle you," he murmured. "Did you lose this?" He held up my cell phone.

The guy's voice was low and steady, but I moved back again out of growing suspicion. He looked like he had taken a step out of a magazine. All his features were perfect, almost *too* perfect, that it was hard to look at him. His dark, wavy brown hair reached right below the center of his neck, messy but flawless at the same time. The stubble over his chiseled jaw complimented his high cheekbones. But what stood out the most were his bright amber eyes. They were breathtaking. As his gaze penetrated mine for a moment, a sense of familiarity washed over me.

Do I know him? No. I would have recognized that face.

I shifted my weight between my feet, ready to take off at the first sign of danger. My entire body screamed at me to run in the opposite direction. I glanced around, looking for anyone else, but we were the only two people in the park.

Fuck. Me.

His gaping stare was unnerving, causing a chill to run through my body. I forced out a smile to assure him I didn't believe him to be a threat and he couldn't frighten me. I wasn't sure what the guy's deal was, but approaching a woman alone in the park the way he had would freak anyone out.

"Yeah, um, thanks," I said unconvincingly. The tremble in my voice was enough to give me away. "I've been looking everywhere for it."

"Here." He held out my phone. I stretched out my hand and grabbed it, putting it in my back pocket.

I willed myself to look away from him and focus on what he was wearing. Dark jeans and a brown T-shirt, all fitted snugly against his body, and his maroon hoodie had been left unzipped. I tried to divert my eyes from the intense gaze he had fixed on my face.

My body also responded in a way I hadn't expected as a smile flickered at the side of his mouth. I felt the warming sensation between my legs while a calming, unexpected energy danced between us. For a second, I lost myself in the intensity.

Why is he staring at me like that? And what the hell is wrong with me?

A wave of dizziness flooded me, and I imagined for a moment what he might have looked like under his shirt.

What the fuck, Mercy?

I shook my head, clearing that image out of my mind. Why would I even think about that? I don't know this guy. Something was seriously wrong here, so I glanced at my car as a plan to escape. Would I be able to make it there in time? Would he chase me? Could I even outrun him?

An awkward silence passed between us before he said, "I'm Caleb. Caleb Blackwell."

Be smart. Don't be an idiot and give him your real name.

"Angie." The lie had rolled off my tongue so easily.

He stepped closer to me and held out his hand. "Nice to meet you, Angie."

I placed my damp palm in his, hoping the wet touch would cause him to recoil or pull his hand away. Instead, he held on longer than I expected him to. I felt my palms sweat between our touch, and I hoped he didn't notice the tremble in my hand because he wasn't letting go.

Why is he not letting go?

"I can feel you shaking," he said with what looked like concern on his face. "I'm not trying to frighten you."

Wiggling my hand from his grasp, I said, "I'm fine." My tone was steady, speaking bravely, but I knew the color under my tanned skin had returned, flushing my cheeks. My back straightened. No way I'd give him the satisfaction of scaring me. "I gotta head home, though." My fake smile was back, hoping that he would leave me alone. "Thanks."

I waved my phone in the air and stepped quickly to the side to walk by him, but he was already moving into my path, blocking me from going any further.

Goddammit.

My stomach clenched, and the hair on the back of my neck stood straight, finding myself staring back into his amber eyes.

I wished I hadn't done that.

There was a tiny glimpse of a smirk on his face before it faded away. "Mercy," he hummed, stepping forward, "relax. I'm not going to hurt you."

Everything around me froze in place while I pushed back the hard sob rising to my throat. Realization washed over me and down my spine like ice water.

It was him—the guy from the accident—who knew my name.

I found myself hyperventilating as I took a step back.

Act like you're not scared out of your fucking mind, Mercy.

"I don't understand. How ... how do you know me?" I stammered.

"Easy, Mercy. I know none of this makes sense. I'm not your enemy nor a stranger to you." He stepped closer again, but my feet moved back. "We've been connected in time for years now. I wish this weren't the case, but you have no memory of me as I have of you," Caleb said, holding up his hands as if trying to calm a frightened animal. "I tracked you down tonight and waited for you to be alone after your friend left."

His intense gaze was fixated on me, as if trying to commit my face to memory. I glanced at the truck again, and he sighed. He moved faster than I could see, grabbing me by my arm and pulling me hard into his chest. The stranger looked down at me, brushing the hair away from my eyes and tucking it behind my ears. The shock of Caleb grabbing me left me speechless. I couldn't force my mouth to scream or my body to fight; I was left staring into his beautiful eyes.

The soft whisper from his lips fanned my cheek. "God, I've missed you," he said before pulling me down to sit on the nearby bench.

Missed me? What?

I shut my eyes, trying not to cry or show this guy how terrified I was.

"Open your eyes, and look at me. Now!" Surprised, I complied, my eyes shooting open. "You're in danger, and it's not from me," he warned. "Someone has been following you, and I know you've seen them. You've felt them, and so have I." His rough hand ran down my arm. "I'm here to keep you safe." He released our touch and slid further down the bench, giving me a little space.

Safe? I feel anything but safe.

"I don't want your help," my voice cracked. "I don't know who the hell you think you are, but you need to leave me the fuck alone. Now."

Caleb breathed an exasperated sigh, running his right hand down his face. "Mercy, I don't know what else I can say to get you to hear me out, but I'm the only one you can trust right now."

He must have been out of his mind to think I'd believe a word coming out of his mouth. Just him being this close to me made me feel numb from utter fear.

As I eyed Lily's truck again, he gripped my wrist, that time with pressure against my skin, keeping me from moving.

"I suggest you come with me willingly, or I will force you into that car. I don't want to hurt you in the process. So, get up and walk."

My legs wouldn't move.

"Mercy, I can lift you over my shoulder and drag you out of here if I want, but I'd like you to make that choice so I don't have to."

Fuck this guy.

With every ounce of strength I could muster, I ripped my wrist from his grasp, leaped off the bench, and grabbed a long, thick branch, bringing it hard against his head. And as he plummeted to the ground, I bolted toward the forest. However, I didn't get far before I felt my body lunge forward and my legs kick back. The firm grip on my ankle caused me to wince. I let out a loud, piercing scream. "Help! I'm being attacked. Someone, help me!"

"Mercy, stop running from me, dammit. Just give me a chance to explain."

I kicked him hard in the face with my other leg until he let go. I jumped back to my feet, sprinting deeper into the forest.

Honestly, I didn't know where I was going, but I hoped and prayed someone would hear my screams.

"Help!" I shouted as loud as I could.

When I turned around, he was gone. A heavy sigh escaped as I crept through the brush and eyed the truck about a hundred feet ahead. Looking around one more time, I sprinted to the car. Once inside, I locked the doors and pulled my phone out of my pocket.

The asshole had turned my phone off.

Shit!

I powered it on, putting my hand back on the keys, which were still in the ignition. I tried again, but the car didn't make a sound.

Please turn on. Please turn on.

I gripped the keys so tightly that the house key dug painfully into my palm.

"Turn on!" I screamed.

A glowing green light shot like a lightning bolt out from my fingertips, instantly starting the engine. I quickly removed my trembling hand, unable to process what I had just witnessed.

"What the actual fuck?" I cried out.

My thoughts returned to the party—the drugs Nick had given me and what I saw because of it.

No. I'm not on anything right now. I'm sober. Clean.

The shock of what had just happened stunned me. I couldn't move or think straight. Was it now fear that was causing me to hallucinate?

I looked up, watching movement ahead coming out of the forest. The stranger was standing there, watching me with those bright amber eyes so wide and, oddly, full of fear.

But why?

Shouldn't he be angry that I got away? Not that I wasn't thankful that I could escape him, but I wanted to know what he was so afraid of.

What is he doing?

His sleeves were now pulled up to his elbows, revealing his muscular arms and the red flame tattoo I had seen after the car accident.

My stomach churned, and I had to choke back the bile rising in my throat. Today was not the first time this man had seen me.

He was my stalker, and he'd finally come out to play.

CHAPTER 7

As I raced home, it seemed like time had slowed to an eerie pace. My screams and cries for Lily when I entered the door could have been heard for miles, and the panic on her face while she made the call to the police would never leave my mind.

Who knew how long he'd been watching me or how long he planned to play this fucked up game? He also wasn't what I pictured a stalker would look like; that was for sure. The man was handsome and charming, but then again, the devil himself was the master of deception.

After the police left, having taken my statement, Lily sat beside me on the edge of my mattress, clasping my hand for comfort. I did my best to explain what had happened, even mentioning the incident occurring right after my car crashed, relaying everything again for her.

It was all pieced together like a puzzle in my mind. That puzzle pointed to *him*: the stalking, the accident, and the incident at the hospital.

I decided not to tell Lily or the officer about the strange green light and the surge of energy flowing through me. Honestly, I was having a difficult time believing it myself.

Yes, Lily believed in witchcraft, but not like this. She used herbs and crystals, not hocus pocus bullshit.

I tried to ignore that I had been feeling *something* going on in my hands these last few months. It was a different sensation than that of my panic attacks. It was not numb and cold; it was warm and felt like energy waiting to be released from the surface of my skin.

"Why didn't you tell me?" Lily asked. "How could you keep the fact someone had been stalking you? Mercy, I could have helped you!"

"How?" I asked. "How could you have helped me?"

Lily pulled one of my throw pillows against her chest and bore her eyes into mine. I saw the fear she tried to mask under her anger.

"You're not to be alone, understand?" she said instead. "I'll find someone to run the café this week." Lily placed the pillow beside her and stood on her feet, reaching to take my hand.

"I'll be alright, Lily. You don't have to change your entire schedule for me," I said. "If anything, I can sleep at Shannon's or Riley's while you're working."

"Are you kidding me? You might have been living alone these last few years, but it's my job to protect you." She sucked in a heavy breath, and I could tell it was helping her calm her nerves. "Listen, Mercy. Whoever this creep is, the police will find him."

I nodded, but I knew the truth. Most stalkers go undetected until the day the girl goes missing, and she becomes one more unsolved mystery.

"I'll open the shop at ten, but plan to be up at eight, just in case the officers have more questions about what happened."

I gave her a weak smile. "Alright. We should both try to get some rest if we can."

Lily squeezed my hand and turned on her heel, leaving me alone in my room with my thoughts.

I plugged my phone into the charger, set it on my nightstand, and pulled out my nightgown from my drawer.

After I pulled off my clothes, I tossed them into the hamper in the corner of my room. God, I smelled terrible after today—a much-needed shower was in order.

Entering the bathroom, I reached up to unclasp my necklace but froze at seeing myself in the mirror. That couldn't be me. There was no way I got away unscathed from everything that's happened this past week, but looking at myself, I must have. Some twigs and smudged dirt covered my skin, but that was it. My skin looked flawless.

I turned around to view my backside, and still nothing, just as I had seen at the hospital. There wasn't a scrape or gash to show I'd been hurt. Nothing—not even scrapes when I fell in the forest by the parking lot.

After rubbing my eyes, I leaned forward.

"That isn't possible," I said aloud, still not believing what I saw in the mirror. "How the hell is that possible?"

"In normal circumstances, it isn't," a familiar voice calmly spoke from behind me.

I screeched and jumped back, banging my back against the towel rack.

"Easy," Caleb calmly spoke. "It's just magic, Mercy. *Your* magic."

I winced at the stabbing pain from the metal edge of the rack but kept my eyes locked on his. It was *him*, standing in my bathroom doorway. I quickly covered my bare breasts, standing there in all my nakedness. My stalker sized me up, taking in my figure with an overconfident smile painted over his lips.

Fucking asshole!

Grabbing the towel next to me, I quickly covered up my chest.

"Lily!" I winced at my own scream, my ears ringing from the noise.

"You can scream until your face turns red, Mercy. She won't be able to hear you," he said, his gaze turning up to meet my eyes. "I put a shield around your room to ensure that doesn't happen." His face was unreadable. Caleb simply pressed his lips together, watching me frozen in complete horror.

Why is he doing this?

"A shield?" I gasped. "What are you talking about, you psycho?!"

I backed up a foot closer to the shower and swiftly looked around for anything I could use as a weapon. I spotted the soap dispenser, gripping it tightly in my hand before I threw it toward his head, but he shifted to the side, letting it land on the floor behind him.

He drew in a breath. "Really, Mercy?"

I screamed for Lily again.

Caleb lifted his left hand and pointed to the walls I now noticed radiated a subtle blue glow. My jaw dropped open.

"It won't hurt you if you place your hand on it," he said, pointing to the walls. "If you'd like to test it out."

Yeah, okay.

I blinked at him and then looked back at the blue light. Touching it would be a stupid thing to do. But if this were all a dream, then maybe it would wake me up from this nightmare.

Hesitantly, I placed my fingers on the light and felt a surge of energy push my hand back, but ever so lightly. It wasn't as powerful as it looked. I could continue touching the light without it forcing my hand back, but it sent a heavy vibration against my skin. The energy beamed brighter the longer my fingers were on it. My eyes grew wide at what I was seeing and experiencing because the inexplicable sight in front of me defied all laws of physics. It was both terrifying and beautiful.

"That shield prevents you from leaving, too." A wry little smirk quirked his mouth.

God, why did I find him so sexy and utterly terrifying at the same time?

"So, I guess we're going to have to learn to get along," he added, "until you allow me to explain myself to you."

My heartbeat picked up, creating a dreadful feeling in the pit of my stomach. This was not a nightmare, this was happening, and I was trapped.

"What are you?" I asked shakily. "How are you doing this?" I looked around the room at the luminous blue light.

He reached behind the bathroom door and grabbed my robe, tossing it toward me. "Put this on. We have a lot to discuss." He turned toward my bed, and I watched him take a seat at the foot of my mattress, making himself at home in my bedroom.

After about a minute of slow and steady breathing to calm my nerves, I wrapped and secured the robe around my body and wiggled the towel down, letting it fall to my feet. If that guy wanted to kill or rape me, I believed he would have done it by now.

I think.

A small part of me decided to trust him. I didn't know why. Maybe it was the magical beam of light around my room. Perhaps it was because he would be able to tell me what was happening to my body. I convinced myself that it didn't matter why I suddenly trusted him, because I could get some answers. Answers to questions I had been asking myself for the last few months.

I took another minute in the bathroom, trying to bring my heart rate to a slower pace. My breaths eventually evened out, and I stepped into my room. I slowly and cautiously moved toward my bed but stopped before I reached him. I eyed the bench connected to my bay window and decided I'd feel safer clear over there. Caleb chuckled as I moved as far away from him as I could. I took a seat, never taking my eyes off the stranger in my room as I watched how closely he watched *me*.

I looked around the room and saw more blue light surrounding the walls.

"Who are you, really?" I asked nervously, as if I didn't truly want to know. "And tell me everything because this—" I pointed to my walls, "Isn't normal, or—"

"Real?" he finished. "It's real, Mercy. Very, very real."

I pressed my lips together. "What do you want from me?"

"Just to protect you," he said. "And I'm sorry I scared you in the process. I didn't know how else just to come out and tell you everything, and—"

"You left me to die on the side of the road and then chased me through a goddamn forest."

Caleb winced. "And I'll regret that, believe me." He averted his eyes from mine as if he were trying to suppress guilt and shame from showing. I wasn't blind to what shame looked like; he wore that face beautifully.

I looked around my room one last time from the seat at my bay window, sorting through the millions of questions I wanted to ask. I'd allow him to explain himself and let my mind be open to the possibility that whatever he was about to tell me might have some truth.

"Why did you leave me injured after my accident?" I asked, raising my brow.

"I was tracking you in my car when I saw you swerve into the forest. I know about your healing powers, so I knew you'd be okay, but you weren't healing fast enough, not how you used to. The last thing we needed was for the police to become involved and ask questions about who I am. I heard someone open their door across the street, so I took off before they could see me with you. I'm so sorry, Mercy. It's not like I wanted to leave you alone out there."

Memories flashed in my mind about what had happened after the crash. Caleb didn't just leave me there, bleeding on the grass next to a puddle of mud, but he had ripped the door from my car and tossed it clear across the ditch.

"What did you mean by me not healing? What does that even mean? I have healing powers or something?" I asked. Then I thought about every injury that had occurred in the past week that had unnaturally disappeared within hours, including the catastrophic ones from the crash.

"You were born with magic that allows your body to heal within minutes, sometimes seconds," he explained. "It depends on the severity of the injury. A lot of times, you have to will it to happen."

My eyes felt like they had grown three sizes as I stared at him, unblinking.

"I know it's a lot to take in," he said.

Yeah, no kidding.

"When I saw you weren't healing as fast as you used to, I realized you had no idea what power you held. I believe that the closer you get to your birthday, the more magic will return to you. My other thought was that since your mother was taking your powers from you your entire life, you didn't know what you were and were unable to tap into the healing abilities."

Wait, what? My mother?

"What do you know about my mom?" Just the mention of her caused my heart to race again. I clenched my fingers together so Caleb couldn't see my hands begin to shake.

Let it go. My mom is locked away.

Beneath my feet, the room started spinning as I closed my eyes tightly. I couldn't keep my eyes open long enough without feeling like I would topple over.

I heard him speaking, but I couldn't look up. "I believe Daniella was using her own magic to take away yours so you could have a normal life."

"None of this is making sense to me." I looked down, pulled the robe back a little, and touched the soft, pink ridge of flesh on my chest. "My scar," I said, remembering the blade slicing open my chest and the wound taking a few months to fully heal. "This is where my mother stabbed me, Caleb. The wound didn't unnaturally heal itself. I have a scar."

"She must have laced the knife with magic or silver. It's the only way it could have penetrated your skin the way it did without your body healing around the blade."

I removed my hand from my scar.

Hearing the words *powers* and *magic* only caused my mind to race again. I felt myself disassociate and stared at the wall as if I wasn't even in the conversation anymore.

My head was so out of focus I hadn't noticed Caleb was now standing right in front of me until I heard his voice. "Mercy, are you okay?" he asked, leaning down toward me and lifting my chin with the tip of his index finger. I quivered at his tender touch—the same way he had touched my skin at the cove. There was also a genuine concern in his eyes.

I opened my mouth to speak, but nothing came out. I took a few deep breaths to help slow down my heartbeat and finally found the question I'd been too afraid to ask.

"What am I?"

The smile on his face was one of pride and sincerity. "You're an entity created for this Earth to bring balance to magic. The world calls us witches. Just like your mom. Just like Lily and Joel. Except Lily hasn't used elemental magic in years. Not the kind of power she was born with, at least."

I blinked at him several times and leaned back. Hysterical laughter spilled out over everything he had shared and how stupid I felt for listening to it.

"I'm losing my mind like my mom," I said, almost in a whisper. "I was right. You're just a figment of my imagination. I might be seeing shadows. The witness said I walked out of my car and wandered into the woods. So, I must have hit my head, and you aren't really here." I pressed the back of my head against the window. "I'm turning into my goddamn mother."

He kneeled before me and carefully wrapped his long fingers around my wrists. "You're not your mom."

At his touch, I felt something flow into my arms and toward my chest. The strange, warm feeling made me laugh even harder, because I had finally reached the breaking point. Magic wasn't real. Absolutely none of this was real. I was finally having a complete mental breakdown and was hallucinating.

Caleb whispered, "Mercy. This is real, and you know it is. That power inside you that you're feeling, even now, as I touch you, that's magic. You're not only feeling your own powers, but you're taking in mine like a sponge. Something you will crave the moment I release our touch."

Sure. Green magic from my fingers. I get it now.

A small part of me wanted it to be real, but it was foolish to believe it. I wanted so desperately to escape from reality that I was willing to cling to anything else. I was ready to stick to the thought that he might be right just so something in my fucked-up life made sense.

"Magic isn't real," I said.

He released my wrists, stood up, and paced in front of me.

Just like that, the energy I had felt simmered down, but only slightly—I still felt my own. Or what Caleb wanted me to believe was mine. There had to be an explanation for what was happening.

Maybe he knocked out Lily.

The neighbors would have heard her scream.

He must have done something to the walls, something high-tech—a sort of soundproofing using blue lasers.

How? It defies all the laws of science.

I must be dreaming.

You know when you're dreaming.

I looked back up at him. "If magic was real, and I'm a witch. How do you know? I've never seen you before in my life."

Caleb smiled. "There isn't anything that stood out to you as odd? Has there been anything you can do that no one else could at any point in your life?"

I recalled memories from my childhood that I'd often convince myself were just dreams. When I would tell my friends about it, they'd call me a liar; they didn't believe me.

Why would they?

I swallowed. "I was never sick. Ever. I ... I saw nature move when I wanted it to if that makes sense. Trees seemed to shift when I'd shift. Branches reached out to me like they were trying to touch my hand." I shook my head. "A child's imagination. That's all I believed it was. All the kids thought I was a fucking weirdo." I looked up. "I never a saw a green glow shooting out of my fingers, though."

Caleb, whose eyes were now full of hope, motioned for me to continue.

I sighed. "There were times, however, that I'd feel this energy in my body whenever I'd get upset. It wasn't adrenaline, though, or even anxiety. As a kid, I would play make-believe that I was a witch and had these magical powers whenever I felt them, but the feelings would quickly fade." I looked up, studying his response in the dim light of my room. "I guess that was my mom's doing?"

Caleb gave me a subtle nod.

"When I got older," I continued, "my mom told me about my ancestors, how we were descendants of some of the accused in Salem, but she told me they weren't *real* witches. That magic and witchcraft were made up, and our ancestors were only innocent victims of a brutal witch hunt. I watched Lily embrace our alleged ancestral practices, but none of it made sense to me. A part of me wanted to believe it was all real. I tried to deny it because it scared me." I let the realization wash over me, the truth of what I felt all these years. We locked eyes. "I really am a witch, aren't I?"

He smiled and gestured to the bench I was sitting on. "May I?"

I didn't say yes, but I moved over a few inches, allowing him to sit. Caleb leaned back against the bay window, keeping his eyes on mine. "I know this is a lot of information to take in at once, but you need to know where you come from, Mercy, and accept who you are."

I looked at him quizzically. "I'm listening."

Instantly, I regretted those words as he smirked. "Well, you already know the answer; you just don't remember."

I stared at him intently. Where had all my fear gone? Every second he was next to me, the calmer I felt.

Why?

I sighed. "Tell me."

A small smile grew on Caleb's face. "I'm going to share with you a story," he said, "about five special children born in 1671 in Salem, Massachusetts."

I lowered my brow. "My ancestors?"

"Not exactly."

Curiosity crossed my face.

"Your mom was right about one thing. Many of those accused during the trials were innocent of magic. The church back then pointed its finger at anyone deemed different. However, some families held that power and tried their best to protect them.

"The five families I speak of were each blessed with a child. The children were born with gifts to help actual witches with their magic."

He brought his hand to my neckline. I flinched. He kept his hand steady, and I glanced at his eyes, which were focused on my necklace. I realized what he was going to do and relaxed, letting him grab the jet stone dangling from the chain. Lily had told me it was a symbol of my heritage. The pentagram represented the five elements: earth, water, fire, air, and spirit.

He rubbed the symbol gingerly with his thumb and said, "You were so powerful back then, and it pained you to see the blood spilled that night ... that you couldn't save them."

It took me a moment to realize what he was implying. "You're lying," I snapped.

"I have no reason to lie to you," he said and tried to reach for my cheek, but I scooted away.

Caleb pulled his hand back, averting his eyes from mine as if he were hiding that my rejection hurt him. "We were both born on May 2nd, 1671," he said, looking back up. "Our mission was to become warriors. We were called the Chosen Ones. After we had turned ten years old, we formed our own coven. Eleven years later, we would go through a ritual, which was called an Awakening."

That word sent shivers down my spine. "What's an Awakening?"

He let out a quiet laugh. "I'm getting there," he said. "An Awakening is when witches turn the age of twenty-one, and during the ritual, they will gain all their powers. Having that kind of power is dangerous for children, so witches aren't given all their magic at birth."

I thought about my twenty-first birthday coming up in less than two weeks; the idea of going through any magical ritual made my skin crawl.

"Our coven," he continued, "decided that once we gained all our powers, we would do another ritual immediately after, making ourselves immortal. That way, we could live forever, protecting other witches and humans without risking our magic disappearing from Earth."

While Caleb spoke, I could feel the walls emitting a low vibration, almost like a cat purring. It was soothing, and I watched as his fingers stretched out to touch my face. Watching his hand, I waited for the sense of fear and dread to come, but it never did. My eyes widened as his calloused hand caressed my cheek. The touch felt warm against my skin. His touch helped me relax, and I looked into his amber eyes. "Why don't I remember any of this? There are clear memories embedded in my mind as a child here in East Greenwich. But they aren't from the sixteen hundreds in Salem. They're from *our* time. Am I really a centuries-old witch?"

Caleb shook his head, dropping his hand into his lap. "No, that's not what I'm telling you." His eyes were somber, and I felt his hand drop from my cheek. "Mercy, you—" His voice wavered, and he took a deep breath. His face contorted in pain, and a tear rolled down his cheek. "You were hanged from the gallows before your Awakening."

CHAPTER 8

My lips parted as I stared at Caleb with unblinking eyes.

"It took me centuries to find a spell to bring you back. I finally had everything I needed to reincarnate you into *this* life."

My mangled thoughts couldn't find the words to speak. I tried to wrap my mind around what Caleb had just told me. If that was true, there was an entire life I had experienced that I knew nothing about.

Who am I?

I sat there, processing all the information, while my heart pounded so hard that it was almost painful.

"My father created a binding spell on the grounds of his farm," Caleb continued, drawing my attention back to him. "The ritual had to be done there to link our powers. I met you at your home that night while the rest of the coven waited in the barn. You were supposed to meet us after you packed your bag, but you never showed up. When we finally found you, the people in our village had already hanged you from a tree for being a witch. It was 1692, and the Salem witch trials had begun." His expression grew somber. "I was too late. We still had a mission, and even though we were all devastated over losing you, we had to return to the farm and complete the ritual."

The vivid images from my nightmare that were burned into my mind, even after I awoke in the hospital, weren't dreams—they were memories of my past life.

Those were real.

I curled forward, my breath uneven and shallow. I remembered the moment that I had seen the woman with my face die. My hand shook. I tightly gripped my arms, trying to remind myself that I wasn't there, that my feet were on the floor, not swaying in the wind as I took my last breath.

I closed my eyes, willing the images of that death away, and searched for the man who would visit me in my dreams. The one who made me feel safe and warm. The one who took all that pain away that I had been dealing with in this cruel world.

Is he real, too?

I looked up into Caleb's eyes. They weren't the same; it wasn't *him*. It was someone else.

"You're immortal, then?" I asked.

He nodded.

"After we went through our Awakening, we immediately followed it by performing an immortal spell. The villagers then found us and hanged us, too. We closed our eyes and waited until everyone left the execution, removed the nooses from our necks, and jumped down."

I ran my hand through my hair, letting my fingers dig into my scalp. I was still half-convinced that this was all just a twisted dream. But I had no logical explanation for what I saw or felt in my life. I didn't want to accept it because then I would have to live that reality, and I wasn't sure I was ready for it.

"Our coven was incomplete without you—I was incomplete without you."

He reached out, but I drew back from his outstretched hand. Guilt gnawed at my stomach. There was an intense pull inside me that wanted him to touch me. I yearned for that same electrifying feeling at the cove that moved between us. But how could I be so careless?

Caleb clearly had feelings for me, but I had to remind myself he was a stranger I had just met. A stranger that, until now, I feared—or that I *should* still fear.

He pulled his hand away, dropping it back in his lap. "It took me years to find the spell to reincarnate someone." He sighed, running his hand over his face. "This wasn't the first time I tried to bring you back. I knew I would need to use someone from your bloodline, and each time a witch got pregnant, I used a spell to bring your soul into the body of the growing child. I tried every spell within my power to bring you back, but no magic held. I had almost given up until your grandfather had two daughters. I then searched for another enchantment with the help of a powerful witch who practices magic linked to the dead. Only then was I able to link the magic to your mother."

Caleb closed his eyes as if remembering the moment. "The spell immediately took hold. I visited your parents months later and told them about the witch growing inside your mom. Nine months after the spell, she had you."

I leaned back; my mind struggled to process his words. My entire life, my mom had known I was a witch.

My dad, though, I never knew him. All my mother shared was that he had left her and me when I was a toddler. That's it. Gone and never looked back.

"Mercy?" I heard Caleb say, pulling me out of my thoughts. "Are you still with me?"

"This is a lot to take in, Caleb," I said, "but keep going."

He leaned forward, resting his elbows on his knees. "When your mom was pregnant, she could feel the presence of an old soul inside of her, even your powers. She could even see visions of your past life when she slept. I told her who you were, your mission, and what to name you. She was to bring you back into this world and train you to know your magic and heritage."

He sat up straight and shifted his body toward me. "We often spoke throughout the years. I explained to your mother what your powers could do and how to prepare you for your Awakening. She'd often argue with me over the phone about you being a part of this life, but I still thought she had been teaching you, Mercy. If I had known she was keeping you in the dark and draining you of your powers, I would have stepped in and taken you from her. I didn't protect you. I allowed her to become addicted to your magic, which eventually led to your attack," he confessed.

He grabbed my hand again and rubbed the tops of my fingers.

I let him.

"Mercy, your powers are stronger than any witch in our coven. The level of magic you were born to have is unlike anything we have ever seen. Your mom was never meant to have that kind of power. When the Awakening happens, it will be too much for her, and it'll kill her."

I quickly looked up, feeling the blood drain from my face.

"You must physically take your magic from her before you turn twenty-one, or she'll die. I believe your mom wanted you dead because it was the only way for her to keep your powers. When you go through the Awakening, she won't be able to hold on to them anymore. They will rip her apart. If a witch kills another witch, the surviving witch will absorb the energy and magic from the other. That's why she attacked you. If you died that night, the powers would have been absorbed into her own, and she'd be all-powerful."

"Why doesn't she simply give them up now if she knows it's going to kill her? It's not like she can get to me now that she's behind locked doors."

"I don't think she realizes what will happen. Or, if she does, maybe she thinks she can get out and finish the job," Caleb said with sorrow bright in his eyes.

I didn't think that was possible, but if my mom were that powerful with my stolen magic, maybe she would find a way to come after me.

"This explains why she told Lily she wants me to visit her," I said.

All this information was like a bitter pill, forcing me to wake from make-believe and face a reality that seemed too bizarre to be happening. But it was the truth, and I had to face this new part of my life, no matter how scary it all seemed. My ancestors were known witches, and I was a member of that bloodline of magic. I started the car today at the park with an energy force that came through my hands, and my body was healing at an incredible speed.

"I'm a witch." I shuddered as the words left my mouth. I hoped that by saying them aloud, I'd begin to believe and accept that part of me.

I still wasn't sure what being a witch meant. I grew up without knowing about magic, and now, I was suddenly supposed to accept it. Caleb was asking for the impossible, yet he made it sound so simple.

Denying the power thrumming softly through me would also be a mistake. It felt incredible now that I knew its true nature. It was as if my body was singing to me—shouting at me to embrace the power at the same time.

Then there was my mother, who had been siphoning my magic since I was a kid. I was more frightened than ever that my mom could escape and come find me. Especially now that I was aware of the reasoning behind why she tried to take my life.

"Why hasn't she used magic to get out of the hospital?" I asked.

"She can't use them behind those walls. That place isn't just any mental institution. This world is known to have many supernatural creatures, Mercy, especially in Salem. This is more of a facility to keep *these* energies confined, for they would use their powers for evil. After she tried to kill you, one of our own used her connection to the legal system to get her transferred to her family's facility. The walls conceal magic, like what I did here in your room, except the shield around your room won't last. I can only hold it for so long because it weakens me." Caleb looked at me intently. "Mercy, please let me help you. You know what I'm saying is true. I can take you to Salem tomorrow and guide you through the process of taking your powers back from your mom."

He raised his hand to my cheek, but I flinched away. He was trying to be affectionate, but I didn't want him to touch me so intimately. I buried whatever desires I had earlier for him away. This was magic at play and some coven connection we had or once had. It wasn't *real*. He may have known who I used to be, but I had no memory of him. Though our connection was clear, none of that mattered.

"Caleb?" I said, thinking about the story he had just shared. He looked up. "Yes, Mercy." His voice came out in a whisper.

"You mentioned meeting my parents before I was born to let them know what was coming. Did you know much about my dad? Was he ... was he like me? Or did he leave because of what I would become?"

I felt a sharp pain in my chest, that aching loss I had accepted because it wasn't like I had known my father. Yet the feeling of rejection was there. It had always been there.

"Your dad wasn't a witch, but I saw how terrified he was when I told them about you. Your father left out of fear, Mercy. He was a coward."

Yes, he was.

Any man who walks out on his family like that *is* a coward. I was still so angry with what my father had done, and I didn't even remember him.

"My mom told me he had left us but never told me why. I assumed being a father was too hard for him, and he ran from his responsibilities." I stood and walked away from the bench, tightening my arms around my waist. "Do you know what happened to him?"

"I'm sorry, I don't," he said, climbing to his feet and walking toward me. That time I didn't back up from him.

"What I do know is that your mother loved you—at least from what I observed before the attack. When she began taking your powers away, she truly believed she was helping and doing what was best for you. Maybe she hoped that if she stripped you of your powers, your father would eventually return, even just for you. Unfortunately, she couldn't stop once she started."

I huffed and shook my head, thinking about Lily now. "Lily and Joel have been lying to me my entire life." I paused briefly. "Lily was planning to tell me something important last night, but I had my accident. This was probably it. Which means she knows about you and knew it was you who had been following me."

Caleb narrowed his eyes and shook his head. "I haven't been following you, Mercy, but someone has been. A few times when I tried to approach you, I heard them. I don't know who it is or what they want, but I promise I will never let them get to you."

"You swear it wasn't you?"

He nodded. "I swear it."

"Okay, but I'm sure Lily knows it was you who attacked me tonight."

He sighed deeply, pinching the bridge of his nose, and closed his eyes. "I didn't attack you," he snapped.

"Oh, give me a break, Caleb. There were better ways to handle all of this. You scared the hell out of me tonight."

I suddenly became aware of how close he was and attempted to move away. He reached out and lightly gripped my wrist, then inched me back, pressing me against the wall until he had me pinned between his arms.

There was a still moment where we only looked at each other, feeling the power of our connection that linked us. I felt shame that I allowed a man I had just met to make me feel so vulnerable.

"Caleb ..."

"Over three centuries of not having you," he said in a low, calming voice. "Like this."

"What are you doing?" I asked frantically, wanting to turn away but feeling myself transfixed again as I had at the cove. "Caleb, what—"

"Do you really want me to stop?" he asked, and I carelessly shook my head no.

His lips crashed into mine while my body became painfully aroused by his hips grinding against me. The sudden wetness between my legs mortified me, as did the way my body begged to let him come closer. The familiarity of his touch and heated breath eased my fear—it felt as if we had known one another all our lives. I had no real memories of him, but him kissing me like this felt familiar, like we never stopped.

But this was wrong—all of it.

You're stronger than this, Mercy.

Caleb released our kiss, even though it should have been me to stop it.

He carefully rested his forehead against mine, and I let him.

"If you only knew how hard this was for me, that you have no memory of us," he said, "to not remember this ... *us* like this."

I shook my head, pressing my hand to his chest to push him back.

"But that's it, Caleb. I don't. As much as my body responds to you, we can't let that happen again. Ever."

There was darkness in his features as I shifted from his grip, moving to the side.

"I'm going to see my mother tomorrow alone," I said, not addressing the intimate moment we had just had any longer.

"What?"

"My mom."

"Yeah, I heard you," Caleb barked.

I scrunched up my face. "Caleb, she owes me answers. All of what you shared with me; I need to hear it from her." His eyes flashed in anger, but I put my foot down. "I think it's time you leave my room."

"Mercy, it's too dangerous without me."

"I don't care." I was suddenly furious about him being in my presence. Mostly, I was angry at myself for letting him touch me like that. "Caleb, I need you to understand I'm not the girl I was in my *past* life. I need time to process everything you've told me." I crossed my arms around my waist. "And honestly, everything we just *did*." A tiny smirk reached his lips despite the frustration written over Caleb's face.

God, he's so arrogant.

"I'll reach out to you when I'm ready to see you again. Okay?" I said.

"Mercy—"

I balled my hands into fists, feeling the muscles in my hands strain. "Stop!" I said sharply. "I realize this wasn't part of your plan. I was supposed to accept your story and blindly follow you down whatever path was meant for me. To fall back right into your arms, right? Well, maybe the Mercy in the seventeenth century would have done that, but that's not me. My own mother attacked me for a magical power I didn't even realize I had, and then I was left for dead in a car accident by someone who supposedly knows and cares for me."

He visibly flinched, but I couldn't care less if I was hurting him.

I continued, "I've also been stalked, chased through a forest, and given a centuries-old story about being a witch. Don't expect me to trust the very person who did most of those terrifying things to me."

I knew it must have been hard for him to understand, but he needed to know the only way I would ever trust him was if he listened to me and did what I asked on *my* terms.

Caleb licked his lips. "You don't want me to touch you? Fine. I don't want you to ever fear me. But it's my job to protect you. So, I'm not going anywhere."

"Get out of my room, Caleb! And knock down this *stupid* barrier!" I pointed to the window. "Please climb down the tree outside my window so you don't wake Lily. I'll ask her how to take those powers away from my mom tomorrow morning. I don't know how much she knows about what I can do, but I'd rather have family help over someone I just met."

Why did I let him touch me? And how the hell did this escalate so fast?

He let out a frustrated growl. "You're just overwhelmed. I get it. Get some rest, and I'll call you tomorrow."

I watched as he waved his hands in the air, and the blue light dissipated. I narrowed my eyes as he walked over to my nightstand, picked up my phone, fiddled with it, punched the keyboard a few times, and set it down.

"Now you have my number, and I have yours. Ask for Leah when you get to the asylum. She'll show you how to take your powers back," he scoffed and padded across the room to the window, opening it up. "Lily doesn't know anything about your magic, Mercy. Not like I do. She won't be able to help you."

The idea of Lily being a witch was still blowing my mind—an actual witch. I was having a hard time wrapping my mind around it. But she still would be a good resource for how this all worked, and I trusted her more than Caleb.

"Listen, Mercy, that shield in the hospital will prevent you from using magic. That means you won't be able to pull the powers back into your body without the facility lowering the shield." He looked down like he was in pain. "Be careful. Your mom may be unable to use her powers on you inside that place, but she's very manipulative. Don't trust anything she says."

He shot me one last glance, then crawled through the open window, disappearing without another word. I gasped and ran to look down the side of the house. Caleb couldn't have made that jump without getting hurt. When I peered over the ledge, he was already running into the forest by our home, unharmed.

Right ... he's immortal.

I sat down slowly on my bed, still trying to make sense of all the information he had given me, then eyed my nightstand drawer. Opening it, I spotted the knife I had kept in there for protection shortly after the attack. Lily hadn't taken it out.

I pulled it out of the drawer, closed my eyes tightly, bracing for the pain, and made a tiny slit right at the center of my palm. I winced and opened my eyes to look at the wound. After twenty seconds or so, I saw my skin seal shut. The pain subsided immediately, and my jaw dropped.

Oh, my God.

I sat dumbfounded. This was really happening.

I glanced at my phone—it was almost one in the morning. I needed rest if I was going to face my mother the next day and make her tell me what she knew. I needed to know, with complete certainty, that everything Caleb said was the truth. If it were, perhaps she would have a change of heart and willingly give me back my magic, especially if she knew it would kill her if she didn't.

CHAPTER 9

As I clasped the necklace around my neck, I took one last look in the mirror. I didn't think I would be ready to face my mom for a while, but I knew I needed to.

Lily was already in the kitchen when I walked downstairs. She smiled and took a sip of her coffee. Her buttered toast was half-eaten, and my stomach clenched painfully at the thought of eating.

"That necklace looks good on you," she said, then studied me for a moment, her voice taking an even softer tone as she asked, "Mercy, what's wrong?"

My face paled at the thought of bringing up last night's visitor. I sucked in a breath before answering her. "Caleb trapped me in my room last night after you went to bed," I said. "He's the one who chased me at the cove."

Her eyes grew wide.

"I'm okay, despite him forcing me to listen to this long tale about what I am and where I came from."

"Oh, shit," she cursed, clasping her hand over her mouth. "You ... you sure Caleb didn't hurt you?"

I shook my head. "I'm hurt, yes, but not in the way you think. I'm feeling a little lost at the moment, and I'm going to do something you don't want me to do."

She set her cup of coffee down, eyes still on me. Her voice cracked. "You're going to see your mom?"

I nodded once.

"I need you to call the hospital and tell them I'm coming."

There was no hesitation in her response. She quickly nodded a yes, because she knew it was the right thing to do.

"Mercy, your mom didn't know what she was getting herself into when she began taking your powers away. She told me a little over a year ago that the time was coming when Caleb would come for you and that we needed to protect you from him. Not that he'd hurt you or anything like that, but she feared the life he'd drag you into. That's what the phone call was about the other day. She knew he was close to finding you and wanted me to let you talk to her before he did." Lily stood up and walked over to me, placing her hand over her heart, tears glistening in her eyes. "Oh, Mercy, I wanted to tell you. I was going to tell you."

"You've known my entire life, Lily. Why wait until two weeks before I'm twenty-one?"

"It wasn't my place to tell you. It was your mother's. Joel and I realized we would have to eventually—you know—after your mom was arrested. A witch shouldn't do their Awakening alone. It's not like you can avoid it. We were just waiting for the right time to tell you."

It all sounded so comical to me.

"Is there a right time to tell me we're real witches?" I asked.

"I guess not."

"Is Caleb dangerous?" I asked her.

"Honestly, I don't know. After you died, Caleb and the rest of your coven created the jet stones by enchanting them with magic to keep the future of witches safe. They had just enough to pass down to each first-born female in each of the five bloodlines. The Chosen Ones proved to us their loyalty, but the way your mom described some of the visions of your past life, with what she saw Caleb do, she said he would only bring you darkness." She rubbed her eyes. "Is it absolutely necessary for you to go see her?"

"Caleb told me my powers are going to kill her when I go through my Awakening if I don't take them back," I explained.

Lily's mouth gaped open. She didn't know.

I told her what I had to do and everything Caleb had shared with me last night. Lily only sat there in complete silence.

"This is why she tried to kill me before I turned eighteen and left for college. She knew I would be out of reach and my powers would become too strong for her to hold on to during my eventual Awakening. She didn't want to give them up, so killing me was the only way to assure my powers would stay inside her."

Lily looked panicked. "The visions your mom had of your former life were terrifying to her. She'd cry day and night every time she caught a glimpse of your previous life. There were days during the pregnancy when she would close her eyes and see them, but she wasn't sleeping. Visions flashed in her mind constantly. She said you were always on the run, fighting evil beings that threatened the witches in your village. Your magic was so dark that she feared bringing you into this world. Caleb and his family used dark magic, and you were always with him. She was afraid you would use that type of magic in this life. She told me she would find a way to take your powers away so that you could live a normal, innocent life. I didn't know what your powers would do to her or that they would cause her to hurt her own daughter."

I threw my hands in the air. "I don't have a choice here, Lily. From what Caleb explained, my Awakening will bring my powers back into my body, but I don't want them to kill my mom in the process. I have to take them back or ask her to give them up."

Lily sucked on her bottom lip before saying, "Okay, I'll go with you, then."

I shook my head. "No. I need to do this alone." I waited to hear her argue with me, but she stayed silent, her eyes filled with understanding and sadness. "That hospital barrier will protect me, right?"

She nodded slowly.

"Then I'll be okay."

I heard her breath hitch, and the color drained from her face. "Please call me when you're heading back."

It was nice not to argue with her as I had with Caleb. I grabbed my purse, turned back to Lily, and asked her, "Why don't you use elemental magic anymore?" Looking around the room, I noted the décor and the little altar she created in the family room. "It's no secret you've embraced it."

"The spells I do now don't involve anyone but myself," she said. "They don't create the kind of power the elements would bring. Besides, even then, my powers don't even come close to the amount of strength inside you." She walked up to me and placed her hand on mine. I welcomed her touch with a slight squeeze. "You're special, Mercy. Joel and I will be here to help you in any way we can."

I flashed her a smile and released her hand. "I'll be back by six, then."

⸻

I arrived at the hospital ninety minutes later and checked in at the front desk.

Glancing down the hall, I noticed steel bars on the windows of each room. One guard near the front desk had a long pipe device attached to his belt. It looked like a stun gun but longer and thinner.

Could that be a magic device to control whatever creatures lie behind these steel doors?

"I'm Mercy Brawling," I told the curly-haired, red-headed woman at the front desk. I handed her my driver's license, and she looked up, her gaze traveling over my face. "I'm here to see Daniella Brawling."

"Hold out your wrist," she said dryly. I reached out my right hand while she placed a hospital band around my wrist. It had my name, the date, the time, and my mother's name.

"Mr. Kriser will escort you to the visiting room. No touching. Got it?"

"Got it." I looked around and didn't see anyone else. "I'm supposed to meet someone named Leah."

The woman looked back up again. "Yeah, Leah's on her way, but she's just running a little late this morning."

The same guard with the pipe device, whose name tag read "George Kriser," opened the door and led me down a long hallway and into another room with a secured door.

I first noticed how simple the room was. A long sectional couch and several tables lined the walls. My mom sat quietly with her arms over the table and shackled at the wrists, staring right at me as I approached.

The unsettling feeling hit me at my core as I heard the door click shut.

My stomach lurched, and I could feel my heart pounding. My mom looked tired, worn, and sick. Were they not taking care of her here? She may have tried to kill me, but she was still a human being, for God's sake, and she was still my mom.

"Daniella, your daughter is here to see you."

The guard looked at me and gestured toward the table where she sat. "We don't allow touching, so sit here and keep your hands on the other side of the table. If at any point you want to leave, just throw your hand up, and I'll take you back. I'll be right over there."

George padded across the room and stood by the doorway, folded his arms, and waited in a wide stance.

"So," my mom's voice cut through the room, paralyzing me where I stood. "I can see that Lily finally agreed to let you come here." She sighed. "If I'd known she'd be so damn controlling with my own daughter, I would have had Joel be your guardian back then."

The smug look on her face was incredibly unsettling. I took a deep breath, reminding myself why I was there. Pulling my chair out, I sat down, resting my arms on the table between us.

"We have a lot to discuss, Mother." My shoulders tensed, but I refused to cower under her glare. I wanted to scream and tell her what a shitty mom she was, but I couldn't. Right then, I only wanted answers. It was the one thing she had deprived me of since it happened. I couldn't get closure, unable to move on with my life, because she made sure I would continue to feel the pain after my wound had healed.

"Well, Mercy, I think that since I called you here, I have the right to speak first," she said. "We don't want things to get ugly again, do we?"

Her threat terrified me, but I kept my breaths calm and steady. I knew these walls protected me, and George over in the corner had a wicked little device I was sure could do some damage if she became violent on me again.

"I didn't come here because you summoned me. I'm an adult, and I make my own decisions now," I said, inclining my head up when I felt myself shying away from the eerie expression on her face.

Her eyes were heavy, and the dark circles under them looked like she hadn't slept much. She appeared like she'd aged twenty years since they had admitted her.

I glanced over at George, contemplating whether being in the same room with her was a safe idea.

Maybe I should have brought Caleb, after all. I thought. *And where is Leah?*

Reminding myself that she was only trying to intimidate me, I cleared my throat. "Lily mentioned you had visions of me while you were pregnant. I want you to tell me about them."

"Oh, I had many visions," she answered, her voice taking on a less aggressive tone, "I saw you do harrowing things with the magic you were born with. Contrary to what you believe about me, I was protecting you in this life, Mercy. You should be thanking me." She lowered her head and stared at her hands that were folded together on the table. "I did what I could to keep you safe and away from that world. I didn't care anymore that Caleb was the reason I had you." She leaned back. "You're *my* daughter, not a pawn in his game, and it was my responsibility to raise you as I saw fit and protect you from him. To protect you from that coven."

My heart ached at what my mother had become, but I could no longer allow myself to cry over her. I didn't recognize the woman who sat in front of me.

What happened to the funny and loving mom I once knew?

"Why are you doing this?" I asked. "Do my powers affect you this much? So much so that the love for your daughter has completely vanished?"

My mother stared right through me and then closed her eyes. I looked down at her hands, and they were clenched in fists.

"You haven't tasted the pleasure of your powers, Mercy." She opened her eyes again. Yet this time, they looked different, almost black. "You've not felt the energy flow through you like I have. It's seductive. You may feel a bit here and a little there, but not like this. I felt your powers trying to leave my body a week before your graduation, and I couldn't give them up. Not then and not now."

My mom relaxed her fists, and for a moment, she looked like she was going to pass out. She held her head and swayed slightly from side to side. It was the image of a person on the brink of death, like she was losing herself.

Do I really want this kind of power? Would I become like this?

"Why did you ask Lily to have me come to see you?" I asked.

"Because I know I'll lose your powers in a few weeks. I can barely hold on to them now. I was hoping you'd see how dangerous they really are for you and willingly give them to me."

My mom really was gone.

She leaned forward and whispered, "There's a way to lower the shield in this place that will allow you to transfer them to me, you know?" She looked over at George and then back at me. "I'll tell you what—surrender your magic to me, and I'll spare your life." She giggled again as if she were laughing at a joke. "You can even help me get out of here, and together, we can be a family again. Wouldn't that be nice?"

She honestly believes I'd buy that.

"You stuck in a knife in my fucking chest—"

"Mercy?" a fair-skinned woman with straight, shoulder-length, light brown hair and teal blue eyes interrupted from behind me. My mom's grin tapered off into a frown. Whoever the woman was, she didn't like her.

"My name is Leah. Will you walk with me for a moment?" Leah straightened the black business blazer she wore over a red blouse and black pencil skirt. She was a petite woman. I would guess she was about five feet without the tall red heels she wore.

She looked familiar, but I couldn't recall from where. "Do I know you?"

"My family owns this institution."

No, that's not it.

She placed her hand on my shoulder, gesturing toward the hallway. "Let's talk out there."

I glanced back at my mom, my eyes drawn to her shaky hands.

"Yes ... yes, of course," I stammered.

We walked into the hallway next to the recreational room, and she closed the door behind us, leaving it open just enough that she could still peek inside the room.

"Caleb just called me," she said when we were alone. "He's going to wait for you in the parking lot when we're done here."

My blood now boiled because I specifically asked him not to come.

"Listen, Mercy. In a moment, you're going to go back into that room. You'll grab your mother's hands when I give the signal and take your powers back. This can be done only if we lower the shield in the room. We can't lower the entire shield in the hospital, for safety reasons, of course. Wear this." She handed me a black stone bracelet. "It's enchanted with retrieval magic. If you wear it when you touch her, you'll be able to draw your powers out of her and back into you."

I glanced at the bracelet, but I immediately drew my attention toward the hallway to our right. I heard cries coming from the other rooms where they'd kept the patients. I wondered how many other witches had been sentenced to this place.

"But be cautious, Mercy," she warned, drawing my attention back to her. "When she realizes the barrier is down, she'll try to use her magic to stop you. Because she also has your magic inside her, she'll be stronger than all of us here combined."

Her warning made my stomach twist into knots. But I also wondered if I should trust her. She, just like Caleb, was a stranger to me. She was also associated with Caleb, who alone made me uneasy every time he simply stared at me.

He makes me feel other things, but I don't want to think about that.

"I'm scared, Leah," I confessed. "I don't know what the hell I'm doing."

Leah smiled genuinely. Her arms hung loosely at her sides, and she leaned against the wall. It was as if someone had flipped a switch, and she dropped her formal persona in the blink of an eye. I felt a little less nervous seeing her relax in the hallway.

"You're the most powerful witch I've ever known," Leah said. "I realize you've lost your memory, but we were like sisters once." She placed her hand on my shoulder again, and I instantly felt a bond and connection with her, as I had with Caleb. It was warm and loving. She was also a witch, and not just any witch from my past; she was part of my coven.

Leah leaned over, peered into the room where my mother sat, and looked back at me. "Put on the bracelet."

I did as she asked, and we both peered inside the room again. "Let's go," she instructed, gesturing to the door.

Leah followed closely to my side as we headed back into the room. My mom observed me as I sat back down and stared into her dark eyes. The only sound was the clock ticking on the wall behind me.

Tick tock. Tick tock.

I then heard a whisper from Leah's lips. "Now."

CHAPTER 10

I reached out my hands and grabbed my mom's wrists. She immediately resisted, as if she knew what was happening. My skin felt like it was on fire against hers—the searing pain burning at my flesh.

She tried hard to pull away, but I was surprisingly stronger. The windows in the room shattered, scattering shards of glass all over the floor, and my mom's eyes grew black like the night she tried to take my life.

"Let me go, Mercy. You don't know what you're doing!" She twisted her wrists from my grip, then wrapped her fingers around my own hands and squeezed against them until I felt every bone in my hands snap into pieces. Her sudden burst of strength was incredible, and I struggled to hold on under the waves of pain.

Fuck!

I let out a scream.

The pain. Oh, my God, the pain.

Leah was suddenly by my side, but she didn't intervene. I gritted my teeth, wrapped my broken fingers around my mother's wrists, and used all my strength to hold her still.

"Leah, make her stop! Help me!" my mother pleaded.

My hands were ruined, but I could feel my powers were already coming back to me. I fought my mother with everything I had while she closed her eyes tightly and her jaw muscles strained under the pain. It looked as if she was battling the worst migraine of her life.

Her voice grew louder as more energy flowed between us, and her screams rang in my ears.

"Stop! Stop!" she cried.

My mother's body slumped deeper into her chair as I continued to take my magic back. I wanted to reach out and help her, but I couldn't break the linked energies. Our powers were now connected, gripping firmly like a tight rope, unable to free us from its hold.

An overwhelming amount of power consumed me as the magic drained from my mom and into me. The bones in my hands repaired themselves instantly, and then I felt my mom's own energy flow into me. I was absorbing her magic as well. I could feel the power shifting from my mom's hands into mine, moving up my arms and filling my entire body. The sensation was unlike anything I had ever felt before. It was powerful and intoxicating.

Then everything stopped as my mom fell from the chair and dropped to the ground.

"Mom!" I cried out, rushing to her side. Slowly, I looked up at Leah, who moved to my side. "What happened? Leah, what is happening to her?"

Pulling my mom into my arms, all I felt was her limp body against my hold. There was a moment of complete silence that followed. The people rushing into the room were talking to me, but I couldn't hear them. I saw lights flash, and a rush of hospital attendees circled us before they tried to pry me away from my mom. I clutched her body tightly, unable to release her. None of it felt *real*—I couldn't even cry.

I lifted my head and looked up at Leah. "Did you know?" I asked, fanning out my fingers and placing my hand on her chest. "Did you know this would happen?"

Her vacant stare was all I needed to answer my question.

I checked my mom's neck for a pulse but felt nothing.

"I killed her. I ... I killed my mom."

Leah kneeled on the floor, hesitated momentarily, and gently placed her hand on my back. "Your mom had a brain tumor, Mercy. It was going to kill her, anyway. Your powers were the only thing keeping her alive for the past three years. She would die now or in a few weeks when you go through your Awakening." She removed her hand from my back and stood up. "You didn't kill her, but I am sorry we didn't tell you."

"But ... why?" I asked, barely able to form any coherent sentence. "Why didn't you tell me what would happen?"

Leah sagged her shoulders and sighed. "You would have hesitated or chosen not to do this altogether. It would have been much more painful for her during your transition." Leah placed her hand on mine. "You showed her compassion this way."

I ripped my hand away. Compassion? I had chosen to trust Caleb and Leah, and now I had my mother's blood on my hands. I killed her for magic. How ironic was that? She wanted to kill me so that she would keep my powers, and I killed her to take them back. I had taken a life, whether it was willingly or not.

I felt the air conditioning running through the building, chilling my skin to ice. I continued to stare at my hands, unable to believe what I had done. My voice wavered as I said, "I trusted the two of you."

Even after my mother tried to kill me, I never wished for her to die. I never craved revenge. All I wanted were answers; instead, I was forced to take her life. It didn't matter how much power was flowing through me at that moment. I felt utterly empty.

Hollow, even.

I wanted to take it back. Take everything back. As the next few hours went by, tears still would not come as I clung to my mom's body.

———

Lily and I didn't want to prolong my mother's cremation, so we made all the arrangements the following afternoon. We decided against a memorial service, as she had no friends in our community anymore. They all knew what she had done. Everyone who had met my mom now feared and rejected her. And those who didn't—only knew her as the monster who tried to kill her only daughter.

Joel flew in the following night, and on Thursday, we spread her ashes over Salem Harbor. We filled him in on the details of the past week. He and Lily helped me learn to harness my powers as much as they could. Joel was a *practicing* witch, but he had different skills than I did. Lily hadn't used her abilities since she was seventeen. Even when she went through her Awakening at twenty-one, she kept them hidden. We both saw Lily's excitement in using her elemental powers for the first time in years. She had missed them.

"So, you can also turn a car on with your hands?" I asked, remembering the first time I saw what my magic could do.

"I may or may not have stolen my dad's car a few times as a kid," she confessed.

Joel and I laughed at her story while he stood up and walked over to the center of the family room. After tucking his long brown strands behind his ears to keep them out of his face, he put his hands up.

"This spell usually takes every ounce of energy I have, but it's my favorite," Joel explained. "A vortex is so complex. The slightest inconsistency or error can collapse the entire thing. William showed me how to do this when I was five." He turned to Mercy. "His magic was the strongest when he could conjure Spirit, pulling out powers that most were too afraid to use ... like teleportation." Joel's smile turned to a frown. "He disagreed with what your mother did by hiding your identity, but he respected it.

He moved his hands around from left to right and from right to left. Yellow energy grew brighter and brighter until it formed a large vertical ring.

"Oh, my God," I gasped. "This is unlike anything I've ever seen ... it's beautiful, Joel." I walked up to it and placed my hand on the outer ring, my fingers lingering near the black hole at the center. My hand went inside when I moved it forward, but I quickly retracted it against my body. "Well, that was wild."

The portal shut down in front of me. "Another day, Mercy."

The things I missed out on growing up—were unreal.

By that Friday, I was exhausted beyond belief. I had just awakened from a restless night again, filled with haunting images of what I now understood to be memories. I secretly hoped the man in my dreams would return, but he hadn't, and that left an empty feeling in my heart. A part of me wanted to ask Caleb about him, but given how it was clear Caleb still cared for me, I didn't want it to get weird.

Opening only one eye, I noticed the time was eight. I quickly climbed out of bed, showered, and ran out the door with plans to meet Shannon at Krista's donut shop for coffee and pastries.

As I walked toward my car, I saw Caleb leaning against the bumper, wearing a leather jacket and dark blue jeans, his hair blown wild from the wind. My heart leaped out of my chest. Part of the reason was because that man was incredibly sexy, but the other part was because the guy terrified me to the core, regardless of his charming looks.

After my mom had died, I stormed out of the asylum and spotted Caleb leaning against his car. My blood burned at the sight of him, but I had turned away and drove off without a word. I was angry because he had betrayed me. However, I was more irritated at myself because I still felt a strange pull toward him again, like we were connected in some soul-bonding way.

Seeing him outside my house reminded me of the betrayal, and I scowled at his presence.

"What the hell are you doing here, Caleb?" I snapped, wanting to slap that pretty face of his.

His shoulders slumped, and his expression changed.

Was it sadness? Guilt?

"I only wanted to say, in person, how sorry I am about your mom," he said. "But I'm glad it was her and not you. You have your powers now, and she can't ever hurt you again."

"You don't get to pretend like you care. You knew from the very beginning my mother would die." I took a step forward, putting myself in his face. My jaw clenched, causing my ears to pop. "You tricked me, Caleb. You used me because you're so hung up on my past life. Well, I hate to break it to you, but that girl is dead. What we did in my room was a mistake. And honestly, did you really think we'd be repeating ourselves after this?"

"Whoa, Mercy. Nothing I have done was to hurt you. Sorry if you disagree with how we handled it, but if she had hurt or killed you, I would never have forgiven myself. I'm sorry you had to watch her die like that. I truly am." He ran his hand through his long hair and added, "But the moment she drove a knife through your chest was the moment I saw her as an enemy and not your mom."

I blinked. Those thoughts used to be mine, too, but that was before I was lied to and took my mother's life. "Move," I demanded. I wasn't going to be swayed by Caleb's pleading eyes. I quickly stepped around him. "Stay the fuck away from me."

Caleb drew in a sharp breath and reached out. "Here."

I slapped his hand away and warned, "Don't you dare touch me again!"

His brow pulled together as he held up his hand, dangling my jet stone necklace by one finger. "I just wanted to give you this."

My eyes widened, and my hand flew to my chest. "Were you in my room just now?"

"I told you. I'm here to protect you. It's foolish for you not to wear this now. Put it on."

I snatched it from his hand, but not because he demanded I wear it. He had no right to bark out commands at me. But the necklace did offer protection, according to Lily, and I wasn't going to make another stupid move again.

"I don't want your protection," I said, keeping my tone steady. "You've done nothing but harm me over and over. I can't trust a fucking thing you say."

I couldn't deal with Caleb's mood swings or the confusing emotions he drew out of me. I was tired of his lies and dealing with his mess repeatedly. He was the last person I wanted to trust, but now that my mom was dead, he was the only one who truly knew what kind of power I possessed and how to use it. I loathed the fact that I needed him.

"We have always been stronger as a coven, meaning when you use your magic, you'll always be more powerful when linked to me or the others," he explained. "So, running from me wouldn't be in your best interest. You'll have to learn to trust that I'm on your side."

I gave him a dirty look. "Not today."

I pulled the chain around my neck and tried to fasten it, but I let out a grunt when I couldn't get it to latch.

"Let me do it," he said. As his hand moved toward my neck, I backed up. I wanted him nowhere near me.

"I've got it," I snapped, trying to latch it again.

He moved faster than I could blink. He latched the hook while tracing my neckline with his fingers. I froze. No one had ever touched me like that, and I wanted to curse at myself as my cheeks flushed.

God, I'm so weak.

I turned around and gripped the stone at my chest. With the magic flowing through me, I felt the connection to him, pulling us through the power that bound us. It was pleasant, and it made me sick. Things between us were different centuries ago. And even though our souls were linked, I refused to allow some weird magic bond to cloud my judgment.

I unlocked Lily's truck, tearing my eyes away from him. "Bye, Caleb. We're done here."

I could feel his eyes on me, lingering on my face. I took an unconscious step backward, but he was standing behind me as I turned around. His eyes bore into mine, and I could feel the tension drain away. His fingers traced up my neck, and I allowed him to. Yet I heard a voice in the back of my mind screaming at me to push him away.

He pulled me toward his chest, and I let myself soak up his warmth before my head cleared.

What he was doing wasn't okay. It angered me. The power under my fingertips jumped at the chance of being used. As that anger brewed inside my body, so did my magic.

I placed my hands on his chest, feeling a surge of fire and strength snake through my arms. I didn't ask for what happened next, but I had no control. That same green light of magic from the other night in the truck ran through my fingertips and blasted him across the driveway.

"Holy shit," I whispered to myself as he landed hard against the gravel. "Caleb! I'm so sorry." I had just meant to push him away. I had no idea I could even do that.

There was a slight smile on his face as he clambered back to his feet.

"What the hell are you smiling at?"

"I'm fine, thanks for asking," he said sarcastically. "Mercy, you're a lot stronger than you used to be."

Honestly, I was too shocked to be angry. The faint green light had faded, but the intense sensation was still running through my hands. I looked down and flexed my fingers, opening them wide. "You did that on purpose, didn't you?"

"Your powers were always the strongest when you were pissed off at someone." He grinned while brushing the tiny rocks from his pants. "Especially pissed off at me."

I quickly climbed into the truck. "I'm leaving, asshole."

As I started the car, Caleb was by my window, tapping the glass. I shot him a scowl and turned on the ignition, ignoring him. He leaned in, speaking through the glass.

"You can't run from this, Mercy. We have a week before your birthday. You don't have a choice about what happens after that." He winked. "See you soon."

Caleb climbed into his own vehicle and drove away before I got the chance to swear at him some more. As soon as he was out of sight, I gripped tightly to the steering wheel, hearing my knuckles crack.

I hate him. I hate him so much. I repeated those words over and over again until I had no raging energy left inside me.

CHAPTER 11

For the next hour, I pushed away every thought and traumatic memory that made my heart pound a million miles an hour. I no longer had to put on a facade; I was just relaxed enough where nothing else mattered but the drink gripped comfortably in my hand and one of my best friends by my side.

Shannon signaled for me to move my knees over to the side, so she could reach for her purse on the hook to grab her fake ID.

The bartender poured me another Moscow Mule and slid it over. Shannon gave me that blank stare she often did when she wanted to judge me but didn't want to sound like a bitchy parent. I had finished my first drink quickly to soothe my nerves and loosen up after that fight with Caleb.

"Come on, Mercy. We're not repeating what happened before summer break, are we?" Shannon asked, quirking a dark eyebrow.

I let out a hard chuckle, remembering the party where I had humiliated myself. It seemed so long ago now, but the embarrassment was still there.

"God, no," I said. "But this is helping me have fun and not give a shit about the rest. This drink and maybe one more glass before we catch a Lyft home."

"I like it!" Shannon said, clinking her glass with mine. "While on the subject of feeling free." She licked her lips and pressed her back into the chair. "So, from what you've told me so far, you've been followed the last few months by a guy named Caleb and keeping this information from us? You gotta fill me with more information than this, babes."

I nodded, feeling my cheeks warm from shame and how it wasn't the entire truth. There was so much more to that than Shannon knew.

"But you know him?" she added.

"Yeah," I said, wanting desperately to tell her how and the secrets I knew I couldn't share with her. Not Shannon. Not Cami. They were too worrisome of me to handle something I couldn't even bring myself to accept.

"Is he dangerous or something?"

"No," I answered a little too quickly. "I mean, he's intense and nothing like Riley. Caleb's kind of an asshole, actually." My thoughts played out the story I had rehearsed in my mind earlier. "We met through a dating app, but I was too embarrassed to say anything because of Riley. You know?"

"Did you—" She brought her voice to a mere whisper, "Did you cheat on Riley with him? Is that why the two of you broke up?"

"Oh, God, no," I said, realizing I hadn't quite thought through my story of lies.

Her expression reminded me I needed to brush up on my line of storytelling if I was going to keep all this from her.

"Caleb wanted to ask me out, but I said no. Then, after Riley and I officially called it quits four months ago, I reached out to him."

"Why didn't you tell us?" she asked. "It's not like we'd judge you for wanting to get laid after a breakup."

I rolled my eyes at her brazen remark.

"I was too embarrassed, to be honest," I lied. "Riley is your friend too, and I didn't want it to accidentally slip and get back to him. I've hurt him enough as it is."

"Chicks over dicks, babe," she said, taking a sip of her cocktail.

I chuckled at her remark. "Anyway, Caleb knew someone was following me because I confided in him about it. He thought he'd keep an eye out."

"By stalking you too?"

"Well, if you put it that way."

She huffed. "Sounds like a creep to me."

The worry in her eyes made me feel like shit for leaving out the most important parts. The last thing I needed was Shannon calling the cops on Caleb to protect me and then him using his powers to escape.

No one needed to get hurt on my behalf.

I nodded. "Honestly, I'm more worried about Cami than I am about the Caleb situation. I haven't seen her since I was in the hospital."

She tapped her fingers on the bar. "At least she texted us back, finally," she said, waving down the bartender.

As she waited for her drink, she shifted back to me.

"Well, what does this guy look like? Hot, ugly, mediocre looking?" she asked, drawing the topic back to the mystery guy. She wasn't going to let up.

"Hardly worth mentioning," I replied and huffed out a heavy breath. "I don't really wanna talk about it."

Glancing at my phone, I found the text from Cami again, trying to get Shannon's mind off Caleb and back to why we were sitting in a biker bar.

"None of this makes sense," I said, holding up the text. "Meet me at The Hideout. Here?"

The Hideout was a bar run by biker gangs living on Newport Island. It wasn't our crowd, let alone Cami's. To say I felt a little out of place and uncomfortable was an understatement.

"Well, we're older now. Things change," Shannon said.

I leaned into her ear. "Not this much."

Every time the front bell chimed, we turned to see if it was Cami. "Oh, come on," Shannon said. "Hot, tatted guys with muscles so big you could only imagine the size of their cocks. I'm in."

"Oh, God," I said, letting out a laugh at the visual of Shannon being taken by the men we'd watched come and go in the bar over the last hour. I could picture her being whisked away on the back of a motorcycle, disappearing for a few hours. Then stumbling back to me in the morning, looking freshly fucked and delighted with herself.

"Did Cami explain what she wanted and where she's been?" Shannon asked, bringing her fresh cocktail to her lips.

I shook my head. "Only that she needed to talk. That's all," I said. "Cami didn't want to do it anywhere in town in case we ran into someone we knew."

Another bell rang. Not her.

"Well, cheers, bitch!" she said before we clinked our glasses.

Another bell chimed. When I turned, my stomach lurched.

"Fucking hell," I said aloud when I had only meant to curse silently. Shannon tilted her head in confusion at my outburst.

While I kept my eyes downcast, Shannon purred in my ear, "Hmm. He's fun to look at." I could feel him stepping closer to me as his warmth made my skin tingle, forcing me to ignore it. "And he's staring right at you."

Caleb's arms were folded tightly across his chest. He looked at me with a guarded, hostile expression that made me squirm and flush even warmer.

"Shannon, this is Caleb," I said, looking up at him to meet his stone-cold gaze. The essence of pine permeated between us. *Fuck, he smells good.* "Caleb, one of my best friends, Shannon."

"Have a seat, Mr. Stalker," she said coyly. "I think Mercy needs another drink."

I stared at Caleb for a moment, wondering what would happen next. Nothing did, thankfully. He only smiled and signaled with his head for the bartender.

I had sunk into my seat, sipping the last of my Mule, before turning to him again. I reminded myself that just because he looks and smells delicious doesn't mean I can't keep my composure.

"I think you're old enough to have a drink, right?" I teased with a slight smile.

His smile matched mine, his white teeth glimmering against his lightly tanned skin before he pulled out his chair. "Old enough."

Caleb ordered a beer and then shifted to me.

"A biker bar?" he muttered. "Really, Mercy?"

"I'm thinking of buying a Harley," I said casually. "What do you think? Can you picture me riding one?"

Caleb narrowed his bright amber eyes at me, but they didn't look friendly. Every ounce of willpower I had went into not letting him see me squirm under his gaze.

"Mercy, why are you guys here?" he asked in a clipped tone. I could tell he was trying to control his anger, but he couldn't hide it with how his jaw clenched.

"Why do you care?" I asked, the picture of innocence as I waited for his response.

"Mercy."

"Caleb."

Another bell rang at the front. Not her.

"Shannon, let's go. Cami's not coming," I said, but Caleb reached for me before I could stand up. Long fingers gripped my hip and held me firm to the seat while his other hand snaked between my legs. My breath caught as soon as the image hit me, but he only went far enough to touch my thigh, stroking me gently as if he wanted to calm my nerves. It was as if he had sensed how I felt without me even telling him.

Of course, he did.

If anything, he was making it worse. So much worse. Not because I was afraid, but because the pulse of adrenaline that hit me only made his touch feel that much fucking better.

I felt the pads of his fingers stroking along my inner thigh, somehow feather-light and rough at the same time. It's been so long since I felt this kind of desire that I hadn't realized how much I missed it. It was all I could do to part my legs slowly for him instead of throwing myself at his mercy.

I knew it was wrong. I knew it was stupid. I took a deep breath in and out, trying to collect myself, but nothing made a difference. All I wanted was for Caleb to keep touching me, setting my skin on fire as his fingers moved further under my skirt.

"Oh, my God," I breathed, prompting Shannon to look over at me.

"What?" She looked entirely oblivious to what Caleb was doing under the counter. My brain scrambled to piece together enough of the English language to keep it that way.

"I just had an idea to pass the time until Cami gets here! Music," I said. "You should pick something on the jukebox over by the window."

Her eyes lit up immediately; Shannon always loved music. Checkmate.

"Done!" she said. "Be right back."

The moment she stepped off the barstool and left us alone, I turned to him, slapping his wandering hand away in the process. His closeness was pissing me off just as much as it was turning me on. I didn't want to give him the satisfaction of seeing how much he got under my skin.

"Are you really this immature?" I asked. "We're in public."

"Wow. You really are different in this life. The Mercy I knew used to love it when I would make her a little ... uncomfortable." He wasn't quite smirking, but one look at the fucking twinkle in his eye, and he might as well have been. God, I hate him.

I narrowed my eyes. "This isn't the same body as before."

His cocky smile was back, so wide it took over his face as he rolled his eyes at me. "Could have fooled me," he said.

"Get over yourself."

"Fine. Dance with me instead," he conceded.

"No."

Caleb planted his feet on the floor and reached over, taking my arm with one smooth glide, then pulled me away from the bar and into his arms.

I could hear that the song Shannon had picked was *God Only Knows* by The Beach Boys.

Caleb snaked his arms around my waist, pulling me into his warm, muscular chest. Turning my head to the right, I could tell Shannon was bored with watching us already. She was taking the hand of some biker guy—a tall, skinny man with a black bandana, leather jacket, and a tattoo across his hairline—and pulling him onto the dancefloor.

Caleb moved my body to the music, and I snuck a glance at the smile he had on his face.

"Fine," I said, surrendering to my growing curiosity. "Tell me about the Mercy that you used to know."

Caleb was the only one who could share that part of my soul's existence, and I wanted to know.

The smirk on his face showed that this is what he wanted, to take a stroll down memory lane together and talk about all the raunchy details of our love affair. He wanted me to know who I was so I could embrace her again.

"Stubborn," he said. "You were very, very stubborn."

"Still am," I teased.

"Oh, I can see that."

I narrowed my eyes. "What else? What did I enjoy doing?"

This was the first time since he arrived at the bar that I could see the humor drain from his face.

"Fight."

"Fight?" I repeated. "Like you and I?"

"Oh, we did that too, but that's not what I'm talking about. You were a warrior. You dedicated your life to saving others from darkness. Helping others who couldn't save themselves. You did it all selflessly because you didn't care about dying. You only cared about protecting others because you were utterly fearless."

I couldn't wrap my mind around it. The last three years had been a nightmare because my mom destroyed everything I used to be. That tiny part of me was happy she was dead; I could finally consider myself free. But hearing Caleb talk about this other life where I was better than I am in *this* body ... made the imposter syndrome choke me like a fucking rope.

"I have another question," I said. "You mentioned that we dated, but how exactly?"

He gave me a quizzical look. "How?"

For some reason, asking that question made a ball of anxiety lodge itself in my throat, but I swallowed it down. Maybe I didn't really want to know.

"Well, you said we dated, right?" I said, raising a brow. "Did we ...?" My voice trailed off as embarrassment colored my cheeks. I had to ask because of how he acted with me in the park, in my bedroom, and what he was trying to do under the bar. What memories had he held onto for the last three centuries?

My body lit up from a simple touch, almost like a conditioned response, and I didn't remember anything about him.

"Mercy," Caleb said, pulling me out of those thoughts. "Are you asking if I saw you naked?"

I swallowed. My cheeks flushed.

Oh, God.

"You know what I'm fucking talking about," I said.

He wanted me to say it.

A playful smile quirked his mouth. "We loved each other in ways no one understood. You and I were something more, yes. But it all changed before you died."

The humor faded a second time, and his expression became unreadable.

"What changed?" I asked.

He pulled me closer and leaned his head back, hesitating for a moment, as if he were trying to connect the pieces of a puzzle; to recount a memory that had been lost.

"Our parents," he began. "They knew us better than we knew ourselves. The two of us being intimate; it was careless. It was a distraction we couldn't afford, so we had to put our focus on our mission. We didn't have a choice, Mercy. Our parents forbade it. We had just turned twenty when they told us they would strip us of our powers if we didn't stop seeing each other."

"We broke up because our parents told us to? Because they threatened us?"

Caleb's mouth gave a slight twist. "Yes. A year before you died. The memories of you and me together like *that* never left me, though. It was as if we were made for each other, body and soul."

"Why did we listen?" I asked. I suddenly felt a little foolish for spending all this energy trying to figure out if we'd ever had sex when really there was a much bigger story I couldn't remember. "If I was anything back then like I am now, I don't understand why I would have."

He frowned. "As I said, we didn't have a choice. The Chosen Ones were sent to Earth on a mission. We were created for a cosmic purpose, and falling in love with each other wasn't it."

I tried to picture what my life might have looked like in the seventeenth century. It seemed so different, so unreachable, and I was baffled by the idea of parents dictating their children's lives like that. But maybe that was the naïve part of my thinking. Plenty of kids in the world don't have the option to disobey their families.

He placed his finger under my chin, lifting it up so I could meet his eyes while the rest of the room continued to dance around us. "There are a few things that haven't changed about you, though."

I raised a brow. "And what's that?"

"Your inability to hide what you're thinking." He pulled me closer, pressing our chests together and giving me a gentle squeeze. It felt like an invitation to fall into the warm solid breadth of him, and I didn't even want to resist anymore.

"You have no idea what's going on inside my head," I mumbled. The lump in my throat was back, and there was no real fire behind the words.

"We're connected in more ways than you think, Mercy."

My face paled, and I jerked back enough to look him in the eye. "Can you read minds?"

Please say no. Please say no.

He shook his head. "No, but I can feel your energy, and you're not as scared of me as you pretend to be. I know you can feel the magic inside of you, and I know it gets stronger and stronger the closer we are to each other. And, more importantly, I know you *like* it."

I gulped. My stomach felt like it was in freefall. Caleb was right, of course. But he was too much of a wild card. Since I took my powers back from my mom, they called out to him. I felt it before, both with Caleb and Leah. The pull wasn't as keen with Leah, but that might have been because of the ritual Caleb used to bring my soul back into a living body. I realized I was probably just beginning to understand the ways in which we were bound to each other.

I felt empty when he wasn't near me. The closer he got, the more I craved his presence. My body felt hollow, a brittle container that I wanted to pour him into and keep inside myself forever. And that was terrifying.

Caleb released his hold on my chin, and for a split second, I could have sworn his eyes were wet with tears.

I had really lived another life ... with him. Though I couldn't remember it, I was curious if those feelings would ever come back. Not just the lust-filled ones, but the kind where I no longer feared what he would do.

"Mercy," Riley called from behind Caleb, prompting me to look up. "Sorry to interrupt, but Cami texted me to meet you all here. She sounded freaked out about something."

My heart stilled as Caleb looked down at me, and Riley's eyes wouldn't leave the back of Caleb's head.

Riley saw me with another guy's arms around me.

Shit!

"Caleb, I have to go."

I wrenched myself away from Caleb, leaving him on the dance floor. I only glanced back once to see him glaring at Riley with naked fury, like he'd already decided that I belonged to him.

When Riley and I stepped onto the curb, taking in a breath of fresh air, I turned to him and searched for the right words to apologize.

"I don't even care," Riley interrupted, turning to me with a smile. "If you want to dance with a random dude from a bar, and that makes you happy, then I'm cool with it."

I swallowed. "Uh, thanks, but he isn't a random guy."

Riley's eyes grew wide as the realization dawned on him.

"Oh. Um—"

"Oh, God. Not that! Riley, I need to tell you something," I said. No, Shannon and Cami's personalities couldn't handle this shit, but I had to tell someone. I had to tell my best friend.

My heart stammered, my breath coming faster as my palms began to sweat, and the thought of telling him my secret felt like a lead weight on my chest.

It wasn't that I was ashamed of who I was, but instead, I feared his reaction. I searched his eyes for a moment longer, gladly taking in the comfort they gave me, before sighing. "I need to tell you something. Something only a few people know."

Riley's brows pulled together. I could see the concern running through him as he focused on me. "You know you can tell me anything, right? Is everything okay?"

I glanced at the bar's front door, hoping Caleb would stay inside and leave me alone for a moment to speak with Riley.

I gestured to a wooden bench leaning against the brick wall.

Once we sat, I reached into my purse and grabbed my defense knife, pulling it out of the holster. I placed the blade on my skin, then slowly dragged it across to leave a minor cut in the center of my palm.

"What are you doing? Mercy, stop!" Riley reached out to grab me.

"Wait," I said, holding up my hand.

After a few seconds, the wound sealed shut.

His eyes widened. "What the fuck?"

"I—" *Steady breath, Mercy.* "—I was born with the ability to heal faster than any normal human. Caleb, the man inside, uses the term 'witch,' but you don't have to. All of this is so new to me that I don't expect you to understand." I waited for a response, but he just stared at me. "Riley, I know Caleb from my past. He's teaching me about my magic, and I need you to stay away from him. As far away as you can until I can figure this all out."

"Are you messing with me?" He half-smiled, but when he noticed I wasn't smiling back, he dropped his grin and lowered his brow. He looked back at my palm. "That's not a trick you're doing there?"

I shook my head. "It all started in 1671."

Though the music from the bar grew louder as more people filed in, I shared with him the condensed version of everything, from being born centuries ago to Caleb and our connection. That what he walked in on wasn't what he thought it was. Caleb from another life meant something to me.

After taking a few minutes, I gathered the courage to tell him what really happened to my mom and why she had tried to kill me.

Riley stared at me with unblinking eyes. His posture was rigid, as if I had just dropped him into the lake during the winter. I searched his face, looking for signs of disgust, hate, or even concern that I'd lost my mind. There weren't any. I took in a breath, relieved that he didn't think I was like my mother or that I was suddenly a new person because I had powers.

"You know," I continued, "I've always felt like there was more than this—more than what we could comprehend. My mom and dad moved to East Greenwich a few years before I was born, but all my ancestors are from Salem. I've felt things throughout my life I couldn't explain. It all just seemed a little too perfect when, in reality, we've been living among people with actual magic. It's a bit unsettling if you really think about it."

Riley covered his mouth with his hands, his eyes wider than before. Taking a deep breath, he ran his hand down his face before turning back to me and said, "My ex-girlfriend is a witch." He was trying to smile as he said it, but his face didn't quite get there.

Riley knew I wouldn't lie to him—even with something weird and unbelievable as what I had told him. Also, the wound healing the way it did couldn't be unseen. *That* happened. It was real.

I swallowed. "Caleb, he—"

"Sounds like a prick," Riley scoffed.

Laughter burst out of me for the first time in who knew how long. "He's arrogant, yes, and—"

"Doesn't deserve you." Riley's voice was soft, but it wasn't jealousy. Only concern.

I was about to speak again when we heard Shannon's high-pitched scream echo from the direction of the alley behind the bar.

"Is that Shannon? I didn't see her walk outside," Riley asked before we jumped to our feet and ran toward the cries.

When we rounded the corner, Shannon was kneeling over Cami, who lay on her back with blood oozing from her scalp, painting a streak of red through her long, blonde hair.

"She just texted me to meet her here in the alley," Shannon choked, "but when I found her, she was like this. Someone hit her over the head. Oh my God." Tears pooled from Shannon's eyes, and she clutched her chest. "Mercy, she's not breathing."

"Riley, I left my phone by the bench. Call 911, now," I told him as I turned, watching Caleb round the corner, staring blankly at us. Suddenly, there was a loud gasp behind me.

"Mercy?" Cami said in a hoarse, strained voice, pulling my attention back to her.

"She's alive!" Shannon said, placing her hand on Cami's chest.

I bent down, coming closer to Cami, reaching out to take her hand. Shannon moved back to give us space as I leaned forward.

"Hey, we're right here—"

"He's going to kill you."

My eyes widened as I looked around at the crowd forming around us that had left the bar.

"Cami," I said, leaning forward, closer to her. "What are you talking about? Who's going to kill me?" I asked her quietly so only she could hear.

"He's coming," she said again. That time it seemed as if she had thrown her voice. "A ... monster."

My skin prickled along my arms. "What are you talking about? Cami, what *monster*?"

Her eyes slowly closed.

No, no, no!

"Cami, stay with me! Keep your eyes open!"

Panic rose in my chest. I couldn't control the sobs forcing their way to the surface.

"Cami, wake up!" I shook her shoulders. "Wake up!"

I pressed my fingers on her wrist and felt a pulse.

There's still a pulse!

My hand stayed connected to Cami's until the paramedics arrived, squeezing her hand once more, then stepping back to give them space. When I did, I accidentally backed up into Caleb's chest, turned around, and shoved him back before I knew what I was doing. I was practically choking on my sudden anger, but I controlled myself enough not to cause a scene. As usual, Caleb seemed to know exactly what I was thinking before I could say anything.

"I had nothing to do with this," he said calmly, as if doing his best not to draw attention.

If he thought that would satisfy me, he was mistaken. Just because I was weirdly drawn to him didn't mean I believed a word that came out of his mouth.

"No? No? Every bad thing that's happened in the last week has been because of you. What do you expect me to think?"

"I expect you to trust me, dammit." He gritted his teeth, looking me in the eye and holding it. Trying to show me how much he meant it.

"Yeah, well, you make it really fucking hard." The fight drained out of me, and I took a deep breath before wiping the tears from my eyes with the sleeve of my shirt. I looked back toward Cami and saw the paramedics taking her away, with Shannon pressing her back against the brick wall, trying to hold herself together. Caleb wrapped his arms around me from behind, pulling me back into his chest. I froze but didn't pull away.

He lowered his head toward my ear. "She's under a spell, Mercy. There's a darkness possessing her mind. I felt it before I even left the bar. There's nothing we can do but find the witch who did this to her."

I turned around, facing him as he released his hold. "Another witch did this?"

I stilled when I realized what that meant. There really was another stalker, and they weren't just targeting me. Whoever was responsible for Cami—intended to hurt the ones I loved just to get to me.

My friend nearly lost her life, and she was still in danger. Everyone I loved was in danger. I didn't need to think too long before the next words left my lips. "We have to find the person who did this to her, Caleb ... and then we have to kill them."

I stumbled back, a hand clasped over my mouth. Had I really said that? I was stunned by my own words, and the way they came out unnerved me more. There was no hesitation, as if killing someone was the most natural thing in the world to me.

"There. Now that is the Mercy I used to know," he smiled fondly. "Find her again because it's that strength we need to win this battle." He stepped closer to me and placed his hand on my cheek, "... because *darkness* is coming."

CHAPTER 12

Riley had taken Shannon home while we waited to hear from Cami's mom, Laurie. She stumbled into the hospital shortly after the paramedics brought Cami in. For the next few hours, Laurie erratically paced the halls, waiting for the doctor to give her an update on her daughter's condition.

But there was no medical condition they could find. Not one that made sense, anyway.

Cami would have to remain in a hospital bed for as long as the unknown witch's spell was in place.

For all everyone else knew, Cami was in a coma, and the doctors were unsure of when she'd wake. The wound on her scalp was severe, but the MRI showed no sign of brain damage. Cami was just unconscious.

Caleb insisted on staying in my room until I fell asleep later that night. While I may not have wanted to repeat what we had done in my bedroom against the wall the other night, I knew I'd be an idiot not to accept his protection.

He sat on my bed while I quickly showered, keeping the bathroom door locked. I had wanted Caleb to stay in the living room, but there would be no way he would get along with Lily, so what was the point? After I pulled on my silk nightgown, I returned to my bedroom, unable to miss how Caleb's eyes followed me as I moved.

I joined him on the mattress and leaned against the headboard while sitting on the covers. I felt the urge to make myself smaller, tucking my legs under myself and staring at the wall as we both tried to make sense of what had happened.

We spoke for over an hour. Caleb was convinced Cami had been possessed for several days. According to Caleb, the energy around Cami was faint, almost undetectable, but because he had spent ages in the supernatural world, he picked it up immediately. This attack was a step in whatever plan the mystery witch had created.

Caleb suggested that whoever hurt Cami was doing it to get to me. To use her to hurt and destroy everything that I loved and valued. But who and why? Aside from my mom, who would want to kill me this badly?

"Was it really someone else watching me?" I asked.

I knew Caleb wasn't the shadow I had seen in the forest, but I had to be sure. The time I've spent around him felt nowhere near like the malice I'd felt when being watched from afar.

"You haven't followed me other than that day in the park? Right?" I pressed.

Caleb nodded. "I always knew where you lived, even if your mom tried everything she could to keep you hidden from me. But I didn't lurk around your home. Whoever is doing this, they're doing it to scare you."

The unsettling feeling of being stalked again twisted in my stomach. It felt sticky and cold inside my chest. I looked out the window into the darkness and wondered.

"What kind of person was I back then?" I asked. "I must have really pissed someone off for them to want me dead in this lifetime."

Caleb looked down and fiddled with his ring, which he had told me bore his family crest. After a long pause, he looked up and brushed my hair behind my ear, a look of hesitation crossing his face. Caleb wanted to tell me something but couldn't—or wouldn't.

What is he hiding now?

"What happened to Cami could have happened to you," he said. "This is why I fight so hard to help you with your powers. Mercy, if you don't know how to defend yourself against the supernatural, something worse is going to happen."

"I didn't ask for any of this, Caleb," I said sharply.

"Neither did I." He looked at my window and sighed. "I have a few leads I'm going to follow up on." He tilted my chin with the tip of his finger, forcing me to look at him. "I know these words don't mean anything to you, but I love you, Mercy." He leaned in and kissed my forehead before standing up. "I'll call you once I know more. Don't do anything reckless, and stay close to Lily. She can protect you until I return."

He loves me?

My mind froze after I heard him say those three words. Did he really love me? No. He may have loved seventeenth-century Mercy, but I'm not her anymore. He didn't even know the real me. Did he?

"There are enemies out there that fear you and will use everything they can to take you out. They know you have your powers again and are about to go through an Awakening." He took two steps back to me and looked down, his eyes boring into mine. "Please let me train you."

"I know now that I need to learn how to harness these powers. After seeing Cami like that, I realized I could use my abilities to save the ones I love, but I haven't a clue what the hell I'm doing," I confessed, feeling completely inadequate next to Caleb, who had been using his magic for centuries. "Whoever this witch is, he has the power to take my friends out. And he's out there waiting for another chance to strike at me ..." I shivered at the thought and inhaled slowly. "Give me a few days, and I'll be ready."

Caleb shut his eyes tightly, clenching his fists until they were white. "Sorry that I've been such an asshole. The other day, I went too far, trying to get you to use your powers the way you used to. I've kept things from you to protect you, but it's not my right."

The wall that I'd been fighting to keep between us suddenly crumbled. Despite the universe-shifting complications, I always wanted to be closer to him, and I was sick of denying myself. I moved toward him with a shocking amount of confidence. I got out of bed, closing the distance between us and reaching out for his cheek, and I held his gaze with total conviction.

"Being vague and keeping secrets isn't going to protect me, Caleb," I said, looking into his amber eyes. "I can't trust you completely if you keep hiding things from me."

"Do you hate me?" Caleb asked. He was always so confident, so slick, but right now, he looked anguished. I wondered if this was the first time I was seeing the real him.

I shook my head as my hand fell away. "No, I don't hate you." I gave him a slight smile and took one step closer, closing the gap between us. "I don't know you enough to hate you." Caleb matched my smile and snickered under his breath before tucking a strand of hair behind my ear. The feeling of him, the smell of him, it was all intoxicating. A curl of warmth moved through me and settled low in my belly as I leaned into his touch.

It was the damn connection again. I hated and loved the thing in equal measure.

Talk about something else, I told myself. *Anything else.*

If I was going to trust Caleb and journey into the unknown with him, and even trust him with my body, he had to be honest with me. I needed to know everything about him, the real him—even the scary parts.

"What is it?" He searched my face. "You want to ask me something, don't you?"

I bit my bottom lip. "Um ... I want to know more about our coven and what kind of magic we possess. Like, what all can you do, aside from creating soundproof auras around a room?"

That brought a playful, sideways smirk to his face. "I can control the element of fire."

He opened his palm, and flames ignited from his hand. I looked at his face, and his eyes appeared even more amber, glowing with vibrant light. The flame disappeared, and he grabbed my hand. He turned my palm over, facing up. Caleb then placed his open palm next to mine. After a moment of focusing on our hands, my eyes widened. The lines on our palms were identical.

How is this possible?

"The Chosen Ones may be from different families—but we're all connected. We have our own unique powers, but our most prominent one is the element we represent. My element is fire, so I can control it." He closed his hand.

"Ah, yes. Your flame tattoo," I said. "And Leah?" I saw his expression change. "I felt a connection with her at Raven's. She's part of the coven, isn't she?"

He smiled and nodded. "Leah can control water." He leaned back against the door. "As I mentioned, we each come from a separate bloodline but formed our own coven centuries ago. Each of us represents an element—from which other witches harness their magic. Tatyana, the angel who created us, believed putting those elements into human form was the best way to restore balance on the earth—witches now having a direct connection to our powers."

It was a surreal feeling to learn I was one of those elements. We were like conduits for limitless witches to tap and use their magic.

"Lily told me a tiny bit about the pentagram and what it meant in terms of the coven. But that's as far as my knowledge of the stuff goes," I admitted.

Caleb held up his hand. "You're different from the rest of us." He pointed to his thumb. "I represent fire. Leah is water." He skipped over the middle finger. "Ezra is the earth beneath our feet, and Simon is the air we breathe." He dropped his hand.

"I'm the middle finger?" I barked a laugh at my lame joke. "How am I so different?"

I rocked back and forth slightly on the balls of my feet, waiting for the answer he didn't want to tell me before—the answer to who I was.

"Though your bloodline represents the element of Spirit, Mercy, you can control all the elements at once. None of us can do that."

I raised an eyebrow. "I control all the elements? Why? What does that even mean?"

"You were the leader of our coven. You were brought here to bring balance and bind our powers. By getting your magic back and going through your Awakening, you'll restore the balance that's been lost for centuries. Without the element of Spirit—and without the power to bring all five elements together—we can't win this fight."

Fight a war ... Caleb wants me to fight a war with him.

"What's going to happen to me on my twenty-first birthday?" I asked nervously.

"You'll go through your Awakening—as we all did. The moment the hour strikes at the time you were born, you will feel all your powers come to you, stronger than they were when you took them from your mom. The only difference is that I'll need to draw some of your blood and bind you to the coven when your Awakening happens. It won't hurt, though. Also ..."

"Also?" I repeated, as if that wasn't enough.

"You'll undergo the immortal spell like the rest of our coven did. I can perform the ritual myself and—"

"No," I said firmly. "I don't want to be immortal, Caleb."

His hands balled into fists. "You don't have a choice," he argued, his brows furrowing together.

Caleb was back to being controlling again, and I didn't want to put up with it. I crossed my arms over my chest and stood up straight.

"My free will sure goes right out the door with you, doesn't it?" I said firmly. "I don't have to do anything, Caleb. Especially that."

I'd thought about becoming immortal a lot since he had told me what they had done. I knew it was coming, but I wouldn't be a part of that.

Caleb let out a quiet grunt and shook his head. "You understand why it's so important, right?"

"Yeah, I know," I said. "You don't want to lose me again."

I did get it. I knew why Caleb wanted this, and some of me agreed. The coven he had spoken of needed my power, and they couldn't risk losing me again. Still, being immortal and living forever, I wasn't sure I could do that. I couldn't watch everyone I loved die while I continued to live.

Caleb bit his bottom lip and groaned in frustration. "Fine. For now, I'll let it go. But I also need you to truly think about what it means and the detrimental consequence if you don't."

I made up my mind.

He touched my cheeks gently, caressing them; the soft, trailing touch left goosebumps in its wake. His eyes seemed to pierce right through to my soul, drawing me in again.

Great, I thought as the anger I had just felt toward him slightly dwindled away.

Caleb could frustrate me to no end one moment and then flip the script without a second thought, making me weak at the knees and wet between my thighs.

He ran his hands down my cheeks, to my neck, and over to my shoulders. His fingers caught at the straps of my nightgown, tugging at them with a whisper of suggestion that sent a buzz of adrenaline and arousal running through me.

"I don't know if this is okay with you?" he asked softly. "We used to fight all the time and then make up minutes later, so this is normal for me but ..."

I shook my head. "I don't want you to stop." My body was drowning in the desire to be touched by him. I still didn't understand how our elemental connection worked, but my body ached to be held and gripped by his firm hands. My mind screamed that it was foolish to relish in something that was purely lust.

Right then, though, I didn't care.

Every doubt left me, replaced by my only desire to be powerless beneath him.

With Caleb, I had to surrender every semblance of control, giving myself up, away from the fears that consumed me every day.

A tiny smile appeared on his face before Caleb gently peeled off the straps of my nightgown, dropping the silky material over my shoulders.

I arched my neck and sucked in a deep breath as his lips pressed into my skin, leaving hot, gentle kisses as he explored me. That alone was enough to ignite a fire inside me. I hadn't felt that vulnerable in so long. I could tell he was trying to go slow and not overwhelm me, but I didn't want that. When his fingers grazed over my breast, I let out a small gasp and pushed into the touch.

That was all the encouragement he needed. Caleb's touch became more confident, taking me into his hands as if he were reclaiming what used to be his. It enveloped me. I could feel my walls come down and my heart completely letting go. Allowing myself to feel loved and protected.

I felt like my old self again.

Stepping back, I brought him with me until my heel hit the bed, causing me to fall back onto the mattress.

A feral growl came from his chest before he moved forward, his knees hitting the mattress, caging me in, trapping me on each side of my hips. Caleb gripped the bottom hem of his shirt and pulled it over his head.

Oh, my fucking God.

My eyes ran over his body, and it was just endless lines of smooth skin over hard muscle, so perfect he could have been sculpted. Sweat dripped down the center of his pecs, and I bit my bottom lip as my eyes etched every part of his form, moving lower.

"Eyes up here," he said. "I want you to look at me while I make you come."

Keeping a slow and steady pace, he moved down further on the edge of the mattress. Caleb's hands crawled up my thighs, pushing my nightgown higher until the hem rested on my belly. His fingers wrapped around my underwear, and slowly, he wiggled them off.

Seeing him in between my thighs alone turned me on beyond comprehension. Any rational thoughts evaporated as I let my arousal take over.

Instinctively, my hands gripped my breasts, squeezing them. All I could think about was Caleb tasting me. The anticipation was driving me mad, and I needed him.

"Fuck, you're so wet, Mercy," he murmured between my inner thighs, giving my skin sweet kisses that made me shudder. Each kiss was feather-light, but it was all that was needed to keep stoking the fire he had set in me.

Before his lips touched me, his finger glided inside with ease, and his thumb rubbed slow circles over my clit, applying light, teasing pressure. I arched back, chewing on my bottom lip to bite back the sounds I already wanted to make.

God, he felt so good.

He knew exactly how to touch me. Suddenly, there was no doubt in my mind that he had touched me like this a million times in the life we had shared before.

I sank into the sensation of his fingers pleasuring me. It rolled through me in waves, my hips rocking in time with his fingers thrusting into me, my legs trembling as I drew in one shaky breath after another.

Caleb hesitated momentarily before his finger slipped out, and he leaned in, licking the arousal that dripped from me. I let out a small gasp, my fingers knotting in his hair to draw him closer.

"Oh, fuck!" I cried out as his tongue moved against me, exactly where I needed him, the sting of his fingers digging into my thigh, a sharp counterpoint to the pleasure. The movements of his tongue were eager and precise, tickling my clit—making me feel like I was losing my mind.

I forced my hips forward, grinding myself against his face—my legs trembling around his head. Caleb let out a loud moan that vibrated against my pussy. The thought that this was also bringing him pleasure made me shiver with satisfaction.

He wouldn't stop, and all I could think about was how much I wanted him to sink his tongue deeper and deeper into me.

"Oh, God ... Caleb, I—" My words were replaced by a loud moan that accompanied the pleasure that intensified in my body, spreading through me. The walls collapsed around us, and I covered my mouth to muffle my screams so Lily wouldn't hear me.

The climax rushed through me like wildfire, burning me up from head to toe.

Arching into the pillow, his hands landed on the bridge of my back to hold me steady, my thighs squeezing his head tighter, my fingers gripping his hair and tugging at his scalp.

When the pleasure finally subsided, I sank into the mattress again as I struggled to catch a proper breath. Caleb emerged from between my legs with a grin; his erection under his jeans was evident now, bringing a coy smile to my face.

"I want you to kiss me," I said.

Caleb's smile reached his eyes, but there was still an intense hunger behind it.

He hovered over me before his lips collided with mine, taking ravenous possession of my mouth. I could taste myself on him, and it felt like the lines between us were blurring. We were becoming one body of pure pleasure.

His erection pressed into my thigh while his hands gripped my wrists, pinning me down into the bed and—

Suddenly, images paraded through my head. I saw my face before me. Not Caleb's.

What the fuck is happening?

All the surrounding sensations were swept away, and a different world materialized. We weren't here in my room, kissing anymore. We were in the middle of a tiny village. Then I saw Caleb again, but he was holding a stick while sharpening the edges. The images were as clear as if I were there. I smelled the haystacks against a barn next to us and the smoke of a fire pit burning behind me.

I snapped back to the present just as quickly as I had left it, tearing myself out of Caleb's arms before I realized what was happening.

"Caleb," I cried, pressing against his chest slightly to move him back.

He stood at the side of my bed, looking down at me in complete horror.

"Where did you just go?" he asked.

"I saw something!" I said. "A ... a vision." My voice trembled as our connection somehow pulled memories from my past life. Seeing myself in another world that wasn't truly mine anymore.

"When I kissed you?" Caleb asked, looking surprised by that.

I nodded. My fear and surprise slowly ebbed, and I let myself move closer to him.

"Kiss me again." My fingers gripped his shirt to pull myself up for another kiss.

Once our lips touched, my mind traveled back to the village. I recognized one of the old buildings from Salem, but many shops that should have been there—weren't. Suddenly, I realized what I was seeing. It really was a memory of my previous life.

"Behind you!" Caleb tossed me the stick, carved out like a stake. I turned around and plunged it into a man's chest, hearing him bellow out a gurgling cry.

The vision disappeared again, and I pushed Caleb away completely that time. "What the fuck was that?" My voice wavered, hysteria clawing at the edges of my rational mind.

"Mercy, relax," he said, even though his own voice was tinged with panic. "It's okay."

"What did I do?" I jumped to my feet, moving away from him and to the back wall, pulling my nightgown back up over my chest. "I just watched myself slaughter a man!"

I panicked, panting as I pressed my back into the wall, clutching my fingers at my chest.

"Relax, Mercy," he said. "Please. I can explain it."

"You helped me kill someone. Oh, my God, Caleb." I turned, bolting toward the door, but he pressed his hand against it so I couldn't pull it open.

"It's okay, Mercy," he said, sounding completely out of breath. "You're not a murderer. What you saw yourself killing wasn't human."

I heard Lily running down the hallway before she burst into the bedroom. She cast her eyes around the room, immediately landing on half-naked Caleb, then me, and the underwear on the floor.

"Mercy, are you okay?" She ran her hands all over me, looking to see if I was injured anywhere.

I shook my head.

Lily's eyes turned back to Caleb. "Get the fuck out of my house. Now!" She moved to stand between us. "I said, get out or I'll call the police!"

Caleb held up his hands in defeat. "It's not what you think, Lily," he said, then turned back to me. "Mercy, fucking help me out here!"

"Lily," I started, my voice trembling so much I couldn't find the words. "He ... he didn't do anything," I explained, "I just need him out of this house."

Caleb scowled at Lily before putting his hands down and pulling on his T-shirt. "Fine," he said but turned to me. "Pick up your phone tomorrow when I call."

As Caleb stormed out of my bedroom, Lily pulled me toward her and held me tightly to her chest. After we heard the door slam shut downstairs, Lily quickly ran through the house, closing and locking every window there was—not that it would stop Caleb from using his magic to get inside.

After checking on me one last time to ensure I was okay, she returned to her room. I didn't tell her about my vision, only that Caleb wouldn't leave when I asked him to. As freaked out as I was, everything I had done with him until that vision was my choice. Caleb wouldn't hurt me like that.

Once I laid my head on my pillow, I tossed and turned for several hours, replaying the moment I had murdered someone over and over until the sun rose above the horizon.

CHAPTER 13

"I'm guessing you didn't get much sleep last night, either," Lily said as she made her way into the kitchen, tightening her robe around her. "I wasn't able to fall back to sleep."

"Lily," I said. I watched as she paused, her eyes narrowed in on me with a look that told me she already knew something was wrong.

She carefully took me by the elbow to help me to the couch. I realized at that moment that the secrets I had cursed Caleb about keeping from me, I was now doing the same to her.

I'd kept Lily in the dark about many things. She had been told about Cami's attack, but not that we suspected it was a witch who did it. I finally sat her down and carefully opened up about the secrets I had been keeping from her. I told her how Caleb and I suspected Cami's coma was caused by a witch who had been stalking me for months and how my dreams weren't dreams, after all. They were visions of my past life. The scene she had run into last night was my reaction to the moment I saw something terrible when I kissed him.

She tried her best not to show how scared she was, but I could tell. I probably shouldn't have told her all of it, but she couldn't help me while left in the dark.

Lily had to head out to the café to open it up, so I splashed water on my face and dressed. A knock at the door startled me. Before I reached the door, I looked at my phone and saw two text messages.

Shannon: *We're coming over.*

Caleb: *Answer your phone. I need to explain what you saw last night.*

The reality was, I wanted him to explain, but not right now.

Riley and Shannon were standing on my porch when I opened the door.

"Come on in," I said, gesturing to the family room.

"You don't look like you've slept," Shannon said as they came through the doorway.

"Yeah, it was a long night."

"We couldn't sleep, either," Shannon said.

Riley's worried expression told me there was something else they needed to talk about.

"I called Laurie this morning," she continued. "There's been no change with Cami. The doctors still tell her they don't know when she'll wake up." She threw her hands up in the air. "They're saying she had drugs in her system, which could explain how unresponsive she's been with the treatment."

"Drugs?" I said.

"That was my response," Shannon said.

My stomach dropped to my knees.

"The police have been interviewing all the patrons from the bar to see if anyone saw anything, but apparently, shit like this happens all the time in that area. They're suggesting she was there for a drug deal gone wrong," Shannon continued. "It's bullshit. She doesn't do or sell fucking drugs."

Riley opened his mouth to speak, but I stopped him with a discreet head shake. His mouth closed, and he creased his brow. He knew my secrets now, so he would need to know what had really happened with Cami.

"Shannon, maybe we don't know Cami as well as we thought." She stared at me as if I had just slapped her across the face. Riley shook his head at me and turned away.

I hated what I had just said, but she needed to let it go. I couldn't risk Shannon digging into Cami's attack. If she did, whoever had hurt Cami could come after her, too.

"What are you trying to say?" Shannon asked me.

I could barely look at her. My eyes shifted to Riley, who snuck a glimpse at Shannon and then back at me.

He placed his hands in his pockets and looked toward the ground. "Shannon—people hide stuff all the time," he added. "It can explain why she'd been ignoring us all week. Why she acted so damn weird."

My heart shattered at the lie we were pushing. I didn't just tell Riley my secrets the night before—I had involved him in this life.

Shannon walked up to me with tears in her eyes and let out a hard sob. "She wasn't on drugs. Cami wouldn't do that." She glared at Riley and me for an uncomfortable ten seconds or so. "I'm out of here," she said, choking back her tears.

My heart sank as Shannon stormed out the door and forcefully slammed it behind her.

"Was it another witch?" Riley asked.

"We don't know for sure," I said, wiping my eyes. "But whoever it was, they're coming after me, and I have to stop them."

There was another knock. I hurried to the front door and looked through the peephole. Caleb stood there, running his hands through his hair, looking frustrated.

Oh, Jesus Christ.

I cracked the door open slowly, but only enough to poke my head out. "You can't just show up here any time you want," I said, trying to remain calm.

"Well, if you had picked up the phone, I wouldn't have had to show up like this," Caleb snapped back.

He stepped into the doorway and placed his hand on the door, pushing it open so he could walk freely into the house. He wasn't going to let this go, so I moved out of the way.

"Fine. You're here. Explain yourself." I was too tired to deal with the shit Caleb had brought into my life. I looked over my shoulder at Riley, standing in the foyer, looking uncomfortable.

"I'll explain tonight, but not here. Not in front of *him*." He gestured his head over at Riley and then looked back at me.

"Riley's cool. Relax," I said. "Besides, he knows. I told him everything last night."

Caleb flared his nostrils. "You shouldn't have told anyone, Mercy. What were you thinking? I don't care if he's your best friend. This life is too dangerous for powerless humans. He'll never accept this part of you." He looked at Riley again as if he were making sure Riley clearly heard his next words. "Unless you want to put his life in danger."

Riley shot Caleb an icy glare and padded across the hallway and into the family room, taking a seat on the couch. It was clear that Riley wanted nothing to do with the conversation, and I didn't blame him.

"Tonight, dinner at my aunt's house in Newport," Caleb said, drawing my attention back to him. "That's where I've been sleeping since I arrived here a few weeks ago."

I realized I had never asked him where he lived. I was curious now. "Your aunt? I didn't know you had family out here," I said, surprised.

"You'll like her." He smiled, cutting through the tension between us. "I'll pick you up at six."

So, his "aunt" was either his descendant or had also performed an immortal spell on herself.

I'll find out tonight. I'd better find out everything tonight.

CHAPTER 14

My dark denim jeans felt snug against my curves as I pulled my red tank top over the waistline, then wrapped my long brown hair into a messy bun. I wasn't going to dress up for Caleb because it certainly wasn't a date. The doorbell rang just as the clock struck six.

I opened the door to see Caleb wearing a black button-down shirt hanging loosely over gray slacks. His hair was a mess from the heavy wind outside, and once he saw me, he ran his hand through it and gave me a charming smirk.

A slight satisfaction hit me, knowing my casual outfit would bother him.

"Please don't mistake tonight as a date, Caleb," I said.

"We can make it a date," he said. "I dressed up and everything."

He flashed that sexy smile again, and despite how that made my stomach swoop with excitement, I was wary of what he was doing. Caleb was the expert at playing that game of manipulation. If I was going to get any answers out of him tonight, I had to play it craftily, too.

"Mercy, who is it?" Lily shouted from the family room.

I quickly shook my head at Caleb, warning him not to speak.

"It's Riley. We're heading to a movie," I shouted back. "I'll call you when I'm on my way back."

Caleb nodded. "You know she'll give you shit if she knew I was here."

I hated lying to Lily, but it was the truth. She'd attempt to keep me from going anywhere with him; that was certain.

He held out his hand. "Shall we?"

Rolling my eyes at the gesture, I wrapped my fingers around him, and he escorted me out of the house and into his car.

We drove across the bridge to Newport, past the mansions, and into a gated community.

Okay, wow. Caleb's aunt is rich.

We hit a fork in the road, turning left through a beautiful garden trail leading up to a castle. The castle looked like something straight out of a fairytale, Victorian style, with century-old gray and red stones. It was several stories high, and even in the car, I felt dwarfed by the looming building.

Massive trees, bent with age, created shadows along the driveway leading up to the house. Caleb parked and rushed to my side to open the door.

"Thanks." I grabbed his hand and stepped out. "What is this place?" My eyes went wide. "Is this her house?" He smirked when he saw how wide-eyed I'd gone at the sight of all this luxury.

"This is the Sherwood Remington Castle. My aunt Abigail lives here with her housekeeper, Desiree."

"Is she a great aunt? Or is she immortal, too?"

Caleb gave me that playful half-smile as if he were hiding a secret and debating whether to let me in on it. As much as his smugness annoyed me, he had my curiosity piqued, and I was desperate to hear the story behind all this.

"Abigail's immortal," he said.

"So, I knew her, then?"

He nodded once. "You did. Very well, actually."

Caleb gestured toward the ridiculously ostentatious house. "This way."

As elated as I was about spending the evening in an opulent castle, it was quickly overshadowed by my nerves about spending it with Caleb. Perhaps being around familiar people might help trigger more memories that would stick.

I gripped his hand tightly as we entered the castle; my eyes widened as I saw the foyer. It was stunning. Candles decorated every corner of the house, beautiful Celtic music played in the background, and the windows were open to let in a gentle breeze. The window curtains danced in the wind, and the elegant crystal chandelier above the entryway table was dimly lit with gas lamps.

The walls were lined with beautiful antique gold and red silk fabrics, still in almost perfect condition. Intricate, ornate designs were carved into the wooden posts in the corners of every room. Old paintings from different eras covered the walls. Sculptures, antique china, and rustic leather-bound books were stacked on the bookshelves surrounding the foyer. Caleb led me into a room to the right of the entry. A highly polished oak table stood in the center of that room with two place settings and wine glasses already set up for us.

Caleb pulled out a chair and gestured for me to sit. He took his seat right as double doors opened from across the room.

A woman dressed in a plum-colored blouse and a long, elegant black skirt entered the room. She looked as if she were in her mid-thirties and incredibly beautiful. She had bright blue eyes, youthful pale skin, and wavy blonde hair that fell right above her shoulders. Caleb and I both stood up as she walked up to my side of the table.

"I can't believe it," the woman said. "Mercy, you're here, in my home, after so many lost years!" She pulled me into a tight hug, then pushed me back at arm's length. "Wow, you're the spitting image of your previous body. It's quite remarkable. Well, aside from your hair color, of course."

Her penetrating stare made me slightly uncomfortable, so I looked up at Caleb, who had made his way over to us. He only greeted my worried expression with a squeeze of my hand.

"I know you don't have your memories, but we were very close when you were a child. Caleb hasn't stopped talking about how thrilled he is to have you back."

Caleb gave a shy smile, then chuckled under his breath. Abigail leaned in and gave me another warm, welcoming hug. I noticed Caleb move in slightly as if to stop us, looking on edge when Abigail touched me. I wondered what was wrong. She was a little strange but looked far from dangerous.

I looked back over at him. "Everything okay?" I asked.

He gave me a reassuring grin and walked back to his seat. "Of course." His warm smile released the tension from my shoulders, and I relaxed a little.

"It's great to have you in my home, Mercy. You're welcome here anytime."

"Thank you." I smiled at her and looked around the dining room again. "Is it just you and your housekeeper here?"

"Her name is Desiree," she affirmed. "We both used to work for the man who built this place, Sherwood. The poor man died a few years ago and left me the house."

"Oh, wow. That's generous," I said, finally allowing myself to relax completely. I straightened my back and gave her a warm smile. "It's nice of you to open your home to us tonight. Whatever is cooking in that kitchen smells lovely."

Lovely? I shuddered at how ridiculous I sounded. I never used words like *lovely*.

Observing everything around the home, what stood out the most was Abigail. Nothing about her appeared out of place. She glided around the table with three smooth strides to greet Caleb. Her movements were full of grace like she was skating on ice.

As Caleb and Abigail exchanged an affectionate squeeze, I said without thinking, "Your house is so lovely."

Fucking hell, not again. What is wrong with me? Heat rushed up my neck.

Immediately, my cheeks flushed, so I gave Caleb a pleading look. I straightened up when Caleb finally spoke with a snicker in his voice.

"So, what's Desiree whipping up in the kitchen tonight?" Caleb asked. I took a deep breath and finally started to calm down, settling back into the chair.

"It smells delicious," I said, making sure I didn't sound like I was trying too hard to be proper.

Caleb laughed under his breath, obviously aware of what I was doing.

"Desiree is preparing you two chicken parmesan pasta—Mercy, yours is vegetarian, I may add—with a special ingredient of mine. And as Caleb knows, I'll never tell *anyone* what it is." Abigail smiled as she grabbed an aged, expensive-looking bottle of wine. "Desiree and I have already eaten, so we'll leave you to your date once your meals have been served."

"Oh. No. This isn't a date," I corrected. I looked up at Caleb, who rolled his eyes at me, and Abigail only smiled back, filling up my glass halfway. The wine was so deep red and dry that I could smell it from here. "Thank you."

She walked over to Caleb's side of the table with the bottle and poured him a glass.

Slowly, I sipped the wine and shuddered as it went down. I wasn't a big red wine fan, and this was dry enough to sting my nostrils as I drank it, leaving an odd aftertaste in my mouth. But I didn't want to be rude, so I continued to drink it without complaint.

"Abigail grows the grapes on her property, and her staff makes the wine themselves," Caleb explained. "They've been producing for decades now."

"Well, it's delicious," I lied. "Thank you again, Abigail."

I wasn't sure if I saw a hint of a smile on her lips because I was too distracted by how she stared at me again as she took a seat on the other end of the table. Her eyes narrowed as she focused all her attention on me, and I resisted the urge to look away. Something told me I was being evaluated, even if I didn't know what for.

What the hell is wrong with this woman? My heart rate picked up as we continued to stare at each other wordlessly.

"Tell me, Mercy," Abigail started. "Do you remember anything about your life before this?" Her fingers drummed against the table.

"Only a few memories have come back to me in visions." I glared at Caleb sternly. He looked uncomfortable. *Good.* "Honestly, it's a strange concept; visions of a past life, as if my brain in this body had something to do with it, even though I know it didn't. I never really believed in souls or reincarnation." Abigail's head tilted to the right, as if my words confused her. "Anyway, Caleb's going to help me make sense of it. That's why I'm here tonight. That's all."

No, that wasn't all. The truth was, as fucked up as that vision was with killing someone, it wasn't entirely terrifying for me now as it had been when it first happened. It had taken me by shock, but now, talking about it only feels like I dreamed it all.

Our attention was drawn toward the kitchen as Desiree entered through the entryway. She was a young girl—maybe fifteen—short, with black pixie-cut hair, a thin frame with a fair complexion, and dark green eyes. She wore a white and blue striped sundress with an off-white lace apron and was carrying a large serving tray.

"Dinner is served. Tonight, we have chicken parmesan with pasta, garden salad, and whole wheat rolls, fresh out of the oven," Desiree said, leaning down and placing a steaming plate in front of me. "Mercy, I made yours with soy protein and topped with our garden's fresh basil. Is that okay?"

I nodded courteously, hiding the confusion I felt.

How does she know I don't eat meat?

"Hey, Caleb," she muttered, putting the second plate in front of him, then turned back to me. "Wow, you sure are beautiful. I'm Desiree."

"It's very nice to meet you, Desiree. As you know, I'm Mercy. Are you also family?"

"Not by blood, but we're pretty much like brother and sister." She playfully punched Caleb in the arm.

He grinned and gave her a friendly wink.

"And I'm your waitress for the evening. Caleb mentioned you liked pasta and don't eat meat," Desiree added.

That answers that question. I glanced over at Caleb.

He acted as if he hadn't been following me before we met at the park, but it was clear he knew a lot more about me than I initially thought.

"Did I eat meat in my past life?" I asked Caleb.

"You did. You have picked up on new likes and dislikes and have formed quite a different personality, but you're still *you*," he said, picking up his fork.

Desiree smiled, took our cloth napkins, and placed them on our laps. Caleb and I didn't say much during dinner. I was too nervous about spilling my food on my elegant napkin. It looked more like a small tapestry you would hang on a wall rather than something someone would use to wipe food off their face.

Abigail had excused herself along with Desiree while he and I ate. After dinner, Desiree cleared the table, and then Caleb grabbed my hand and lifted me up from the chair.

"Care to dance with me?" he asked.

Caleb, acting like a gentleman, escorted me across the dining area and to the room behind us. As we entered through the double doors into a large ballroom, I heard beautiful violin music playing over the speakers strategically placed throughout the room.

"You should have learned the last time we did this, Caleb. I don't dance," I said shyly.

"You used to be a fantastic dancer." He bowed while gesturing toward me.

"Yeah, but in this life, I have no rhythm," I joked. "No, seriously. I'll step on your toes if you attempt to waltz with me."

"Oh, come on, Mercy, you used to dance with me all the time." He tenderly grabbed my hand and pulled me in closer to him. I tensed as our chests touched, and his arm slid around my waist. As charming as he was at that moment, I knew what he was doing, and I didn't have the time or the inclination to deal with his flirtatious little game.

"I came here for answers, Caleb. And all you're doing is stalling."

"I told you I plan to tell you everything, Mercy." He leaned in until he was so close that his lips grazed my ear when he spoke, his warm breath ghosting over the back of my neck in a way that made me shiver. "I just really need you to relax before I do." He used his hand on my waist to pull me in, holding me tight to his chest. I wanted to pull back, but the way my pulse raced, and a warm flush climbed up my neck told me my body was enjoying the contact, if not my mind. Pressed against him, I could smell his woodsy, masculine scent, and it was distracting me, even as he continued talking. "Just one dance. Because *this*. Right here. This is what I miss. The two of us together when we're not saving the world and just living in it. Relaxing with each other."

"This isn't relaxing, Caleb," I retorted. "This is making me un-easy."

"Liar," he said with a teasing smirk.

None of this was about dancing. It was about what we used to have over three hundred years ago.

Caleb kept his smile as he readjusted us, putting a little distance between our bodies. I ignored how my skin felt ice cold wherever he wasn't touching it. He kept his right hand on my waist while the other came up to grab my hand and hold it out. Before I could realize what was happening, he positioned us to waltz.

Great.

"I'm going to step on your toes," I said. "Also, I know what you're doing."

"Do you?"

I hated how smug he looked, but I couldn't wait any longer. I needed answers, and there was one way that guaranteed I'd get them without having to navigate any more of Caleb's oh-so-witty repartee.

I forcefully pulled him by the collar toward me, taking hungry possession of his mouth. It was painfully difficult to avoid not feeling aroused as his lips touched mine.

Like the last time we kissed, it caused my entire body to melt and ache for his touch. The moment was short-lived, as my mind drew me into another vision, just as I suspected.

Caleb and I were standing over a woman lying on the ground. She was begging us to let her go. To let her live. He reached down and dragged her by the hair as she kicked and screamed for him to release her.

What is he doing?

"Caleb, let go of her, now! I need to speak with her first!" I screamed at him in the vision. "Please!"

He threw her onto a pile of bodies and lifted his hands, and yellow flames appeared at his fingertips. As he leaned down to touch one of the woman's legs, the fire took hold of the flesh and cloth, erupting around her and the corpses. The screams were unlike anything I had ever heard. I shut my eyes to block out the scene. It was clear I hadn't wanted any of that to happen. I didn't want anyone to die at Caleb's hand.

I broke off the kiss and backed up, causing the memory to disappear.

"Fuck," he cursed. He must have seen the fear on my face. It was clear I had seen something terrible—something he didn't want me to know about—something more sinister than the previous vision.

"Back the fuck away." I held up my hands, my magic thrumming under my skin.

Just then, Abigail barged into the ballroom. "Mercy, you need to leave now. Caleb, don't you try to stop her."

Caleb didn't say another word, but he heaved a heavy sigh, watching me back away from him. I said nothing, either, as I turned and ran out of the ballroom, grabbed my purse hanging from my chair, and exited the castle. I opened the Lyft app to request a ride home and stood at the end of the driveway waiting for them, shaking from the cold and, more intensely, from the nerves.

I'm such a fool to have trusted him.

Were Abigail and Desiree safe from that monster? I turned around and contemplated heading back into the castle, but she must have known what I was thinking. She was so quick to enter the room, as if she knew I had discovered Caleb's darkest secret and was trying to protect me from a murderer. At first, I thought maybe I was the killer in these visions, but this time, I had begged him to stop as he ruthlessly burnt that screaming woman to death. I didn't want the woman to die; I wanted to speak with her, and Caleb ignored my plea. He was trying to control me, just as he had done in the seventeenth century—*his* little soldier.

What didn't make sense was that he had told me I was the coven leader. But wouldn't he have listened to me when I told him to stop if I was? There were so many bodies burning because of his hands. What did that woman do to deserve to be killed with such brutality?

My driver arrived, and we headed toward my home. I texted Lily that I was on my way back and put my head in my hands. As the tears flowed down, I switched my constantly ringing phone to silent. It was slightly after ten before I arrived home and quietly snuck back into my room.

Aside from that horrible vision in the ballroom, I was nowhere near having the answers I needed. The night had not gone as I had planned. I had to think of another way to get my memories back, because I wasn't going anywhere near Caleb again.

CHAPTER 15

As I lay in bed that night, I thought about what to do next. I didn't trust Caleb enough to know if he was truthful. He had been hiding too many things from me, and as attracted as I was to him—or how he made me feel when he was tender and showing like he genuinely cared—I wasn't going to kiss him again to see into my past.

It wasn't worth the horror I saw in those visions, nor my dignity, to give myself to someone who wasn't treating me with respect or as an equal.

I did some research online about paganism and witchcraft, and a witch shop in Providence popped up on the top search results. It wasn't exactly where I thought I'd have to go to receive my answers, but I didn't know what else to do.

"What am I doing?" I said under my breath as I parked in front of Patricia's Witch Shop, then hopped out of the car. I looked at the front of the shop, noting the oddities in the windows and its quaint aesthetic. Taking a deep breath, I gripped the door handle and swung the door inward. A light chime echoed through the store from the bells dangling on the doorframe. It was dimly lit inside, and there was a faint smell of incense hanging in the air.

"Good morning, darling. Welcome," an older Black woman with deep brown skin and tiny freckles along her nose greeted me as I entered. She wore a long blue dress, and her gray hair was wrapped loosely into a yellow silk scarf. "I'm Patricia." The woman sized me up. "You look as if you've seen a ghost," she added. "Come on in."

Seriously, what am I doing?

Hundreds of books lined the glass shelves that stretched toward the back of the shop. I ambled along the side wall and scanned over them. Most of the books were novels about witches and the supernatural, but a few were books about the history of witch-craft. Patricia stalked around me and picked up a crystal globe on a shelf beside the entrance. She smiled and walked to the back, disappearing behind a beaded curtain. A few minutes must have passed before I realized how long I had been reading the book titles.

"Is there something, in particular, you're looking for?" she asked from behind me, pulling my gaze away from the shelves.

"Honestly, I have no idea," I confessed. I giggled softly to myself, turning my attention back to the books. "I don't even know if you have what I need." Out of the corner of my eye, I could see that she tilted her head and slowly closed her eyes, took a breath in, and opened them back up. There was an unusual light in her eyes now.

"If I could get a reading on you, I'd say you're seeking answers as to who you truly are, but you're afraid of what you'll find," she asked. "Am I right?"

When I glanced back at her, I saw she was still holding the globe.

"Are you a psychic?" I asked.

Patricia nodded. "I can do an official reading for you ... if you'd like. I'm just setting up my table for a client, but they won't be here for another fifteen minutes, so I have time."

I shook my head. "I appreciate you offering that, but I'm okay," I responded, eyeing the bookshelf again. "What about spell books? Are these books authentic?"

The peculiar woman walked past me and placed her hand on the shelf, closing her eyes again and gliding her fingers across each book until she stopped.

"This one is from 1725. I found it during my travels in Europe a few years ago. It's not for everyone who comes through that door, though. I can't sell this to you unless I do a reading."

I looked at her quizzically. "You really want to do a reading on me, huh?"

She smiled and pulled the book from the shelf. The lady's deep brown eyes turned to stare at me, and without another word, she walked to the backroom again.

Okay. That was bizarre.

I looked again at the books on the shelf, but nothing stood out. I turned back around, browsing through the shop. Over in the corner were a few more shelves with herbs and stones, like what I've seen Lily decorate her home with.

If Lily could see me now ...

I spotted a few stacks of herbs tied off and picked up three of them and four jet stones. These probably had no powers like the one on my necklace, but it didn't hurt to have a few extra on me. I placed them on the counter by the register and rang the bell. She didn't come. I rang it again but only heard Patricia clearing her throat from the back.

I guess I'm doing this.

The beaded curtain rattled as I made my way through it. I instantly drew my attention to the small round table in the middle of the room. A deep red cloth covered the table, and the globe sat innocently in the center on a bronze pedestal. My eyes hurt from trying to make sense of the eccentric decoration of the walls, so I focused on the woman sitting at the table.

Her eyes were closed, her petite left hand resting on the book she had taken from the shelf. I shifted uncomfortably in her presence. Even before discovering I was a witch, I'd always been very skeptical of the profession. My unease stemmed from being thrown into the supernatural world. I believed it was better to be cautious of so-called psychics.

"You want me to sit right there?" I gestured to the chair across from her. She didn't answer, so I sat down anyway. Right then, she opened her eyes, which were now as white as winter's snow. My jaw dropped.

"I dreamed about you last night," she started. "I knew you'd be coming here today."

I was unsure if it was some parlor trick, but *fuck,* I was freaked out. "Can I, uh, just please buy that book? I'll pay double just so that I don't have to do a reading."

Yeah, coming here was a mistake, I told myself.

Patricia's eyes fluttered and turned back to brown, and she looked up. "Didn't you come here for answers?"

I nodded. "I don't know if I believe in psychics. Sorry."

"Ah, you used to not believe in witches either." She rubbed the top of the book before opening it up, then flipped through several pages before pausing. When she spoke again, she had my undivided attention. "You're an old soul. This spell will help you remember."

My heart raced. *How could she know that?*

"You're not a psychic, are you? You're a witch."

"I'm a witch who can see one's future and their past. So yes, I'm also psychic. I know nothing about your life before this. Your soul now is only bound to this body and this life. Last night, my dream showed you arriving at my shop and that you're seeking to understand your purpose. That I can help with. Let me do a reading."

She lightly tapped her fingers on the open page, drawing my gaze to the book.

Should I trust her?

There were so many things I needed to learn, and having another way to tap into my past life would help me understand myself and Caleb better.

"What do I need to do? Are you going to read my palm or something?" I asked, only half joking.

Patricia stood and walked toward a shelf in the corner of the room. After grabbing a stack of cards and placing them on the table, she retook her seat. "I'm going to draw tarot cards."

"Oh, okay." I was expecting her to use her powers to glow and read out my future, not calmly sit there and read cards.

Patricia shuffled the stack of cards a few times and then closed her eyes again. Then I felt the slight hum of magic in the cards and watched in fascination.

How had I not seen this earlier? Or felt her magic?

"Mind and body, life once well," Patricia started. "Memories taken, hear this spell. Take her mind and make it whole. Return the life that death hath stole." She pulled the top card over and displayed a blade. "Your journey never ended; it's only just begun. You were once a warrior in another life. Your purpose in coming back was to train again and learn to defeat the darkness that—" She stopped, and her freckled hands trembled slightly. "I ... I'm sorry."

"What is it?" I asked, but after seeing the fear in her eyes, I knew she had a vision.

"You're afraid," Patricia said, her eyes fixed on mine.

That was obvious.

Whatever she saw terrified her.

Nothing is that easy.

The more I learned about the supernatural, the more frightening it was. I had been falling down a rabbit hole, scrambling to grab at any form of reality. Strangers have come into my life, telling me stories I don't remember, and worse, my friends are now being targeted.

Her voice pulled me from my own troubled thoughts.

"A man has come into your life," she said. I assumed she was referring to Caleb, as he was the only new person I had seen. "Despite your reluctance, you must follow and trust him to guide you down this path."

Easier said than done. Caleb is dangerous and unpredictable.

Was she really telling me to trust him? Caleb, who had a silver tongue and had no qualms about tricking me into doing whatever he wanted me to do?

I looked at the card more steadily, focusing on the blade. It wasn't shiny gray like a kitchen knife. It was possibly carved from a tree. It looked exactly like the one from my vision that Caleb had been sharpening.

She flipped the next card. It was a red heart outlined in black. "You loved someone once but were taken from them tragically."

My death.

She flipped the next card. On it was a swirled circle that started out broad and became smaller until it met in the center of the card with a green triangle encasing it. I hadn't looked at it longer than a few seconds before I felt my eyes roll to the back of my head, and my inner thoughts fell open to a different world around me.

In this realm, I saw a woman I somehow knew was my mother, Mary, from my past life, cradling me in her arms. A midwife wiped me down with a wet rag and wrapped me in a cream-colored blanket.

"We shall call her Mercy," my mother said to the man I knew as my father, Alexander.

The scenes flipped past quickly, like scenes in an old-timey projector. First, there was me as an infant, wailing in a bassinet, while my mother shed tears into my father's arms, saying she wasn't good enough.

Good enough for what?

Next, I saw my childhood friends: Caleb, Simon, Ezra, and Leah. I saw myself grow to love them as my family. Next, I stood in a room with instructors teaching us how to fight. I threw punches at Caleb's father; his name was Roland. Suddenly, I turned around to see someone I didn't recognize charging toward me.

"Here comes one of them, Mercy," Roland ordered, throwing me a wooden stake.

A stake?

As I turned around, I felt a blunt force slam into my chest as the strange man with ashy brown hair and dark, eerie eyes threw me to the ground. I wrestled with him, gripping tightly to the stake.

"Mercy, now! What are you waiting for?" Roland screamed.

I clutched the weapon as hard as possible and plunged it into his chest. The body of this man exploded on top of me, covering me in gray ash.

"Wake up."

My eyes shot open when I heard Patricia's voice.

"Oh, my God," I gasped.

"What did you see?" she asked.

"The symbol had triggered the visions from my past life. I've had visions before, but nothing like this. This time, I felt things and touched them. I remember a huge part of my life from back then." Pointing to the symbol on the card, I asked, "What does this mean?"

She looked at me with genuine fear in her eyes. "It means you're a—vampire hunter."

Patricia and I spoke for over an hour. She shared how she had learned about a particular coven sent to Earth centuries ago. Still, the history books never mentioned that their purpose was to fight vampires. They only knew that each witch possessed an extraordinary power to help other witches manifest their own. They had only heard tales that vampires once existed, but the undead hadn't been seen since the Salem trials.

My vision's unsettling feeling came over me as I sat in my car in front of the small shop. Fighting vampires wasn't an inconsequential part of my past life; it was the reason for my existence.

My phone beeped, and I looked down to see who it was.

Shannon: *An animal attacked Riley last night. Meet me at his place.*

My pulse jarred in my throat.

Me: *An animal? What animal?*

Shannon: *His dad isn't sure, but his leg got pretty cut up.*

Me: *On my way.*

Not Riley. Please, God, help him be okay.

⁓ele⁓

When I arrived, Shannon was waiting in the driveway for me.

"I texted you," I said, inching toward her. "I'm so sorry for what I said yesterday about Cami. I didn't mean it."

She caught me off guard and wrapped me in a warm hug. "I know you didn't mean what you said. You're just upset. We all are."

I gave her a tight squeeze before I released her. "Let's go inside," I said.

As we entered the kitchen, we met with Mr. Davis, who told us what had happened.

"Yesterday morning," he started, "when Riley was heading back from your house, he stopped by Goddard Park to take our boat out. A girl going for a run found him lying in the parking lot with a huge bite mark on his leg. There was so much blood that she rushed him to the hospital and called 911 on the way. They released him a few hours later with over thirty stitches and antibiotics. I thought he was alright until this morning when Riley complained about feeling sick."

I looked up at Mr. Davis. "Sick?" I asked.

Riley's father frowned as if recounting his son's story had disturbed him. "I thought maybe it was a dog bite at first, but that's not what he told me. He was sure it was a wolf, given its size." He ran his hand down his face. "There ain't no wolves in these parts, Mercy."

I shook my head. "I may have seen one," I said, remembering the animal that dashed in front of my car right before my crash. It was massive, much bigger than any creature I'd seen in East Greenwich. It could have been a wolf.

He gestured with his finger out the window. "Naw, not around here," he said, "when was the last time you saw a wolf in East Greenwich?"

I didn't answer because I was still trying to understand it myself.

"Can we go see Riley now?" I asked. We needed to ask him ourselves.

"Yeah, go on up," he replied.

We heard Riley calling out to us; his voice sounded weak. When we walked in, he was curled up in the fetal position on his bed, holding his stomach.

"He's been like this since this morning," Mr. Davis said.

"What's wrong with him?" Shannon asked.

"We thought perhaps an infection was starting, though his wound today doesn't look nearly as bad as it did after the attack. He's been throwing up, and his temperature spiked to 104 an hour ago, so I called the hospital again. The doctor doesn't think it's related to the attack, more like flu symptoms. If it worsens by the end of the day, I'll bring him back in."

I walked up to Riley and rested my hand on his head. "You're so warm."

"Temperature's gone down a bit," Mr. Davis said.

Mr. Davis grabbed a wet cloth from the bathroom and handed it to me, and I placed it over his forehead.

"Here, this should cool you down," I said as I rubbed the back of my hand over his cheek and then gently shook him. "Riley, we're here." His eyes were dark; I could tell he was hurting. Tears welled up in my eyes. "I'm so sorry. We didn't know what happened until this morning."

Riley looked up to meet my eyes, smiling weakly. He placed his hand on mine. "Don't apologize, Mercy. I'm okay, really." His voice was hoarse and strained.

A lone tear rolled down my cheek and fell on Riley's hand.

"Oh shit, sorry," I whispered. We both chuckled, but I was still crying through the tears.

"Quit it, Mercy," he breathed. "This isn't your fault." He wiped another one of my tears away, then looked at Shannon. "I don't want you two getting sick, so I'll call you once I'm better. Hopefully, before this weekend."

My stomach dropped. Riley knew about my Awakening on my birthday, and Shannon was sitting by us, who was still left in the dark.

"This weekend?" I asked, giving him a hard stare. Maybe with him being sick, he had forgotten all the secrets I had shared.

"Your birthday dinner, Mercy," Riley said. "Did you forget about your own birthday?"

I smiled nervously. "That's right," I said. "Though, I might just stay home and eat pizza and cake with Lily.

"And me," Shannon added.

I gave her a weary smile. "And you."

Not sure how I was going to get out of this one. We had been planning my birthday dinner for months.

CHAPTER 16

I felt numbed by everything that had happened in the last few weeks. I should have been excited when I awoke in the morning—after all, it was my birthday—but I wasn't.

The day was filled with long discussions with Lily about how to prepare for my Awakening. I also shared with her my newfound knowledge of hunting vampires.

Lily swore she had no idea that the creatures I fought in my past life were the undead. In fact, vampires were only legends in our history books, at least the parts her own parents shared with her.

I couldn't stop thinking about the man I had killed and the woman Caleb threw into the pile of bodies in my memories. It all made sense now. They were vampires.

Fucking vampires! My God.

My mind had a hard time wrapping around the fact that vampires existed. I could barely accept that I had magic and lived an entirely different life hundreds of years ago.

It didn't matter how many times I ignored Caleb's text messages to explain himself and his need to be with me tonight as I transitioned. If I faced him about my discovery of being a vampire hunter—letting him know what I saw; everything would change.

It would no longer be a memory. It would be my life, and Caleb would take full advantage of that knowledge. This is what he wanted all along.

I hurried downstairs and into the kitchen, watching Lily place her dinner plate in the sink. When I turned, Joel was leaning up against the wall with a massive smirk on his face.

"Joel!" I cried out, leaping into his arms for a tight hug. "I didn't think you'd be able to come back out. I thought you had the opening for Derek's recent work this weekend."

"And miss my niece's ascension?" We released our hug and looked at each other at arm's length. "Derek understands."

I pressed my lips together and gave him a nod. "Did Lily fill you in?" I asked.

"Yeah, it seems like we're learning new things about you by the day now," he said, folding his arms across his chest and leaning his back against the counter. "I don't know how to kill the undead, Mercy, but I can teach you how to control your powers if you feel overwhelmed."

I glanced at the clock. "I told Riley everything—well, almost everything," I said. "He wants to be here tonight, too, to see it happen. Thankfully, whatever made him sick a few days ago has passed."

"Mercy told Shannon he was still sick, and she caught it too," Lily added. "So, if she shows up here with soup and cold meds—"

"We play along," Joel said, giving my hand a tight squeeze. "How's Cami doing?"

I swallowed as he released my hand. "Still in a coma, or what the doctors think is a coma."

"There are spells that might break whatever the witch did to her. I'll try to swing by the hospital and see what I can do in the next day or so."

That hope for Cami pulled at my heart.

Could he really help her?

"Joel, Lily?" I started. "What should I expect tonight?"

"I won't lie, Mercy. It'll be overwhelming," Joel explained. "But not as big of an ordeal as you think it'll be. You could literally sit on the couch with your feet propped up while it happens. The sensation mostly feels like a stream of water entering your body, but you can breathe it in without drowning."

"But they're not here," I reminded her.

"And that's a good thing," Lily said. "It's your choice what you plan to do after this, Mercy. Let's focus on getting your powers back to you first."

"We'll be right by your side, though. Okay?" Joel's assurance brought me a tiny amount of comfort, but the fear of what I'd be experiencing still lingered within me.

Lily and I had an extensive conversation this morning about Caleb's need to be the one holding my hand through the Awakening. So much so that he had threatened through text messages that he would track me down tonight, and the immortal spell would happen right after, whether I wanted it to or not.

So much for not bringing it up again, fucking liar.

To him, it was my duty to the world to live in immortality to protect the mortal world.

To me, he could fuck right off.

I hurried to the window when I heard tires along the gravel. Riley's car was parked at the end of Lily's driveway, but he hadn't gotten out of the car yet.

"Give me a minute," I told Joel, who had placed a few ritualistic gems and herbs along the coffee table. "He might be on the phone, but I'm going to go check." As I peered through the window, I saw his headlights were on, but I couldn't see his silhouette through the windshield.

"Once Riley is safe inside, I'll put up a protective spell around the home to keep any uninvited guests out," Joel said.

I nodded before stepping out onto the porch. "Riley?" I called as the wind blew up the surrounding leaves.

Something isn't right.

"Riley, where are you?"

I took one step to the right to see his door ajar, but only slightly. What looked like a wallet lay on the ground next to his door.

Shit!

"Caleb?" I called out, forcing back tears that something had happened to my friend. "Where the fuck are you, Caleb?" My voice carried through the wind, but I feared Lily or Joel would hear. He could hurt them if they came out and confronted him. I didn't want him to harm my family, too.

"Riley's fine," Caleb said, appearing from behind the trees next to the property. "He's sleeping comfortably in the forest."

"Sleeping?"

"A simple spell."

"Fuck you. I'm so sick of you trying to destroy my life!" I scowled.

Caleb cocked his head. "I'm not your enemy."

"Oh, the fuck you are. You've done nothing but use, manipulate, and lie to me. You're the definition of my enemy."

The hum of magic filled my veins—the raw power harnessing down to my fingertips. Now I understood what my mother felt; it was like a drug; the more I used it, the more I wanted to use it. If this were how I was when I barely scratched the surface, then Caleb would feel the wrath of what I could do when he hurt those I loved.

"I don't want you here," I said through my teeth.

Caleb's eyes widened as he watched the green light dwindle at my fingertips. "Put down your magic, Mercy. Now."

"I'm not going with you," I said, but my threat did nothing. Caleb walked toward me with his own power in the palm of his hand—fire, lighting up the space around him like a beacon.

I took a step back, feeling fear blanket my body because I hadn't a fucking clue how to control this magic. I could feel my energy slipping away as my hands shook at the sight of his flames.

His presence of true power circled me as he stood within a few feet, powering down his magic but keeping his hand still outstretched.

"Please don't make this so difficult," he pleaded. "I don't want to hurt you."

I gave him a stern look. "My family is whom I want with me when I go through the Awakening. Because, unlike you, they would never force me to do something I didn't want to do to get what they wanted."

I felt the surge of my powers completely dwindling away. It was as if the fear of Caleb's presence numbed my core to where I could no longer focus enough on my magic. I didn't know what to do with it.

Caleb dropped his power, his hand reaching out to pull me close. As I shoved at his chest, his other hand landed on my head. Before I could scream, my eyes rolled back into the darkness.

—⁓—

When I opened my eyes, we were pulling up to a little cottage in a wooded area. Caleb parked the car, and I glared at him until he looked at me.

"Did you seriously kidnap me? For fuck's sake, Caleb, do you have no respect for me?" I scolded.

Caleb turned the ignition off and leaned back, his face contorting in pain, or at least, it appeared that way. He had to know from my tone that I was pissed.

I looked down at my phone, which Caleb thankfully hadn't taken from me, and I had six missed phone calls between Riley, Lily, and Joel.

At least Riley's alive.

I hissed, "Am I allowed to use my phone? Or are you going to take that away from me as well?"

He rolled his eyes. "You aren't my prisoner, Mercy." He gestured to my door with his finger. "You can leave if you want."

This had to be a trick.

I didn't understand him. Now he regrets it? He knocked out my friend, stole me from my home, and what? He was giving me choices?

My hand hovered on the door handle, but I didn't get out. Slowly dropping my hand to my side, I took hold of my phone again and opened my text messaging app.

"I'm not going to hurt you, Mercy." He gestured to my phone. "Let them know you're safe and follow me inside when you're done. I'll tell you everything you want to know."

Thinking about the situation, that was what I wanted. No more secrets or lies. Just the truth. If I ran now, I'd be alone during my Awakening, and I wasn't sure if I'd survive that. But if Caleb really was a threat—

His hand touched mine, and I turned to look into his pleading eyes. "I would never hurt you. Please, for the first time since we met again, trust me."

His expression was unreadable, but the longer his hand was placed against mine, the stronger I could read him through the link between us. The unspoken bond was unlike anything I had ever felt, and I wanted to hold on to the hope that what I was feeling was real.

Caleb removed his hand, placing it back on the steering wheel. I unlocked my phone's screen and created a group text between Lily and Joel.

Me: *I'm with Caleb. I think I'm safe.*

My hands felt clammy as I scanned my messages again, looking for Riley's name.

> **Me:** *Hey, Riley, I'm sorry Caleb did what he did. I'm safe. Stay with Lily and Joel.*

I kept it simple. Any extra detail about what Caleb had planned would set off an alarm of worry between the three of them, though I'm sure Riley had already called the cops.

After I texted everyone, I decided I was *safe* with Caleb. I had to get information from him, and I reasoned that maybe it would be good to have a member of my coven guide me through my Awakening after all.

But if he forces me to do anything against my will, I'd fight him at every chance I can.

I powered my phone down and put it in my pocket. I got out of the car with Caleb and followed him inside the home through the front door. There was a log in the fireplace, and the scent of the recently burned wood lingered in the air. The cottage felt warm and inviting and was filled with old furniture and antique sculptures. A collection of artifacts looked centuries old, covering the dusty shelves against the walls and paintings that reached from the floor to the ceiling.

"Whose place is this? It looks like a museum," I asked as we walked over to the couch.

"Mine," Caleb answered before disappearing into a small room.

I sat down on a black leather couch and looked around the room. The cottage wasn't what I expected. The truth was, I didn't really know what I had expected. I might picture it as a family home, with parents and children laughing and playing games, not as the dwelling place of a powerful flame-throwing witch.

Caleb returned to the family room, stepped toward me, and kneeled down. He looked into my eyes and took my hand. "I know you disagree with my methods, plus I've kept things from you, but I did it to help you learn who you are. We grew up learning about our powers from childhood. You didn't have that luxury. I had to tread lightly with you, so you could use your powers as you're supposed to. We don't use spell books, Mercy. We act on instinct, and with you not understanding what's happening to you, it's shielding you from your gift."

He watched me as I sank deeper into the cushions. "I know what I am, Caleb." I reached out and wrapped my arms around one of the soft pillows. "I know I'm a vampire hunter. Or at least, I used to be."

His eyebrows rose a notch. "I've wanted to just flat out tell you, but—"

"One secret at a time?"

He smirked. "How did you find out?"

"I saw it, actually. Through a vision." I rose and turned toward the fireplace, sauntering across the room to a bookshelf, and placed my hand on one of the books. "You speak of spell books like they're a bad thing, but the truth is, there are answers on paper or *cards* that hold power, just like what we do with our magic," I said and then withdrew my hand from the book. "A psychic from a witch shop in Providence showed me a symbol from a tarot card, and it triggered every memory up until I was maybe thirteen or so." I smiled, proud of myself for being able to figure it all out on my own, at least part of it.

"Mercy, you went to a psychic?" he asked incredulously.

I huffed. "Well, she's a witch, too, if that makes a difference." I pressed my lips together. "Look, it doesn't matter how I found out. But I now know, and Caleb, I don't want that life from what I saw. I don't want to *kill* people."

"They're not people," he tried to explain, but I shook my head again and sat back on the couch, clutching my legs against my chest. He joined me, raising his hand toward my face, and brushed the hair from the side and away from my eyes.

"You're not a murderer," he whispered, raising my chin to meet his eyes.

"But I was," I corrected. "Whether it was a vampire or a human, I still took a life."

Caleb shook his head and ran his hands through his hair. "There's more to this story," he said.

"I'm ready to hear it. I don't care if it's good or bad anymore. I need to know everything. You need to tell me, Caleb."

He leaned back into the couch. "Centuries ago," he started, his voice calm and steady. "An angel named Tatyana came down to Earth. The Upper World sent her to stop a demon from destroying humanity. Instead, she fell in love with the demon and helped him create the very thing she was supposed to stop. Their union created a half-breed—part demon, part angel."

"A vampire," I said. "Beauty on the outside, but with a dark and evil soul."

"Vampires don't have souls," he corrected.

"Well, that's unsettling." A chill crawled up my back.

"Yeah, and they spread like wildfire. Vampires were creating more vampires, and the destruction was more than the witches on Earth could handle. Our purpose in being born was to rid the world of these beings. After you died, we struggled to keep the balance. Our coven split. We each went on our own journey and did our best to kill as many vampires as possible." He closed his eyes and drew in a breath. "It felt like there was an empty hole in my chest after the church hanged you, as if a part of me had died that day too." He opened his eyes.

I was a vessel that was lost. That must have been horrible to my kind.

"Why didn't the angel who created us just bring me back? Surely, she had the power to do so."

He shook his head. "We couldn't find your soul. It was as if your spirit died with your body. The first time I felt you after you were gone was when the spell worked with your mom. We don't know where you went. My guess is, neither did the angel." He grabbed my hand gently. "When you go through the Awakening, you'll be a tool for all the witches in this world. You're going to help them become strong again. We can't do this without you." He held up his hand, and instantly a flame appeared on the tip of his thumb. "When a witch draws the powers of fire, using my element, I give that to them, no questions asked." He shut his hand, and the flame disappeared.

"What does the power of Spirit actually do?" I asked.

"Spirit is a little bit different than the rest. You bind all our powers together and amplify them. You control the power of healing, nature, and telepathy. When you died years ago, the power to heal someone was taken from Earth. It was the key to what your magic represented. Witches haven't been able to heal anyone for centuries. We needed that power, but it was gone. When I brought you back, we could all feel that element again, but your mom began to shield it from us. Once you awaken, we can do so much more with your gifts. We can start saving human lives again."

I thought back to my childhood and how I knew I was different. Hearing more about my magic brought a feeling of sadness and anger that my mom had hidden that part of me. The people I could have helped, the lives I could have saved, were no longer here because of *her*.

Caleb continued. "You can move objects with your mind and telepathically speak to someone. Spirit allows you to use all five elements without having to pull them directly from us like others would have to."

"This is crazy," I said, still trying to wrap my mind around this new information.

He smiled at me and gingerly brushed my cheek with his hand. I moved back, removing his touch from my cheek.

"You kidnapped me, Caleb," I reminded him. "You don't do that to someone you care about."

"I would never hurt you, but I also know what's best for you. You don't have your memories, and you don't truly understand what's at stake. I can't have Lily and Joel trying to stop what we need to do. They don't understand," Caleb explained. Still, it didn't make me any less irritated by how he had handled the situation. "You were destined to fight evil and save other witches from being destroyed by the demons created to kill them. The angel couldn't destroy her own child, but she hated what she had helped create. So that is what we're to do in her stead."

I had read a few books about vampires and werewolves, but I suspected nothing like this could be real. I searched for my thoughts. "What else is real?" I asked. "Dracula?"

Caleb snickered. "Come on, Mercy. You know that's fiction."

"Doctor Frankenstein?" I always tried to be funny when I was nervous, but this time, I was serious. If witches and vampires were real, what else could be?

"Also, fiction."

I paused for a moment before I said, "So, I killed a vampire." I hoped saying it aloud would make me feel better about what I had done, but I still felt sick.

"I couldn't just come out and tell you everything in your room the first time we talked. It would have overwhelmed you. Finding out through visions wasn't exactly how I wanted it to play out, either, but now you know."

"Now I know." I looked up at the ceiling and rubbed my eyes. The lack of sleep the last few nights was getting to me.

"What did the male vampire I killed do to deserve death?" I asked.

"That vampire had just slaughtered an entire village. Women and children were killed, and bodies were left to rot on the streets. You were protecting humankind, Mercy. You're a hero."

It felt better hearing that—but only a little.

"And the woman you killed in my vision? The people you burned alive?"

Caleb closed his eyes tightly and balled his hand into a fist. "Oh, that one and *her* bloodsucking clan killed my mother, turned my father into one of them, and took your father prisoner."

I quickly sat up and looked at him in disbelief.

Oh, my God.

He looked so upset, as if he were living it all over again. "I was enraged because of what they had done. I had to kill her; make them pay." His eyes watered, but he wouldn't allow the tears to fall. This was the first time I had seen Caleb so brokenhearted.

"Why did I try to stop you, then?"

"Because we didn't know where they were taking your father. You thought if we kept her alive, we could torture her for answers, but I couldn't stop myself. You hated her just as much as I did, but you wanted me to stop so that we could find your father. For that, I'm so sorry, Mercy."

So, another thing he lied about.

If I hadn't asked, would Caleb ever have told me about my father from my past life? Would things have been different if my mother hadn't gone crazy from my magic, and I knew of my Awakening well before now?

I shook my head to myself. No, things don't change that much. I sighed. "Did you ever find him? My father?"

"No. We searched, but we couldn't find your dad."

The pressure on my chest grew, and I could barely breathe.

Was the father from my past life still out there as a vampire, an immortal ... or had they killed him?

The feeling of anxiety tightened in my chest, and I had to steady my breathing, or I was going to pass out. The vampire I killed had murdered children. I did what I had to do.

Right?

I still felt like he was holding something back.

"Is that everything?" I asked nervously.

"There is ... one more thing."

That didn't surprise me because there was always something else with Caleb that he was keeping from me.

"Your blood is special, Mercy. Especially to a vampire."

Well, I wasn't expecting that.

"And by *special*, you mean ...?"

"One drink and it'll allow them to walk in the sun."

My eyes grew wide.

Jesus. That's not what I expected to hear.

Caleb saw my expression and shifted in his seat. "Yeah, and once you go through the Awakening, they'll come after you for a taste."

I gulped. "Are you fucking kidding me right now?"

"Do you honestly believe I could have just dropped this on you before you had a full grasp of your purpose here?" Caleb asked while I studied his face, watching his eyes leave mine for a moment.

There's more. Always fucking more.

He shifted uncomfortably in his seat, and I immediately understood why. "That's the reason you kidnapped me, isn't it? You knew Lily and Joel would stop you because the next step in your plan is to make me immortal."

"You being a mortal is a problem, Mercy," he explained. "Vampires are hunting you, and they won't stop." I looked away from him, staring blankly at the floor. "Look at me, Mercy. They know I brought you back."

I shook my head. Being immortal was a big fucking deal, and he wasn't giving me a choice. I felt his hand on my back, but I shifted my shoulder to the right, brushing it away.

"Some vampire clans know what will happen tonight after you turn twenty-one. If you get caught, some will not be able to stop when they drink your blood. They will kill you, Mercy, whether they want to or not." Caleb bowed his head. "I won't lose you again."

He looked at me with a tortured gaze. I saw how much it hurt him to see me protesting something he had probably been thinking about for centuries. The desire to bring me back and finally complete that last step to making me immortal. Just like the rest of the coven.

"I don't know if I can watch the people that I love grow old and die while I continue to live."

I collected my thoughts and asked myself if there was any other way. If I died, the element that was crucial for the survival of the witches would be gone again. But if I became immortal, I would watch Lily, Joel, and my friends die, and I would be fighting monsters for eternity.

Caleb pulled me out of my thoughts and placed his hand on my cheek again. "I've loved you since the moment the stars aligned and brought us together for the first time. You won't lose everyone, Mercy. You have a coven that will walk with you in this life. A coven who loves you."

This isn't love.

"We don't allow the stars or the universe to decide our fate!" I pounded on my chest once with my fist. "We decide, Caleb. We do."

His face scrunched up at my words. "Then decide ... now."

Caleb's words sent my heart racing, but I was confused about what that meant.

He wanted me to decide to change my life completely and become an immortal warrior—vampires against witches, for the rest of my existence.

Then there was Caleb. It didn't matter that I was attracted to him. He lied, kidnapped, and held things from me—something no one would do to the person they loved. I didn't know if the feelings I had before for him were lust or love, but I felt something at moments ... and I hated myself for it.

CHAPTER 17

I sat in Caleb's car, staring at the Danvers City Library entrance for a solid ten minutes before I decided to break the silence.

"Why this library?" I asked.

Caleb kept his eyes on the building but snuck a quick glance my way. "There used to be a farmhouse here, which my family owned. The cellar underneath the library was our meeting ground when our coven joined together. Our village was a few minutes from here. We would meet at a cabin built here to perform spells and train to fight. We couldn't train in the village, as people started becoming suspicious about witches' existence. The very first day we trained was right here."

My vision. This is where I saw my memories stop during the reading I did with Patricia. "You mentioned you'd have to draw blood to bind us?"

He nodded, turning to me. "Just a little to link the elements."

"I mean, is it going to hurt?"

"Not much. You'll be fine, Mercy. You heal faster than a were-wolf, and they heal pretty damn fast."

I blinked rapidly.

"Yes, werewolves exist," he said casually. "But they aren't a threat to witches. They despise vampires just as much as we do. Werewolves have felt a bond with witches throughout the centuries. They protect us, as we always have with them. It's an alliance against evil."

Holy shit.

"Alright," Caleb said, halting me from asking more questions about werewolves. "We need to go inside."

When we reached the door, he placed his hand on the handle and then stopped. "My heart broke when you died, Mercy. It nearly destroyed me." He grabbed my hand gently. "If you die again, we all die, and I need you to stay alive. We need your strength and your power, but most importantly, I need to be able to look into the eyes of the woman I love for the rest of time. Whether or not you choose to be mine."

At that moment, I knew that his words were meant for someone else. It wasn't about what he and I had years ago. It wasn't about how he felt about me romantically; I couldn't give him my heart when I wasn't even sure who I truly was.

The memories I recalled during my vision with the psychic flooded my mind; the echoes of emotions flowed through me as if they had never left. I remembered caring for Caleb as a kid, and I felt things in this life when we touched. It was a connection I couldn't deny, but I had to remind myself that the girl from my visions wasn't me. The woman he had loved long ago ... wasn't me.

I thought more about why the coven was formed—the reason I was born. I needed to understand the relationship between who I am today and who I was in my past life. I couldn't deny the reason Tatyana gave me these powers. My purpose, then and now, was to protect this world from evil. If I deprived the witches on Earth of my power, it would be the most selfish act I could ever do, and I couldn't live with myself if I turned my back on them. My life belonged to the coven.

"Okay," I said, looking at the door we were about to walk through. I put my hand to my chest and let out a slow exhale. "I'm terrified, but I won't fight you on this any longer. I've decided this is what I want."

With a smile, he grabbed my other hand, unlocked the front door, and escorted me inside the library. We took the elevator down into the cellar. As the doors opened, my eyes immediately drew to an engraved pentagram on the wooden floor.

I sat at the center as he instructed. Caleb sifted through his backpack, pulling out a few candles and placing them around the circle, lighting each one. Then he checked the time on his phone.

"The spell to make you immortal will take place immediately after your Awakening, which is just a few minutes away. Ready, Mercy?"

"I'm scared," I admitted.

"I'm right here," he said, running his hands through my hair in a gentle touch. "Close your eyes."

After I shut my eyes, Caleb began to speak in a tongue I didn't recognize—incoherent sentences that seemed to be all flowing together at once. I couldn't decipher any of it. I felt him move closer to me, and I opened my eyes again, watching the look in his own eyes that seemed distant ... like he was afraid this moment was going to be our last.

Caleb leaned forward, cradled my face in the palms of his hands, and kissed me gently upon my lips.

As he deepened the kiss, a gray cloud formed under my eyes and parted, revealing an image before me, just like I had seen during the spell in the witch shop.

In the scene before me, my mother from my past life was cooking something over an iron stove. The room was dimly lit by candle-light. The kitchen appliances weren't like anything we had in the twenty-first century. It was my old home.

She turned around and looked straight through me.

"Mercy, go to your room," she said. "I need to speak with Caleb."

I heard the floor creak from behind me, and when I turned around, I saw my past self, but with copper-red hair and deep blue eyes.

"Mother, I want to hear what Caleb has to say."

My mother slammed her hand on the counter. "Go, Mercy. Now!"

"No! I'll not be kept from my coven. Not anymore," the former me told her mother defiantly.

Caleb was there, dressed in black slacks with a buttoned-down white shirt under his long coat. He took a few steps toward my past self and grabbed her hand gently, still facing her mother.

"We're doing the ritual tonight. Mercy and the rest of us will become immortal because it's the only way she'll be safe. Look what happened to your husband. Alexander could be dead for all we know. And what about your daughter, Faith? She needs her sister to protect her. Mercy will be able to protect you both. It's a witch hunt out there, Mary. Why would you not want this for her?"

"Roland lied to you, Caleb. Your father knew more about this prophecy than he shared with us. You'll never be safe. If vampires knew she was immortal, knew any of you could not die, they would take you and torture you. They would feed on you over and over again. Not to mention, Mercy's blood will allow them to walk in the daylight, putting us *all* in danger."

He stepped in her direction, but she moved back as if she were afraid of him. "I'll protect her," he promised. "We all will protect her."

Caleb caught hold of Mary's shoulder and squeezed. She didn't fight back. Her dazed look terrified me because of the amount of power he had over her. She was utterly helpless as he chanted a spell, followed by her collapsing to the floor.

He turned to my old self. "We must leave the village as soon as the ritual is done. It won't take long before the vampires know what we've done. Grab enough clothes for a few days and meet me at the barn. I need to go find the others," he instructed.

After Caleb left the house, the other Mercy ran upstairs and stuffed a bunch of clothes in a sack. She picked up a book from the dresser and a few small blankets and stuffed them into her bag. She then stopped by her bed.

Is she having second thoughts?

She heard a knock at her door.

"Mercy."

"Dorian, what are you doing here?" A handsome man with dark brown hair and brown eyes stepped into the room. He was built like Caleb, strong and tall, with smooth, slightly fair skin. He wasn't rugged, no five o'clock shadow. It was clear to me—he was a vampire.

My stomach fluttered wildly as I recognized him. He was the man who had been visiting my dreams before all of this happened. He was the one who kissed me under the moonlight night after night, who had suddenly disappeared when Caleb walked back into my life.

Dorian stopped by her bed. "Your mother is right, Mercy—you cannot allow Caleb to make you immortal. The vampires know you're doing the ritual tonight, so I came here to warn you. Maurice is on his way. Once the ritual is completed, his men plan to take all five of you and enslave you behind their walls. I'm not strong enough to stop them." He took her hand, pulling her closer to him. "You saved my life once, love. Let me save yours."

"I'm dead either way." She gripped his hand and placed it over her heart. "Do you feel that, Dorian? My heart is steady. I'm not afraid. At least if I were immortal, I would be stronger, fight back, and not need you to protect me anymore.

"I'd rather for you to be dead than tortured by them. At least if you're dead, you'll be free."

She shrugged. "We'll be apart either way." She squeezed his hand and released it.

Did she care about that particular vampire?

She was a hunter. Well, I was a hunter, and I wasn't trying to kill him. Was I not the ruthless hunter I was told I was?

These memories weren't like the ones I had after looking at the symbol on my hand. These were more like watching a film, whereas the others were actual memories coming back. I didn't feel any emotion; I only watched. I had to have met this vampire between the ages of thirteen and twenty-one, as I had no recollection of him from when I did the memory spell with Patricia.

She stepped closer to him, touching her forehead to his. She sucked in a deep breath as if she were taking in his scent for the last time and treasuring every moment she could before she had to say goodbye.

He also closed his eyes but hesitated in pulling her closer—he loved her deeply.

Mercy stepped back and walked to the door. "The coven is waiting for me, Dorian. I ... I must go." I watched as she rushed down the stairs.

Dorian moved with lightning speed toward her, trying to stop her at the door. Her hair flew up like it was caught in a breeze from the speed of his movements. "Mercy," his voice wavered. "You don't have to do this. You can choose death. If the vampires catch you after you become immortal, you'll want to die, believe me."

Mercy dropped her bag at her feet and looked at him, tears glistening in her eyes. They didn't speak as she closed her eyes tightly, her mouth hardening into a thin line. When she opened them back up, her tears had dried, and she gave him a nod.

"I love you, Dorian," she said. "I love you more than my own life. Nothing in this world has ever meant more to me than the moments we've shared this last year. Every kiss. Every touch. Every moment of pleasure."

Slowly, she opened the door, and I heard loud cries throughout the forest outside her home. She turned to Dorian, rushing back into his arms, their lips colliding and tears flowing down their cheeks.

Mercy released their embrace, stepping back to create distance between them. "Don't forget me, Dorian," she said before walking out the door and into the night.

I could only watch with sadness as she walked outside the house, fell to her knees, and put her hands up in the air as a crowd of angry villagers formed around her, carrying ropes and lit torches.

The woman had chosen death—*I* had chosen death.

Dorian backed away from her, blending in with the crowd, unable to hold back his sobs. Clearly, he didn't want her to die, but he must have known it was the only way she'd be free from the endless torture that awaited her.

The villagers couldn't have known Dorian was a vampire because they ignored him as if he were just part of the crowd. They were focused solely on her.

"Witch! Witch!" one called out.

"Hang her now!" another shouted.

Two men, each grabbing an arm, held on to her tightly and dragged her across a long field. Once they reached a clearing, I saw a wooden platform with rough ropes hanging from a tall tree, and people screamed and chanted in increasing fervor.

"Hang her! Witch!" voices cried over and over again.

I watched as they pulled the woman up on the platform, but now, I could feel their hands on my skin like it was happening to *me*. They placed the rope around her neck, and I felt the thick fibers around my own skin.

I didn't understand why I wasn't using my powers to stop them. The truth was, death was better than being sucked dry for eternity, but I could have at least fled. Fled the ritual, fled this town. I, this woman from my previous life, didn't care anymore.

The opening under my feet felt wobbly, and the noose was rough against my skin. I was no longer viewing the memory, but

I was *her*, standing in front of an angry crowd, cheering for my execution.

I smelled horse manure and the sweat from the man who tied the noose around my neck. I saw Dorian in the crowd, smiled softly, and whispered to him, "I love you."

Tears flowed freely down his cheeks faster than my beating heart. I wanted to reach out and hold him one last time, but the villager's cries echoed loudly in my ears.

"Witch!" the villagers chanted in unison again.

"Hang her now!" a man bellowed.

Everything went black after that, and my eyes popped back open.

I started coughing as if the noose was still around my neck. Caleb held on to me, comforting me as I trembled. I looked up, and his face was painted in horror and sadness. "Mercy, are you okay?"

"You ... you weren't my last kiss," I whispered, feeling Caleb's arms slip from my body, pulling back until we no longer touched.

He remained silent.

"Dorian," I said, watching Caleb's eyes dim. "Where is he?"

Caleb now sighed heavily, because he knew. He knew I saw the last secret he wanted to keep from me.

"He's a vampire, Mercy," he said. "You fell in love with the very thing you were sent here to kill."

"Where. Is. He?!"

Caleb swallowed, his lips set in a hard line. He wasn't angry; he almost appeared defeated.

"He attacked the coven the night you were hanged. Simon was forced to kill him."

My heart hammered in my chest. *No!*

"That can't be true." A lone tear fell down my face. "Dorian was kind. He loved me. In that vision—the last moments before I died—I didn't just see things; I felt them, including how I felt about Dorian. I knew what kind of man he was."

"He was a vampire, Mercy. He wasn't a *man*."

I recoiled at his comment because I knew in my heart that it wasn't true. "There are good vampires out there, Caleb. I never felt threatened by Dorian. But you, you made me believe that you and I loved each other until I died. No. I had moved on and found true love. From *him*."

"As I said, he attacked us," Caleb said bitterly. "Dorian was angry at himself for letting you go, and he wanted to die to punish himself. He provoked Simon so that he would end his life. Our mission is to kill vampires, Mercy. We didn't have a choice."

Caleb lifted the dagger he held, and I winced as he slit the center of my hand. "Does any of this change your mind?" he asked.

I shook my head. "No." Another tear ran down my cheek, but I wiped it quickly with the sleeve of my sweater.

"The Awakening will happen in thirty seconds. The blood needs to be drawn at that very moment to link your powers with the covens. It's going to bind you to us."

I had to push back the pain from the betrayal and the knowledge I now had that the man from my dreams would never be mine again. He was gone.

Caleb wrapped his fingers delicately around my palm. "Sorry, this will sting just a tad." He squeezed the skin around the wound, and blood dripped down to the center of the circle.

My ascension was happening, and it was happening now.

He squeezed my hand, urging the blood to flow freely as he chanted again. My blood dripped to the floor, and we both looked down as he released my hand. Blood swirled around like a vortex forming from the pentagram and wrapped around my body. I felt warm and then increasingly hot. It was like my body was melting, but at the same time, the heat was comforting and pleasurable. I closed my eyes as the red mist wrapped around and swarmed my body. A massive burst of energy flooded through my chest, and I fell to the floor. The moment was brief, but my body felt like it had been running for hours. The blood dissipated all around me, and I felt like my entire body was about to explode. It wasn't painful, just overwhelming. Every inch of my body burned as the magic settled itself into me.

I flinched as Caleb laid his hand on my overheated skin. His touch was icy, and I could barely focus on the string of words coming out of his mouth. Every part of my body felt like it was being ripped apart. I screamed in sudden agony as I dropped to the floor, digging my nails into the wood to take away some of the pain from my mind. The energy was like a wave, crashing hard over and over against the rocks on a shore. Suddenly, a sharp pain stabbed my stomach. The cold metal under my skin made me nauseous. I forced my eyes open, seeing Caleb's hand on the dagger as it pierced right into my gut. I knew he wasn't trying to kill me—it was part of the immortal ritual—but it still hurt like hell. I refused to scream again, absorbing the pain shooting through every cell of my body. As soon as the dagger was removed, I felt my skin knit back together.

It's over.

My eyes rolled back into my head, darkness blanketing the pain. I felt myself go limp and land on the ground. Slowly, the pain subsided, and I opened my eyes and sat up. I rubbed the area where the stab wound should have been and looked at Caleb.

"Is that it?" I asked nervously, not wanting to endure that level of pain again. "Is it done now?"

"That's it," he said, gently helping me to stand. We both stood up from the circle. I felt a little disoriented, but overall, I still felt like the same person.

No, I feel better than before. I feel strong.

"What now?" I asked.

But before he could answer, we heard the elevator ping. We quickly turned around as Abigail emerged from the shadows. "Thank you, little nephew." Her grin was sinister, and it made my skin crawl.

"Abigail, what are you—" Before I could finish my question, fangs protruded from her mouth.

I knew something was off about her, but I didn't expect that.

"Step back, Abigail. You're not touching her." Caleb pushed me behind him, sheltering me from his own family. But she ignored his commands as she licked her top lip and stepped forward. She wanted blood—*my* blood.

"I only want a tiny drop. I won't even bite you," Abigail muttered.

"Caleb, tell her to put her fangs away before I kill her," I warned.

He stepped toward Abigail as if ready to fight her to protect me.

"Oh, don't be so dramatic, Caleb. Just a few drops will do," Abigail continued to plead, but something told me that no matter her intention, the moment she took hold of me, there would be a bloodbath.

Her eyes were now crimson red as she stalked in my direction, probably smelling the blood soaked into the wooden floor. She inhaled deeply, as if the scent in the room alone brought her pleasure. A smile crossed her lips. "I'm sick of staying inside during the day. Let me have a taste, and I'll be on my way."

I gulped right before she lunged at me, but in an instant, I felt my body pull back through a thick wall, thrusting me down toward the floor. My vision spun, and I held my head as my eyes adjusted. I looked around the room, realizing I was kneeling in Lily's kitchen.

CHAPTER 18

H *oly shit! Did I just teleport?*
     I looked around the kitchen, scanning over the walls. I could smell something smoky lingering in the air. Shards of glass littered the kitchen floor from a smashed wine bottle, and one of the chairs was overturned. I whirled around as I heard an exhale, electricity ready at my fingertips. Seeing it was Joel, I released the energy from my fingers, dropping my hands to my side. He immediately rushed to me, placing my head in between his hands.

"Mercy! Thank God you're alive."

Joel was shaking, and the adrenaline rush of having just been teleported across state lines faded away. I realized that something was wrong. His eyes were wide, most likely still stunned that I was standing in front of him after being missing for hours. I glanced at the table to see candles and the source of the potent scent lurking in the air. Burning herbs. "What's going on, Joel?"

The panic in his eyes caused my heart to race. He stared at the shattered glass on the floor and ground his teeth.

"Lily was taken," he said.

The second those words left his lips, I felt the blood drain from my face. The glass crunched under my feet as I looked closer around the kitchen. That deep, rich color of wine looked so much like blood. It covered the tile floor and refrigerator and spilled out into the hallway.

"We ... we waited for you to return to the home with Riley," Joel explained. "When you didn't, Lily rushed outside and saw Riley stumbling out of the woods. He told us what had happened to him and that he believed Caleb had taken you. We quickly grabbed the items needed for the locator spell to find you. But it wasn't enough. Riley helped me find a personal item from your room needed for the spell, leaving Lily in the kitchen alone with her wine bottle to calm her nerves. It all happened so fast after that. We heard a crash, ran downstairs, and she was gone." Joel ran his hand through his hair, tugging at the ends. "I didn't even hear a scream."

Joel had been speaking so fast, his words stumbling over each other, that I was still trying to register what he said.

This isn't happening. Lily can't be gone.

"Where's Riley now?" I asked.

"He took a call shortly after and said he knew someone that might be able to help us."

"We have to find her, Joel. Now!" My voice cracked, and my hands became unsteady. I felt my powers climb to my fingertips, and Joel placed his hands on mine in a soothing gesture.

"Mercy." Joel's voice caused me to look up. "I know it's hard to control your powers right now, but you need to relax. Just take a deep breath. Nice and easy."

My hands shook as I tried to quiet the power. I clutched my hands to my chest, not trusting myself to touch anything around me. I struggled to slow down my racing heart. I sucked in a breath, feeling like I was drowning in the sensation of raging magic.

"I'm okay," I assured. "It's like fighting an uphill battle, where there never seems to be an end. I'll be able to have more control once I'm used to this magic flowing through my body. Right now, it feels like a pinball is out of control under my skin." I straightened my back and walked over to the table, pointing to the items he had laid out. "Maybe I can help?"

Joel solemnly shook his head. "I've been trying, but it's not working. Something is blocking me," he explained.

I picked up a stack of burning herbs and smothered the glowing embers; the thick smoke hung in the air, filling the space between us. "What about her phone or car?" I asked, hoping that maybe she was able to escape.

"They're gone, Mercy, but you know she wouldn't have taken off like that, even if she were being chased. Lily would have fought back or screamed out a warning for me." He tightened his fingers around the back of the chair. "Whoever took her did something to silence her before they even left the house."

I nodded, rolling the herbs around in my palm, trying to think of any clues I could have missed from the last few weeks that might lead us to where they'd taken her. And, more importantly, why?

Joel took the stack of herbs from my palm and was about to place it on the table when he paused. His brows furrowed. "What about you? Did Caleb—?"

"No. Caleb took me, but he didn't hurt me. But he did help me through my Awakening." I bit the inside of my cheek. "I'm immortal now, too."

I refused to look Joel in the eye as I heard the heavy sigh escape him. Both he and Lily tried so hard to protect me from this life and to do something I knew he'd oppose; I felt like I'd betrayed them.

"Mercy ..."

I could hear the disappointment in his voice. The room went silent, aside from the crunching sound of herbs between his fingers.

"I didn't have a choice, Joel."

His other hand rested on my shoulder. "We always have a choice," he hissed.

I hated that he was right, but at the moment, I felt like that was the only choice—the only *right* choice. In my past life, I chose death over my coven and look at what happened to the world. Vampires were growing in strength and numbers every single day, and I had the power to finally end it. For once, I wanted to have a chance to live my life how I wanted to. I wanted to be able to protect my family and friends, but I could only do that if I were immortal.

"Let's focus on Lily right now," I said, reminding him that every second we argued about my poor life choices was a moment someone could hurt her.

Joel nodded. "Do you know who could have done this?"

"I have an idea who the fucker is, but I don't know who they are, exactly." I saw the look of confusion on Joel's face, and I dropped into the chair next to him. "Seems to be someone who has some personal vendetta against me. They went as far as possessing one of my friends to hurt me." I scrunched up my face from the memory of Cami covered in her own blood.

He grabbed his keys from the counter. "Any clue where they could have taken her?"

I shook my head frantically, realizing that this wasn't something I could solve in a few days. I had joined a centuries-old war without a clue what was going on. I took whatever Caleb said with a grain of salt. This wasn't some fantasy where everyone would be okay in the end. People were going to die, people had died, and there was nothing I could do to change that.

What if we can't find her?

Frustrated tears welled in my eyes as I shook my head.

We were interrupted by my phone ringing. When I looked down, it was Lily. I fumbled to answer the call.

"Lily?" my voice stammered, pitched with a mix of panic and relief.

A low and eerie voice answered, "Hello, Mercy."

I swallowed as my stomach churned, realization hitting in a bitter wave. "If you hurt Lily—" my voice hitched. I had to control my anger until I saw she was safe. Threatening this psychopath probably wouldn't be the best idea. He could retaliate and hurt her.

Laughter rang out loudly on the other end of the line. It wasn't a playful laugh—it sent shivers down my spine and left a foul taste in my mouth. I clenched my jaw, causing my ears to ring. "Where did you take Lily, you piece of shit?"

Maybe name-calling wasn't the best choice when dealing with a dangerous person, but I couldn't help myself.

"It is quite beautiful out here," he said. "I can see why you and your friends are so drawn to this place. The moon's reflection on the water, the gorgeous trees, and the peaceful silence—are simply breathtaking."

There was a beep as the line dropped, and I slammed my phone on the table, swearing under my breath. I had no idea if Lily was alive or injured. I banged my fist on the table, causing it to splinter from the force, and looked up at Joel.

"Where is she?" he asked.

"Goddard Park," I answered. "Let's go."

Joel instantly jumped up and conjured a portal, concentrating on each motion of his hands. Together, we sprinted into the vortex.

The park was empty except for Lily's car sitting at the end of the parking lot. I scanned the area and spotted her brown hair shimmering in the moonlight near the lake. My breath hitched as I realized she was sitting on the same bench where, not even a few days ago, I had sat with Riley.

I shouted as we ran toward her, "Lily, we're here!"

It only took seconds to reach her, and I started to panic when she didn't move. However, her chest's gentle rise and fall calmed the raging power surging through me. I moved to unbind her hands when I heard a groan. I whipped around to see Joel collapse behind me. Caleb stood behind him, holding a bloodied rock in his hand.

CHAPTER 19

"Caleb, what the hell are you doing?!" I didn't wait for a response before I got my answer.

His eyes were midnight black, and the look on his face was filled with pure distaste—he was possessed, just as we suspected Cami had been.

"Seems a little cowardly, don't you think?" I taunted. "Using my friends to get to me instead of fighting with your own hands."

When his expression didn't change, I grabbed a large rock from the ground and threw it with every amount of strength I could muster. It hit Caleb's head, grazing the side of his temple. It wasn't a direct hit as I had aimed for, but it was enough to make him lose his balance and topple over a large branch behind him.

I needed to lure him as far away from my family as possible, so I spun around and ran toward the forest, hoping he'd chase me. With my hand outstretched, I was about to reach the tree line when a blaze of flames lit up in front of me, blocking my path. I skidded to a stop and swung around. Caleb's hands were raised, but only for an instant, then brought back down to his sides. I could tell that getting him into the forest would no longer work. I had to think of another strategy. Without hesitation, I held up my hands toward the water and started channeling the green light into my fingertips. Caleb stopped moving, threw his head back, and started laughing.

Ignoring him, I used the power from my hands to pull Joel closer to where Lily was sitting. Then I harnessed my magic to direct the nearest fallen tree branches toward them, wrapping their ankles and waists to the bench to keep them secure.

The entity inside Caleb looked on curiously, tilting his head, dark eyes glittering. I had to act fast. My hands flew up toward the bay, and with my mind, I commanded the waves to pull toward the forest and cleanse the burning trees. The water did as I commanded, pulling up into the park and sweeping away the blazing fire around us. It reached only up to our ankles, but it wasn't enough.

Caleb was in front of me in a split second and pushed my arms to my side, keeping me secure in his grasp.

I smiled. "You're too late, fucker." The water came crashing down over our heads in a massive tidal wave. Caleb's grip faltered, and I held my breath as the water pulled us under. We were being washed back out into the cove, but I was able to make my way to the surface as the torrent started to calm down. Caleb was already on me and grabbed my hair. I spun around and punched him straight in the face.

He screamed, releasing his grip. "Bitch!" he cried out.

I hoped my punch would slow him down, even for just a moment, so that I could escape. I quickly swam to the shore, which took every ounce of energy I had, but before I could reach Joel and Lily, Caleb was behind me, grabbing me by the waist. I kicked my legs frantically, trying to get away from him. He walked steadily toward Lily's car; unfortunately, my struggle didn't slow him down.

My breaths were labored as he forced me into the passenger seat. Fear rose to my heart.

What is he going to do?

"Mercy." I winced at my name coming out of his mouth, but I realized the tone had changed; it was gentle.

"Caleb?"

He looked at me, the amber in his eyes fighting through the darkness like flashes of bright lights. "Are you still wearing the necklace?" he asked with a clenched jaw. I fingered the stone resting on my chest, under my sweater, as I watched him grip his head in pain.

"Caleb, is that you?"

"Mercy, I need to make sure you're wearing it so it doesn't latch on to you, too," he snapped, removing his hand from his forehead and throwing the back of his head against the car seat. "Mercy?!"

"Yes, it's right here," I answered quickly. "It's on."

Caleb placed his hands against his head, using his magic to fight the creature inside him that fought to latch on, to gain control again. "Get out!" he shouted. "Get the fuck out!"

I reached for the door but froze when black smoke leaked through his eyes and down his neck and chest. I slapped my hand over my mouth—it looked like a scene straight out of a horror movie. The black smoke oozed out of him, and my stomach rolled at the sight. I didn't want to watch, but my eyes were glued to his face. The black smoke moved my way but only hovered near my chest before disappearing out the other window, leaving the car.

Caleb groaned, coming back to himself. "Are you okay?" he asked.

He closed his eyes, and while I couldn't see the black color, I knew he was back, and the darkness was gone.

"Are you?" I let out the rest of the breath I was holding in. "Holy shit, Caleb. You were possessed. How did you even get here or know where to find us?"

Caleb panted, gripping his fingers around the steering wheel. "The portal Joel created was still open, so I hitched a ride here. As I saw you approach Lily on the beach, black smoke took over my body. I think I must have touched your jet stone while we fought, allowing me to gain enough power to force it out.

"What do we do now?" I asked, but before Caleb answered, I drew my gaze to the front window of the car.

Several feet away, a tall, slender man with frosty-white hair stared back at us. He smoothed his hands down his long, black coat while his dark gray slacks moved slightly against the wind. His thin lip curled, showing his pearly white fangs.

He wasn't a witch, as we had suspected; the creature in front of us was a vampire. I shivered at the look of malice in his eyes. He might look beautiful, like an angel, but nothing was angelic about him. He reeked of evil. My heart pounded painfully as the blood rushed to my head. I gulped. "Who is that?"

Caleb paled and shook his head. "Ah, shit."

I gripped his arm, not daring to look away from the horrifying creature in front of me. "Who or what the hell is that?"

Caleb turned in his seat, but I couldn't tear my eyes away. "Remember the demon I told you about who had mated with an angel, which resulted in the vampire race?"

The hysteria in my voice was rising. "That's the demon from that story?!" *This is not what I signed up for.*

"No," he corrected, turning his eye to the creature. "That's their child. The very first vampire to ever exist."

I looked back toward the vampire. "Oh, great." My throat tightened as I panicked. Though I had hunted vampires in my past life, that creature before us was nothing like what my visions had shown me.

I turned back to him. "Caleb, we can't drive away. Joel and Lily are still on the shore. We need to fight back. It's not like he could kill us, right, being immortal?"

He put his hand on his waist but froze. "The dagger I used during the ritual," he said. "It's gone. He must have taken it."

"Why the hell do we need that dagger again? Aren't wooden stakes for killing a vampire?"

There was a lot I still needed to learn, and my mind raced so frantically for my own plan, but it left me with nothing. I didn't know how to do this.

"The dagger wouldn't be for him, Mercy. It would be for us."

I looked over at the vampire, who seemed to be reaching for something. I gave him a stern look. "Are you telling me that your dagger can kill an immortal? And now that vampire has it?"

Caleb nodded. "Son of a bitch."

We looked back at the smug, red-eyed demon; he held the dagger in his left hand and tapped it against his leg. He stood in front of the car now and sneered at us.

"My name is Kylan, Mercy. It's a pleasure to finally meet you face to face." His smile reached through me as if it had touched my soul, freezing me in my seat. "I was hoping to stop the ritual from happening, but you weren't at your home like I thought you'd be. So, I took your lovely aunt to draw you out. Then that idiot came through the portal, carrying this dagger, and it was all too easy to take him over." He flashed an evil grin and showed his creepy fangs again, his face contorting into a disgustingly vile expression.

Caleb didn't take his eyes off Kylan as he spoke. "You're his biggest threat, Mercy. With you being back, he knows we will destroy everything he created. He's trying to stop us before the other vampire clans reach you." He slammed his fist against the steering wheel. "Fuck! I wish I had put it all together earlier that he would be the first to come after you. He would have known about you long before the ritual." Caleb cursed again, slamming both hands against the steering wheel. "I didn't know that he could harness magic. I just assumed it was a witch."

I placed my hand on his. "Hey, this isn't your fault. We both knew that it was a risk to do the ceremony. I'm at risk just because I'm alive. He's the son of a demon and an angel. There was no way to know he had magic or wasn't like the rest. It could have been anyone, Caleb." I swallowed, feeling the painful ball in my throat slide down. "Now, let's get out there and kick that mother fucker's ass together."

Caleb looked at me and nodded, then we exited the car, slowly and cautiously, walking in Kylan's direction. Caleb moved to the left, and I to the right, in a flanking position.

"Oh, how precious is this?" Kylan's lip curled. "Look at the two of you, back together again after decades apart. Too bad you're about to die together. In a way, it's like a tragic love story."

His laughter sent chills down my spine. I had never been so terrified in my entire life. Despite the overwhelming feeling of fear, I was furious. He was hurting the ones I love. I felt my new powers radiating through my body, and I vowed I wasn't leaving this park until that creature was dead.

Kylan took a step closer to us, and I braced myself for his next move. I watched Caleb shift into a fighting stance, hands alight with gold flames.

"Mercy, run!" I heard Joel's voice cut through the air. I looked over and saw that Lily and Joel had regained consciousness and were breaking off the branches I had used to secure them earlier.

Kylan stalked toward us—the dagger he held giving off an eerie red glow. I lifted my hands, harnessed my energy into a single point, and fired a beam of green light toward his left hand. The beam slammed into the blade, knocking it out of Kylan's grip and across the parking lot. He hissed viciously, his eyes glowing even brighter as he glared at me. The magic I had at my fingertips was still sparking, and I shuddered at the power running through me. I thought it was intense before my Awakening, but that was nothing compared to this.

Lily and Joel, still standing by the bench, clasped hands together and chanted a spell, creating a ring of fire around Kylan.

"Parlor trick?" he hissed, scanning the circle of flames around him. When he looked back up, the blaze glowed in his eyes. "Do you have any idea how long I've been around? Fire cannot hurt me, you imbeciles."

"No?" I questioned. "Then walk through it."

Kylan glared at me and slowly clapped his hands together as if we had just concluded the ending scene of a play. "You know, I've decided to kill Caleb first. That way, you can watch him die a slow and painful death." He cocked his head to the right and curled his lip up. The slow hesitation in his movements made my skin crawl.

"The spell will only last a few more minutes," Lily shouted. "We need to stand in a circle around the fire ring and be ready when it burns out! We can strike then."

Kylan scoffed, "I'll rip your throat out before you can even lift a finger against me." Lily's brows furrowed as she concentrated, not bothering to acknowledge Kylan's threat. She and Joel had now moved by our side, and we clasped our hands to form a circle around him.

Kylan lifted a brow. "As the son of an angel and a demon, I was given a little magic, too, when I was born. Did you forget already?" He raised his hands, and there was a flash of black smoke. I could see Joel, Lily, and Caleb immediately stopped moving, their expressions blank as their hands dropped to their sides. Lily turned to me, and her eyes were midnight black.

Oh, fuck.

I reached out and shook her shoulders. "Lily, it's me. Wake up. Fight it, dammit."

Lily's hand opened with her palm up, and I felt a tug from the inside. It clenched at my chest, and my heart felt like it was being squeezed. It was hard to move as life pulled out of me.

My eyes widened as I realized Lily was attempting to draw out my power, using me as a Spirit conduit to use telekinesis magic. I saw the dagger lift from the ground and fly toward her hand. She clasped her fingers tightly around the handle and lunged toward me, throwing my body off balance. I landed painfully on my back, my head slammed on a large rock, and I winced. The jet stone pulsated with energy, holding back the darkness that held Lily in its grip.

"Lily, wake up!" I shouted. "Force him out of you!"

She tried to plunge the tip of the blade into my chest, but I held her back with all my strength. But the metal slowly sank into my skin, blood staining my sweater. I stared up at her, and for a moment, her face was replaced with the face of my mother. I shook my head, suppressing the memories of that night, erasing her face.

I resisted the urge to throw up as the flashback threatened to consume my senses. *No, this is Lily.* My sweet aunt was possessed by a monster. She wasn't like my mom. If Lily could resist his power, she would.

I flexed my fingers as the power begged to be released, but I feared I'd hurt Lily if I used them. She may be a witch, but she couldn't heal like me, and I didn't want to risk it.

I decided to try a different tactic, and I grabbed the dagger at the hilt and summoned fire to my fingers to heat the metal. It quickly grew red hot, and Lily yelped, releasing it. I caught the warm end of the blade and tossed it again behind me. I reached for her temples and used my element to pull the smoke out of her eyes. She fought me, trying to keep Kylan's magic inside, but my power was stronger.

I shielded my face as Kylan's power exited her body. For a second, I felt it trying to enter my mind, but my necklace lit up and pulsated against my chest. The power of the pentagram had repelled the dark force away from my body and back into Kylan. The beast stood with his hands in fists and fury in his eyes.

He isn't going to win. I won't let him.

Kylan grinned, showing his sharp fangs again. For an ancient, all-powerful vampire, he wasn't fighting much. In fact, *he* wasn't fighting at all.

"It's over, Kylan. Let them go." I pulled myself out of my fear, jumped to my feet, and helped Lily to hers. She was in a daze and held her hand to her head like she had a vicious migraine. "It's okay, Lily," I said. "You're safe."

Kylan lifted his right hand and froze Lily like the others. He snarled between his teeth. "So be it. I'll find another way to get rid of you."

I felt conflicted. I could fight this monster and kill him, but not at the risk of having him kill my family and Caleb. I held out my wrist, not knowing what else I could do at that moment. Maybe I could bait him and direct his focus to only me.

"Drink my blood," I begged. "Here. Just take it. That's the other way. My blood will allow you to walk in the daylight, Kylan. Don't you want that? Here. Drink!" My voice cracked. "Drink from me, dammit!"

It was reckless to give in to being sucked dry by that monster, but I didn't know any other way to fight him. That's what he wanted; that was what they all wanted. So, I'd give it to him to keep the ones I loved safe.

"I don't want your tainted blood," he said distastefully. "It isn't desirable to all of us."

I blinked. *What?*

His lip curled up at the baffled expression on my face. I had no idea what was happening. If he wanted to kill me, wouldn't he have done it already?

What is he waiting for?

The fire spell burned out around him, and he walked over to the dagger on the ground and picked it up. Instead of using it to attack, he flipped the handle toward me and thrust it in my face.

What the hell is happening?

"Take the dagger and plunge it into your heart, or I will gut your aunt right in front of you with it."

I could feel my breath growing shallow from panic. I didn't know what to do. How was I supposed to stop the original vampire? My memories of battles I'd fought in my previous life were brief. I couldn't recall any training that I could use right now.

I'm surprised I'm not already dead. Why am I not already dead?

"You're making me take my own life?" I asked. "But why? Why not kill me yourself?"

He frowned. "It's more poetic."

No, that's not it. Something isn't right.

I looked down at the dagger. This didn't make any sense. "No." I handed it back to him, but he wouldn't take it. This was his chance to use the one weapon that could end an immortal, so why was he hesitating?

He looked down at the dagger and then up at me. "No?"

Nothing was adding up, and I was starting to have a good idea of why he hadn't killed me already. I was taking a gamble, but I needed to know. I lifted my chin and met his eyes. "You do it, you bloodsucking piece of shit. Just make it quick, though ... please."

He frowned again, and his eyes twitched in irritation. "Take this dagger and kill yourself with it, witch! You don't want to see what horrible things I will do to your aunt, do you?"

I looked over at Lily and back at him. A soft smile curved my lips. "You can't kill me, can you?" I asked. "Because something is not allowing you to do it. And you can't possess me, either, because I'm wearing this necklace." I ran a finger over the jet stone dangling from my neck, and Kylan hissed through his fangs. "That's why you used Cami ... because you can't do it. You can't kill any of us. You need a human to kill on your command." I narrowed my eyes at him. "Let me guess. Cami fought back against you and forced you out. So then, you possessed someone else near that ally to knock her out before she told us what was happening? She called us that night to warn me of you."

This may be easier than I thought.

"Why can't you, though?" I asked. "Why are you not able to kill me?"

His eyes narrowed at me like a serpent ready to strike but then shrugged, indifferent. "After I ripped my father's head off—" He rolled his eyes as I gasped before he finished his sentence, "—my angelic mother put a curse on me. She rendered me unable to take human lives, so I had to resort to other means."

The sadistic bastard killed his father. But then again, his father was a demon.

"I don't understand. You created vampires. Don't humans have to die to transition?"

"I only turned *one* into a vampire. Her name was Valentina. She went paralyzed with fear of what she'd become after I fed her my blood. That fear led her to take her own life. She didn't realize that was the final step in her transition. Once you die, you're reborn as an undead. It's a delightfully ironic thing." A sinister smile played on his lips.

God, he was sick.

He loved seeing people in pain ... he thrived on it.

"Her bloodlust was stronger than mine," he continued. "She began to turn humans into vampires, and her creations then turned others, and a vampire race had begun, just like the devil wanted. It was like a plague that would never stop spreading. It was the perfect solution to end the humans and claim the Earth as my own." He laughed again so hard he flung his head back and balled his fists. When he lowered his head again, the red in his eyes had turned black. This inhuman *thing* was pure evil. He had to die, and now.

CHAPTER 20

"I don't know how long you've been following me and preparing for this moment," I told Kylan. "But what a waste of time." I raised my head, looking him dead in the eye. "Every life is valued in this world. I'll never *take* mine, no matter what threat you hold over me. I'll continue to fight by my coven's side until each and every last one of you becomes a pile of ash. Starting with you, the pathetic monster who can't even harm a fly."

Kylan's face twisted in pure rage—his facial features contorted into something much more sinister and grotesque. His sneer was absolutely demonic, and I turned away briefly, feeling violated by the evil look he sent me. What human features he had melted away into something unspeakable.

When I slowly glanced back up, Kylan spoke again with a deep, growling voice. "That necklace may keep you from being controlled by me, but all I need to do is wake Lily or Joel. I'll possess them like I did Caleb and make one of them overpower and kill you with this dagger. Then I'll force them to drown themselves in the cove." He gestured to the weapon. "Push this through your heart, you little abomination, and I will spare their lives."

I wanted to wipe that cocky smirk from his face. He thought he had won, that this fight was over.

It is far from over.

My nostrils flared with rage. "No, you'll not touch them. You will never touch any of them, ever again." His smirk faltered, and I took that moment to toss the dagger behind me, lifting my hands and focusing on my thoughts. I pushed through the power to create a barrier around Caleb, Joel, and Lily. The shield encircled them in a bubble Kylan couldn't penetrate.

Through shaky breath, I chanted, "Power from my hands, create this flame—make him feel every ounce of pain. Send this demon straight to Hell; for all I have, I create this spell."

Kylan lunged forward but screeched when the magic flames encircled him. He tried to walk through, but the power repelled him, trapping him within the ring. When he raised a hand to use his own magic, Kylan paused, held in place by my power.

"What is this?" He looked down at his body in horror. "What the hell did you do to me?"

Oh, my God. It worked.

His body was melting, but he didn't scream in pain. The look he gave me was not that of agony but pure loathing. I felt the surrounding power willingly bend under my hands—the chaotic fire hummed gently between my fingers.

I kept my eyes on Kylan, his flesh melting from his face to the point where he was no longer recognizable.

"Stop this, you fucking witch! You think I can die?" he barely cried out before the sound was cut off as his mouth melted, and his jaw fell to the ground like warm wax dripping down a candle. Underneath the melted flesh, I could see his demonic form writhing and burning with the unholy countenance. I had seen the face of the angel, and now I saw the heart of the demon. I had to end this.

I spotted a fallen branch near where Caleb was frozen, yanked it free from the ground, and split it in half with my knee. It was slightly damp, but it was sturdy enough. I ran toward Kylan with the sharpest end pointed at him. I entered the fire, untouched by its searing heat, and grabbed Kylan by his melted shoulder. Kylan looked too weak to fight back; there was hardly anything left of his muscles to defend himself. He couldn't even shield his heart with his hands, but he did backhand my cheek the moment the wood broke through his skin. The force of the impact caused me to fall to the ground. With the branch now embedded deep into his blackened heart, I met his stone-cold gaze and smiled. The ear-splitting screech he let out at the sight of my smirk was pure satisfaction. As he screamed, Lily, Caleb, and Joel were released from the spell and fell to their knees. They all looked up just in time to see Kylan explode into ash.

I let out a sigh of relief before breaking the spell, then turned to pick up the dagger. The moonlight hit the metal and gave off a slight red glimmer. The weight of the blade felt heavy in my hand. It felt surreal to hold something that came so close to ending the existence of myself and my coven. I dropped the dagger as Lily ran to me, wrapping me up in her arms. The tension from the fight faded away as I held my aunt tight.

My family was safe. But the thought lingered in my mind ... for an ancient vampire, that was too fucking easy.

Caleb clambered to his feet. "We need to hide the dagger," he said, picking up the blade carefully. "As soon as we can."

"I know of a place," Joel mentioned as he lifted both hands in the air and created a portal. "I'll teleport it there now."

He chanted a spell, and the dagger slipped from Caleb's hands and zipped through the portal entrance.

I cocked my head to the side. "Where did you send it?"

Joel opened his mouth to speak, but Caleb interrupted, "Don't tell us where. There are mind-reading witches out there, Mercy. The fewer people who know, the better. It's safer this way."

Joel nodded.

I turned to Lily but felt Caleb's hand wrap around my arm. "We need to go. Every witch felt it as soon as your Awakening happened, and some witches are aligned with vampires. They would have reported to the clans by now. Your blood is very desirable to them, and their witch allies will lead them to you. We must take you somewhere safe until we can devise a plan."

I wormed out of his grasp. I was done with him dragging me wherever he wanted. He took me away from my family during my Awakening, and we were only in this situation because of it.

"Joel?" I called, turning to my uncle. "Where can we go?"

Caleb rolled his eyes and spoke before Joel could answer, "St. Peter's Cemetery in Salem. Can you teleport us?"

Caleb's eyes were on mine, pleading for me to stop pushing him away. I looked down but didn't resist this time when I felt his hand wrap around my fingers.

Goddammit.

Joel let out a heavy sigh. It was evident how exhausted he was. The side of his head had dried blood from where Caleb had struck him, and I was aware of what the teleportation spell did to his energy.

"Honestly, I can take you anywhere you want to go," Joel said, "but why there?" I felt admiration welling in my heart. My uncle was willing to do anything to keep us safe, even if it meant taking every ounce of energy from him.

Caleb hesitated for a beat, but when I drew my brows together, he understood his vague responses had to stop. He continued, "There's a safe house under one of the mausoleums. One that has protected witches for decades."

Once everyone agreed this was the safest place to hide, we followed Joel into his portal, passing through space until we reached Salem.

—*ele*—

"I've been here before," I said, looking over at a large stone mausoleum across the cemetery. "In a vision, anyway."

Caleb nodded. "It used to be a vampire lair. You and I snuck in once to take out a vampire planning to strike a werewolf pack. We owed that pack a favor."

"At the time, I thought it was only a dream," I explained. "Someone threw me down the entryway from behind."

Bits and pieces of that vision came back to my mind. "I had looked down some stairs inside a coffin in the mausoleum. They had come up from behind and pushed me inside."

Caleb smiled as if recounting memories of his own. "Yeah, that guy got what was coming."

I looked at him curiously. "That actually happened?"

"It was as if they knew we were coming. They struck you from behind, and a crowd of angry vampires surrounded you when you landed." He smirked. "But don't worry, we were right behind you." He winked at me and grabbed his phone from his pocket. "I need to call Abigail. She's going to worry about me."

"Are you serious right now? Your aunt Abigail? The one who followed and attacked us at the library?"

"She's not going to hurt you, Mercy. She's on our side. I'm sure she couldn't help herself when she smelled your blood. She didn't mean it."

I scrunched up my face. "Are those words actually coming out of your mouth?" The disbelief on my face as he dialed her number caused him to smile.

We entered the mausoleum's doors, and there was a coffin at the center. Joel slid the coffin lid open, and there stood a long set of stairs that led under the ground, and Joel went in first.

"Climb down in a few minutes," Joel instructed. "I just need to make sure it's safe first."

Five minutes later, we entered the lair, and I looked around. It was bigger than I had imagined. There was furniture in every space of the walls; there was even a kitchen and a few bathrooms.

After an hour of exploring the safe house and securing it with a shield spell, we heard a tap at the door.

"Do you really think she'll be safe here, Caleb?" Abigail said as she walked inside. "A vampire's lair?"

Caleb lit up when he saw her, relief clear on his face. He truly cared about Abigail, regardless of her earlier moment of bloodlust. "Not anymore. This place has been abandoned for years.

He walked up to her and gave her a warm embrace, then pulled away, but only slightly, his arm resting around her shoulders. "We could use your help, Abigail," he said.

"Of course you do, Caleb," she boasted with a sideways smirk, and Caleb rolled his eyes at her remark.

Abigail walked in my direction and sat on the couch next to me. Now that my family was here, I wasn't as afraid of her as I was when she caught us off guard in the library. I wanted to trust her.

As I turned to face her, Abigail inhaled a breath of annoyance. "Sorry we got off on the wrong foot," I said, waiting for her response, but she only folded her arms across her chest. "I mean, you did try to bite me."

Again, Abigail stayed silent, turning her gaze away.

Great. I'm not sure how to fix this one.

After a long pause, she finally turned to me. "You're a fool if you believe any of us can control our bloodlust. It doesn't make me selfish to succumb to my basic needs as a vampire. The dangers you're about to face, Mercy, with blood as potent and powerful as yours, doesn't even scratch the surface of what it did to me back there."

I couldn't possibly understand that craving. The idea of drinking someone's blood was repulsive. However, I realized at that moment I needed to learn everything I could about the vampire race. What drove them to blood? What weaknesses did they have? If I were completely ignorant of it all, I'd never be able to defeat them.

"May I ask who did this to you?" I said.

Her forehead creased. "You mean—who turned me?"

I nodded.

"No one has ever asked me that before," Abigail stated. She looked away and shifted again in her seat. "I was thirty-two when I turned. As you know, I was born a witch, but that all changed after you and your coven began to train. I didn't feel like I belonged there anymore, so I left the village to find my purpose. Then, three years after I left, there were stories of the witch hunt and that you had died." She looked back at me. "I felt our hope for survival in this world had been lost, and I no longer had a home to return to." She crossed her legs and folded her arms around her chest. "I didn't belong anywhere, Mercy."

I thought about placing my hand on hers as a gesture of comfort, but something told me she wasn't the touchy-feely type, and it was best to keep my distance to get on Abigail's friendly side.

"I met a handsome vampire named Lucas Carmichael shortly after Caleb and the rest of your coven fled Salem," she continued. "At the time, I didn't know he was a vampire. He was so charming, and he treated me like a princess." Abigail smiled wanly. "I wanted so desperately to live forever like my nephew, but the Chosen Ones were the only witches allowed to perform the immortal spell. I envied what they had, so when he told me what he was, I was drawn to it. This was my moment to live forever but in a *different* way."

"So, you asked him to turn you." It wasn't a question.

Abigail uncrossed her arms and gave me a hint of a frown. "After Lucas turned me, we moved to a clan in Warwick. Being a vampire wasn't like anything I had expected. I missed being able to use magic, take walks in the daylight, and not feel the ever-present hunger. It was a sacrifice I had to make for immortality."

I hadn't realized that. If a witch were turned, they'd lose their power.

"I grew to love the vampire clan who took me in," she said. "They were kind to me, and Lucas had hidden from them that I used to be a witch. Vampires and witches were enemies and always will be, and the punishment for turning a witch was death. We lived there for several years, and no one ever found out."

"How is it that witches today know very little about vampires?" I asked. "The stories clearly were a huge part of their history."

"Because, Mercy, after the Chosen Ones became immortal, vampires feared them, so they hid. If they killed a witch or human, they were discreet about it. They were no longer slaughtering villages and making a bloodied scene everywhere they went. It would have only drawn Caleb and the others to them. Witches didn't want mass hysteria, so they didn't write about it or tell anyone about them. A few stories made their way into our history books, but for all witches know today, they were no longer a threat, or they were simply a myth."

I looked up at Caleb, leaning against the wall, watching Abigail and me. His hands were in his pockets, and he had a faraway look on his face.

I turned my attention back to Abigail. "What took you away from that clan?"

Tears formed in Abigail's eyes. It was weird seeing her so vulnerable. When I first met her, she seemed too flawless to show weakness, or what some may perceive as weakness. It was as if there was an impenetrable wall around her.

She continued, but her voice became stern, "Lucas brought me a child who introduced herself as Emily. She was around fourteen years old but looked much younger. I thought he had adopted the little girl for me. As a vampire, it's impossible to conceive a child, and he knew how much I wanted children. I fell in love with her immediately. All I wanted was to hold and keep her safe. I realized what was really going on, though, and it had nothing to do with taking in that girl."

My lips parted. "Did Lucas—"

"Kill her?" she finished. "Lucas grabbed her by the hair and shoved her toward me because he wanted me to feed on her. I looked at the young girl, who had tears streaming down her face. Emily was so frightened and was begging me to let her live. Seeing her terrified face awoke something within my heart. I was feeling emotions that were almost impossible for a vampire to have. Lucas was becoming angry, and I had no choice but to obey him and drink her blood. As I went to sink my teeth into her neck, I felt a force pull me back, like someone grabbed onto my head and pulled me from her. I looked down at her neck and saw her wearing a black stone necklace. A jet stone, Mercy."

I placed my hand on the stone around my neck.

Abigail nodded. "That same stone I saw you wear the night you came to my house. As I'm sure you already know, the stone protects witches from demons like me. I didn't realize then that your coven made this enchanted stone as protection against evil, but I still knew she was a witch."

I stared blankly at Abigail as she continued her story.

"This child was about to become another victim of something dark and evil. I had asked a vampire to turn me into a monster so that I could live forever. I was so selfish that I didn't think twice about the lives I would have to sacrifice for my needs. I also knew I couldn't kill Emily; she represented a part of who I truly was and still am inside. I may have lost my powers as a witch when I was turned, but it will always be who I am deep down. I told Lucas I couldn't kill my kind. This, of course, angered him because I chose a witch over the vampires. The bastard then ripped the necklace from her neck and sunk his teeth into her throat himself."

CHAPTER 21

"Lucas made me watch the girl slip away as punishment."

Poor Abigail. I can't imagine watching a child being killed in front of me.

Abigail placed her hand over her heart as if she was experiencing chest pain, and tears slowly fell down her cheeks. "Everything happened so fast after that; I was overcome with rage. I broke the leg off a dining chair and lunged toward him. No one there even saw what had happened as I staked Lucas in the heart and turned him to ashes. I went to help Emily, and I could tell she was losing too much blood. I had to save her, so I turned her into a vampire. After her transition was complete, we fled the clan. Several decades later, we met Sherwood. He gave us a place to sleep, and he fed us."

"You mean, he let you feed on him," I guessed.

"Not at first. Sherwood didn't know we were vampires. We did our best to stomach the human food he served us, but we had to find blood to survive. We would walk through the woods at night and find animals near the forest by his house. It wasn't the same, though." Abigail cringed and shook her head. "It's not natural. Over time, Sherwood noticed we weren't getting older, so it forced us to share our secrets if we were to stay with him. Sherwood loved us and accepted us, no matter what. The animal blood was weakening us, so he let us feed off him from then on so we'd have our strength. But I knew when to stop—I didn't hurt him. Ever.

Emily was afraid her old coven would try to find her and destroy her if they discovered she was a vampire. So, we changed her name to Desiree."

I gasped, staring at her with wide eyes. "Your housekeeper?"

"She's my daughter, Mercy," she corrected, seemingly annoyed that I would assume anything else.

"Of course," I said, shame painting my cheeks pink. "I'm sorry."

To kill the child in order to save her and turn her into one of the undead must have been awful for Abigail. I couldn't imagine what those two had gone through, and listening to Abigail share the most vulnerable parts of herself proved that she was one of the bravest women I knew.

Lily and Joel had been gathering snacks and water for everyone in the food storage closet. When they re-entered the room, Abigail shifted in her seat; her story was done.

I stood up. "I need to keep my friends safe, Caleb. We need to bring them here."

"You're not leaving this lair, Mercy," he ordered.

I scowled at his abrasive response.

"No. I'm not saying I have to leave." I turned to my uncle. "Joel, can you teleport them here?" I asked.

"Sure," Joel said. "I'll need their name and where they are, though. I need to be able to hone in on their exact location."

"I can't reach Riley, so it will just have to be Shannon until I can reach him. I'll call her now."

Caleb threw his hands up, exasperated. "Oh, yeah, that sounds like a responsible plan, Mercy. Let's bring all your friends down here. You need to keep them away from their families and hide them here, where the vampires are heading," Caleb snapped.

"You can tone down the sarcasm, Caleb. You don't need to be an ass. If I can protect the people I love, I'm going to do everything I can to keep them safe, and if that means keeping them inside a safe house for as long as I can, I'm going to do it." I pointed toward the ceiling. "I can't keep them safe when they're up there, defenseless." He turned away from me and folded his arms.

I didn't understand why he was being such a prick.

I stood and put my hand on Abigail's shoulder, trying not to let Caleb's obnoxious attitude bother me. "Thank you for telling me your story."

Abigail didn't look up or acknowledge me anymore, and I accepted that. It probably took a lot for her to open up about that part of her life to me.

Caleb cursed in the distance.

"What the fuck is your problem, Caleb?" I asked as I approached him.

"I don't like this," he seethed. "I can't protect *you* while worrying about the safety of your friends."

"I can't fight when worried about *their* safety," I snapped.

He walked up to me, slid his hand around my neck as if he had a right to touch me, and pulled me in. "Stop being so stubborn." With his other hand, he gently ran his finger under my jaw. "And stop pretending like you still hate me. I know I haven't been honest. I know I've lost your trust, but we've done this a million times before in your past life, and we always worked this shit out." He dropped his hand and stepped back, swallowing down the nerves I knew were running wild in his body.

My heart raced, but I couldn't allow myself to feel anything right now. Yes, I remembered my friendship with Caleb and the coven when those visions returned to me. But I don't remember the parts where we dated. The visions stopped when I was thirteen. What I felt was only what our bond gave me. I felt love, but I felt hatred, too. After all these centuries, Caleb never changed who he was; he was still as stubborn as he was as a kid. But I *had* changed. I wasn't the same person he knew. I couldn't have been. We fought in the past just as we have fought in this life, and every time, I forgave him because our bond was too strong. But I knew better now, and I knew what this bond truly was.

It was toxic.

I placed my hands on his chest and pushed him away slightly, giving us some distance, and backed away from him. I pulled my phone from my pocket and heard Caleb mumble something under his breath.

Shannon's phone rang once before she picked it up. "Jesus, Mercy. You scared the hell out of me!" she said. "Are you okay?"

"Yes, and no," I said, trying to hold back my laugh from her immediate response. "Look, Shannon. I don't have a lot of time to explain, but—"

"Riley found me after he left Lily's," she said. "He told me she had gone missing and how Caleb took you and—. I swear to God if Caleb laid a finger on you ..."

"No, I'm okay. Caleb didn't hurt me," I said.

I heard an audible sigh of relief come from her.

"Listen, Shannon. I need to explain something to you that you might want to sit down for." I suddenly felt nervous about telling her.

I heard a heavy breath on the other end of the line. "Is this about you being a witch and vampires are after you?"

"Wait, how?" I gasped.

"Riley told me," Shannon said. "The call was brief, but he let me know so I could hide out for a bit since your friends were being targeted."

"Wow," I said. "Shannon, it took me, who has felt the powers running through my blood, at least a few days to grasp that it was all real."

"Oh, come on, Mercy," she said. "We've known each other since we were five years old."

"What the hell does that mean?"

"It means that sometimes things happen to us that scare us so badly that we have to deny it so we don't have to face the gravity of the truth. That's why we have best friends to help us come to accept that you can be a little weirdo, and that's okay." Shannon and I both laughed. "I knew you were different. We all kind of did."

"And about the vampires?" I asked.

"Yeah, that might take me a while. It's no secret our world isn't as it seems. But vampires. I need to process that one."

I nodded, even though she couldn't see me. "I need to get you here and quickly. Okay? We're being hunted at the moment. I can't let what happened to Cami happen to you."

I heard a gasp. "A ... a vampire hurt Cami?"

It was clear she struggled even to say the word.

"Yes," I said. "Possession, but I killed the son of the bitch. Unfortunately, there are others coming."

Shannon sighed heavily. "This is unreal, Mercy. I knew you didn't mean what you said. I'm sorry I didn't understand at the time," she sounded like she was on the verge of tears.

"Stop, Shannon, all of this is my fault. I can't fix what happened to her, but I can save you and Riley. I don't want to risk your life trying to travel up here, so my uncle is going to teleport you to a safe house."

I waited for another gasp, but it was much louder than expected.

"Holy shit!" she cursed.

I had to pull the phone away from my ear until she calmed down. After she stopped screaming on the other end of the line, I instructed her to pack a bag for a few days and stay on her couch until we brought her here. She agreed, but a part of me felt she doubted the entire story of witches and vampires, despite what she suspected when we were kids. I knew this kind of news wasn't the easiest to believe. Even though I couldn't physically show her my powers at that moment, I knew being pulled through the walls of her home and into a vortex would be proof enough to no longer doubt.

I tried Riley's phone again.

Please, Riley, pick up my call.

His phone rang a fourth time before I got his voicemail.

Dammit. Where was he?

We spent the next hour devising a plan to draw out the vampires into the open before they found me first. The last thing we needed was someone to sneak up on us and catch us off-guard. We needed to keep my friends down here while we scoped out some of Salem's most prominent vampire clans. The problem was that they'd smell me a mile away, compromising the group, and we'd be ambushed. We needed to find a spell to mask my scent.

Shannon texted me that she was sitting on the couch and ready. I wasn't sure how long we'd be at the safe house. These vampires weren't going away after this weekend, but keeping her close until we saw what we were up against was the wisest and safest move. Riley still wasn't answering his phone, but I left a message about where to find us.

My next call was to the hospital where Cami was admitted. I spoke with a nurse who informed me she had woken up an hour ago but wasn't talking to anyone at the hospital, not even her doctor.

She's at least alive.

"Cami's awake," I told everyone, shutting my phone down.

Lily's entire face lit up. "Thank God!"

"The spell must have been broken when Kylan died," Joel explained.

"She's still not safe, Joel. Can you bring her here, too?" I asked, hopefully.

Joel shook his head. "No, Mercy. She's been through enough. Pulling her through that portal could be what ultimately kills her. I don't think it would be the best thing for her health to put her through that," he said.

It pained my heart to hear him say that, but I understood. I knew it was best not to put Cami's body through any more stress, but not having her here, where I knew she'd be safe, worried the hell out of me.

Kylan may be dead, but the danger was still out there. The threats weren't going to stop.

Joel lowered his eyes and caught my gaze again. "The only spell I can think of is a cloaking spell. The nurses and doctors will be able to see and tend to her, but she'll be shielded from the supernatural. Meaning, not even *you* can see her."

I nodded. "Do it, then. Please. It's the best chance she has," I said optimistically.

"But Mercy, I can only do it for one person because it's linked to me. We will need to secure Shannon down here and hope no one penetrates the locks."

I nodded.

"Okay. Do it." I looked up at the clock and saw that it was half past two in the morning.

Joel immediately went to work on the cloaking spell from the kitchen and building the portal through which he'd teleport Shannon.

They'll be safe soon.

———

Shannon's eyes went wide with shock as she scanned the safe house. It looked like she was finally seeing the world for the first time, as it really was. Her hair had been disheveled from her journey through the portal, and she was shaking profusely. The amount of supernatural information was probably overwhelming her, so I waited until she spoke first, giving her a moment to let it sink in.

"Mercy, I ... it's like I took a pill to wake me up." Shannon shivered and braced herself on the wall next to her. "I'm a little bit scared," she admitted.

"You're allowed to be," I said.

Abigail stood quietly in the doorway to the kitchen, looking into the dining area where we were.

"Why is that woman staring at me like that?" Shannon asked, her voice trembling. "I mean—she's not a witch, right? Is she something else?"

Abigail rolled her eyes. "Oh, for God's sake. I'm not going to bite you."

Shannon stepped back until her rear hit the wall. "Stop looking at me like that, then!"

"If I were going to eat you, I would have done it before you could ask that ridiculous question."

Shannon gulped but kept her eyes locked on Abigail's. Caleb was in the lair's training room, pounding out his frustration on a boxing bag, while Lily and Joel were working on making Cami invisible for the time being.

Lily broke from Joel and welcomed Shannon with a hug.

"It's a lot to take in, I know, but you'll be safe here," Lily promised. "We'll keep you safe with magic."

I turned to Shannon when Lily released their hug.

"Did you ever get a hold of Riley?" I asked her.

Shannon nodded. "Yes. Finally. He's with his new friend, Amber. They should already but on their way."

"Amber?" I asked. "Amber, who?"

Shannon shrugged. "I don't know her last name, but apparently, she's the girl who found him after the animal attack.

Amid the chaos, I hadn't even thought about the girl who had saved him. However, I was grateful for all she did; I just wasn't sure bringing a stranger to the safe house was the best idea. It could expose us to vampires, and this place would be threatened.

I checked my phone one last time to see if Riley had tried calling me before turning back to Shannon. "Okay, we'll start without him, and I'll fill him in when he gets here."

I brought Shannon up to date on the events of the evening, going into great detail about what I had left out of our phone call. I explained the ritual, my mission, my sole purpose for even being in this world, and all the powers the element of Spirit possessed. Finally, I confessed my immortality and told her my destiny was to protect humans on Earth. Surprisingly, she expressed her acceptance of the new *me* and her desire to help in any way. Though she suspected something was different about me when we were kids, there was a lot more she didn't know, and now this was her reality, too.

Caleb emerged from the training room after pouting there for the last hour. Sweat dripped from his neck with each heavy breath.

He hastily interrupted us by clearing his throat. "We need Mercy to train so she can learn to fight with her hands." He looked over at me, giving me a warm smile. "Your powers will come naturally to you but fighting with your fists won't."

"You want Mercy to fight?" Shannon said. "This should be interesting."

I playfully rolled my eyes at her as I stood from my chair—following Caleb into the training room.

It was quieter than the rest of the lair, closed off from the open space. It had a padded mat and various steel and wooden weapons stretching to the ceiling. Caleb explained witches created this place after they took over the lair. The adult witches would bring their children to the safe house to train them just in case they needed to fight other witches who were into dark magic. Back then, before the Chosen were born, vampires weren't a threat to witches, but not all covens were allies.

Caleb padded across the mat and over to a radio hanging on the wall. He turned the knob until a rock station played loudly through the speakers. He lowered the volume and turned back to me.

I shook my head in disbelief at the clear music coming out of the speakers. "You get frequency down here?"

"It's the only station that isn't just static." He laughed softly. "I hate training in silence."

Caleb pulled a hairband from his pocket and wrapped it around his hair, pulling it into a low ponytail. He then removed his T-shirt, revealing a black tank top underneath. The fabric stretched over his muscles, showing the definition of his abs through the thin cotton material.

He is beautiful. I'll give him that.

Caleb handed me another rubber band, and I wrapped my hair into a messy bun.

"Thanks," I said.

Caleb then walked behind me, unclasped my necklace, and placed it on the table by the radio.

Even though the spell Joel had cast around the safe house offered protection, I felt a little naked without my jet stone.

Once Caleb returned to the mat, he said, "It's probably going to get pretty hot in here." He winked for his not-so-subliminal sexual reference that didn't go unnoticed. I snickered as we moved toward the training mat. Once we reached the center of the room, he held up his palms. "My hands are your target. Don't hold back."

"Oh, don't you worry," I said, winking back, "I won't."

CHAPTER 22

Over the next few hours, Caleb showed me how to properly kick, jab, swing an uppercut, sweep, punch, and strike. My body sure hated him with every second of it. I hadn't done any physical activity since my junior year in high school before I quit cheerleading.

"Come on, Caleb. I need a break."

"Mercy, this new body of yours is weak and skinny. We need you to be able to side-kick your opponent and actually knock them down."

"Okay, I get it. I'm a frail little girl that no one in their right mind should trust to save them. Caleb, I can just use my magic. I'm much more powerful now, right?"

Caleb huffed, clearly exhausted by my excuses. "Mercy, if only it were enough." He walked up to me and placed his index finger under my chin, lifting it up slightly. "Your physical strength has heightened since the Awakening. You need to learn to use it."

"Fine." I backed up from his touch. "Just go easy on me, alright?"

"Not a fucking chance," he said with a grin. He quickly shifted behind me and put his arm around my neck into a chokehold.

"Now, try to pry my arm away." The heat from his breath tickled the back of my ear, weakening me at my knees. "I'm your enemy right now, Mercy. Do what I showed you."

I gulped and closed my eyes. As Caleb had shown me before, I grabbed his arm, pulled it down from my neck, stepped to the right, and elbowed him in the chest ... hard. He winced and backed up slightly, giving me an opening. Now, taking his arm, I twisted it behind him, holding it in a firm grip. "Don't hold back, Caleb," I teased.

His face scrunched up, and blood rushed to his cheeks. "I'm not, Mercy. That was all you." Caleb let out a low grunt. "You can let go now." I released him, and he let out a heavy breath. He rubbed his arm, making it look like I had hurt him.

It hurt his pride, most likely.

Caleb straightened his back, his hands into fists, and moved his left foot in front of him in a fighting stance. "Now kick me," he ordered, and I did just that.

I shifted my body slightly to the left and side-kicked him, but in a split second, he grabbed and twisted my foot. My entire body bent, and I fell to the floor. He was on me before I could get back on my feet and laid his chest against mine, pressing down on me. He forcefully grabbed my wrists and pinned them above my head. While he stared into my eyes as if he were devouring me, that tingling feeling shifted from my belly to my nerves. I wiggled out of his grasp, placed my hands on his chest, and blasted him off me. He flew so high up he slammed into the ceiling above and then plummeted to the ground. That time I didn't apologize because I knew he was okay.

"You see," I said, "I can just use my magic."

Caleb proudly smiled at me and rose to his feet. He leaned down and kissed me on the forehead.

"Let's get some water."

We both took a swig of water and quickly returned to the mat. Before we could start again, we heard a commotion coming from the main living space of the lair. "Stay here," he barked.

"No way. I'm coming with you." Caleb shook his head and cursed under his breath again. We walked in and saw the others on their feet; they were looking at the entryway door.

"We heard the coffin lid opening," Lily explained, then stepped back until she was standing next to me. "Someone's here."

"It's probably Riley," I said. "He did say he was on his way here with Amber."

"He wouldn't have gotten here that quickly after I got off the phone with him," Shannon explained. "Would he?"

Caleb's phone rang. He answered it but didn't take his eyes off the entrance. I heard another male's voice at the end of the line while Caleb nodded.

"Okay, got it. Thank you for the warning." He hung up. "That was my father, Roland."

"Your father?" I remembered Roland from the brief memories I had of him, but I also remembered Caleb telling me how his father had been turned into a vampire centuries ago. So, the Roland I once knew and loved like a father and mentor was someone else now.

"A vampire was at the cemetery when we arrived here and went back and reported it to her clan. They're going to strike by sundown."

"Does Roland not have allegiance to his clan? Wouldn't he have reported to them about me and our arrival here, too?" I asked, but he didn't answer. "Caleb, is your father on our side or not?"

He looked back at me. "Yes and no. He's faithful to his clan, but he was sworn to protect the Chosen Ones, and he will. Right now, he's on our side, but if we come after his clan, he won't be able to protect us."

Joel ran up and interrupted our conversation. "I hear them again. They're on the ladder, so get ready, just in case it's not Riley."

The reality of my new life hit me. My chest tightened at the thought of using my powers against an actual enemy at that moment. I quickly stood in front of Shannon, ready to fight for her life—prepared to fight for all our lives.

As we waited for something to come crashing through, we heard a familiar voice behind the door.

"Open the door, Mercy. It's me." We all sighed with relief. It was Riley's voice!

Riley came in, and he pulled me in for a warm hug. I could feel my knees shake with relief, and I didn't want to let go.

He's safe.

A girl with long black hair pulled into a tight French braid, with rose-colored lips and deep blue eyes, stood quietly behind him. I glanced over his shoulder.

"You must be Amber," I said.

As Riley released me, she held out her hand for me to shake. "Nice to finally meet you, Mercy."

I only looked at her. "Nice to meet you, too."

I knew I was acting rude, but it was weird timing—her suddenly coming into our lives amidst everything going on these last few weeks. Why would Riley bring her here? I punched Riley hard on the arm, and he barely flinched.

"Mercy? What the hell?"

"I've been worried, Riley. Where the hell have you been? I've been trying to call you for hours." My voice echoed against the walls, and Riley backed away slightly from how loud my voice was, like his hearing was too sensitive. "And then I have to tell you we're in trouble by leaving a voicemail! Not to mention, you contacted Shannon and not me! If that wasn't bad enough, you bring a stranger, whom we don't know, to our safe house." I turned to her. "No offense, Amber, but a lot is going on right now, and we don't know anything about you." I expected her to get upset, but she stayed silent. At least she had some sense in her.

A low growl came from Abigail, who had entered the main room, causing Amber to tense from the sound.

"Abigail, what is it?" I asked, watching her fangs appear. "What are you doing? Stop!" I ordered as if I was chastising an untrained dog.

Amber sighed. "It's okay, Mercy. It's her nature to want me dead."

"No, Amber. She doesn't kill humans." I looked back at Abigail and gave her a stern look. "Stop. They're friends."

Abigail looked at me fiercely. "You didn't mention you were friends with werewolves."

"Wait, what?" I looked back at Amber. "You're a werewolf?"

Amber stepped in my direction. "I was the one you almost hit with your car when you crashed that morning. I spotted Kylan in the forest ahead, and I didn't want to lose him. Trust me, Mercy, I felt like shit after you crashed."

"It's fine," I said, now feeling uneasy that Kylan was so close to me this entire time.

Amber took another step toward me. "I wanted to morph into my human form that day and help you, but I couldn't risk it. Kylan, though, was too fast. I lost him.

I bit down on my lower lip, and a proud smile formed. "I killed Kylan tonight." A feeling of gratification hit me. I knew that in my past life, I was a vampire hunter. However, it was a new feeling to have the satisfaction of killing one with my own hands, not just watching a memory about it.

Amber had the same proud look on her face. "We saw. We arrived at the cove right as he turned to dust."

"You were there?" I asked.

She lowered her head as if she were ashamed of something. "Yes, and that's why I'm here, too, Mercy."

She looked over at Riley, who moved to lean against the wall sometime during our conversation. It was strange. I hadn't seen or heard him move away from Amber and me. I was usually so aware when Riley was in the room.

Amber scratched at the back of her neck. "I needed help. My pack has been missing for months, and it was my duty to continue to watch you with or without them—trying to protect you from Kylan and others like him. That monster sometimes dawdled right outside your own backyard."

While we suspected it was Kylan who had been following me, we couldn't be sure, not then, at least. My hands shook as I took in her words.

How long had he watched me?

"We're about to face some very dangerous enemies. They're coming after you, Mercy," she said. "Some had planned to take you the night of the Salem trials. They aren't going to give up now. You've been a target since the seventeenth century. The vampires will never stop hunting you. Kylan, he was only the first."

That wasn't news to me.

"Werewolves have always been aware of the prophecy that the Chosen Ones would come to Earth and protect us," she continued. "We want to win this fight just as much as you do. Without a pack, I'm nothing. I *needed* help."

The way she emphasized the word *needed* sent an unsettling feeling to my gut. Like she was desperate, obligatory—willing to do almost anything.

"What are you getting at, Amber?" I had a bad feeling as I looked over at Riley again. "Amber, what the hell did you do?" Panic rose in my voice. There was a moment of silence before Shannon walked toward Riley and looked deep into his eyes.

"Abigail," Shannon called to Caleb's aunt, but her eyes stayed on Riley's. "Why did you say werewolves and not *werewolf*?"

Abigail sighed deeply. "Your friend Riley is one of them."

I was stunned and silent for a moment, then walked over to Riley and looked at his face. The expression he gave sent my heart thundering.

He can't be. Not Riley.

"Mercy, it's okay. I want this," he tried to explain, but I covered my mouth as utter panic overtook me.

I ran my hands down my face, my fingers digging into my skin.

"No. No! You didn't ask for this, Riley. She turned you against your will." I waved my finger at Amber.

"I feel stronger than ever," he said. "It's the most incredible feeling in the world. Now I can help protect *you*."

"Oh, Riley. It's not your job to protect me. I told you this before. I didn't want you to get involved." I grabbed his hands, and Caleb, whom I hadn't noticed until now, was by my side. His shoulders stiffened when Riley's fingers touched mine, clearly uncomfortable with Riley being so close to me. But I didn't care. Now wasn't the time to act all alpha male on me. I looked over at Lily and Joel while still gripping Riley's hands. "What do we do now?"

Joel straightened up. "Well, now that we have werewolves on our side, this will be a much easier fight."

I sighed heavily. "No. Absolutely not. Riley is not fighting."

"Mercy, we're going to need all the help we can get," Joel added, still trying to convince me it was a good thing Riley was no longer a normal human being. "I know you don't want to hear it, but he's strong now, and you need to trust him. That's why Amber turned him in the first place; he is as close to you as any of us. With werewolves on our side, we have a fighting chance."

Riley squeezed my hand gently. "Joel's right, Mercy. I can handle this," he said. I shook my head, turning away. He stepped closer to me and spoke again in a near whisper, "This isn't your decision. Besides, werewolves can heal just like a vampire can. It's going to take a lot to kill me."

"Like a silver bullet?" I sneered, looking up into his eyes, which looked a little brighter than they used to.

Riley rolled his eyes, flashing me a slight smirk. "Yes, Mercy, like a silver bullet. If the vampires aren't expecting us to be here, it is unlikely they will have one of those on them." He sounded so confident, but it didn't make me feel any better.

I had faced a vampire before, and I had taken him down, but I'd had the powers to do it. Riley might have been able to heal quickly, but he could still die. I knew we needed help from werewolves, but at what expense? Would I so willingly put my friends in danger for them to protect me? It wasn't Caleb, Riley, Lily, or even my human friends they wanted; it was me. I also knew I couldn't stop Riley from being a part of Amber's pack and jumping into this fight. He loved me and would take a bullet for me if he needed to—even a silver one.

I squeezed his warm hand, feeling the heat from his touch pierce my skin.

"Okay," I hesitantly agreed. "I'm putting my trust in Amber right now." I turned to her. "I appreciate everything you've done, but I need you to promise me something. You are to keep him safe if you plan to drag him into this. No matter what you must do."

She nodded. "You have my word, Mercy. Nothing will happen to Riley. I'm the alpha, and it's my job to protect my pack—"

Amber and Riley abruptly snapped their attention toward the entryway and sniffed, moving in front of me. They were on edge and sensed something that I couldn't.

"What is it?" I asked, feeling incredibly out of the loop.

"Someone is outside," Amber answered, tilting her head and closing her eyes as if she were listening to the space around her. "They're about a hundred yards from the tomb. I can hear their feet hitting the surface above us. They seem to be searching."

Riley sniffed the air again. "It's not human."

"Hm," Amber hummed. "It's not a vampire, either. It's almost dawn now, so they wouldn't be out hunting. I don't know what that is."

What else is out there?

"We need to leave now," Lily interrupted us, a worried look creasing her forehead. "Whatever this thing is, we can't have it drawing unwanted attention here when the lair isn't completely secure. If we can lure it away and kill it, we can buy more time."

I nodded and ran to one of the storage closets Caleb had pointed out earlier. I reached in and pulled out a gray and black hoodie. Despite it being summer, I could use the hood to temporarily conceal myself as we made our way out into Salem. After donning the clothing, I re-tied my hair into a bun and joined the others. Joel and Caleb grabbed some weapons and headed toward the ladder that led outside. They went to work, securing the main entrance with trap magic and a secondary shield spell, should that fail. We ushered Shannon to the secured vault and gave her the code to unlock the door if she had to. A landline was also inside, and we instructed her to call us if anyone breached the lair.

Shannon turned around after we ushered her inside. "I can't believe this is happening. My friend is in a coma caused by a vampire possession, and my other friends are a witch and a werewolf. This happens in movies, Mercy, not in real life."

I pulled her tight to me and squeezed. I, myself, never wanted to be a part of that world, and I hated that I was dragging her into it.

"I won't let anything happen to you. I swear it." A moment of doubt crossed my mind, but I couldn't tell her that. I feared I wasn't good enough to protect anyone. But I wouldn't stop trying—I would give it everything I could.

"I'll be back for you once we know it's safe."

Should I really promise that?

Two weeks ago, I was a semi-normal human, oblivious to the supernatural world. I didn't know I was a reincarnated witch, blessed by an angel. I didn't know vampires and werewolves roamed the streets, and I most certainly hadn't figured out I was the weapon that could bring it all to an end. Fear engulfed every part of my being, and nothing I promised Shannon would make her feel better. How could it? Our plan was fucking stupid. We hadn't a clue where these vampires lived. They could smell and find me with little effort, not the other way around. How was I going to fish them out? Our plan was to run in the opposite direction and *play it by ear.*

Abigail stayed behind to stand guard until whatever lurked outside lost interest and left.

"I'm ready," I said, stepping toward the ladder that led back up to the graveyard, but Caleb yanked on the back of my sweatshirt, pulling me toward him.

"Not that way." He pointed to a hallway next to the training room. "Behind that door at the end of the hallway, there's a bookshelf that has an entryway behind it, leading into a tunnel. That tunnel will lead us to the other side of Church Street and take us over to Harrington's Antique shop."

As we ran, Caleb told us we'd have to steal a car once we reached the tunnel's exit. We wouldn't last long on foot, and Joel's portals could last for ten to fifteen minutes after they were opened. It would be too risky to let whatever was out there follow us through the portal and catch us off guard.

Once we reached the end of the tunnel, we spotted a gray SUV across from a bar on the other side of the antique shop. It was right after four in the morning, so someone must have had too much to drink and got another ride home.

Lily placed her hand on top of the car, closed her eyes, and recited a spell. The car unlocked and automatically started up.

A little Winchester magic, thanks to my grandfather.

"I honestly didn't think that would work. It's been a while." She smiled with pride. She'd definitely missed using her magic.

We pulled out onto the road and headed west. We needed to get whatever was following us away from the safe house, so Shannon and Abigail would be safe. It was still very early in the morning, so there weren't any people on the road yet.

"We don't even have a plan," I huffed, feeling increasingly incompetent to fight against our enemies.

Caleb poked his head out the left passenger window, searching for whatever was following us. "Well, the plan is to kill it, whatever *it* is, that's tailing us," he said.

"We've got this, Mercy. Have a little faith, kiddo," Joel said as Lily pressed her foot hard on the pedal.

"Can you still smell it?" Amber asked Riley.

He sniffed the air. "I'm not sure anymore. What I smell now wasn't what I smelled at the safe house," he explained. "It smells *almost* like a bird this time, maybe? I'm still trying to figure out these new senses of mine."

Lily sped up again to about ninety miles per hour. Whatever creature was following us was foreign to the newly formed wolf pack, and they were fast.

"I think it's behind us, guys," Lily said while looking in the rearview mirror. We heard a high-pitched whistle above us as an enormous bird came crashing into the windshield, smashing the glass with large talons. Lily slammed on the brakes. Glass shattered all around us. She quickly pulled over on the side of the road and turned toward the back seat. "We can't outrun it. Get ready to fight," she said.

CHAPTER 23

I looked through the shattered windshield as an abnormally large eagle soared upward. Seconds later, the animal circled around the car and started a nosedive toward us. That time, it crashed through the window on Riley's side and began pecking at his arm. Riley didn't flinch, but he screamed angrily and punched at the bird, forcing it back outside. Joel moved to the side as Riley and Amber jumped out of the car and ran toward the eagle.

Before they could react, the eagle grabbed hold of my hoodie through the broken window. I screamed for it to stop and hit it several times on the head, but it latched on, unbothered by my blows. Caleb grabbed my right arm from the front seat while Riley snatched the bird's tail and pulled it off me. The bird flew back up in the air as Riley lost his grip.

We heard a loud grumble from behind the car. When I turned to look out the rear window, I spotted Amber on all fours, her canine teeth sparkling in the glow of the streetlights. Riley scrambled after her, taking off his shirt and pants as quickly as he could before he dropped to his knees, joining her. He gritted his teeth as he arched his back like a frightened cat. His spine was visible against his skin. Coarse hair follicles rose tall, and his face pulled forward, forming a long muzzle. The transition into his wolf form was much faster than I'd seen in movies. The good thing was that he didn't appear to be in pain, but the transformation left me shaken.

Whoa.

With so much going on, I didn't even realize that Caleb, Joel, and Lily were out of the car. Caleb threw a ball of flames at the massive bird as it came back down. Lily used her powers to accelerate the flame faster in its path. The eagle dodged the flame, flew back to the car, and grabbed me tightly again, digging its claws into my shoulder.

"Son of a bitch!" I screamed. The bird dragged me out the window and onto the road. I could feel shards of glass slice into my legs, and I lifted my hands and released my energy force toward the bird, hoping it would injure it enough to back off. The green energy knocked it to the ground, its feathers scattering around the street. But it recovered within seconds and began beating its wings, my shoulder firmly in its massive talons.

Joel ran from behind the car toward me. "I think I know what this thing is, guys."

"Shapeshifter?" I heard Lily respond. Riley swiftly ran toward us and leaped at the eagle's throat. His teeth glistened as they barely missed the thick cowl of feathers. The eagle was gaining altitude as it yanked me off the ground.

The eagle pulled me higher and higher into the air. I tried to hit it again with magic, but I couldn't concentrate enough to pull up any energy. Desperate, I grabbed its legs and pulled its talons apart using my heightened strength, causing it to screech and finally release me. I landed hard on the ground next to the car, and Lily and Caleb were immediately by my side.

"So that isn't just an enraged bird?" I asked, panic rising in my voice.

"That creature will be back!" Joel shouted. "We have to move now!"

"Joel, I think you should teleport us somewhere if you have the strength. If it follows us, so be it," Lily said while trying to catch her breath. "We at least know what to look for if it hitches a ride."

Amber and Riley joined us, and everyone formed a protective circle around me. I looked at Lily, then at Caleb, who peered up at the fading night sky with his hands open, creating a new ball of fire on his palm. He searched for the bird with such intensity—waiting for it to come back down.

This will never end.

I cried out, "No!" Everyone turned to me, and I shook my head, knowing they would fight me on what I had planned. "We can't keep doing this, guys. I won't risk any of your lives when it's me they're after." I knew running would never end until we knew who or what would come for me. If I allowed myself to be taken by them—my friends would be safe, and maybe, just maybe, I could find a way to take them down from the inside. I would gladly let myself be taken in their place. They didn't deserve to be wrapped up in my mess. It was *my* destiny.

"Get in the car, Mercy!" Caleb growled through his teeth.

I shook my head again. "No, Caleb. You can't save me this way. We're just running." I threw my hands up. "Where are we going to go? How many lives will be lost from you trying to protect me? I refuse to lose my family."

I looked over at Joel and Lily coming toward me. Caleb's hands were clenched into fists, and Riley and Amber circled the car in their wolf form. I gulped down the guilt that was coming, but I couldn't let them sacrifice their lives for mine. I bit my lip and took a few steps back, quickly throwing up my hands, creating a force that pushed Lily and Joel back.

"Mercy, stop! What are you doing?" Lily cried out, unable to move her legs forward anymore. Riley and Amber were also held in place, pushed down to their bellies. I could see the pleading in Riley's blue eyes, and I had to look away.

"Mercy!" Caleb hissed again, straining against the energy that held him. "You better get in the goddamn car before I drag you in myself!" Caleb's face turned bright red. "Now!"

Joel pleaded. "Don't do this, kiddo. Please."

"I won't let any of you get hurt because of me," I said, releasing the energy force. I could hear their feet pounding against the pavement as they chased after me. But I didn't look back. I didn't stop. The sound of massive wings flapping echoed across the sky.

"Here!" I shouted, waving my arms. "Over here!"

Seconds later, I felt the eagle's claws dig into my shoulders, pulling me up into the air. The talons punctured my skin this time, and the pain was intense. As I watched the ground and my family disappear from sight, I took a deep breath, trying to plan the next step.

The truth was, I wasn't giving up. I would still fight, but the farther the creature was from my family, the better their chance of survival.

I tried to communicate with the bird verbally, but it wasn't responding to me. I tried to speak to it telepathically, but still nothing. I lifted my hands to use levitating power on its talons to pry them from my skin to ease the pain, but I remembered I was now extremely high up, and it would be awful if I fell. I closed my eyes, trying not to think of the pain, knowing I'd be able to heal myself once we landed, but the feeling was unbearable. Time seemed to slow, but as my body felt like it could no longer bear it, I looked down, seeing the Salem Witch Museum. The eagle tilted its wings, and we started descending. It gently set me on the ground and removed its grip from my shoulders. Fresh blood was soaked around the puncture marks in my hoodie, but the actual wounds sealed up immediately.

The animal lowered its head between its front claws, and its body suddenly grew larger and larger. The feathers seemed to fold into themselves while human skin formed around them. There now stood a very well-built man before me.

He was incredibly tall, taller than anyone I had ever seen. He was probably well over six foot eight, with a bulky, athletic build. He had dark brown hair that went below his shoulder, and a goatee framed the sharp line of his jaw. A large black tattoo adorned his golden-bronze skin, wrapping around his chest and down his muscular arms.

Under the glow of the streetlamps, I could see that his glittering eyes were also a light shade of brown.

His tattoos resembled mostly animals: an eagle, a bear, a wolf, and a lion specifically, all on his chest alone.

He walked over to a nearby trashcan, lifted a plastic bag, pulled out some clothes, and proceeded to get dressed. I thought about using my powers on him, but whoever sent the shifter would send another. Not to mention that people were walking around the area now, and using magic would put them in harm's way. The only way to fight these monsters was to start from the inside, from wherever he was taking me.

At least I have some protection, I thought, placing my hand on my chest to touch the jet stone.

Oh. Shit! The training. I had left it in the training room.

The man sauntered over, and I noticed he held a metal bracelet in his hand. He grabbed my arm gently and fastened the bracelet around my wrist. I tried to pry it off, but I saw it required a key.

"What is this thing?" I tried again to pull the bracelet off, but it was still no use. I tried to call up fire magic to melt the metal off, but there was only an empty feeling there. "What did you do to me? Take this off."

"Sorry, Akasha. That bracelet prevents you from using your powers." His voice was low and masculine and had a hint of an accent.

And I'm officially fucked. Also, what did he call me?

"Akasha? My name is Mercy." I fiddled with the bracelet again. "Fuck."

I can't fight them without my powers.

"Akasha is what vampires call you. It means Spirit or Fifth Element." He frowned. "What would you rather me call you?" He was oddly polite.

"My actual name," I said. "Mercy."

"Alright, then. Mercy, we walk from here." He grabbed my arm and escorted me to a nearby park.

"Where are you taking me?" I asked, but he stayed silent. I moved around, hoping he would ease up on his grip, but he didn't. "Will you at least tell me your name?" I asked, hoping a simple question would get him talking.

He glanced at me. "Noah. The master sent me to retrieve you."
He gestured ahead. "We aren't far from the house."

Master? What the fuck?

Noah clearly wasn't much of a talker. I tried to engage in conversation as we walked, but he wouldn't respond. I even tried making a few jokes to ease the tension as fear rushed through my body, but he didn't even crack a smile. We walked for about thirty minutes before arriving at a tall black gate in front of a beautiful, dark, gothic-style mansion. By now, the sun had risen, and I was becoming uncomfortably warm in my thick hoodie. I could feel sweat forming on my hairline, and my legs were aching.

I was exhausted, and all I wanted to do was lie down, even if it was in a strange and dangerous place.

Noah rang the bell on the outside of the gate. "Open the damn door. I have Akasha with me."

The gates opened slowly, and the shapeshifter gently escorted me through the entrance and along the long, stamped driveway. Once the gate closed behind us, Noah released my arm. I took in the rest of the house—my prison.

My mouth gaped open as I looked around. It appeared to be everything I'd pictured a vampire lair to look like. Just like the vampires themselves, the beautiful house reeked of something sinister. It was over-the-top glamorous, gray stone walls with detailed carvings. The wide windows on each story of the gorgeous mansion had been draped with dark curtains. I swallowed as my eyes landed on the stone gargoyles decorating some balconies. They seemed to glare down at me as if they were alive. My heart skipped a beat as I took in the view above me. I feared what was ahead, but I wasn't going down without a fight.

After entering the house, I drew my eyes to the front room that was filled with three black couches and a machine of some sort sitting in the center. It was a clear case with tubes that protruded from the inside and into small glass vials surrounding the device.

"I'm afraid to ask," I said, twisting my body to look at Noah. "But what is that?

He, as expected, didn't answer me.

"Noah, I'm not your enemy."

He looked at me expressionlessly. "You really want to know what that machine does?" I nodded. "If one of the humans the vampires drink from tries to run away, we execute them. We then place them inside the glass chamber. Then we hook them up to those pipes and drain them until the last drop of blood is emptied into the vials. You see—the vampires here don't waste blood, so if they're going to kill them, they might as well take the blood while it's fresh and pumping through their veins. They store the blood in a cooler downstairs."

I'm going to throw up.

As the bile rose up my throat, I tightened my jaw. I quickly raised my fist to my mouth, choking it back. Noah just looked at me and shrugged, unfazed by the horror he had just told me.

"You see, Mercy. I *am* your enemy."

I'm starting to think that sacrificing myself was a mistake. If I fail to take this place down, I could easily end up in there as an eternal meal.

I drew my attention to loud laughter coming from a room down the hall. Noah was staring at the double doors in front of us, but we didn't enter. The suspense of waiting to see what my future would look like in this place drove me mad. I stomped in the room's direction but felt a pinch at my scalp as Noah gripped my hair and yanked me back.

"Ouch! Quit it!" I whined.

"Yeah, you're not going to want to go in there right now," Noah said.

I was so exhausted from the last twenty-four hours that I almost didn't care what had happened to me.

Almost.

"Honestly, Noah. I just want to lie down. I may have powers, but I'm also in a human body, and humans need sleep."

No response. Asshole.

"Noah," I tried again, "aside from your muscular and very intimidating build, you don't seem all that scary. You don't belong here any more than I do. You're not like them," I said, pointing toward the door. Noah started to give a sideways smirk, then quickly became serious again as he heard a door open. It caught us both off guard.

I looked down the hall, watching another man close the doors of that room behind him and walk in our direction.

Once he was in front of me, my neck craned to look at his stunning appearance. His face looked youthful, but his fair skin also seemed to emphasize the gray circles under his eyes; he was strikingly handsome. The man's skin looked like someone had carved him out of marble.

The vampire smirked. It was clear that my terrified expression amused him as he stalked around me, tightening the muscles around his strong jawline. His medium-length, dark brown hair looked wet, as if he had just stepped out of the shower and had slicked it back over the top of his head. His body was lean, and he moved elegantly. The muscles under his shirt rippled as he passed by me. It was like looking at a panther as the guy was covered head to toe in black attire, his long trench coat brushing the floor as he circled my trembling body. Hunger peeked through his vibrant, hazel eyes, churning my stomach the moment he stood directly in front of us—staring at me intently. It was unnerving. It was like I had just been served on a silver plate for him.

I instinctively stepped back and tumbled backward into Noah's chest. My fear appeared amusing to the vampire before me, who lifted his hand and stroked my cheek in a gentle caress. I recoiled at his touch, and he removed his fingers from my skin the moment I did.

Noah cleared his throat. "Master, I brought her to you unharmed, just as you asked," Noah said. "I assure you that this is Akasha."

The vampire's eyes turned venomous as he sized me up. I suppressed a shudder at the man who was looking at me, less like a creep and more like I was cattle for sale.

"Hm, and what of the immortal spell?" His voice was calm and eerie; it sent an icy chill up my spine.

Noah nodded.

The vampire licked his lips. The news of my immortality obviously satisfied him. He stalked around me slowly again, touching each part of my body. I quivered as he ran his fingers through my hair and lightly touched my neck with his cold fingertips. Goosebumps continued to trail up my spine as my stomach rolled with nausea. He then put his hands on my shoulders and rubbed where Noah's claws had been embedded.

"What the fuck happened here?" he said, continuing to trail his fingers near the marks. "I told you she wasn't to be harmed, Noah." Though the vampire's tone was eerily calm, he shot Noah an icy glare.

Noah's breaths were shallow as his shoulders shook. The man before me was as evil as they got, and I knew right away he would make my life a living hell if he wanted to. No, he wouldn't grant me any sort of reprieve. He was a predator who would play with his toys because he could.

"I'm sorry, Maurice. I tried to avoid injuring her, but she kept squirming under my grasp. The wounds healed immediately; I assure you."

I made a mental note of the name, which was now the name of my greatest enemy: Maurice.

As I repeated the name in my head, memories of my past life ached to show themselves, but they seemed lost behind a mental haze. I hadn't met the man before, not in this life or in my past. However, his name, I had heard his name before.

Dorian!

Dorian had said it in my vision. Maurice was coming for me, but I had escaped through death.

Now I was within his clutches, trapped behind his walls.

Maurice's devilish smirk returned, and I wasn't sure what was so damn funny. He placed a finger under my chin and lifted it, forcing me to stare into his eyes. His nails were painted black, sharpened to a point, and the tip of his nail dug into my skin. Then he slowly traced his thumb over my lips. "You're so beautiful." His lip curled. "And such beauty will now belong to me."

No, it fucking won't.

"What the hell do you want from me?" I managed to say, but my voice hitched, showing my enemies how terrified I truly was.

He raised a brow and slightly bit his bottom lip. "What every vampire who knows of your existence wants." His tongue slid out, licking his lips. "That incredible, powerful blood of yours."

"Well," I responded with false bravado, "you can't have it."

I shocked myself at how fearless I sounded right then, especially knowing that it was a ridiculous thing to say. My powers were bound, and Maurice could take my blood at any moment. In different circumstances, I could do damage to his pretty face. Still, everything that made me powerful and invincible was trapped under that bracelet, and I had just poked the beast like an idiot. I wasn't anything special to him—I was a toy he could play with and devour at any given moment, and his dark and evil eyes warned me he had planned to.

He ignored my defiance with a heavy sigh. "I'm the master of this house, but you'll address me by Maurice." He glanced at Noah, who was now right in front of him. "Thank you, Noah, but you can leave us now. I'll get your report tomorrow."

"Thank you, Maurice." Noah proceeded down the hallway and through the double doors.

Maurice turned back to face me. "Akasha." He said that damn weird name again, and I hated it even more coming from him.

"You can call me Mercy," I mumbled under shaky breath.

He laughed under his breath. "*Mercy* doesn't exist behind these walls." The smile that followed sent a wave of unwelcome goosebumps over my skin. I wasn't a praying person, but I said a silent prayer that I'd find a way to get the bracelet off, so I could show them how powerful I really was.

"You escaped my clutches centuries ago, you know, and then sacrificed yourself like a damn fool before I could reach you."

And there it is.

Maurice smiled again, sending another wave of fear through my entire body. "I've stood by for years, waiting for this moment." The vampire's fingers trailed slowly down my shoulder. "The moment your purpose in the human world dies, you're reborn into a life behind my walls, at my mercy."

I swallowed. "For someone who seems to know so much about me, you don't appear to be afraid of what I can do to you with my magic." A hard lump pressed painfully against my throat. And it wouldn't go down. My words were empty threats because I didn't know what the fuck I was doing.

Maurice licked his bottom lip. "Not with that bracelet on your wrist, you won't."

He was right. I was defenseless without my magic, but I wasn't going to let him believe I was feeling so defeated.

"People aren't possessions, Maurice," I argued. "I'll never willingly give you my blood." I instinctively took a step back, but his hand reached out and grabbed my throat but didn't squeeze. It was merely a threat to how much power he had and how easy it would be for him to cause me pain.

"Oh, I don't expect you to give it freely," he said calmly. "Makes this more exciting, doesn't it?"

God, he's sick.

The corners of his mouth twisted wider into an even more sinister grin. He released my throat, trailing his hand down until he reached my wrist, clenching it. "Come. I want you to meet the others."

"Oh, I can't wait," I said sarcastically.

We walked toward the double doors. I deliberately slowed my pace a few times as Maurice tightened his grip into a possessive hold, leading me to the doors at the end of the hall. He slowly opened the room filled with around twenty to thirty vampires.

Oh. My. God.

What I witnessed wasn't what I expected to see behind those doors.

Half and fully-naked vampires spread out over beds and leather couches. Several sprawled out on the floor. Some of them engaged in positions that were beyond my imagination. It seemed like no space was off limits for them as they gave in to their two most primal needs—sex and blood. Humans served as the instruments of their dark desires, draping in their arms as the undead bit down into their tender flesh.

Fucking and feeding at the same time.

Loud moans laced with pleasure and pain intertwined with the sounds of heavy breathing and bodies slapping against each other. It echoed through this den of sin I found myself in. My cheeks burned as my gaze wandered around the room. Logically, I knew I should have looked away, but for some reason, it was hard to remove my eyes from the sight that had me in somewhat of a trance.

One vampire, a tall man with dirty blond hair and a bare body that one would believe belonged to a Greek god, thrust violently into a woman from behind. One of his hands clutched on her hip, while the other tightened its grip around her hair, yanking her head back as their bodies collided against each other, again and again. Blood dripped from a deep wound on her neck, serving as evidence that he had just finished feeding on her and was now scratching another itch that resided within him. His movements grew more forceful as he announced his orgasm with a loud growl, his body buckling visibly for a moment. The woman seemed to be close to her release, too.

"Don't stop!" she begged, and I watched him as he slammed his hips into her one last time before his large hands yanked her head backward, breaking her neck. A small gasp escaped my lips as her lifeless body plopped on the floor. My eyes darted around the room; no one seemed to care the slightest bit about the murder that just took place next to them.

I think I've descended into hell.

Another woman, possibly human, straddled a man's lap, her hips moving in a circular motion controlled with the utmost, hypnotizing precision to the beat of the music. As she slid down on his cock, the man pleasured another woman that rode his face. As her eyes rolled back, her head tipped as she allowed her hips to grind against his lips. The blissful expression on her face undoubtedly showed that she was in another dimension.

I stared at her, watching her thighs tremble as he grabbed them with his firm grip, holding her in place. His head shifted to the side, and his fangs sunk into her soft flesh. That tipped her over the edge—she let out a loud, broken scream, her entire body convulsing with a never-ending pleasure.

Around them were women fucking women, men with men, and then some were joined together, taking each other all at once.

Cravingly.

Shamelessly.

Hungrily.

An unexpected arousal hit me at my core, awakening a single spot inside of me I didn't want to react to. Not even the scent of blood bothered me at that moment.

I cursed myself for responding the way it did, clutching my legs together as I prayed for the sensation to disappear as quickly as it overcame me.

Once the first vampire noticed me, hissing bounced off the walls. Some stopped what they were doing, while others continued to fuck and watch me while they did it. It was as if they were beckoning me closer and asking me to join them.

Long fingers wrapped around my arms from behind, and I felt Maurice's presence behind me as he pulled me into his chest.

"Do you like what you see here, Akasha?" he asked, his cool breath tickling the back of my neck. He was standing so close to me that I could practically feel his lips against my skin.

I shook my head. "This is beyond repulsive, Maurice. I haven't done a fucking thing to you or anyone else in your clan. There is no excuse to subject me to this. I don't want to be a part of it!" I turned to look at him, trying to plead with my eyes. With nothing left to lose, securing my safety was the only thing I had left.

"Hmm," he hummed, gingerly reaching out to run the back of his finger along my cheek. It was the weirdest feeling; his bitter touch barely brushed against my skin, sending an electrifying sensation through my entire body. "Such nasty words from a lady." Raising the side of his mouth, he laughed to himself and showed his fangs as if he were mocking my words. "How about this, Akasha? I promise not to torture you, but I can't assure you I won't inflict a little pain." Maurice's hand then trailed down my neck, between my breasts, with a long stroke. He didn't stop until he touched the waistline of my pants, tucking a finger under the fabric. Gently, he dragged his sharp nail along my stomach, causing my belly to do an involuntary flip. "And pleasure."

Turning myself in was foolish, but standing in a room full of sex-addicted, blood-thirsty vampires without my powers was terrifying.

I swallowed a little, at a loss for words, which wasn't something that happened to me often. That only seemed to entertain Maurice more. His hand dipped a little lower, inching toward the place that burned with revolting desire now—taunting me as his eyes remained glued to mine. It was as if he was waiting for a reaction I sure as hell wouldn't give him.

I was a child drowning in a sea of darkness. My measly knowledge was nothing compared to what I was witnessing. At that moment, hope was snuffed out, and the sight before me, of blood, torture, and captivity, became my reality. I was a toy for them, a walking blood bank, and there wasn't anything I could do to stop them.

CHAPTER 24

"Quiet down!" Maurice shouted, raising his hand in the air to silence the room.

Everyone slowly came to a halt, which seemed to satisfy him: obey immediately, and you won't die.

"I'd like you all to meet the newest member of our home," Maurice said, gesturing to me. "The element, Spirit, or the name the angel gave her—Akasha."

Everyone cheered and shouted, but their voices dimmed once Maurice raised his hand again to quiet the room. "When we first heard of the prophecy that a witch would be our undoing, I must admit, it intrigued me," he continued. "Not because I feared she'd try to kill me, of course ..." The room burst into laughter, "... but because the second part of that prophecy contained what we've been waiting to do for centuries. The Fifth Element would give us the ability to walk in the daylight." He pointed at me. "Akasha's blood has the power to give each one of us that gift." I heard a few audible gasps from around the room. "That which we've all been searching for is finally ours."

There was another round of applause, even from some humans. I heard whispers from those around us discussing my presence there, and a low growl came from Maurice. Vampires lived long lives, but it seemed the older they were, the more entitled they became. This was *his* palace, and he wasn't pleased with all the interruptions.

"Listen!" he shouted, and the room instantly hushed. "Just because the gift exists doesn't mean you're all worthy of it. First, I'll be the only one to taste Akasha's blood. Then I may choose to share her with chosen individuals. Once they've proved themselves." His eyes narrowed on a vampire in the corner of the room whose gaze was boring into me. "And if anyone were to touch her without my permission, I'll tear off your head and turn your body to ash."

A red-headed woman stood up—her oversized bosom spilling over the top of her silky dress. Her Irish accent echoed throughout the room. "Can I 'ave a taste, Maurice?" she asked. "And then later, fuck her while you watch?"

Then a roar of chattering and pleading filled the room.

"Enough!" Maurice screamed. Several vampires looked away in shame.

The woman's eyes grew wide. "Forgive me, Master. I should not 'ave asked," she apologized, lowering her head in shame.

Maurice glided across the room until he stood in front of her, reaching out to raise her chin and present her mouth to him. While he kissed her, his hand skated down and then under the hem of her dress. He bit into her neck savagely, without warning, and she let out a moan of pleasure that echoed through the room. I could see the shadow of his fingers working her over under her dress. He kept his fangs in her neck as she climaxed, blood dripping down between her breasts until he finally pulled away.

He took a moment to lick his lips as if he didn't want a single drop of the precious ruby elixir to go to waste, and then his hands found her temples. The way he touched her seemed gentle. Affectionate, even.

"A farewell gesture to you, Ava. I'm sure going to miss those lips," Maurice said. With a smirk, he twisted her head so fast it wholly disconnected from her body in one smooth motion. The rest of her turned to ash. He tossed the head against the wall, where it dissolved into gray dust.

I couldn't hold in my scream. I turned on my heel and bolted for the door. I knew I wasn't going to get far, but I couldn't stop my feet from moving as far away from the sight of a decapitated head as I could. Two fully clothed vampires quickly jumped in front of the door to stop me. Without looking up, I tried to move around them. But I was grabbed by my shoulders and swung around to face the room again. The other vampire's hands gripped tightly around my arms, forcing me to look Maurice in the eye.

"Let that be a lesson to you all," Maurice warned as he stalked back to me. "You will never ask for Akasha's blood and never broach the subject with me without my permission. Let's pretend we're all in a classroom and start raising our damn hands. The only topic that is forbidden is *her*."

I was so repulsed by the sight of him, by him standing so close to me after committing such a disgusting act. I leaned into the other vampire's chest, whose arms wrapped around me. I didn't even care that the other one was probably just as evil as Maurice. I had to find comfort in someone. The closer Maurice came to me, the more I clung to the body holding me still. I turned from the master and buried the side of my face in the other's chest, not looking up.

Maurice placed his hand gently on my shoulder, trying to turn me around. I felt like a scared little mouse burying myself in a corner. I couldn't keep my body from trembling.

"You need to let her go so that she can face her reality," Maurice barked at the one I sought comfort in.

I felt a firm yet gentle hand run down my arm as if they were trying to soothe me.

"I said *let her go,* Dorian."

My gaze snapped up when I heard that name.

I felt his hands fall from my shoulders as I stared into the eyes of a familiar face. It was Dorian. *My* Dorian.

Oh. My. God!

My mind suddenly ripped itself out of the present and into another time. I was in the barn, training with Caleb. We were there with Roland, and there had been an argument.

"You're forbidden to see each other outside of training. You cannot fight the vampires while you're distracted by love —*if* it's love," Roland told us. Caleb had his arms folded, and he stomped out of the barn.

"Is there no other way?" I asked. "We're just supposed to be alone for the rest of our lives? This isn't fair, Roland."

"You were never supposed to come here and fall in love, Mercy. You're a weapon."

My past self didn't flinch at those words, but I did.

"We promised we wouldn't let it distract us from the mission," I pleaded. "Please, Roland. Don't make us do this."

"Whenever the rest of the coven is in danger, the first one Caleb saves is you. You cannot fight this way." He shook his head. "The answer is no, and I have your mother's support on this." Roland pointed to the ground. "Pick up your stake. We'll continue to train until dusk." I looked down at the wooden stake, picked it up, and held it loosely between my fingertips.

I shook my head and placed it under my waistband. "No," I said. "I'm done for today." I then turned and ran out of the barn.

I looked around frantically for Caleb, but he was nowhere to be found. As I approached a small hill by the farm, I heard shouting from a clearing.

"Caleb!" I called. When I reached the top of the field, it wasn't Caleb. It was a man and two women. One of the women, blonde hair loosened from her coif, was on the ground, backpedaling away from the others. I could hear her weeping and praying to be spared. I hid behind a tree and watched. The two standing were vampires but seemed to be arguing; the male refused to feed.

"Kill her, Dorian. Do it," the woman commanded, but he shook his head.

"Look at her; she's terrified. Please, don't make me do this," Dorian pleaded. "I didn't *want* this!"

He began to help the frightened young woman to her feet, who was shaking profusely. That only infuriated the one giving him orders.

"You're right, Dorian. I should have never turned someone so useless." She leaned down and picked up a branch from the ground. I saw her snap the end off, creating a sharp point. She then turned to Dorian, who was still helping the girl stand up and had his back turned.

No!

I ran as fast as possible while reaching into the holster around my waist and pulling out my stake. I leaped toward the vampire woman and plunged the weapon into her heart. She exploded into ash in front of me. I turned to the man she called Dorian, whose eyes were wide and terrified. "She was going to kill you," I said, grabbing him by the hand. I didn't fear him; yes, he was a vampire, but his kind eyes spoke to me as no other had ever done.

"Mercy, back away from him," Roland shouted from the opposite end of the clearing.

I looked back at Dorian and whispered, "Run."

The images wouldn't stop coming, giving me a vague snapshot of what happened in my past life. I watched the seasons change, taking me through an entire year of memories with Dorian. From the moment we met to the night I gave up my life.

I never saw him as the monster everyone claimed he was. I had a duty, but even so, I was attracted to him—an attraction I shouldn't have allowed to continue, as it would put everyone at risk. But I couldn't stay away. Through the visions, I saw how much we loved each other. I watched as Caleb tried to break us apart, but I wouldn't allow it. I understood why he had chosen his father over me, and even though I still cared for Caleb, I loved another man who would love me openly.

The memories faded in my mind, and I no longer felt like a stranger watching stories I had no recollection of. Each memory felt like it belonged to me—as if it had never left. My life played out until a rope snapped my neck.

I felt myself blink and come back into the present. Despite having a year's worth of memories with Dorian flow through me, only a minute had passed since the redhead's decapitation. Maurice still had his hand on my shoulder.

I looked up at Dorian, wondering if he even remembered who I was. There was no emotion in his eyes. He wasn't ripping Maurice's head off in my honor. Dorian was acting like I was a stranger. He was acting like—one of them.

Why hadn't Dorian come for me? Simon had never killed him, as Caleb told me. Caleb had lied—again. Why hadn't Dorian come for me after I came back to life? Did he know who I was?

Dorian caught my eye and shook his head discreetly. He adjusted his shirt as if he were uncomfortable with me looking at him now.

Was that expression a warning not to let Maurice know we knew each other?

Dorian had the same face, but his hair was shorter than it was in my memories. He had messy, medium-length hair that stood taller on the top than the sides, but he had the same beautiful light brown eyes from my dreams. Dorian was dressed in all black, and a long red scarf adorned his neck. His eyes met mine again, and his face went still.

Our locked gaze was torn apart as Maurice grabbed my hand and escorted me out of the room. I looked back at the man I once loved and gave him a pleading look.

"*Dorian,*" I said silently. "*If you can hear this, please help me get out of here.*"

I wasn't sure if he could hear my thoughts with the magic bracelet on my wrist, but I hoped he could.

We walked in silence as Maurice led me up a long spiral staircase near the front foyer. It was black marble, carved with various monsters on the handrail. His shoes clicked on the floor, echoing throughout the narrow hallway once we reached the top. The doors we passed were black, with enormous iron knockers on each of them. It looked like we stepped into an old gothic film, and I had no doubt that these decorations were the original furnishings when the place was built.

Maurice stopped at the last room at the end of the hall, pushing open the tall door with his finger. I first saw a gaudy canopy bed with intricately carved posts. They draped a ruby red silk cloth over it, hovering over the metallic blue comforter and way too many throw pillows than needed. I spotted a gray vanity in the corner of the room with a maroon, framed vintage mirror. The closet was open; many dresses hung on the racks, and heels lined the walls.

It was apparent they had been planning my arrival for quite some time.

"You'll sleep in here for now," he said flatly. "Just because you're a prisoner doesn't mean we won't show you some hospitality." He turned to me. "However, if you disobey me, you'll spend the night in a caged dungeon below." Maurice's warning made my blood run cold.

With his overly heightened vampire senses, I wondered if he'd be able to hear how fast my heartbeat picked up.

He placed his hand on my cheek again. I really fucking hated it when he touched me. "In time, you'll submit to me willingly. Until then, I want you to feel at home here, Akasha. However, you're still my prisoner. I expect you to obey every order I give you, or I'll be forced to punish you for your disobedience." He gestured to the bathroom behind me. "You'll have your own shower, and your closet is filled with clothes your size that Kyoko, my right hand, picked out for you. You're expected to be presentable when you leave this room. Press the speaker button here if you need anything, and Kyoko will come to your aid."

I nodded because, at that moment, I was too exhausted to fight. "Maurice?" I said.

His lips curled. "Yes?"

I swallowed. "Are the humans and witches you keep here ... *all* prisoners?"

He snickered. "Surprisingly, most come here of their own free will. Not every human lives in fear of the undead. Many of them enjoy the lifestyle we give them and are so willing to donate their blood to satisfy their masters. And, in other ways."

Everything that had just come out of his mouth was vile. And wrong. Why would anyone sacrifice themselves to be fed upon and imprisoned like this? Why would they give their bodies to fucking monsters?

"Yeah, sounds like a blast with you psychopaths," I said but pressed my lips together, instantly regretting those words. I closed my eyes tightly, anticipating a hard blow. When it didn't come, I opened my eyes to see an amused smirk on Maurice's face.

"Get some sleep," he ordered. "Kyoko will be at your door later in the day with breakfast."

Maurice leaned in and kissed me on the forehead, and my body stiffened.

Suppose he believes we're going to have that kind of relationship. Maurice will have to fight me in that case because I'd never willingly give it.

I held back the urge to quiver, focusing on my breathing so he didn't sense my fear. He was a killer, a sadistic predator who was keeping me against my will and had plans to feed on me or worse. He enjoyed every fucking moment of how terrified he could make me.

"Goodnight, Akasha. I'll see you soon." Maurice shut and locked the door behind him; the sound of the lock sliding into place was the last straw, and I dropped to my knees. My mind was a mess, but I didn't even try to figure anything out because I needed to sleep. I told myself it was okay to cry, and I needed to, but I couldn't. I eyed the clock, groaning when I saw the time. It was eight in the morning, so I threw the ridiculous number of pillows off the bed and drifted asleep.

CHAPTER 25

I wasn't sure how long I had been out before I heard a knock at the door. Assuming it was Maurice's right hand, I rolled over and looked at the clock on the nightstand. It was two in the afternoon.

"Come in," I called through the door.

I heard the door unlock, and a woman with long black hair, slightly fair skin, and dark eyes entered the room. She carried a serving tray with two bowls of fruit and a plate of hotcakes. "Good morning, Akasha. I have your breakfast," she announced. "My name is Kyoko; I hope you like the clothes I bought for you." She opened the armoire next to the bed. "You should wear this black strapless dress today, with your hair down with that red clip in your hair." She pointed to the dresser. "Maurice will love that," she said as she walked back toward the door. "It's very nice to meet you."

"I don't care what he likes," I snapped.

"That's bold to say in his own home. I'd be careful with that tongue. It's far better that you comply, believe me." She placed her hand on the door handle, but her eyes stayed on mine. "He'll make the process less painful if he likes you."

"What do you mean by *process*?" I asked. "Like when he drinks from me?"

"It'll only hurt if you fight it." She winked and then shut the door behind her before I could say another word.

Is she a prisoner, too, or completely delusional?

Now, alone in the room, I thought about my friends and family. Were they safe? A part of me wanted them to bust down the door and help me take down these evil bastards, but that would just put them in danger. Besides, they had no idea where I was. I needed to find out as much information as possible about this clan, find a way to escape, and then use that information to bring them down with the help of my coven. We didn't think when we ran from the safe house. We had no plan on what to do because we didn't know what we were up against. I now knew, and I truly believed with my coven, Lily, Joel, and the werewolf pack, we could take them out.

My thoughts turned to Dorian. Would he come with me when I escaped from here? Or was I kidding myself into thinking we could once again have what we had all those years ago?

After I ate and showered, I opened the armoire to pick out my outfit for the day. I decided against the black dress and chose a blue spaghetti strap tank with black jeans, then pulled my hair up and put on some light makeup they left me in the bathroom. I didn't want to be punished for not looking somewhat presentable. Sitting on the edge of the bed, I waited for someone to get me. After an hour, nobody came, so I walked up to the speaker and pressed the button.

"Hello? Um ... Kyoko?"

"Heading back up."

Ten minutes later, I heard a knock at the door before Kyoko entered. She sized me up and shook her head, clearly annoyed with what I had picked out to wear. "I said to wear the black dress, Akasha." She let out a heavy sigh. "I guess that'll do," she said dryly. "But I'm going to warn you again. You don't want Maurice as an enemy. It's best you cooperate and make the best of a shitty situation."

I gave her a stern look. "Maurice is already my enemy, Kyoko. And you obviously don't know much about me if you think I will let him do whatever he wants with me."

Her eye twitched, but she sucked in a breath, most likely her way of stopping herself from saying something she'd be punished for later. "He's waiting for us. Come on."

We headed downstairs, and I had to ask her the question lingering in my mind since I'd met her. "So, Kyoko. How long have you been a—"

"Vampire?" She smiled for the first time since she came to the room. "Longer than you've been a witch."

I shrugged. "Well, I don't know about that. My soul has been around for centuries."

"Yes, I guess you're right," she said, followed by a quiet chuckle. "I was a human over a hundred and fifty years ago. My family and I had settled in California from Japan in the late eighteen hundreds, my father taking a job working on the railroads. We wanted to have a fresh start in America. But it was not meant to be. Ten years later, a vampire from this clan killed my parents in front of me and then fed on me. I still remember the pain I felt while I was being drained. It didn't hurt if I lay still, but when I struggled, I wanted to rip my heart out. He took so much blood from me that he could either kill or turn me. So, he turned me and brought me back to the clan. He thought he could control my life and make me his submissive. Unfortunately for him, I couldn't forgive him for what he had done to my parents, so I drove a stake through his heart. Maurice found it admirable of me, so he asked if I'd oversee the clan when he could not.

"And then you had your own human to feed on?" I asked.

"Every human the clan takes is assigned a vampire who lays claim to them. They are yours, and you are theirs. The older vampires have seniority over the witches brought in. The blood from a witch tastes so much better than a human, but the blood from *you*, Akasha, has been prophesied to be quite delightful."

Gross.

"This is the reason Maurice wants you all to himself," she said. "The power he'll gain from drinking your blood, well, he'll stop at nothing to have it."

This cannot be my reality now. I have to get the fuck out of here.

We heard laughter coming from two men in the dining area. I recognized Maurice's laugh, but I wasn't sure about the other.

We entered the room, and Maurice was sitting next to a man I hadn't expected to see. It was Roland, Caleb's father. He was as strikingly handsome as I remembered, just like his son.

Suddenly, another memory sprang into my mind, covering my vision in darkness.

Not now. Not now.

I was back in the training room at the age of thirteen with Caleb, Leah, Simon, and Ezra. It was the same memory the psychic had brought out of me. Roland reached out his hand to bring me to my feet after I had just turned my first vampire to ash. He brought me in for a warm hug.

"I'm so proud of you, Mercy. Well done," Roland said.

I felt a sharp sting on my face. "Wake up." Maurice was standing over me.

Did he just slap me?

"Where did you go just now?" The tone of Maurice's voice demanded that I answer him.

"I don't know. I spaced out or something. I'm used to having coffee first thing when I wake up."

He let out a derisive snort and glanced over at Roland. "Humans are so pathetically weak." He turned to Kyoko. "Have the help brew some coffee for our guest."

I sat down directly across the table from Roland as Kyoko rushed to the kitchen. I looked into his eyes, and my heart ached a little. Roland had stepped in like a father figure, and now, he was part of a malicious clan that was keeping me against my will. "Akasha, this is Roland," Maurice said.

Roland held out his hand, but I didn't take it.

"I know who he is," I snapped. I felt rage build up inside me. Roland helped raise me, and now he was sitting here as one of my captors.

He's a traitor.

"You remember me?" he asked, tilting his head.

"Oh, I know exactly who you are!" I fumed. "But apparently, you've forgotten who I was to you back then."

Roland may have warned us about the clan coming to the safe house, but he wasn't trying to rescue me. He was sitting next to Maurice—his ally. This was just a sick and twisted game to them.

"I've not forgotten, Mercy," Roland said. "Many years have passed, though, and our roles have been slightly divided since then."

Maurice glared at Roland.

"Relax, Maurice. I helped raise this girl. I'll call her by her given name," Roland said and then tilted his head toward me. "Has my son been training you?"

"When was the last time you saw Caleb?" I asked, ignoring his question.

"Akasha, hold your tongue!" Kyoko snapped at me while placing my coffee on the table.

"It's okay, Kyoko. She has every right to be angry with me," Roland said.

At that moment, staring into the eyes of someone I had once loved as family, I wondered if he was indeed on my side.

"Don't ponder too hard on that thought, Mercy. I'm always on your side." A voice echoed in my mind. Roland kept his eyes on mine and gave me a discrete nod while Maurice asked Kyoko to call in Dorian and Noah.

What game is he playing? I asked myself.

One thing was clear—we shared the gift of telepathy. It amazed me how Roland could still use his powers after being turned into a vampire. Not to mention, he heard my thoughts without me deliberately projecting them. I wondered if it was just that gift alone that he could use or if there were more abilities he still had in that form. I also hoped that when I projected my words to Dorian, he may have heard me after all.

Roland looked away and focused his eyes on Maurice.

What's he planning?

I turned to Maurice. "You have to let me go. You can't just keep me here. I'm not some kind of servant to your psychotic whims." I needed to distract Maurice somehow.

"Clearly, the reality of your situation hasn't quite set in," Maurice said and leaned forward until I felt his breath fan my cheek. "I can do whatever I want to you, Akasha," he warned, "And I'm very much looking forward to it. The sooner you realize you're just a thing and not a person, the easier all of this will be for everyone."

My heartbeat thumped so hard against my chest that my breath caught.

"I can hear your heart beating," Maurice hissed. "Is that excitement, or have you finally accepted your fate?"

"Look, asshole—"

"Easy, Mercy. Just let me drink from you," Roland told me telepathically, cutting off the rest of my insult.

"You're out of your fucking mind," I projected. *"Get out of my damn head."*

"You're quite brave to run your tongue like that in my home. I'll forgive you just this once," Maurice said, licking his lips.

Roland spoke aloud, "Mercy, your blood is very much desired here in this clan. Maurice has allowed me, and only me, to drink from you, other than himself. That was the deal for me for giving up your location."

"You son of a bitch!" I silently screamed.

I folded my arms over my chest, that time, speaking out loud. "No, thank you." I glared at them both.

Maurice laughed again. "Isn't she adorable? She's so defiant." His demeanor quickly changed as his face grew stern. "I never break a promise, and I won't start with Roland. He gets the first drink."

"How could you do this to me?"

"Trust me, Mercy."

"Well, I don't!"

Shit. I'd said that out loud.

I was getting confused about what was in my head or from my lips.

"Excuse me?" Maurice asked, puzzled.

"I ... I said I don't want anyone to touch me."

"You still don't get it. Do you?" Maurice snapped.

"Well, I get that you're a sadistic creep whom I can't wait to slay someday." I waited for a slap, but all he did was laugh.

I understood Roland wasn't warning us earlier at the safe house; he was fishing us out of there, so I could get caught. I suspected he had a plan, but I wasn't sure if it was in my favor or against me.

"Just think, moments from now, I'll get to enjoy the warm rays of sunlight on my face," Roland gloated. "It's the only thing I despise about being a vampire." He looked at Maurice, and they laughed in unison. "But I guess that won't be a problem anymore, will it, Mercy?" Roland flashed me a mocking grin.

There was a moment of silence while two strikingly handsome bloodsuckers stared at me. A shiver ran down my spine. I was more disgusted than afraid.

Roland stood up and walked toward me slowly while Maurice held both my shoulders in a tight grip, his nails digging into my skin. "Seriously, Roland, don't do this," I pleaded. There was no hint of love or compassion in his eyes. He wanted my blood—and he wanted it badly.

I'm not ready for this. It's a complete violation.

At that moment, Dorian entered the kitchen to inform Maurice that everything was set for tonight. "Perfect," Maurice said. "Send Noah in as well."

Dorian's eyes passed over mine before continuing out the door, as if he hadn't even realized I was in the room.

He did. But he didn't care.

Roland was now by my side and placed his hands on my shoulders, every muscle in my body tensing the instant he touched me.

"What's going on? Do you have an update?" Roland asked Noah, who stood at the door.

Noah didn't say a word. After a few more minutes, Dorian walked back in. He looked at me nervously and drew a deep breath while Noah approached Maurice. I kept my eyes on Dorian.

What is happening?

Maurice placed his hand on Noah's shoulder. "Where's the rest of the coven? You said this morning that you saw more than just a couple of witches. I want your full report."

Noah straightened up. "I counted three other witches, a human, a vampire, and two werewolves. The witches and werewolves were the ones helping her escape. I didn't see the other elements there."

A disapproving sigh came from Maurice's mouth, and he grimaced. "Werewolves, Akasha? Really? You have werewolf friends?"

"At least they would never turn their backs on their own kind." I glared up at Roland, who just shook his head at me.

Noah cleared his throat. "Once the wolves could smell me, they took off toward the tunnel. They think we don't know about the stupid tunnel; it was too easy to follow them. I don't know what they're up to, but after Mercy—" He stopped and cleared his throat again. "After Akasha surrendered herself, they returned to the safe house. They didn't sleep all night. They are planning ... something."

"You surrendered yourself?" Maurice paused. "Interesting."

I kept my lips shut.

"Maurice," Roland interrupted, and I couldn't have been more relieved to have Maurice draw his attention to someone else. "I'd like to test daylight while we still have it. May I feed on her now?"

"Yes, of course, Roland. A deal is a deal." Maurice gestured toward me. "Go on," he instructed casually, as if I were just a tasty appetizer he was serving a guest.

"You mean, right now?" I cried out.

No! This can't be happening right now.

Roland's lips parted. "Relax, Mercy. It won't hurt you if you relax."

So, I've heard.

Roland pulled my ponytail to the side and leaned down toward my neck. I felt a cool chill from his breath crawl up to my ears. The only thought going through my head was, *why the fuck was I just sitting here?*

Without thinking of the consequences, I pushed the chair back, toppling Roland onto the ground, and sprinted for the door. It took only one second before Noah had his massive hands on my shoulders and yanked me back, placing me back in the chair.

Dammit!

"Noah, allow me." Dorian walked up to my side, and Noah stepped back. He pulled my ponytail again to the side and gently tilted my head, keeping me in place. His touch was soft and gentle, and I immediately relaxed. With my eyes closed tightly, I took a deep breath, picturing Dorian comforting me. It was like all those times in the past when I was scared. I held on to the feeling of his fingers touching my skin, keeping me safe.

Roland walked up behind me while Dorian continued to hold me still. That was when I felt sharp fangs pierce my skin.

CHAPTER 26

The bite didn't hurt as I had anticipated. If anything, it was weirdly pleasurable. As my blood was being drained, I felt the pulse of it moving through my veins. Now and then, the skin around Roland's fangs tried to knit back together. A sudden wave of relief hit me when I realized I could still heal quickly, even if the bracelet blocked my powers. After he let me go, a brief cloud of euphoria hit me, and I lost my balance, falling to the floor.

Dorian moved quickly, reaching out to catch me before I could hit the tile, and then he pulled me close and cradled me against his chest. I looked up, staring back at the familiar face—the face of someone who no longer loved me. I hoped the moment wasn't real; I longed to reach up and touch his face—and feel his cold skin against my fingertips. But I couldn't.

He isn't mine anymore.

In his arms, I was at peace. I could block out the pain. I could ignore the fact that he worked for monsters like Maurice. That wasn't the Dorian I knew and loved. Maurice was always the type of creature he fought against becoming. He hated that he had to feed on humans to survive. Even from the moment that Dorian was turned, he never had the urge to drink from humans. At least, he never admitted that to me.

"I don't want to waste any more time, Maurice. I need to make arrangements." Roland licked his lips and then wiped the remaining blood from his chin with a kitchen towel. "It was nice doing business with you, as always." They didn't shake hands, and Roland didn't say goodbye to me. He spun around and headed toward the front door. The vampires in the room shielded themselves from the light outside as the door opened and closed.

I wasn't a person to any of them. I was property, and this was a vampire testing out the merchandise. I closed my eyes and fought back the burning tears. I felt violated and alone in that quiet, dark moment, but I refused to give Maurice or his friends the satisfaction.

My wounds healed over before Kyoko could tend to them, but I was still covered in my blood. Dorian helped me to my feet, and she moved to grab a wet rag from the kitchen. He dabbed at it with another damp towel, but Maurice yanked the rag from his hand and signaled him to move away from me.

"We need to burn this rag, Kyoko," Maurice said, "Then escort Akasha to her room to clean herself up. Noah, find someone to mop the floor until every drop of her blood is gone."

My strength was coming back to me, and I was able to stand straight again. I looked at Dorian, but he wouldn't even look at me.

Is he ashamed he hadn't helped me? Could he help me?

I didn't want him to risk his life for me, but I needed to know if I really had an ally inside these walls.

Maurice turned to exit the room, but I needed him to know I would be the worst prisoner he had ever had. I wasn't afraid; I was fucking angry.

"What are you waiting for, you piece of shit?" I asked through gritted teeth. "For someone as egotistical as you, I'm a bit surprised you let someone else feast themselves on something you think belongs to you." Maurice hissed, and for some stupid reason, it fueled me. "Drink from me, asshole. Get this ridiculous shit over with."

I wasn't sure where my bravery was coming from, but a week ago, I would have cowered under his control.

Maurice's laughter came out over the top as if mocking my defiance. I honestly thought he'd strike me this time, but it appeared my insult only amused him.

"The first time I drink from you, my love, I do it as part of a ceremony." He stepped forward, his eyes sizing me up. "It will bind you to me. Once I feed on you," he said, stepping even closer. "You'll then feed on me."

The fuck I will! I felt sick.

"I have a loyal witch that performs a ritual while I take my first drink. The magic will bind us to each other. I'll always know where you are and what you're feeling, just as you will for me. Don't worry. Any disgust you might have for me won't linger. You'll *want* me to feed on you." He stepped closer. "You'll want me to fuck you." The smile he held slowly flattened into a heated, animalistic scowl. "You'll crave it as much as I'll crave you."

No, I didn't like the sound of that.

"Tonight, we do the ritual," he exclaimed excitedly. "And to ensure you don't fight it, Noah is bringing me some leverage."

My eyes narrowed as I stared at him. "What kind of leverage?" I gulped.

"A little human friend seems like a nice appetizer for me, don't you think?"

No! She was supposed to be safe. I was supposed to keep her safe!

"Maurice, I swear I'll kill you if you touch her." My hands balled into fists. "I promise you, I'll make you a pile of ash before dawn, and I don't need my magic to do it."

Anger flashed in his eyes as his hand swung back to strike, but he stopped the back of his hand at my cheek. I flinched, turning to him with a look of pure, raw hatred.

Before I knew it, Maurice had smoothed over his anger and replaced it with his usual expression of haughty, contemptuous amusement. He smirked as he leaned into me and whispered, "I know that's meant to be threatening, but believe me when I say I would love to spar with you." My fingertips dug deep into my palms as he moved even closer, his breath chilling my neck. "I'm going to bathe you in Shannon's blood."

Without thinking, I leaped out of my chair and lunged for Maurice. My magic might not have been working with the bracelet on, but I still had my strength. Also, I learned a little kickboxing from my training session with Caleb earlier, and I used everything in my body to knock Maurice flat to the ground.

I went down with him and didn't waste a moment, turning to kick him in the face and making his skull crack against the tile floor. He was up on his feet before I could kick him again, trapping my hands with one hand, twisting painfully as he wrapped his other arm around my neck in a chokehold. He slammed his knee into the back of my legs, and I winced as my kneecaps hit hard against the floor.

"You're no match for me, witch. I'm eight hundred years old." He let go of me by shoving me to the floor. I heard Maurice stomp out and signal Noah and Kyoko to follow, but Dorian stood by the wall.

He walked over to me slowly, reaching out his hand. "Let me help you up." Dorian's familiar voice calmed my nerves.

"Um, thanks." I took his hand in mine, relishing his touch, and pulled myself to my feet. My heart clenched painfully as he let go of my hand and turned to walk away. I grabbed his wrist, keeping him from leaving me again. He turned around but wouldn't look into my eyes.

"Look at me, Dorian," I pleaded. "You know who I am, don't you?"

He looked up, his eyes meeting mine. "Of course, I know who you are—you're Akasha. The one who can save us." He wiggled his wrist from mine, releasing my hold.

"The one who can save you? Why are you pretending not to know who I am? Dorian!"

"Keep your voice down!" he whispered sternly. The look he gave me, that tortured stare, was familiar; I had seen it a thousand times before. It was the same way he had looked at me when the crowd took me away to be hanged. The look told me he loved me but couldn't stop what was about to come.

Dorian turned from me, heading to the door, but I quickly stepped in front of him, blocking him from leaving. "Do not walk out that door, Dorian. Please, talk to me." There was so much desperation in my tone that my voice cracked. He turned back around but didn't speak. "Dorian," I whispered again.

"Shh, not here," he whispered while signaling with his head to a camera tucked in the corner of the ceiling.

We're being watched.

Kyoko entered the room and glared at us suspiciously. An uncomfortable silence loomed in the air as Dorian straightened out his shirt and walked away from me, leaving me standing alone in the corner.

"I'm supposed to brief you on today's activities and the house rules, but we need to get you cleaned up; that shirt is stained," Kyoko informed me. "I can still smell your blood from across the house." She glared at Dorian. "What are you still doing here? Get back to your assignment."

Dorian nodded. "Sorry, Kyoko, there was a bit more blood that needed tending to." He looked over at me one last time, face blank. "I'll leave the two of you alone."

Tears fell as I sank down at the kitchen table; my body was numb, and I couldn't help but absentmindedly rub at my neck where Roland had bitten. It healed, but I still felt his sharp fangs in my neck. It was clear that Dorian still cared—I saw that now—but it didn't mean he'd save me. Roland used to see me as his child, and even so, he was willing to feed on me.

I drew my eyes to a large painting on the wall of a nude demon with scarlet red skin and black bat-like wings. It looked like the devil I had always imagined. In his arms was a beautiful woman wearing a long white dress. The demon's mouth was open, showing shiny-white fangs as he gazed at her neck with lust-filled eyes.

He didn't look anything like the vampires I'd met. The vampires here were all beautiful and humanlike.

Kyoko walked toward me, placing a knitted bag on the kitchen table. I tore my eyes away from the painting and glanced at the bag.

"You like that painting, don't you?" She gestured toward it.

"Not really. It's a little too terrifying for me," I admitted.

Kyoko sat down and stared at the painting with me. "His name was Misha. The devil had a plan for him to change this world forever. He was only a baby when he was sent to Earth thousands of years ago. In a small village, there was a couple who couldn't have children of their own, and they took him in. They raised him like their own son, and as terrifying as he looked, they loved him deeply."

When Caleb first talked about the existence of vampires, he mentioned an angel who had a child with a demon, who they named Kylan. Then Kylan became the very first vampire to walk the earth, spawning a plague of monsters to consume humankind. It was a dark story, and I hated that I had to know about it. Hated that I had to know without a doubt that vampires are real, as is the devil, and I'm trapped in the story as some beacon of light to lead an army of good against evil. But despite the hollow sadness that it filled me with, I wanted to know more.

"His parents tried to feed him milk from a human breast and food from their farm, but he threw everything up. One night, they found him covered in the blood of their sheep. The desire for blood was all he could think about—all he wanted. His instincts brought forth the craving for it, yet he had no idea why. It was the only way for him to survive. He also grew at an abnormal rate. Within a year, he was fully grown."

As disturbing as the story was, the more I learned about vampires and their original creator, the easier it would be for me to expose their weaknesses and fight back. Kylan may have been the original vampire, but this was the demon that created him in the first place: his father. I wanted to know more, so I stared at her intently and nodded. My gesture caused her to perk up, eager to share more of their dark history.

"Then one night," Kyoko continued, "while Misha was sleeping, he had a dream. In the dream, the devil appeared and told him why he was sent here in the first place. He told him he was here to create an army, and humans were destined to be their food supply. Misha was filled with so much evil and hatred that he obeyed the devil's instructions without question. He slaughtered the people who raised him and fed upon them. It was Misha who gave us the name *vampire*. His mission was to feed a human his blood and then kill them. Once they awoke, they had to feed on human blood. After that, the transition would be complete, or so he thought."

"It didn't work at first?" I asked.

She frowned. "It never worked," she said. "The humans he turned had transformed into what Misha looked like, unlike the vampires you see today. Their outsides were red, demonic, and frightening to humans. He knew this would be a problem. It's much easier to charm someone to be their victim when their appearance is beautiful and approachable. He also had no control over these vampires. They were like rabid beasts with no intellect or self-control. He knew he had no choice but to kill all he had created and start over."

She stood up and walked toward the painting. My eyes followed her around the table, and she stopped in front of it, placing her hand on the elegant white dress the angel wore.

"It was then that Misha had another dream, where the devil told him there would be an angel sent to Earth to put a stop to their plan." Kyoko removed her hand from the painting and looked over at me. "The devil told him to destroy her. So, one day, while tracking the forest by his house, he saw this angelic, blonde-haired woman. Misha couldn't take his eyes off her immaculate beauty."

I looked back at the painting.

"Her name was Tatyana," Kyoko said.

Kylan's mother.

"She was wearing all white, and her hair was golden like the sunrise, and it fell straight down to her waistline. Misha was taken aback by her presence and was determined to have her, even though he knew this was the angel the devil had told him to kill."

Kyoko joined me back at the table. "We don't know if Tatyana was forced or mated with him willingly, but together they created a child. Misha wouldn't destroy the angel sent to stop him, but he would use her to build his army.

"Their union created a half-breed. His son would be the one to create vampires. He'd make them demonic on the inside, like himself, but beautiful on the outside, like Tatyana. They would also have half of their human traits inside them, but they'd lose their soul." Kyoko smiled. "Tatyana named her son Kylan."

I cringed at the sound of his name.

"When Kylan was born, Tatyana was relieved he didn't have demonic traits like Misha. He was beautiful and perfect, just like her. Kylan couldn't eat human food either, so Misha fed him only blood. Misha would fetch the blood first, then serve it to Kylan because he didn't have fangs yet to pierce the victims' skin. It took her son a few years to grow into a man, but then, like Misha, he stopped growing.

"One day, Tatyana was cooking supper when Kylan came into the room covered in blood. As she looked closer, she could see Kylan's fangs were out and his father's head in his hand."

I remembered that unsettling detail when Kylan told me how he had ripped his father's head off.

Kyoko's face hardened. "Tatyana knew Misha would not be the only victim of Kylan's bloodlust. It was at that moment she placed an angelic curse on Kylan. According to the curse, he could never take a life with his own hands. Unfortunately for her, he had the gift of possessing others and making them do what he wanted. He turned one human, who completed her transition on her own by taking her own life, and through her, Kylan was able to create more vampires. His charisma allowed him to spread the vampire race.

"Angelic curse?" I said. "Wouldn't that be a gift? To make someone not able to kill another person?"

She shook her head, appearing annoyed by my question. "Tatyana abandoned her son after what he had done. She could no longer stop him once the vampires started to spread all over the world. The vampire race grew so large that witches and werewolves could no longer defend themselves.

I rolled my eyes at that comment. "You speak about witches and werewolves like they're dispensable. Who are vampires to dictate who lives or dies?"

Kyoko's lip curled, sneering at my comment. "Tatyana apparently did. She had failed to protect humanity, so she created the

Chosen Ones." Her voice came out harsh when she said my coven's name. "Your coven has slaughtered more vampires than vampires have killed humans since the dawn of our existence." She turned away from me. "Fortunately for us, we stopped Tatyana's plan by capturing the key element needed to make her plan a success. You." She smiled to herself as if she were the one who had brought me here.

I wanted to share with her how much Kylan suffered as he died at my hands, but I had to keep that part a secret ... for now.

"Why did Kylan kill his father?" I asked.

She beamed—a sudden shift in her mood. "I love this part of the story. Kylan was hiding in the stables when he saw the devil from the Underworld demanding Misha kill his wife. The devil knew the plan had been delayed because of her, and he wanted her dead. Kylan could never let anyone hurt his mother, even if she tried to turn on him and Misha. He confronted Misha, and they had a vicious fight. In the end, Kylan ripped his father's head from his body and was then cursed by his mother. The rejection led to rage, and Kylan soon took up his demonic father's cause. Making the army take the world in blood."

Caleb never told me that much detail about the origin of what brought us here. I learned so much about the vampires' history, my coven's creation, and why I was so crucial to the world.

"Kylan created this painting to remind him of his origin." Kyoko looked at the clock. "I'd better start explaining the rules of the house. But first ..." Kyoko grabbed a silver bracelet from the knitted bag. She stepped to my side, exchanged it for the one I already had around my wrist, and snapped it tightly shut before removing the first one. "There you go. It fits perfectly."

"Why did you change them?"

"Like the other one, it blocks your magic. But this one also has a mechanism that will send an electric current through your body, completely paralyzing you, should you try to escape. A cord running around the property boundaries will trigger the device if you pass over it." She giggled to herself like a little child. "It's like one of those invisible fences humans use for their dogs."

As tears formed, I grabbed my wrist and lowered my head. I wanted to be brave. I was angry, and there was no doubt I would fight for my life at every possible chance. But at that moment of exhaustion and fear that they'd hurt the ones I loved, I couldn't stop the tears from falling.

"Please don't cry, Akasha." She placed her hand on my back. "Every woman and man here would jump at the chance to be with Maurice."

I huffed. "I doubt it. Maurice is as evil as they come."

"That's where you're wrong," she said. "You don't know him, as I do. Believe me when I say that you're one of the lucky ones. He'll be gentle with you when he drinks your blood. I promise. To be chosen by Maurice ..." Kyoko scooted closer to me. "Anyway, there are only a few rules here in our home. Obey your master. Don't try to run from them. And you need to eat plenty of human food so you have your strength. The only light sources you will have are the lamps and candles that are always on during the day and night. The shutters are locked during the day, so we'll provide you with vitamin D supplements."

I lifted my head. "You don't sleep in coffins during the day?" I asked innocently.

She let out a little laugh. "No, we don't need to sleep. We only have to ensure all the outside light is shielded from entering the home during the day."

I looked at her with pitiful eyes. "Well, Kyoko, I'd rather die."

"I know," she breathed. "I've been in your shoes before, remember?"

I don't know what I was thinking, but I'd also be a fool not to try. I lowered my voice to a near whisper, remembering the camera in the corner of the room. "Then take this off my wrist. Help me escape," I begged.

Kyoko's face drew into a scowl. "Don't confuse my kindness with me liking you," she hissed. "You're still a witch, and I'm a vampire. You're only *food* to me." She sat up, straightened her clothes, and grabbed her bag. "Follow me upstairs. You look like shit."

I was stunned by how quickly her tone had changed, but not entirely surprised. All I knew was that I was in this prison alone, and then, more than ever, I had to find a way to get out of this mess.

CHAPTER 27

B ack in my room, I pulled my hair over my right shoulder and traced my fingers to where Roland had bitten me. I felt utterly violated. Fear was taking over me at the realization that Maurice would soon feed on me himself. I also knew it was only a matter of time before these creatures brought in Shannon as *leverage*.

I decided to make the most out of the day and learn everything I could about the clan, hoping it would, in some way, help me. After changing out of the bloodstained shirt, I walked throughout the house, noting various rooms and hallways, trying to get a sense of the place.

I spoke with several humans and witches held in the lair against their will. When the vampires were not feeding on them, they allowed the prisoners to wander the house and interact with each other. They had books for them to read, several televisions, and plenty of food to keep them healthy. They had specific meals for the captives because, as Kyoko had explained, the healthier the food, the better the blood tasted. There was always a vampire watching them. The vampire assigned to me when Maurice was away was his brother, Colin.

Colin was turned after he noticed Maurice wasn't aging. Maurice knew he would have to leave their town as he no longer aged and wanted company along the way. He turned his own brother to have him at his side through the years. Colin looked in his mid-twenties and wasn't as handsome as Maurice, but he still had some of the same features. He didn't have a lot of power with the clan. Maurice was the master, and Colin abided by his brother's commands. The way Colin's eyes were fixated on me with every single move I made was unnerving.

It was a relief for me to meet other witches and learn about the unique powers they held. They all talked about having the same experience I had with being bitten. If you relaxed, the bite wouldn't hurt. Fortunately, I regained my strength right away after being bitten, unlike the rest.

Mid-afternoon, I hurried into one of their great rooms and gravitated toward Sarah, a witch who was also held against her will. We had to do our best to speak quietly whenever we were around Colin or Sarah's vampire, Troy. Vampires had a strong sense of hearing and were always listening nearby.

It was hard, though, to keep quiet when Sarah first mentioned her power.

"You can do what?!" I lowered my voice by the last word as Sarah, a blonde woman with lightly tanned skin, gave me a sharp look with her hazel-colored eyes.

Troy wasn't far from where we were sitting. Though we weren't plotting an escape, I wasn't sure yet what was acceptable as a topic of conversation amongst the witches. Despite these bracelets shielding our powers, I strongly suspected we still made them nervous. They may have fangs to bleed us dry, but if we could use our magic, they'd have no fighting chance.

"I can make people see things that aren't there or manipulate someone's face to look like someone else," Sarah explained patiently. I hadn't even heard of powers like those before. "If I could use magic right now, I could make you see flowers blooming in my hands or trees growing in through the windows." She glanced over at Troy, leaning his back against the wall, his arms folded across his chest. "Troy over there." She gestured with her head. "I could make him look like Steve Buscemi, and everyone would see it."

I giggled at the mental image, glancing at Troy from the corner of my eye. As I looked, a pale-white, red-headed vampire on the other side of the room called out for Troy, waving him over and out of the hall.

Finally, we can speak normally again.

"That's fascinating, Sarah," I said. "I'd love to see you use your magic someday."

Her expression changed. "Yeah. Me too." She sucked in a breath and looked over at a group of girls sitting by the fireplace. "You should ask around later, hear what some others can do. Like, you see April over there?" Sarah pointed at a curly-haired brunette with light brown skin, slim and slightly older than Sarah and me. "She can manipulate light and camouflage her body to blend in with her surroundings. And Rachel can make plants grow faster. I don't remember what else she can do, but she used to have a lovely flower shop before ... before they brought her here."

My excitement dulled again as I looked at Rachel, who had been staring at the covered window, and imagined how much happier her life had been back then. "She must miss it," I muttered.

"Everyone misses their old lives, Mercy," Sarah shrugged. "Everyone lost something." The way she said that last phrase struck me.

"What did you lose?" I asked before I could stop myself, realizing those words could have offended her. I had no idea what she had gone through, and I hoped my question wasn't prying too much into her life.

Sarah sighed, looking away. "Almost everyone, back then."

What does that mean? Did she lose her family?

As if she could see the questions on my face, she frowned and continued, "Things aren't black and white, Mercy. Maybe my life wasn't exactly ideal before I was brought here. It's not like I wanted this, but I'd been running from someone else, and my vampire's not a bad one."

I didn't know how to respond.

Her vampire wasn't a bad one?

April hesitated as she walked past on her way out the door. "You okay, honey?" she checked, looking concerned at the expression on Sarah's face. Not angry, but certainly not happy.

"Yeah, I'm fine," Sarah reassured her. "Have you met Mercy yet?"

I let Sarah change the subject and smiled at April.

"No, I haven't!" she chirped. "I heard about you, of course. I could feel your Awakening yesterday. We all did. Like there was this sudden strength we'd been missing our entire lives, you know?"

Actually, I didn't know that. I knew my Awakening would make a difference, but for everyone to feel it immediately? I hadn't really expected it.

April, Sarah, and I talked together for a while longer. They told me how they and the other witches had heard stories about the Chosen Ones coming to Earth centuries ago. Yet they didn't know our purpose, nor did they know vampires existed until they were caught and brought here.

We shared stories about our pasts. Some witches, like Rachel, used their powers in everyday life to support themselves. At the same time, they had been taught to hide their skills. Making one mistake in the wrong place, in front of the wrong people, had brought them to this hell house. In return, I told them how my mother had taken my powers hostage my entire life and that when we all escaped from the lair, they'd be able to use their respective elements, including Spirit, from there on out.

At the mention of escaping, a few witches froze. Sarah tilted her head to the left, and I noticed a vampire standing off to the side and staring right at me.

He heard.

A chill ran down my spine as our gazes locked. The vampire tucked a strand of long, raven hair behind one ear and held one finger to his lips, as if telling me to be quieter before going on his way. Was he going to pretend he hadn't heard anything?

"That's Silas," Sarah murmured. "You're lucky. He's not a monster like the others."

"Every vampire I've seen since I've been here has shown me otherwise?" I said.

"Not every vampire wants to be the way they are," she reminded. "There are a few vampires like him in here; they want to survive, but they don't enjoy having to do it this way. They'd choose to be human again if they could."

It got me thinking, *how many vampires were like Silas?*

He wasn't the first vampire who disliked being undead, but how common was it for a vampire to feel that way? Kyoko came strolling around the corner with her head held high, flaunting her superiority over us, silencing the room. She was tiny, but she wasn't someone to mess with, not while our powers were concealed.

"Akasha, let's go," Kyoko said. "We need to get you ready."

She led me into my room. I glanced at the clock; it had been over twelve hours since they trapped me inside the lair. It was almost sunset.

After she left, I washed my skin in the shower until it turned raw, trying to scrub off any trace of those monsters from my body. I didn't even try to fight this time. If Kyoko wanted me to put on rose-colored lipstick, I would do it. I brushed on light bronze eyeshadow and heavy mascara, remembering Maurice's warning to be presentable. I then slipped on a beautiful blood-red, formal gown that, again, I wasn't allowed to protest. The symbolic choice of colors didn't go unnoticed. Kyoko instructed me to wear my hair in a high bun so it didn't impede Maurice from drinking from my neck.

When I was done getting ready, I heard a knock at the door. Kyoko said she would take me to the ballroom at eight. It was seven forty-five, so she was early. When I answered the door, Colin was standing in a sleek black suit. The first thought that crossed my mind was that there was a slight change of plans, and Colin would be the one escorting me to the ballroom. However, when his fangs protruded, and his lips curled, I realized he was only there for one thing—my blood.

Fight for your life, Mercy. Don't give up. Fight.

He grabbed me firmly by the shoulders and pushed me down onto the bed. I screamed while kicking frantically at him, my nails digging deep into his cold flesh. I turned to the left, looking toward the nightstand for anything I could use as a weapon. The only thing my fingers could reach was the alarm clock. After I yanked it from the cord, I slammed it hard across his head, but of course, being a vampire, he barely flinched. That only fueled his animalistic rage, and he slapped me firmly across the face. It stung, but it didn't stop me from fighting.

"Get the fuck off me!" I screamed again, hoping someone would hear me. "Maurice will kill you!" Colin was too strong.

"I just want a taste of your blood," he hissed. "I just need a few drops." Colin licked his lips, and I turned away, desperately trying to choke back the bile in my throat. He gripped my jaw, pulling my face back straight so I'd look back at him. "I'd like you to look me in the eyes when I take from you," he said. "Fucking whore!"

I'm going to be sick.

"Maurice would never allow that, Colin. Please don't do this," I cried out again.

"I could smell your blood from outside the door." Colin leaned in closer to my neck. I froze. "Why should my brother get to walk in the daylight while the rest of us suffer in eternal darkness?" He snarled, gripping my wrist tightly. He squeezed so hard I felt my wrist pop. "He'll allow that piece of shit Roland to drink from you, but not his own fucking brother."

Fight, dammit. Fight!

I lifted my leg, ready to knee him in the groin, but Colin bit down on my neck. The pain was so excruciating that my body began to tremble. It wasn't as easy to relax that time, so my struggle worsened the pain. I closed my eyes and thought about Dorian. It was the only way to get through the experience. The pain started to subside, and all I could feel was blood being drained from my body. Colin released me after a minute and climbed off the bed. I stayed on the mattress, looking up at the ceiling as tears stung painfully in my eyes.

I waited for him to lick his lips as Roland did, but his reaction was unexpected. Colin sat there for a few minutes with a blank stare, blinking rapidly.

What the hell is wrong with him?

He squinted and opened his eyes as wide as he could before rushing to the bathroom and puking all the blood he had stolen from me. A moment later, I heard him spit the last remaining blood from his mouth onto the floor. When he exited the bathroom, he just stood there and glowered at me. I climbed off the bed and stood in my fighting stance, ready for him to strike.

He's not going to touch me again.

"Your blood is disgusting," he whined. Colin turned toward the door and ran out faster than he had entered. I relaxed my stance.

Disgusting?

Kyoko had said the taste of a witch's blood was like no other, especially the blood from Spirit. I ran into the bathroom to look at the two wounds on my neck that I expected to be already closing up. Yet my eyes immediately drew to the bathroom floor, covered in my blood.

Fuck. I have to clean this up, or they'll know.

There was no way I could tell Maurice what had happened. He would think I gave myself to Colin, and then he might punish *me* for it. It would have to be my secret, and I prayed he wouldn't notice Colin going out in the daylight before I escaped from there. *He did throw it up, though. Is there enough of my blood in his system for the daylight powers to even work? Or I might get lucky, and he'll simply burst into flames.*

After I cleaned the dried blood from my neck and chest, I started wiping down the bathroom floor and the toilet as much as possible. I gathered up the bed sheets stained with blood and hid them in the closet. Once the comforter was neatly made over the mattress to cover up the missing sheets, I sat quietly on the bed, trying to compose myself before Kyoko came for me.

A knock at the door startled me, and when Kyoko entered, her eyes immediately targeted the bathroom. She sniffed the air.

"Akasha, what happened?" Instantly, I realized I should have cleaned up better.

"While touching up my makeup, I dropped the powder compact, breaking the mirror. I cut my fingers on the broken glass while cleaning it up."

She looked at me suspiciously before saying, "Let's go. Maurice is ready for you."

We entered the family room, and all the witches, humans, and vampires were waiting for their master, who hadn't joined them yet. Sarah was the first to speak when Maurice entered the room.

"Everyone, on your knees," she instructed. "Bow!"

They all fell to one knee and bowed to Maurice. I didn't move but glowered at him as he approached me.

"Mercy, you need to get down on your knees," Sarah whispered while keeping her head down.

Maurice stood in front of me with a blank look, but when he sized me up, a slow smirk reached his lips—being in that dress obviously pleased him.

"You look stunning," he said, holding out his hand.

"I won't bow down to a vampire," I scowled, only looking at his hand that I refused to take. "I don't care what you can do to me."

Gasps came from all corners of the room.

Maurice chuckled, and the vampires began to laugh uncomfortably around him while the humans and witches looked frightened for me. Maurice lifted his hand as if to strike, but I only stood there defiantly. I was done being afraid.

I will not give him the satisfaction of scaring me. Not anymore.

Once again, he didn't hit me like I thought he would. Instead, he turned my head to expose my neck, running his thumb over my jawline. My heartbeat quickened. I thought he would see the wounds from Colin's bite, but he only continued to stroke my skin with a gentle touch.

"No reason to give you any more punishment for speaking to me the way you just did. Especially when you're about to be fed upon," he said coldly, with a wicked smirk. The crowded room was silent, waiting for his instructions. "Come on, everyone, join me in the ballroom," he ordered.

Maurice grabbed my hand softly and escorted me to the beautifully decorated hall. Everyone followed closely behind. As we reached the door, he leaned in until I felt a chill against my ear, and with a firm tone, he hissed, "I'll not be disrespected in front of my clan like that again." His warning made my skin turn to ice. "If you do, I'll not only feed on your blood, but I'll make you watch as I drain one of the dispensable witches I have at my disposal. Their death will be on you."

Despite how brave I wanted to be at that moment, his words sent a sudden panic coursing through me. His threat wasn't just a warning, it was a promise that he would punish me or others for what I had said, and he'd show me no mercy when he did.

He straightened up. "Noah will be here shortly with your friend, and you won't have much choice but to abide."

My heart told me it was just an empty threat. Abigail was protecting Shannon, and I trusted she'd fight to protect her at all costs.

"Fuck. You!" I fumed. "When I find a way to get this bracelet off my wrist, you'll be the first to die at my hands." I instantly regretted that threat. The look on his face was pure rage.

"Oh, Akasha. You threaten like a stubborn child," he mocked. "When all is said and done, it is you who will be left defenseless and afraid. You'll be under *my* control." He gestured to the large wooden door. "You belong here now ... with me. Your friends don't know where you are, and even if you were to escape, I'll hunt you down and drag you right back here and into my bed, where I will keep you chained forever. You ought to tame down that arrogance of yours and enjoy the festivities that are about to take place."

He squeezed my wrist harder, but I pressed my lips together in a flat line, trying to hide the fact that it hurt like hell. I didn't have a comeback. My mind went blank for the first time since I arrived here.

I looked around the ballroom and focused on the other vampires taking their seats. They seemed ready—or anxious—to watch me get devoured.

CHAPTER 28

My eyes immediately turned to a black dais holding up a low marble altar with gold patterns carved on its side. It sat right in the center of an extended platform—the floor covered in red and black roses. I was led to the altar and unceremoniously shoved down to sit and stay put.

This is too creepy and a little pretentious for my taste, I thought, trying to find any distraction to ease my nerves.

Colored stained-glass windows covered the wall, bringing color to the night sky. Smaller windows were slightly opened, letting the breeze blow through the room, shaking every leaf from the trees, some knocking right against the glass. I smelled the gentle scent of rain and the freshly trimmed, grassy lawn. The light from the room poured out through the windows, showing the juniper bushes lining the mansion walls. The need to be out of the mansion, taking in the fresh air, overwhelmed me.

I eyed the rows of seats and noticed every vampire had their human or witch sitting next to them. Most of the women had their hair styled up, just like mine. I knew then there was going to be a bloodbath the moment Maurice took a bite out of my neck, like a cult-like mass feeding.

Dorian stood next to the stage with his hands clasped together. He stared at me with his dreamy eyes. Ever since I had arrived, I'd noticed Dorian didn't have someone to feed on, unlike everyone else. Once I made eye contact with him, he walked toward me and pulled the thin, red scarf off his neck that I had seen him wear several times before. He proceeded to wrap the scarf around my bun.

"What's this for?" I asked him softly. Being this close to him again made butterflies flutter inside my stomach.

I inhaled the scent of iris from Dorian's shirt as I stood so close to him. It reminded me of the flower fields I used to sneak into so we could see each other or the woody bark of our favorite tree. He smelled like the lake we would walk across in the winter.

Dorian smelled like *home*.

"It's just tradition." He tightened the scarf around the bun and stepped away from me.

"What are you doing, Dorian?"

My lips wobbled, and I bit down on them to stop the sob caught in my throat. Dorian frowned. "Mercy—"

At that moment, Maurice approached us and bellowed, "Dorian, where is Colin?"

The nostalgic scent from Dorian was replaced by the pungent smell of Maurice's cologne as he waved Dorian away with his hand.

"I haven't seen him," Dorian replied. "Do you want me to search the house?"

Maurice shook his head. "No, I've waited long enough." He bent down, sniffed my neck, and protruded his fangs. He then pushed me down on my back until I was lying flat on the altar. I glared up at him in a warning.

I'm going to fight you, Maurice. I am going to fight.

A woman with dark brown skin, ruby red lips, and a beautiful black sleeveless gown walked onto the stage. Her eyes met mine for only a moment. If I had to guess, she almost appeared like they forced her to be there. Her face looked pained to see me bound and ready to be fed upon.

It made me wonder if they forced every witch here to do Maurice's bidding.

The witch recited her chant and gently wafted the smoke from the herbs around us. She circled me a few times till an earthy, herbaceous scent covered the stage.

I had to think of something—and I had to do it fast. Maurice was the last vampire in the world who deserved the power of my blood. He placed his arm under my back, lifting me toward his mouth, and arched my neck. As he did that, I felt the sensation of an object slipping from the red scarf around my bun.

As it was about to hit the altar, my hand reached back and caught it. Moving it around in my palm, I figured out what it was—a key.

Holy shit! A key!

Dorian *was* on my side, trying to save my life.

I let both my hands dangle loosely behind my back, avoiding touching Maurice's hands, which supported my body, and unlocked the bracelet from around my wrist. My magic surged through me like a spring, and I felt whole once again.

Steady. Breathe.

I slowly tucked the key and bracelet under my rear while keeping my wrist hidden from his view. Maurice tightened his hold on me as the witch concluded her chant.

I closed my eyes and did what I had done with the water at the cove. This time, there were no chants, herbs, or spell books. My mind was the only thing in control as I mustered all the energy I could.

How much power am I truly capable of?

I stretched out my fingers, and with my palm facing up, I focused my energy on all five elements. The strength came crashing through me, almost causing Maurice to lose his hold of my waist.

"What the hell are you doing?" he hissed.

The green energy in my fingertips sparked, and the sound of a bucket wobbling in the corner of the room caught Maurice's attention. For a few quick seconds, I looked at the trees outside the walls of the house. Their branches were shuddering and waiting for my command.

Maurice looked back at me, his eyes saturated with fury, and opened his mouth, ready to bite down.

"Trees," I whispered, "save me."

A shock wave of energy shot through my body, blasting Maurice across the platform. He quickly jumped back to his feet and charged at me, but I swiftly planted my hands on the ground and used my feet to kick him away from me as hard as I could. The force of my kick caused him to go flying across the stage again.

I turned to the witch next to us and used my strength to throw her against the wall—so hard it knocked her out.

My physical abilities had heightened even further. The astonishment of what I had done loomed over me for a moment. But my mind was abruptly drawn back to the ballroom. Hisses and gasps came from every vampire in the room while I looked down at my hands, illuminating a bright green glow.

The chandeliers shook, the walls cracked, and everyone scurried around the chamber like roaches. I coughed as Maurice gripped my throat, but I wouldn't crumble under his strength. I stayed still as magic flowed out to my fingertips.

I lifted my hands above my head and threw my arms out to the side, allowing the green power to leave my body and slam into the walls. Suddenly, a crash from the windows lining the hall echoed in my ears. The trees broke through the glass, shattering it to pieces. Their branches moved swiftly, stabbing the hearts of the vampires who tried to run in the opposite direction.

My eyes narrowed in on a black-haired female vampire running toward me. The roots from one tree blasted through the floorboards, stopping her in her tracks. She tried to run in the opposite direction, but the roots grabbed her by the leg. Her body twisted and soared up into the air. She screamed and punched the tree frantically with her fists. Still, the roots only squeezed tighter and tighter around her body until she exploded into ash.

Maurice turned around to look briefly at what was happening behind him. I quickly kneed him in the groin, causing him to screech and release me. One vampire promptly jumped toward the stage, trying to stop me, but I kicked him in midair, and he plummeted to the ground.

Maurice was right behind me. He grabbed my arms and bent them backward, forcing me to fall face forward onto the stage and lose focus on what I was commanding the trees to do. Everything came to a standstill. I tried to get up, but three other vampires were already holding me down. One of them put the bracelet back on my wrist.

Shit! I was so close.

I looked around the room, trying to locate Dorian, but I didn't see him anywhere.

Panic ran through me at the thought that I had hurt him.

Several vampires shrieked from the wounds that hadn't healed yet. Others lay on the floor looking at the numerous piles of dust. All the while, the rest stared at me with fuming rage as I kneeled proudly on the stage. Several humans and witches cried for their now-deceased vampires. I didn't understand it. Shouldn't they be happy they were free from them?

I looked up at Maurice, who was ready to sink his teeth into my neck. His anger seemed to grow as he observed all the death and destruction I had caused in a matter of minutes. I scanned the crowd for Dorian again and spotted him coming to his feet. He was covered in his own blood.

What have I done?

The bloodied scene didn't seem to concern Maurice anymore. Apparently, all he wanted was my blood. He licked his fangs and moved toward me while the other three vampires held me down. He stopped moving when a loud voice echoed off the walls.

"Stop! Maurice, don't do it!" Colin called out while running toward us.

Maurice grunted. "What the fuck, Colin? Where the hell have you been?"

"Don't drink her blood, Maurice. It's all a lie! All of it," Colin told him.

"What are you talking about, brother?" He signaled the vampires to pull me back up to my feet.

What the hell is happening?

"I'm sorry, Maurice," Colin said, "but I was tempted today to drink her blood. I couldn't stop myself." Colin backed away from his brother's expression.

The look of malice in Maurice's eyes said he wanted to kill his own family in that instant.

"Noah, seize him," Maurice commanded.

Noah dashed to Colin and grabbed both of his arms. Maurice drew near his brother and slapped him firmly across the face. But then Maurice quickly stepped back, his eyes widening in horror. The skin on Colin's face turned bright red where he had been hit.

"Colin?" Maurice cried.

"Yes, brother. I'm human. Blood is pumping through my beating heart, and I feel weak and powerless. I can *feel* my heart beating." Tears formed in Colin's eyes.

More gasps filled the hall as vampires heard what he had said. My eyes grew wide as I realized what his words meant.

CHAPTER 29

"No fucking way," I breathed as the realization hit me. "My blood will allow you to walk in the daylight, not because of some temporary power, but because it turns you back to a human," I said. "Roland knew it this entire time, too. He betrayed you, Maurice." I smiled. "This was the reason for my existence. *Spirit* brings light to this world." I turned to Colin. "Your soul is *that* light. My blood reunites the body with the soul that was lost when a vampire goes through the transformation." I laughed and turned to Maurice again. "Oh, you didn't honestly think it was going to be that easy, did you?"

"How is this possible?" Maurice cried and flung his hand toward my throat.

Dorian leaped toward us, but Noah grabbed the back of his shirt and pulled him back before anyone else noticed.

Noah must know about us.

Maurice squeezed my neck with brutal force seconds before he threw me across the stage. I slammed hard against the wooden floor and winced.

"This is impossible!" he screamed. Maurice stalked toward me as I lay on the floor in agony. "I didn't wait centuries for you just to be deceived." He gripped the bun on my head tightly, pulled me to my feet, and then held me high. "I love being a vampire. Nothing is better than the strength I hold and the power I have over *you* pathetic humans. I'll not have you destroy what we have built here." He paused for a beat to compose his rage. "How do you reverse it?"

I shook my head. "I don't know. I had no idea my blood would do this," I confessed.

Maurice released me, dropping me to the ground, and approached his brother with his fangs still out.

"Stop, Maurice," Kyoko said fearfully. "You don't know what will happen if you touch him. Don't risk it."

He stopped for a moment and then turned back to Kyoko. "You're right," he said. "Kyoko, feed him your blood."

"Maurice?"

"Just do it!"

Kyoko bit her wrists, and Colin gladly drank from it. They all watched Colin as Kyoko backed away.

While that was happening, I looked around and saw several vampires watching me and licking their lips. I knew not every vampire in Maurice's clan desired to be what they were. If they had a chance to be human again, they'd take it.

I stealthily picked up a piece of broken glass scattered all over the floor without anyone seeing. I went to slice my hand, but Dorian was in front of me before the sharp edge could touch my skin.

He shook his head. "Yeah, that's not going to happen," he said, taking the glass from me and tossing it back on the floor. "Let's get you out of here instead."

I looked down at his bloodied shirt. "Dorian, are you okay? I hurt you."

"I heal quickly, too, remember?" he said. "The branches never pierced my heart."

Dorian placed both his hands on each side of my cheeks and smiled. "You kept your promise."

I pulled my brows together. "My promise?"

"You ... you came back to me."

My lips parted right before I heard Maurice clear his throat. "Dorian?" Maurice held up the key to my bracelet. "Did you lose something?"

No, they can't take him from me. Not again.

I gripped his arm and held on, but Noah and another guard grabbed Dorian by the shoulder and pulled him away.

Noah shot Dorian with an apologetic look. "Sorry, brother, I don't have a choice."

"Get him the fuck out of here," Maurice commanded. "Put him in the dungeon, and I'll deal with him later."

They escorted Dorian out of the ballroom, and Maurice went over to Colin again, grabbed his neck, and snapped it. Colin fell lifelessly to the floor.

I jumped, shocked at Maurice's sudden impulse to kill his brother. They all stared at Colin for a few minutes, waiting for him to wake, but he didn't move.

"Get up, Colin. Wake up!" But there wasn't any movement. Maurice screamed and kicked his brother several times in a row. "Wake up!" he shouted again.

"You see, if you do that to a human, they die. Since Colin's soul returned to his body, vampire blood would no longer turn him.

This is permanent, Maurice. You just killed your own brother." I said to him with a slight smirk across my lips.

Maurice screamed and stomped toward me, slapping me hard against my cheek with the back of his hand. Right at that moment, the lights in the ballroom went out.

Someone came from behind me, covered my mouth, and pulled me behind the stage curtains. One arm was wrapped around my waist as another pulled around and placed a hand over my bracelet. I felt the sensation of burning around my wrist. I winced as the bracelet melted off and fell to the floor. The strong arm wrapping tightly around my waist was familiar. It was Caleb.

I twisted around and threw my arms over his shoulders, holding him tight. "Caleb! Where is everyone?" There was panic in my voice as I tried to catch my breath.

"They're safe. We were able to hide Shannon before they got to her," Caleb explained as I released him.

Those words sent a wave of relief. "And Cami? Has anyone checked on her at the hospital?"

"Joel sent Lily through a portal to the hospital so she could move her. Don't worry. She's safe at your home, too." I could finally let go of the air I had been holding in.

My friends are safe. I sighed in relief.

"They told me they captured her."

"They lied," Caleb said. "I'll explain everything on the way."

He grabbed my hands and led me off the stage.

"Wait! We need to save Dorian. They're going to kill him," I said. "I can't leave him."

"We can't save him right now, Mercy. We can come back for—" He stopped. The look on his face showed me he knew I was aware he had lied to me.

I frowned at him. "Yes, the same Dorian you claimed Simon had killed. You lied to me, Caleb. Yet again."

His face grew grim. "I was protecting you from a world of pain. He joined this clan on his own. I wanted you to have positive memories of him."

"That's a lie!" I said sharply.

His face turned pale. "This isn't the best place to have this conversation. We need to go. Now!"

We heard Maurice barking orders to his men, and I knew Caleb was right. We needed to leave, but I would come back for Dorian. I would be back for everyone behind those walls that didn't want to be there.

It took us over ten minutes to find the door that led out to the vast garden on the side of the property. It was so dark out that we couldn't see where we were walking anymore. Caleb held up his hand, and a flame lit on each fingertip.

"What are you doing?" I asked.

"We can't exactly see without light," he explained, holding the fire as we continued down the driveway.

The air around us felt invigorating as it entered my lungs. I took several deep breaths as we tiptoed through the rose bushes. I was free. Well, almost free.

"How did Shannon escape?" I asked. "They said they got into the safe house."

"Some of their men disconnected the power lines to the vault, and the door we had her locked behind was no longer secured.

Abigail got her out in time through another passageway through the sewers. She took her to Lily's house," he explained as he quietly opened the gate that led out of the garden. "They were right behind them, but Abigail was faster. She was able to make it into Joel's portal before it closed."

I sighed with relief, but it was cut short as the floodlights turned on as we approached the front gates. We turned our attention toward Maurice as he cleared his throat. Standing on each side of him were Noah and Kyoko.

"Going somewhere, Mercy?" Maurice asked.

"It's over, Maurice. The only reason you wanted me was for my blood, and well, I don't think you'll be drinking from me anytime soon, will you?" It wasn't wise to provoke him with his people around him, but having Caleb beside me made me feel a little braver.

Caleb pulled his hand out of his pockets, and a ball of flames hovered over his palm. He only held it there—as a threat to our enemies.

"You can't stop us," I warned.

"Maybe not now. But I know about that dagger,' Maurice said. "And I won't stop until I find it."

"I guess I'll be waiting for you then," I said.

Maurice turned around and moved to the side, letting us pass. It puzzled me why he would just let us go until I saw Riley and Amber approaching the tall black gates in their wolf forms. Caleb closed his hand, extinguishing his flame. Maurice and Kyoko looked terrified at the sight of two massive wolves circling their driveway.

"As I said, you can't stop us," I repeated as we crossed each other, slightly bumping my shoulder against his arm. I looked up into Maurice's eyes as we passed. "Goodbye, Maurice."

Caleb and I picked up our speed and ran toward the pack. Caleb led me to an open portal about a mile from the house. We were then teleported to the front porch of Lily's home. Once I saw the house, I just stood there. Relief and sorrow hit me all at once.

We were safe, but Dorian was not.

CHAPTER 30

"Everyone's inside," Caleb said. "Leah, Ezra, and Simon—they're all waiting for you." He gestured toward my house, and I could almost hear the secret words revolving inside his brain.

We're a coven again.

At that moment, I wanted to be happy. I hadn't seen my friends since before I died. I met Leah briefly, but now I was getting a second chance to make it right. They were a part of me, and I was a part of them. But I wondered if they'd like the new version of me. Back then, I made a choice to save myself from an eternity of torture by choosing death instead of the coven. Would they forgive me for that?

As I gathered up the courage to face my past, a bright light appeared. I turned around, and my mouth gaped open, shielding my eyes from the blinding glow. The light rapidly dimmed, and a beautiful woman in a long, white dress stood in front of me. I recognized the angel from the painting hung in the lair.

Tatyana.

Caleb moved in front of me to stand between us.

"I think that's close enough," he growled.

Her voice was soft and tender. "I'm not going to hurt her, Caleb," she said.

"No? I find that hard to believe after she killed your son." I looked at Caleb and then at the woman. She didn't appear to be a threat, but what did I know? This was the first angel I had ever met, and it was true, I did turn her son to ash.

Tatyana gave me a friendly smile. "The world has one less monster, Caleb. I only came back to thank her for what she's done. As a mother, we accept our children's flaws, no matter how evil those flaws may be. But the Chosen Ones were also created by my hands, regardless of not sharing the same blood. You're my child, too, Mercy. The tragedy of losing you all those years ago and being unable to bring you back—" She looked down to the ground and back up to meet my eyes. "Mercy, I hold no malice against any action you had to make to save the ones you love. You came back to this world to make *my* wrongs right."

I bowed in solidarity and moved around Caleb, meeting her halfway. He tensed as I walked toward her. I turned slightly, shooting him a glare not to follow me. I didn't need his protection any longer.

She held out her hand, and I hesitantly took it. When our fingers met, I was engulfed with warmth and power as it filled my body. I looked over my shoulder. "Caleb, please leave us."

He clenched his hands together at my order and shook his head. He made a move in my direction. "Not a chance," he said.

Caleb froze at the glower I shot at him, freezing him in his tracks. I snapped, "I'm not asking for your permission. I'm giving you a direct order as Spirit."

Caleb glared at me for a hard moment and threw up his hands in defeat. He walked to the side of the porch and plopped down on the rocking chair by the front door. He looked upset, but he knew it wasn't an argument he would win. After I saw he wasn't going to protest any longer, I followed Tatyana toward the driveway so we had some privacy to speak.

Tatyana turned toward me and smiled. "Thank you, Mercy," she said. "You did what I could not. Kylan would have destroyed this world if he had killed you. The five of you are my greatest creations."

It was such a weird thought that an angelic being had created us to kill the very thing she had made in the first place. I knew, though, that I couldn't do this without her guidance.

"I don't know if I'm strong enough to do this, Tatyana," I admitted. "I need help. I need *your* help."

"Of course, you can. All of you can." Her voice was so calm, very much expected from an angel.

I clasped her hand again, thinking back to the man I had to leave behind. I couldn't be in two places at once, and as much as I wanted to chase after Dorian, I knew it wasn't possible then.

My voice was soft as I pleaded with the angel. "Will you save Dorian from Maurice's clan? Please? Save as many as you can from that place. They took him for saving me. That is, if they haven't already killed him."

She nodded once. "I will try to save Dorian and take down that house. I will rescue those who want to be saved from behind those walls, but it's your mission to be the one who fights against them, Mercy, not mine anymore. I failed once, and now it's your turn to restore the balance lost because of my mistake."

I glanced back at Caleb and sighed. "How do I do it? I'm struggling with a million emotions all at once. It's not a simple task trying to balance what my mission is and what my heart wants. I'm fighting the undead while constantly worrying about the safety of those I care about. I wasn't born in this life to be a warrior, Tatyana. How do I become the hunter you created me to be?"

She smiled warmly. "You love them both, don't you?" she asked. Understanding what I had meant.

I nodded, looking over at Caleb again. "Caleb is complicated and frustrating," I said, knowing he'd see my lips move but not hear my words. I looked back to Tatyana. "I feel something for him in this life, whether it be love or lust. That aching feeling when we're close; that it's more about what we used to have versus what we do or what I want ... now." I breathed in slowly. "And Dorian—" I paused, tears filling my eyes. "—Dorian was, and is still, the love of my life."

She leaned forward to whisper in my ear. Her hair tickled my neck, and tears burned in my eyes as I listened to her advice.

When she pulled away, her smile was gone, and I knew I had one more sacrifice to make in this battle. Tatyana bowed her head and took off into the sky; a soft "Thank you" left my lips as I watched her fade from view.

Caleb hopped down from the porch. "Roland's almost here."

I wiped the tears from my face. "You can't trust him, Caleb. He purposely led me out of the safe house at the cemetery so I'd get caught."

"I know."

He what?

My fingers sparked as I turned to look at his face. "You knew I was being led to those monsters?"

"I didn't know then, of course," he explained. "But after Roland became human, he came here to help us. He needed your blood to become a witch again. He's powerful, Mercy, and he needed to be human again to use the kind of magic we need in this fight. Maurice wasn't going to let him leave if he didn't give you up."

"And what about Dorian?" I asked. "Was he all part of that plan, too?" Caleb was silent and dared to look guilty. "You knew he was alive, Caleb. You lied to me."

He hesitantly placed his hand on my cheek. "Mercy, please don't."

I pushed his hand away. "Stop, Caleb! You purposely kept me from him. Why?"

"Because I love you, and I'm a selfish asshole. You and I had something special, which was ripped apart by parents who didn't understand our love for each other. Then you met Dorian the day they forced us to stop having a relationship. You gave your heart to *him*."

He stepped closer, causing me to step back so we weren't touching.

"I also thought keeping that secret would protect you from being in the arms of someone I never trusted. We have a chance to start over again. You and Dorian could never have what we had." He put his hand under my chin and lifted it gently. "He's a vampire, Mercy."

"That isn't your decision to make, Caleb!" I hissed, grabbing his hand and removing it from my chin. "Your father and Abigail are vampires, and you still love them."

"They're my family."

"And Dorian is mine!"

He flinched. "I'll fight for you."

I gingerly touched his hand, centering myself on calming my frustration. I was about to hurt him significantly, and I didn't want our last moments to be out of hostility and anger. "I do love you, Caleb. But I also love Dorian." I lowered my head but kept my hand gently in his, afraid of the words that I had to say next. They were words he had to hear and something I had to do to fulfill our given mission.

"Tatyana is going back to rescue Dorian from that clan and anyone who wants to leave. Yet the fight isn't going to stop there. There are more clans to destroy and humans and witches to be saved." I choked back the sobs caught in my throat.

Caleb stood there in silence, tears streaming down his face. I let go of his hand. "I can't let my feelings for you and Dorian distract me from what we were sent here to do. Your father was right all those years ago. We were never sent here to fall in love."

He reached for me, but I backed away. "Please don't, Mercy."

I closed my eyes as a ray of white light poured from my fingertips. When I opened them back up, I formed a bright white ball with the light. The ball grew larger and more radiant. My hands swarmed around it, keeping it stable and bright. I whispered to myself the words to the spell Tatyana had spoken in my ear. I pulled the ball firmly to my chest, almost falling over by the force of energy entering my body.

He reached out to me—his eyes wide with worry. "What are you doing, Mercy?" he asked. "What the fuck did you just do?"

I looked up at the man that I once cared for. All the feelings I'd had for him in the past and my current life ... were gone. I thought about Dorian and everything we used to feel for each other. I reached my memories and pondered those feelings and felt ... nothing.

They were two beautiful men I knew cared for me, but the only things left in my heart were the memories.

Panic rose in his voice like it was threatening to choke him. "Mercy!" He stepped closer to me. "Mercy, what did you do?"

"The angel showed me how to take it away, Caleb. I had to take it all away."

He stumbled back, falling to his knees. That was the moment he realized what I had done, what I had to sacrifice to become the hunter Tatyana created me for.

"I'm sorry, Caleb," I said. "All I want now is to purify the Earth as the elemental power Tatyana created and bring an end to the evil that soaks the world in blood.

ABOUT THE AUTHOR

D.L. BLADE

D.L. Blade has always been passionate about creative writing, focusing on poetry during her younger years. One night, after having a vivid dream, she was inspired to pick up her pen and write her debut novel, *The Dark Awakening.*

Initially, Blade had focused on writing young adult fiction, but she has since shifted her focus to adult fantasy, paranormal, and dark romance. Through her stories, she takes readers on a journey into a world of unconventional love, morally gray men, and deliciously handsome villains.

When she's not writing, Blade enjoys reading, spending time with her husband and two children, attending rock concerts, and exploring new restaurants in Denver. She dreams of continuing to create exciting novels for her readers and taking them on a journey through the magical realms that spill from the pages of her books.